THE BROTHERS

ADRIANA GUYTON

Published by AG Publishing Australia
www.adrianaguyton.com

ISBN 978-0-9943087-2-6

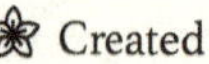 Created with Vellum

~

There are no goodbyes for us.
Wherever you are, you will always be in my heart

Mahatma Gandhi

PART I

1

—————

THE MOUNTAIN

Julia woke from a dream, the kind she can't remember. It slips from memory, a thief in the early morning light of possibilities.

A rosy glow slips through the gap between the blind and the floor, casting a skinny shadow on the carpet. She pushed herself up on one elbow and gazed at Patrick. Fast asleep, his eyelids twitching, his brain playing out stories like a sleeping cat who dreams of the hunt. She reached out her hand, tempted to trace the contours of his face with her fingers. Reluctant to wake him, she turned away and gently eased herself out of bed.

Opening the outside door, Julia watched as their dog Alfie trotted across the terrace, his sleek black coat gleaming in the morning light. He makes his way across the manicured lawn, still sparkling with dew, in search of his favourite tree.

Julia wandered outside to the terrace, her diary and mobile tucked under one arm and a cup of steaming peppermint tea in the other. The tiles beneath her bare feet are already warm from the early morning sun with the promise of a beautiful day ahead. She enjoys this time of year before the proper heat of summer begins.

Up here on this magic mountain, with its mist and rain and wind and amazing beauty - she can almost believe she's fulfilled by her life.

Blue sky, not a breath of wind and the sun already warming her face, she pulled the silk Kimono robe tighter around her waist and sat down ready to write her list of tasks for the day.

As she sipped the last of her tea, her eyes were drawn to the view across the valley. The early morning mist still hovered above the forest of Eucalypts. She'd seen photographs like this in travel magazines and she'd watched the ad campaigns on television promoting Australia as the go to destination. Food, wine, beaches, spectacular scenery, and grand lifestyle.

The reality, Julia believed, was different. Whilst the adverts accurately represented part of the truth - beneath the beauty, lay a brutal, unforgiving country of extremes. Every living plant and creature has to fight to survive in this harsh land – a fight Julia has accepted she can't win.

'Morning darling.' Patrick stood in the doorway, dressed ready for work, but still towelling his wet hair.

'You're up early, did I disturb you?' Raising her arm, to shade her eyes from the sun.

'No, I have an early meeting, a full day ahead of me, and I need to leave the office before five for an appointment in Hawthorn.'

'What's in Hawthorn?'

'Don't be nosey. I will reveal all tonight, it's a surprise.' His face alight with mischief. 'I need to go, sorry, no time for coffee or breakfast.'

'What's the surprise? Tell me. Don't be secretive.'

'I'm not telling you. I'll surprise you this evening. It will blow your mind. Gotta run. Love you.' He turned and walked to the front door.

Julia followed behind and reached out to take the wet towel from his hand throwing it over her shoulder. 'So, I can't tempt you back to bed then?' He hesitated, car keys in one hand, his laptop bag in the other.

'Well, I hate to turn down a wonderful offer, but it will have to wait until tonight.'

She closed the gap between them, reaching up to kiss his lips. He pulled her in close so her nose was against his neck and she could smell "Eternity" the after shave she bought for his birthday a week earlier.

He would say happiness is the elixir of youth. 'I'm happy. Being happy keeps you young. That's why you still have the look of a young girl Julia, so you do.' She'd pooh-poohed this remark, at the same time inwardly pleased he still viewed her with such transparent adoration.

Young university students swooned over him, but he said he never noticed. She often wondered if this could be true. He was not a vain man, but was he blind to their ego flattering attention? She didn't think so.

'What time should I expect you back, Mr Mysterious?'

'Maybe seven, seven thirty. I'll phone you when I'm near.' He laughed, recognising she hated him keeping secrets.

'It's not a secret Julia, it's a surprise. You won't make me spoil it so give up graciously.' He tenderly kissed her mouth, before brushing her lips with one finger, tracing where his own lips had just been - their own special love message to each other - thankful it had not been lost in the maelstrom of their lives.

'I know what you're thinking, but I can't stay. Not because I don't want to.' Gazing at her, knowing how lucky he was – his wife, his lover - mate of his soul.

'I know that. Shame,' she said, smiling back at him, 'it will keep. What's the surprise?'

'Can't say. I have to go, see you tonight.' Grinning to himself he opened the car door and could see in the rear-vision mirror Julia wave before she turned to go back indoors. With the car window down, Patrick could hear her call to Alfie and watched as his dog turned to follow with the reluctance of a grumpy child denied a treat.

The trees they'd so lovingly planted in blocks of five down the long driveway three years ago - now tall and willowy like teenagers following a growth spurt waved gently in the light breeze as if farewelling him on his journey. The grass, vigorous and emerald green, making the most of the moisture before the fierce summer heat would scorch it - he made a mental note to cut the grass at the weekend before it became too long.

Patrick turned from the driveway onto the main road. His car cruising around the twisting, curving bends and he marvelled at the beauty of the mountain. This stretch of road so familiar, yet constantly surprises him by its enchantment. Never the same, never dull, and this morning with the sun's rays filtering through the Ghost Gums and tiny jewels of water glistening from the enormous tree ferns, the forest's beauty is nature at her most glorious.

His thoughts settle on tonight's meeting. With the agreement signed, he will write his letter of resignation. It's a thrilling plan.

No longer will he have to endure the department politics, the tedium of students with little or no talent but plenty of opinions, and nor will he have to tread carefully around some of the young female students who signal their attraction to him before he's even finished handing out their study notes.

He's tired of teaching and tired of Australia and he longs for the moment when he can lock himself in his music room and compose. He loves the mountain and the home they have built. But Australia no longer holds him in its embrace the way it did in the beginning.

He's kept his thoughts to himself, unwilling to share them with Julia. He was the one who had the amazing opportunity to take up a new position on the other side of the world, and she'd been the one vehemently opposed to leaving London.

Her acquiescence had both surprised and thrilled him. Now, although his time at the university has been challenging in all the right ways, he knows in his heart he needs to move on. After tonight, they will be free to choose what happens next. Will they stay or go? Julia can choose.

She's unhappy at work – her despondency is palpable, but her reluctance to share her thoughts and feelings has caused him to doubt the wisdom of raising the subject with her. To ask might mean he has to accept she hates her job and can't find it within herself to love Australia. She's sacrificed her own happiness to please him, and that thought fills him with a mixture of guilt and sadness.

He turned onto the ramp for the Monash Freeway and waited to merge with the traffic pouring into the city - he won't miss this junior every morning and evening.

Once he resigns, it will be a matter of working out his notice period, which could take months while they find another suitable head of department, but he will use that time to make plans with Julia. They both miss London and the frequent visits back to see his parents in Ireland and her son Jack in Switzerland. But what does she really want? What is it that will make her happy? He doesn't know the answer.

His thoughts settle back to Ireland and the holidays spent there with his parents and brother. There was a time when he'd been jealous of Julia's relationship with his younger brother Carrick. Now this is a distant memory, one that has left him feeling embarrassed at his own insecurity.

He's learned to accept Julia and Carrick have a special bond. She's relaxed and in some indefinable way, more at peace in the presence of Carrick. Patrick's relationship with Julia has always had a unique energy surrounding their love, passion, and loyalty to each other. Not exactly an edge, Patrick mused, just a different something - he searched for the right metaphor - a distinct vibration, he decided.

He's watched Julia fight the storms inside of herself. Random events triggering dark ghosts from the past that rise up to claim her from time to time. Her fears come from another place and time, and there is no connection to him. He's been patient during these times until the storm has blown over and life resumes its normal rhythm. Safe with the knowledge that she loves him. But he's wondered in quiet reflective moments - if she has ever been *in love* with him?

Did her love for him blossom from watching the relationship between himself and her son Jack mature into the strong father-son bond they share today? Was that more important to her back then? He doesn't know the answer and has never asked.

2

———

REFLECTION

The water was cooler than Julia expected, fooled by the warmth of the sun. The sudden cold upon warm skin takes her breath away. She swims several lengths before her body accepts the water is no longer glacial. Resting against the side of the pool, she listens to nature and enjoys the view across the valley. Now the mist has lifted, Julia can see the Currawongs swooping and diving in the distance, their distinctive call bouncing around the valley floor and back across to her in stereophonic fashion.

Soon she will have to leave the pool and check her emails, but the soothing effect of water and the sun on her face make her linger a while longer.

Alfie, lazing on the opposite side of the pool, his head resting on his paws, his eyes steadfastly watching her, remind Julia of the time he fell into the pool as a puppy before they'd installed the cover. The lesson had been a good one and despite his love of water; the Flat-Coated Retriever is now older and wiser and has learned to keep a respectful distance from the pool's smooth edge.

She lay on her back and floated, weightless and relaxed. The sky above like a giant blue room dotted with soft white scatter cushions.

In the past, she would not have permitted herself the luxury of relaxation. Patrick has taught her to relax - to chill as he frequently tells her. He's taught her to understand the importance of taking time for herself.

Her mind drifts to the subject of work and her distinct lack of enthusiasm for what she now does. Returning to the world of family law is no longer an option, she left that behind in England and now she works in insolvency and liquidation, but the office dynamics and her increasing desire to spend more time at home are making her doubt her commitment to law in any form. What else can she do? Law is what she knows, understands and what she once loved with a passion.

The question hangs in the still morning air as she pulls herself out of the water and sits on the edge of the pool, letting the warmth of the sun dry her skin.

Her inability to discuss her feelings with Patrick concerns her. She's sidestepping what she needs to face. Avoidance becomes the easier path to tread. Patrick is so happy in his job – how can he possibly understand how she feels when he is so content. She reassures herself that continuing down the path of avoidance is the best option.

He's a born teacher, and music is his lifeblood. It courses through him with such vigour. Julia longs for something to course through her veins with equal strength.

Her arms rest on the side of the pool and she lowers her head, resting her chin on her hands and looks back to their home. They built it with the love, care and dedication normally reserved for a child.

The house sits on a gentle rise that slopes gradually away on each side. In front, the views extend across the valley to the wide forest below. Ghost Gums, Blue Gums and Mountain Ash provide a canopy of shade for the majestic tree ferns flourishing on the forest floor. To the rear across sweeping lawns, they have a close-up view of the forest which bounds their land.

The house design is that of a horseshoe with sheltered seating areas front and back. It's in harmony with its surroundings. Julia loves their home, but in moments of quiet reflection admits it is all she loves about being here in Australia. If she could cocoon herself in this house on this mountain, she may just find contentment.

3

―――――

THE STORM

I t's late afternoon and Julia has almost finished the client report she's been working on. It only needs one final read through before emailing. She takes a break and makes herself a pot of tea. While she waits for the kettle to boil, she switches on the TV to catch the latest news.

'Heavy rain and gale force winds to hit Victoria by late afternoon,' the solemn weatherman tells her.

Glancing out the window all she can see is brilliant sunshine. Perhaps this weather change won't stretch as far as the mountain, she thinks. Maybe they will be spared further rain. After a soaking winter and spring, the prospect of warm sunny days without wind and rain is pleasing, although Julia knows she will eat her words come summer when she'll long for rain, a welcome respite from the heat.

Last summer was hot, even on the mountain where it's cooler. The 40-degree days burnt their trees and hardened the ground until it cracked in places. She hoped this summer would be a kinder one. She has never adjusted to this unpredictable and brutal Australian climate and longs to feel the green fields of England beneath her feet.

Two hours later Julia could see from the lounge window the

bright blue of earlier has been replaced by a tar-black sky. Large slate grey clouds are gathering, the rain is coming. Remembering the washing on the line, she hurried outside to gather it in.

Playing on the terrace with the neighbour's cat, Alfie looks up at her expectantly. Their seventy-year-old neighbour Nancy owns a large tabby cat called Hagrid – a name he wears with the perfected sense of superiority that cats possess.

Alfie is no match for Hagrid's sly games of hiding and pouncing, but the two share a special relationship. Julia steps around them avoiding a swipe from Hagrid's outstretched paw.

The strange stillness in the warm air reminded Julia of New Zealand right before an earthquake when you could sense the building rage beneath the earth's surface. There is something in the darkening clouds which leaves her feeling uneasy.

A swirl of cooler air as the first fat drops fall and Hagrid takes his leave, making his way across the lawn to home. He does not enjoy being caught out in the rain.

Alfie retrieved errant pegs in the grass and helpfully brought them to Julia dropping them at her feet. She picked up the now full clothes basket and hurried for the shelter of the covered terrace.

Moving from room to room, Julia closed windows which earlier she had opened to welcome in the early morning sunshine. The rain falls in grey sheets. Lightning discharges, brilliant shocks of white ripping the graphite sky, flickering silently behind and between the roiling heavy clouds - a backdrop to the jagged bolts linking sky to unsuspecting ground. The shortening pauses as the storm draws closer before the crashing boom of thunder, reverberating echoes, reminding inhabitants of the mountain - of their place in the face of nature's fury.

The wind howls with violence and the raw power of an angry God. Giant trees, their branches heavy from an unusually wet winter and spring, are ready to break and crash to the ground. A groan from a Ghost Gum echoes across the mountain as a bolt of lightning splits the tree in two.

Finally, as the centre of the storm recedes, an eerie, sombre feeling envelops the house. Julia poured herself a wine and added the final touches to the salad she's made.

Fresh salmon fillets are on the kitchen work surface, marinating ready to grill when Patrick arrives. She's hungry and becoming increasingly agitated that Patrick is yet to call to let her know he is almost home.

By eight thirty Julia has given up waiting and sets about grilling her fish and sits with a plate on her knee watching QI. She loves Stephen Fry whether his guests are celebrities out of their depth or the sidesplittingly funny professional comedians, the show always makes her laugh.

She has tried phoning Patrick but his phone rings out and by nine o'clock she's furious at his thoughtlessness. He's never been good at keeping to a time, a barb in their relationship that Julia feels has pierced her too many times.

THE BLUE LIGHTS from police vehicles illuminate the slick road, voices shout orders. Flashes of yellow as first responders in high visibility vests assess the scene. The giant Ghost Gum straddles the road, blocking it from both directions. The car, unable to avoid the tree, hangs precariously over the edge of the steep bank, its airbags inflated on impact.

They make a call for an ambulance. The paramedics will have to negotiate the mountain from the other side, taking a longer, slower route, but it may already be too late for the driver in the car.

Tail-back traffic stretches down the mountainside for miles. Commuters will be late home tonight. A police officer approaches the first vehicle requesting the driver turn around and make his way back down the mountain in search of another route home. Others follow. The road is impassable for the rest of the night.

Firefighters begin the process of carefully manoeuvring the

vehicle up and away from the edge of the bank. Time is of the essence, but decisions made in haste could cause the vehicle to tumble over into the valley below. Heavy rain and howling winds make progress slow and cumbersome.

4

THE AFTERMATH

Julia and Jack waved a teary goodbye to Jack's wife Kat, Patrick's parents, Rose and Brendan and Patrick's brother Carrick.

Rose, desperate to contain her emotions, her face sagging under the weight of so much sorrow. Her eyes, Patrick's eyes, looking into Julia's and for a moment Julia found herself mesmerised, unwilling to say the last goodbye. Rose holding her close, shaking with the effort of restraint.

They would visit back to Ireland, but it wasn't the same as having them here, right here where Julia could reach out and absorb a little of Patrick every-time she looked at them. Turning to Brendan, Julia taking both his hands in hers, the sadness surrounding him palpable. Such an exuberant man; reduced to a father in great pain. No parent should have to bury their child - it wasn't right.

Within 24 hours they would be home. Back to their life, their beautiful, uncomplicated life – referred to by the family as "the most beautiful place on God's earth".

.   .   .

JULIA LEANED back against the headrest and closed her eyes. Images of the summers they'd spent in Baltimore County Cork and the delightful Christmas breaks floating before her eyes. It was the perfect place for two high school teachers to retire. A picturesque gem, packed with history and renowned for its sailing and fishing, pursuits both of which Brendan and Rose adored.

Patrick would tend the BBQ grilling freshly caught Gilthead Bream, drizzled with lemon olive oil and Rose's freshly baked home-made bread, no bread-maker for her!! Lazy summer days spent sailing, something Julia had never experienced until she met Patrick. Having spent most of his childhood sailing Ireland's West coast with Carrick, he was an expert on the water, as were his parents.

'You will come won't you Julia and you too Jack and Kat? You will come and visit, stay with us for as long as you want.' Brendan had said, his voice shaking with emotion as he spread his arms wide to embrace Jack and Julia.

'Try stopping us,' they'd chorused. 'You will always be in our thoughts and prayers. We love you both very much.' Reaching out to pull Rose into a hug one more time before they headed for the airport security gate. Carrick turned one last time to wave to her, his face ravaged with grief.

Julia glanced across at Jack in time to see him swipe at an errant tear, knowing he felt as wretched as she did. It was painful saying goodbye. Patrick's parents had loved and welcomed them into the bosom of their family from the very beginning. Rose and Brendan caring for and loving Jack as though he were their very own grandson and equally loving Julia like the daughter they never had.

As Jack drove through the Burnley tunnel and merged onto the freeway, Julia glanced across at him and wondered how he would cope, and her thoughts came back to trying to imagine what life would be like without Patrick. What did that mean exactly? She did not understand how to live without him. How to be without him. How to feel without him. Especially not here in Australia. Somehow, she thought it would be easier to manage her grief if they'd still been in London. The pain of grief was so overwhelming. She'd grieved before, but not for a husband.

'Stop grabbing at the door handle Mum, I'm not driving fast.' Jack looked across at his mother, reaching out his hand to touch her arm.

'I'm sorry, I feel so nervous, I just can't help it. Stupid really, it wasn't me in the car with him.'

'You know what don't you? You should get back behind the wheel sooner rather than later. You've always been such a confident driver. Well, apart from when you were teaching me to drive; that was a disaster.' He smiled across at his mother.

'Patrick was so much better than I was at teaching you. So patient and thorough. It was irrational when I look back. I just wasn't in control and couldn't shake off an overwhelming fear that we could or would crash.'

'Bit like now Mum. It's still irrational and you're making me nervous, so the sooner you get your confidence back, the better.'

Julia knew her son was right. But this wasn't the same as teaching him how to drive. This was something entirely different. If asked to differentiate one from the other, she wouldn't have been able to say – she just knew she couldn't trust herself behind the wheel. Not yet anyway. Maybe in a few months she'd feel differently.

'So, are you going to go back with Lizzie to Spain for a month?'

'Yes, I've decided I will. I'm taking a leave of absence from work. Not even sure I want to go back there. I might move onto something else – I need time.'

'Are you going to take Carrick up on his offer of using his London apartment?'

'I think so. Lizzie thought it would be good to have a week in London before Spain.'

'Is Carrick going to stay on in London with you?'

'No idea. Why?' The coolness in Jack's tone caught Julia by surprise, but she recognised it was coming from a place of pain, of grief, of disbelief. Jack adored Patrick, and his sudden death had rocked Jack's world.

'You know he's in love with you?'

'What? Who?' It took Julia a moment to register Jack's words.

'What are you talking about?' She said sharply She was finding her mind wandering like a sleepwalker drifting from room to room in a long-abandoned house and each time Jack spoke it pulled her back to the present, away from that empty place.

Since that knock on the door, Julia's reality had turned on its head and she struggled with so many simple tasks, concentration being one of them. Tolerance was another victim of her state of mind. Waspish comments and angry reactions seemed to bubble up from deep within with little regard for appropriateness of time or place, or to whom she was talking too. The weight of grief lay heavy on her heart.

'Carrick. I'm talking about Carrick.'

Julia looked across at Jack as he turned his head to face her briefly before turning back to focus on the road ahead.

'Don't be ridiculous. We've always gotten along. I'm like a sister, that's all it is and to think and say otherwise is disrespectful to both of us.' As the angry words left her lips and she saw Jack's expression tighten, she knew that she had overreacted and that should have been disturbing, but she was finding she couldn't stop herself and realised she was seething with anger. Such a stupid, stupid thing to be saying, and it wasn't true.

'You're angry, and I know his attentions are not something you've encouraged, and Patrick knew too.'

'This is inappropriate Jack,' Julia snapped. 'What gives you the right to say these things?'

'Because he spoke to me about it. Ages ago. When you were still in London and he came across to see me in Geneva.'

'What did he say?' As fast as it flared, Julia's anger suddenly subsided like a spent balloon.

'Oh, I can't remember exactly Mum, it was ages ago. Something about when they were boys in Ireland and Carrick having a crush on Patrick's girlfriends.'

'Patrick could get quite aerated with Carrick. They're such distinct personalities. Carrick is so like Rose in many respects. The calm measured way they have. Patrick is far more flamboyant. His students love him.' Aware she was using the present tense and unwilling to correct herself. Unable to believe she'd lost him.

Sensing the moment of tension had passed, Jack continued. 'Yes, maybe you're right. Anyway, it never worried Patrick. He trusted you implicitly. Lizzie said Carrick reminds her of that character in "Love Actually" who comes to the door and holds up that sign to Keira Knightley. Do you remember?'

'Yes, I know the scene exactly.' Julia laughed, the sound foreign to her and immediately making her feel guilty that she should allow herself a moment of light-heartedness. It felt wrong to be laughing and at once she felt saddened at the realisation that Lizzie's remarks were not made kindly but were mocking Carrick. She suddenly felt a little ashamed that she'd laughed so freely at the comparison.

'I don't believe for a moment that Carrick is in love with me. He's always shown me the utmost respect. He's funny and kind and generous, well philanthropic really. Anyway, it's irrelevant, I married Patrick, and that's that. He's made me the happiest woman alive, and the thought of my life stretching out ahead of me without him by my side is unbearable.' Julia wept again, unable to hide her grief from Jack.

'Hey, sorry, it's okay. I didn't mean to upset you. You have time to decide if you want a week in London. Lizzie's not going back for another fortnight and nor am I. I thought maybe we could fly back together, and depending on my work schedule, Kat and I might get across to Spain and visit.'

Julia pulled a tissue from inside the glove box to dab at her tears. 'That would be wonderful if you were able. Did you speak with your office yesterday?' Eager to learn that there had been no fallout from his work, Julia recalled the fraught discussion she'd over-heard Jack having with Kat several days ago.

'Tell Julia, Jack, she will understand.' Kat's heavily accented voice drowned out by Jack's louder and agitated tone.

'I'm not ready to go back home yet and work will just have to understand that.'

Julia had asked later that day, 'I heard you talking with Kat. Jack, if you need to go back to work earlier, I totally understand.' Jack had been standing with his hands in his pockets the way he used to when he was behaving petulantly as a young boy, Julia thought. He was facing away from her, looking out across the sweeping lawns to the bush beyond, and turned to face her when she'd questioned him.

'Work has emailed, nothing bad, just asking for a timeline for my return. But I can't go yet Mum, I'm not ready.'

Julia had gone to him, pulling him to her and hugging him tightly, relieved that he would stay a little longer; the thought of finding herself suddenly without her son by her side frightened her.

'They're fine with me staying an extra two weeks as long as I can look over the changes to the musical score they've made and get back to them with my comments by the end of the week.'

'Are they going into recording soon?'

'Yes, but not until I'm there, they've agreed to wait. Kat will be back if they need clarification. She knows the piece well. But I need to be present when the musicians are in the studio. I'm never happy just hearing the recording. I like to see them in action, know that they are *feeling, living* the music that I've written, if that makes sense?'

'Absolutely. Patrick was the same.'

'I know, he taught me to "feel" music, way back when I was first being tutored by him.'

'Did you know I saw his solicitor yesterday?'

'Yes, but I didn't like to ask anything in front of Rose and Brendan. What did he say?'

'He was there, with his solicitor, the day he died, completing a deal.'

'What sort of deal?'

'He wrote a musical score, something he did a long time ago - when he was still running the academy. Anyway, it seems some film director has approached him and wants to use the score in a new movie. Patrick has sold the rights.'

'Wow, that's quite something. Do you know what genre, how much he wrote? One piece or many?'

'I didn't ask. Sorry, I couldn't take it all in. Carrick came with me - he may remember more about what the solicitor said. All I could think of was seeing Patrick waving goodbye to me, smiling and winking that he would reveal all that night, only he didn't. Somehow, and I know, this might sound unkind.... but I can't help it. I feel so angry with him. Angry that he was there chatting with his solicitor until late, much later than he'd said he would be while I was waiting for him at home and, well..... maybe if he hadn't stayed so late then he wouldn't have been driving in the middle of that awful storm.' Julia grabbed at another tissue, holding it to her eyes to stem the tears.

'Mum, it's okay. I understand, I really do. I can't believe, just like that.' Jack clicked his fingers. 'His life is over and he's gone from us.'

Gone, yes, Julia thought, but it wasn't only Patrick's life over, she felt she was holding her own life in a precarious balance on a cliff edge - stable ground on one side, but one step away from a fatal drop onto the rocks below. One little push and she'd lose herself. She glanced across at Jack, his face flushed with emotion, and it reminded her once more of the unfairness of it all.

'He phoned me in Geneva the week before. You know how he was, always checking in with me, seeing what I was up to. What musical score was I working on? Was I still playing a bit of live stuff? He was always so interested and supportive......' Jack trailed off, lost in thought and too choked with the freshness of the memory to carry on. And there was nothing Julia could say or do that would make the pain go away for either of them.

They'd just turned off the freeway onto Ferntree Gully Road, in another forty minutes they would be home and Julia wondered for the umpteenth time, how was she to carry on living on the mountain, in their home without Patrick? A memory from the funeral pushed its way to the surface. She'd successfully blocked out most of that day, but now a conversation floated to the top.

A young couple recently arrived from the UK. The husband had just taken up residency at the University in the department Patrick ran. What was his name? Julia silently asked herself. Jacob, Julian? No, it was Jason; that was it. Jason and Sarah something.

'Patrick was very welcoming to me, only been in the department a month, but he made me feel like I belonged. His concern for us staying in a motel was touching. We don't know our way around and haven't found a suitable property to rent or buy.'

Julia struggled to recall the rest of the conversation, too numb with grief at the time to even take it on board, but now an idea emerged through the fog and she wondered if it might be possible.

5

LIZZIE AND JULIA

Lizzie was sitting in the lounge nursing a glass of wine when Julia and Jack returned. Julia noted a full wine glass never seemed to be far from Lizzie's reach. She had hoped in the intervening years since they'd left England that Lizzie may have curbed her drinking and instead found solace in the art galleries and history of Spain, in the turquoise brilliancy of the sea view she enjoyed from her large penthouse in Palma and in the group of ex-pat friends that surrounded her.

Sadly, Lizzie was still trying to find answers in the bottom of a wine bottle. Michael's sudden death five years earlier had been not only a shock but had revealed a secret part of his life.

Lizzie had never come to terms with what she learned after Michael's death. The man she thought she knew, loved and had devoted sixteen years of her life too, a partial stranger to her. Lizzie had not coped with the seesaw of emotions, from grief to feeling betrayed and had disintegrated until she was a shadow of the strong, amazing friend Julia had loved since their school days.

'So, what have you been up to?' Julia asked Lizzie, flopping down into her favourite chair.

'Not a lot. Just wondering how life can hold so much promise and the next there's a knock on the door; you answer it expecting a courier with a box of vintage wine for the cellar but find it's the Grim Reaper leaning on his sickle and wearing a cruel smile before announcing – *Have I got a surprise for you?*'

'I'm sorry. Me trying to cope with Patrick's death must bring back a lot of awful memories for you?' *And sitting there nursing a glass of wine, probably the umpteenth already today, filling your head with maudlin thoughts is not the answer.* Julia was not sympathetic towards Lizzie's drinking.

'No, not really. This is different. Patrick didn't have a heart attack - and I'm confident when I say this,' she said rather harshly. 'Patrick doesn't have a closet full of unsavoury secrets. He was a straightforward, gorgeous man.' A loud cry escaped into the room.

Julia wanted to reach out and comfort her friend but couldn't. She was far too raw. Instead, she leapt from the chair and left the room, walking swiftly through to the far end of the house to the bedroom. The room she'd shared, until two weeks ago with Patrick.

She wanted to run to him. Stepping into the walk-in wardrobe, Julia grabbed at Patrick's clothes, pushing her face into the fabric, inhaling deeply, finding solace in the smell of the after-shave which still lingered on his jumpers and jackets. His shirts, laundered and pristine, Julia ran her hands over the fabric - remembering when he wore this one or that. Imagining how handsome he looked dressed in a suit or sports jacket and open-necked shirt. *Where are you now? Why don't you come to me, show me a sign, any sign that you're around, still by my side like you've been for these past years?*

When Lizzie came looking, she found Julia curled in a ball on the floor of the walk-in wardrobe clutching an old and much-loved jumper of Patrick's rocking back and forth, tears drenching her cheeks.

Crouching down, Lizzie reached out and took Julia's hand. 'I'm sorry, Julia. That was thoughtless of me to mention Michael. Come on, get up, Jack's just poured himself a beer, he'll be wondering where you are. Don't let him see you like this.'

She hauled Julia up by the arm, carefully taking the jumper from her, re-folding it and putting it back on the shelf, before leading her to the ensuite, encouraging Julia to dry her tears and freshen up.

'I'll cook dinner tonight. I know you don't feel like eating, but you must Julia, at least try to have a little something.'

This was like the Lizzie of old, Julia thought, as she splashed her face with cold water. The Lizzie who was always there for her, picking up the pieces and putting her back together again and who had been absent for such a long time.

Julia dried her face quickly before applying some light make-up, eager now not to let Jack see her so distressed. He was struggling, as was she, and it worried her what would happen when he went back to Geneva. Perhaps he would be okay with Kat by his side. Strong, resolute and loving in equal measure, Kat would help him the way Julia knew she couldn't.

During the next two weeks before they departed Melbourne for Europe, Julia frequently stepped into the walk-in wardrobe, sometimes standing there without realising; eyes closed, breathing in the faint lingering scent of Patrick. Other times she'd take an item of his and hold it close to her heart, aching to have him near, to hold him, just one more time. She'd taken one of his jumpers to bed with her every night, clutching it like Jack had done with his black and white Panda bear as a child.

She would take his favourite jumper with her when they left for Europe, it would help him find her if he returned to find an empty house – *Oh what a mad thought Julia, he won't need a jumper to follow you like a bloodhound. He'll be able to see your love like a beacon wherever you are in the world and come straight to you. Still, maybe she should take his favourite jumper anyway, just in case.*

BEFORE KAT, Rose, Brendan and Carrick had flown back home there had been a night as sleep embraced her, when Julia's senses had drawn her back to consciousness, to the sound of music playing. She lay for a moment transfixed, unsure whether she was dreaming, before swinging her legs to the side of the bed and barefoot moved swiftly through the house to the lounge. As she approached, the music faded, and the house became silent once more.

The room illuminated by the full moon suspended like a giant orb in the dark sky, Julia could see the expanse of green lawn outside the door and an overwhelming sense of loneliness engulfed her. She was sure she'd heard music but realised it must only have been a dream.

She turned to the Bose music system and quickly selected from her playlist the song she was looking for. Turning the volume down so she wouldn't disturb anyone, she sat crossed legged on the floor and let the melody wrap her in its embrace.

It was then she saw him. Patrick, standing on the lawn outside, smiling back at her. At last he was here, she thought. I knew he'd never leave me. This has all been a terrible mistake. A cruel, crazy dream, but it's over. He's here waiting for me to join him.

Julia listened to the words of the song they both loved - Leonard Cohen's *Dance Me to the End of Love*, and as the words drifted over her, she turned the volume up so Patrick could hear every word and ran to greet him. They clung to each other and swayed as they'd done so many times to this very song. She felt his hands run over her body, her back arching at his touch. The whispered words in her ear - *Dance me through the panic till I'm gathered safely in...*

As the sound of the music echoed around the garden, Julia felt him let go of her hand as she lifted her face to his. She called out again and again before she felt Jack's powerful arms encircling her tightly.

'It's alright Mum, I'm here. It's okay, it's okay.'

Julia collapsed spread eagled on the grass, feeling its dampness penetrate her silk pyjamas, her eyes searching the night sky for answers. The first drops of gentle rain brushed her cheek as Jack lay down beside her, his hand entwined in hers, and as the rain gathered momentum, it washed away the pain leaving a barren space in her heart.

Julia hadn't woken until late the following morning. Images of the night before flashing by like a movie clip. Snatches of music and emotions floated before her, but she couldn't hold on to a solid memory. The ache in her heart was overwhelming, so much pain, how would she learn to live with this agony? She would later learn that Lizzie had given her a sleeping tablet, which accounted for the long sleep and her inability to hold on to any coherent memory. She hated sleeping pills. Hated that lack of control.

Hours later when Julia was sitting at the kitchen table, the images from the previous evening clear and concise in her mind, she tried to explain what she'd seen.

'He was here, I know he was. I saw him, felt him.' She looked at the assembled group of Lizzie, Jack, Kat, and Carrick, seated at the end of the table, drinking coffee and letting her talk. Rose and Brendan had taken themselves off for a walk and Julia was grateful they'd not heard the music the previous evening nor been witness to the scene. She wasn't sure what was worse, hearing herself saying the words or listening to their silence. Julia realised, as she looked from one blank face to the other, that she needed to get away. Away to Spain. Lizzie was right, a change of scenery is what she needed.

A sudden wave of anger welled up inside her. She fought to control these crazy swings of emotion but failed. She was furious with Patrick, the feeling so strong she wanted to tear all his clothes from their hangers and destroy them. To burn his suits, his jumpers, his jackets. Smash his guitars and wreck his music room. The need to punish him for tricking her into believing he was still alive - her grief and anger were all-consuming.

WHEN JULIA HAD ACCOMPANIED the police officer to the morgue to identify Patrick, she thought about the number of times she'd watched this scenario being played out on television. Mid-Summer Murders or Inspector George Gently - now she was the character who stood waiting for the sheet to be drawn back to identify the face of her loved one. It felt surreal. Flashes of Martin Shaw as George

Gently rushed to the surface, his voice so clear in her head, he could have been standing beside her. She wanted to stay within the world of television drama and not face the reality of whose body lay beneath the cover.

Seeing Patrick lying there, cold, damaged - not like her Patrick, Julia wanted to shout it wasn't him, they'd made a terrible mistake and that somewhere out there her husband was still alive. But that would have been a lie.

When the morticians had done their magic, Julia had insisted on bringing Patrick home. She couldn't bear the thought of him alone in a cold, clinical undertaker's room.

So he came home to her and she could see him and talk to him every moment of every day until the funeral and his ultimate cremation where her beautiful, talented, kind and generous husband would be reduced to fine ash, and she would have the neat little urn which was somehow meant to provide comfort from its place on the sideboard, instead of reminding her of the vibrant living person it had replaced.

Julia would need to find the courage to set him free. Free from the entrapment of his ornate urn.

Some acquaintances had found the prospect of an open casket at home macabre, peculiar even, while others had found kinder synonyms to describe what they saw as Julia's disturbed behaviour. But it had comforted real friends and family, knowing they could see him, talk to him, tell him stories and come to terms with their loss before saying their final farewell.

Alfie had barely moved from beside the casket from the day Julia brought Patrick home. He lay stretched out, head on his paws, barely eating and only venturing out to toilet. It was heartbreaking to see, and only when Nancy arrived each day, did he show signs of enthusiasm. She would crouch down beside him, stroking his ears and whispering messages which Julia wasn't privy to. It would be weeks before Alfie showed any genuine enthusiasm for life.

Patrick's casket had sat on the Undertaker's trolley, raised high enough for him to see the view stretching out across the lawn to the forest beyond, or at least that was Julia's thought process in placing him there. He would be at peace and it was important to her, that despite the brutality of his death, somehow being here at home, surrounded by the things of beauty he most treasured, this would make his journey to the other side a gentler one.

JULIA LAY STRETCHED out on her bed and acknowledged all that had happened that night, everything she thought she'd heard, saw and felt was just a manifestation of her grief. Patrick was dead. Patrick had been in the open coffin. There was no mistake. The storm had taken him. The impact of his car hitting the fallen tree as he swerved to avoid it had killed him instantly. He hadn't suffered they said. But do they always say that? Julia wondered. How does anyone know if someone has suffered or not? How do they know if in that split second before Patrick died that he wasn't aware it was the end and conscious he was alone with no one by his side?

A FREAK ACCIDENT, they called it. A vicious storm which had felled many trees and left roads awash with water and debris. The wrong place at the wrong time. She hated hearing these clichés. Hated people trying to rationalise why.

6

SPAIN

They had seats in business class, courtesy of Lizzie and as the plane lifted off the runway at Heathrow, climbing and banking across London, Lizzie sensed the tension in Julia ease and recognised that temporary feeling of relief that for a while she would leave behind so much sorrow, the way Lizzie had when she'd departed London for Spain after Michael died.

Jack had flown from Melbourne with them as far as London before they'd said their emotional goodbyes at Heathrow. Katharina was waiting for him; she'd flown across from Geneva, wanting to be by his side and know that he was okay since her earlier than planned return from Melbourne due to work pressures.

She was wonderful, Lizzie thought, kind and loving - the perfect wife for her godson. The knowledge that Jack had Kat by his side would comfort Julia.

Julia had visited Lizzie only once since she bought her penthouse in Palma. She'd travelled out to say goodbye before she started a new life in Australia. It raised painful memories for Lizzie.

Lizzie had been depressed at the thought of Julia leaving for a *new life down under*, as people referred to it, worsened by Julia's apparent light-hearted lack of distress about moving so far away from Lizzie and their friendship.

Lizzie had understood that Julia needed to follow her new husband's dream opportunity but couldn't stop herself from feeling resentment that Julia hadn't shown more concern for what this meant to Lizzie.

When Lizzie compared her time with Michael to Julia's with Patrick, she felt that Julia's *dropped bread of life* always seemed to land *butter-side up* and she could feel the worms of envy, regret, sadness, anger and bitterness twisting inside her even as she happily contemplated the prospect of rekindling the closeness of their friendship.

Lizzie knew Julia had been looking for an excuse not to move out to Australia, there hadn't been one to find. She couldn't use Jack, he was married and settled. There was no excuse.

WHEN JACK GRADUATED from Juilliard and returned from New York to London, he announced he was heading off to travel around Europe for 'six or maybe twelve months, depending on what opportunities come my way.' He'd spent four months travelling with a friend when he met Katharina in a bar in Stockholm.

He'd phoned Lizzie to tell her all about this amazing woman he'd met- phoned Lizzie before his own mother and this had not only surprised Lizzie, but it had warmed her with smug glee that he'd chosen his godmother over his own mother to convey his excitement and starry-eyed love for the woman who would later become his wife. Lizzie had been in London when Jack had brought Kat out to meet everyone for the first time.

'He was a dangerously good-looking boy, I thought.' Kat would later recount to the little gathering of Lizzie, Julia, and Patrick. 'A mix I found too irresistible. My heart would say to me, Katharina, you are a foolish Swedish girl with your head in the Ostrich. He's too good looking to be nice. But I learned in time I was wrong on two counts. You can be good looking and a good person, and my English was not so good, and the Ostrich was in the sand.'

They'd laughed until tears ran, and they'd all warmed to Kat instantly. They could see the attraction and knew, given time, she would marry Jack.

'He's chosen a blonde version of you, Julia.' Patrick would tease. 'Don't you agree, Lizzie?'

'Don't be silly, she's nothing like me.' Julia had retorted, whilst smiling despite the denial. Lizzie had a different view to Patrick but decided against sharing it.

When an opportunity for both Jack and Kat to work in the music industry in Geneva presented itself a year later neither hesitated and that's where they had been ever since. Lizzie had been secretly pleased that at last Jack had set himself free of his mother's apron strings. Lizzie felt it healthy that Jack should live his own independent life and, always eager to be part of her godson's world, she kept in regular contact to share news and ideas and offer advice and wise counsel when she thought he needed guidance.

'WE'LL GRAB a taxi when we get outside,' Lizzie said as they towed their suitcases along the concourse at Palma de Mallorca Airport. 'I should have thought to ask my neighbour to come and get us.'

'A taxi will be fine. At least it's warmer than in London,' Julia said.

'I know, bloody freezing there. Now you know why I live here.' Lizzie laughed as she exited the arrivals door and headed towards the line of taxis.

'And the air is fresher. I couldn't believe how smoggy London was.' Julia remarked.

They'd enjoyed their week-long stay in Carrick's Bloomsbury apartment despite the cold, grey London days and pollution. Carrick had flown to York for work in the early evening of the day they'd arrived. It had been obvious to Lizzie that he was escaping the attraction of Julia.

'I can imagine Carrick is kicking himself he couldn't spend time with you in London. Apart from the loss of his brother, which he is distressed about, he doesn't get to spend time with the woman of his dreams.'

'Oh, for heaven's sake Lizzie, these insidious innuendos you keep trotting out have to stop.' Julia interrupted. 'I'm like a sister to Carrick, that's all it's ever been. The number of different women he seems to date, I hardly think he has time to moon over me.'

'Rubbish, he's smitten. You must be careful.'

'Thanks for your support, dear friend.' Julia responded sarcastically.

'Portixol please driver.' Lizzie said, ignoring Julia's tone, watching as the driver lifted both suitcases and dumped them carelessly in the taxi's boot.

They rode in silence the short distance from the airport to Lizzie's apartment. Lizzie could sense Julia's irritation and wondered briefly if it had been such a good idea inviting her out here if she was going to be this up-tight for the rest of her stay.

London had been a buzz, plenty to see and do, and it allowed Julia a temporary reprieve where not every minute was a painful memory and reminder of what might have been. She had made an effort to get out and explore London and be more upbeat rather than drifting around Carrick's apartment grief stricken and barely able to function as she had been in Melbourne.

Now it was just the two of them, and Lizzie wondered again how it was going to work if Julia kept provoking Lizzie's latent feelings of resentment and anger fuelled from the hidden depths of Lizzie's own depression.

JULIA HAD a young couple renting her home in Melbourne. It had overwhelmed them, her generosity, especially given the size of the property and the low-rent Julia was asking. She'd even arranged for a gardener to come in each week and look after the grounds, but they had insisted that Julia cancel the gardener and they would do it. Jason and Sarah, it seemed, were keen gardeners and happy to attend to everything that needed doing. When Julia left Spain, she would head to Ireland to spend time with Rose and Brendan, and Lizzie wondered how long it would take Carrick to make his move.

Lizzie thought Julia was naïve to believe this had not been an orchestrated positioning on Carrick's part to suggest she spend time in Ireland with his parents. It would make her easy prey. Grief stricken - vulnerable and ripe for the taking. Dead brother's wife or not, Lizzie believed Carrick had one intention and one intention only.

Lizzie had observed one Christmas a long time ago now - when they'd all travelled out to Ireland to Rose and Brendan's; watching as Carrick smoothly negotiated his way between the simmering hostility of his brother and the girlish charm of Julia. She'd always had this hold over men. A spell rendering the male species helpless in her presence. It had been that way since their early school days. Lizzie constantly living in the shadow of the much taller, more beautiful, more elegant, enigmatic Julia.

'God, you could never get sick of looking at this view, Lizzie, it's so gorgeous and you've certainly changed a lot of things since I was here, not least the décor.'

Her stream of conscious thought broken; Lizzie looked across at Julia standing at the floor to ceiling windows unsure if Julia's comments had been praising or criticising the changes.

'Yes, I'd only just moved in when you visited. But you know me, I need to put my stamp on things.' Her tone was slightly defensive.

'It's only natural, I would have done the same.' Julia rushed to reassure, and Lizzie was fully aware of how prickly she was being, and bit back the sarcastic retort she was about to unleash.

She knew she'd moved with speed out of London and here to Spain; the ink had hardly dried on the Probate documents when she'd sold the home she'd shared with Michael in Henley before flying out to Spain whilst telling no one.

She'd just as quickly sold the tiny apartment Michael owned in Tarragona, getting an unbelievably good price for it, before settling on Palma as the place to start a new chapter in her life, searching intensively for several weeks before buying this beautiful penthouse.

With four bedrooms, a large terrace and her own private swimming pool, she'd made a glorious choice. She watched as Julia appraised the changes she'd made. Knowing Julia as she did, there wouldn't be much she would miss. Everything was different. This was her home, her choices. Had Michael been here, his taste would have dictated everything, but he wasn't here - there was no presence of Michael.

'Feel like a drink on the terrace, might catch the last of the afternoon sun before it gets too cold?'

'Sounds great, what have you got on offer?'

'Well, let me see,' Lizzie answered, bending down to check what she'd left behind in the fridge.

'There's white wine, vodka, gin, and red wine in the pantry. What do you fancy?'

'A white wine would be nice, thanks Lizzie. Do you want me to get it?'

'No sit down, enjoy the view. I'll get the drinks sorted and bring them out to the terrace, then we should think about where we want to eat tonight. Tomorrow I'll get some food in.'

JULIA

Lizzie was busy pouring the wine, giving Julia the opportunity to look around the apartment again. The artwork differed completely from anything she'd ever known Lizzie to buy. Both Michael and Lizzie had been keen art buffs. Some of Michael's choices were a bit out there for Julia's more conservative taste, but Lizzie had an excellent eye and now, without Michael's powerful influence, Julia could see where Lizzie's freedom had led her.

'Here you go.' Lizzie said, handing her a glass of white wine. 'Let's retire to the terrace, shall we?' Lizzie smiled at her and Julia felt the tension ease between them and the prickliness of earlier appeared to have dissipated

'I'm really pleased you came back with me. A change of scene will help, it really will.' Lizzie reached across the table and squeezed Julia's hand. 'And Jack and Kat will be out to visit in another 10 days, can't wait.'

As Julia gazed out across the city, her eyes settled on the yachts anchored in the tiny harbour and the familiar overwhelming sadness threatened to swamp her thoughts once more. Patrick would have been down at the harbour's edge ogling all the yachts before he'd unpacked his bag; he wouldn't have been able to help himself.

They'd never stayed at Lizzie's apartment together and in agreeing to come back with Lizzie, Julia had naively thought she may find a little slice of peace without the constant reminder of Patrick everywhere she went, but here it was, right in front of her. All those times they went sailing together in Ireland and in the Greek Islands, the memories assaulted her in painful waves, all the things that would never happen again or be reminisced over during intimate evenings.

The waves of sorrow rolled over squeezing from her the oxygen of hope that she would ever be happy again, tears welled in her eyes. In the space of moments she felt like a vicious street mugger had attacked her emotions with a baseball bat, smashing and bashing at her fragile belief that she could get through this nightmare and build a worthwhile life again, that she could somehow cope with this crippling loneliness and fear of facing her future alone.

The breath seemed frozen in her chest and she could feel panic rising in her throat under the assault of the emotional mugger. She put her glass on the table and stood hastily to escape to the bathroom.

'You okay?'

'Just need the bathroom. I'll be back in a minute.' Julia moved swiftly through to the main bathroom, shutting the door quietly behind her and letting her head rest back against the door.

It wasn't the first time she experienced a panic attack like this but they were getting worse, often unexpected and uncontrollable and for a woman like Julia, renowned for her considered and controlled demeanour, unsuccessfully trying to tame them or rationalise what was happening to her was terrifying.

'Now then,' Julia chirped in a strained attempt at cheerfulness as she walked back outside to the terrace, 'where shall we go for supper?' She'd washed her face in cold water and given her reflection a good talking to in the bathroom mirror before returning to Lizzie, determined she would not allow emotions to spoil the evening.

Surely, she could have one night free of despondent thoughts and memories?

'You okay?'

'Yes, just a funny tummy, probably gulped down that white wine too fast on an empty stomach. What do you fancy for supper, I know it's early, but we can have fun deciding?' She was babbling and Julia knew Lizzie would recognise she was trying to cover up her emotions.

'It's okay to be sad Julia, just because we're out here, there will still be reminders. It's impossible to block them out. Well, at least that's what I found, anyway.'

It was as though a dark cloud had swept across the sky and was hovering over Lizzie's apartment, and it reminded Julia once more of the depth of Lizzie's heartache over Michael. It may have been five years ago, but Julia could see Lizzie was struggling with her own demons.

They'd eaten that evening in a small café at the end of the street. Brief conversation passed between the two and Julia sensed there was much Lizzie wanted to say, but either couldn't or wouldn't.

It bewildered her, the change in Lizzie, and she could no longer blame the tension between them on Lizzie's drinking. There was something else. Something heavier on her friend's mind.

Later that evening when they'd both retired to bed, Julia lay awake, her mind drifting back to the week they'd spent in London. Lizzie had behaved oddly, Julia recalling the day they had arrived and after Carrick had departed for York, when Lizzie went marching through the house, straight up the hall to Carrick's bedroom only to find the door locked.

'How weird, who locks their bedroom door?'

'Maybe someone who doesn't like people snooping Lizzie. This is Carrick's home; he can lock whatever doors he wishes.' She'd barely contained her disapproval of Lizzie's actions. 'What on earth was she thinking and what was she expecting to find, a collection of blow-up dolls, mirrored ceilings and pornographic videos?' she bristled with indignation on Carrick's behalf.

Then there had been the scene over Julia catching up with her old boss and legal assistant. She couldn't understand why Lizzie had become so angry especially as she'd been out with her own friends at the time.

'So, I thought you didn't want to go out and see people, Julia? Then as soon as I'm gone, you make plans. Did you not want to come out with me?'

Lizzie had been so hostile. The words spat at Julia like some jealous lover. 'I contacted George and Maria before I left Melbourne, I told you that. George sent me a text message to say he would be up at Petries London office and if convenient, we could meet up. What's your problem with that?'

'There isn't a problem. I just thought it was odd you turned me down, but then made other arrangements, that's all. I would have liked to have caught up with George and Maria.'

'What for? You don't even know them. You've met George once and Maria not at all. Why would you expect or even want to come along?' Julia had been furious at Lizzie's attitude and stupid remarks. She didn't need or want hostility. She was finding it hard enough coming back to London with all its memories and no Patrick to share them with.

'You're being pedantic, Julia. I might not know them personally, but I feel I've known them for years. You worked with them and talked about them a lot.' She'd poured herself another wine, Julia noting it was the third in an hour. *Not that she was counting...* well yes, she had been, she was always counting and Lizzie's need to drink all the time was a worrying trend.

Julia had walked out of the kitchen and into the lounge, desperate to escape Lizzie's foul mood. Going out to meet up with Lizzie's friends had not been something Julia was remotely interested in doing. She'd met some of them a handful of times and found they had nothing in common. Why would she wish to sit in a London bar talking to people she barely knew and trying to remain upbeat and smiley when she'd only just said goodbye to her husband?

Now they were out here in Spain, Lizzie didn't appear any better. The barbed comments about Carrick, the defensive tone when Julia had commented on the apartment, it was tiresome. Perhaps tomorrow would be a better day. Holding onto this hope, sleep finally claimed her.

AS THE DAYS drifted by in Spain, Julia felt herself beginning to relax. Lizzie had become more tranquil, drinking less and behaving more like her old self. They'd explored Palma's old town and Castell de Bellver and spent hours at Es Balaurd, a contemporary art gallery. They'd eaten out and found a delicious array of fresh foods at the local markets to take back, prepare and cook.

Jack and Kat were to arrive in two days. Jack had phoned to say their stay would be shortened as they were behind schedule with the assignment they'd been working on. This news upset Lizzie when Julia told her they would only be out for four days at most.

'I was so looking forward to seeing them. I thought we could at least have 10 days, four seems hardly worthwhile.' She'd swept off to her bedroom for the afternoon which Julia felt was a strange over-reaction to the news, disappointing as it was.

Later in the day when Julia offered to cook, Lizzie responded that she wasn't hungry. Sitting on the couch flicking through a magazine - Julia knew she wasn't even looking at the pages or reading the articles, behaving like a truculent teenager denied the opportunity to attend a party where alcohol was being served.

'I'm going out for a walk, and maybe I'll grab a bite to eat. Do you want to come?'

'No. You go. I'm happy here.' She looked far from happy, Julia thought, but wasn't prepared to press the point.

Julia dressed warmly and set off along the beach for a walk and to catch the last of the sun. As dusk approached, she found a beach bar where she ordered a cocktail and sat watching the sunset. Glancing at a menu, the simple but diverse range of dishes made her mouth water, so she ordered a platter of cheeses, and homemade salamis with olives and flat bread.

After she'd eaten, she ordered coffee and noticed how the bar had filled with locals all chattering animatedly, gesticulating wildly as they spoke. She moved away from the bar and found a table out the front by the outdoor heater, content to drink her coffee in relative peace with an uninterrupted view of the ocean. They had cranked the sound system up and suddenly Julia found herself transported back to another time and place.

They'd had dinner at Byblos, their favourite restaurant. It over-looked the Yarra river and after their meal they'd walked back across the city to the Forum Theatre where Patrick had tickets to a Johnny Marr concert with an up-and-coming Melbourne band headlining the main act. He always liked to support local talent whether it was London or Melbourne.

Julia had never been to the Forum Theatre before and marvelled at the unique Gothic-Romanesque architecture. The exterior had an exotic design that continued as they stepped through the doors.

Lavish moulded plaster, gold paint and reproduction casts of famous Greek and Italian sculptures lined an auditorium interior topped with a soaring blue ceiling punched with stars designed to look like an open sky. She loved it and as they settled themselves at a table with large leather chairs; she imagined they could have been at a venue in London's West End.

Julia returned to the present as she felt the lump forming in her throat, but she would not cry. Not tonight, not here in such a public place, but as she listened to the music, she allowed the memories to take hold and could see herself lean into Patrick and whisper 'who does the drummer remind you of?' He'd turned and grinned at her.

'He plays just like Jack, even left-handed. It's the same rolling, rhythmic style. They're an amazing band, I love their stuff.'

As she sat immersed in memories, a young waiter cleared away her coffee cup.

'Excuse me, can I get you another coffee, cocktail perhaps?' She looked up into the smiling face of a young man, sleeves rolled up exposing tanned muscled arms.

'Maybe I'll be a little wild and have another cocktail. I'm loving this music.' She smiled up at him as he finished wiping her table and collecting the empty coffee cup. She thought she detected an Australian accent.

'The staff take turns each night in selecting something they like. It's my turn tonight.' He flashed what she could only describe as a beautiful Colgate smile, which Julia thought had probably cost his parents a fortune in teenage orthodontic care.

'It's a Melbourne band, Flyying Colours, have you heard of them?' Before she answered he continued. 'I'm from Melbourne and they're the best band we have, probably the best in Australia.'

'I've seen them live as a matter of fact at the Forum.' She sat back in her chair smiling smugly, feeling like she'd just answered a popular culture question on a TV quiz show.

'Nooo,' he said, almost dropping her coffee cup with excitement. 'Don't you think they're the best? Are you an Aussie, you don't sound like it?'

'No. I'm a Kiwi and I thought they were an amazing band and I'm not normally into that music. What do you call it? Psycho shoegaze?'

He laughed out loud, flashing his beautiful white teeth at her. 'You mean psychedelic shoegaze.'

'Probably. Anyway, I thought they were great, and it has been lovely sitting here listening to this compilation.'

'Well, don't go away, I'll bring you out a cocktail, my special, something I picked up in Rarotonga when I was doing a bar job there for a few months. Back in a jiffy.'

He sounded so stridently Australian - she felt her spirits lifted by his youthful exuberance. Here she was - thousands of miles from Australia and she meets a barman who is a fan of a band she and Patrick had seen play live and had a vinyl record of - 2 degrees of separation as they referred it to in New Zealand.

The cocktail the young barman brought out was delicious. He called it an Atiu Special, but Julia didn't care, she enjoyed every sip and as she sat watching the sun go down, listening to Flyying Colours and the track *Mellow* she felt the weight of grief shift a little. As the track ended and the music changed to something from Fleetwood

Mac, she left behind a generous tip for the barman and made her way back to Lizzie's penthouse.

As she walked, she felt she'd achieved a tiny goal in not falling down that black hole of grief. It was a relief to remember Patrick and enjoy vivid images of him without losing control to that psycho little mugger wanting to beat up on her emotions with his baseball bat.

There was no sign of Lizzie when Julie let herself into the apartment. She'd left a lamp on in the living area, otherwise the house remained still and quiet. She tiptoed into her bedroom, deciding she'd skip her nightly routine of make-up removal and night cream. She undressed and pulled herself under the covers. Sleep came almost immediately, a first since that knock at the door.

8

TO BREAK A FRIENDSHIP

Jack and Kat had flown back to Geneva on an early evening flight, so Julia and Lizzie were eating supper in silence. The moon hung low in the sky illuminating the ocean beneath and had the mood not been one of antagonism, Julia would have enjoyed the view as the night reflected its beauty on the surface of the ocean.

'Why did you have to keep harping on about Patrick to Jack? Julia, couldn't you see he's as grief stricken as you are?' Lizzie announced, breaking the silence and increasing the tension between them.

'I wasn't harping on about Patrick. What are you talking about Lizzie, or is this just the booze talking again? For God's sake, stay away from the drink, it's not doing you any favours.'

'What fucking right have you got to be lecturing me? This is my home and I'll do what I like and if that doesn't suit you, then piss off back to London. Back to the arms of your love-sick brother-in-law and don't say I haven't warned you. He'll make his play for you soon enough.'

'That's bullshit, Lizzie. What is it with you and Carrick? Why all the hostility? He's done nothing to hurt you.'

'He's like any bloke, Julia. Running around the world, probably got a woman in every town and still thinks he can get lucky with you if he hangs around enough. You need to stop encouraging him, give him the flick, quick smart.' Lizzie sat opposite Julia, a look of belligerent resentment in her eyes.

'Carrick isn't like that, Lizzie. I don't think he's looking for a girl in every town and as for me, he's just a kind and supportive friend who's looking out for me.'

'Looking at you more like! Panting along in Patrick's shadow, while you keep him keen with little scraps of affection that you toss his way. Do you think no one else is good enough for him, Julia? Not smart enough? Not attractive enough? Do you really believe you're the only one he has eyes for?'

Julia's eyes hardened. 'What the fuck are you saying Lizzie? He's both a womaniser and has the secret hots for me and I'm what? "treating him mean to keep him keen" because secretly I don't want him to be looking at anyone else while I'm working through grieving for my dead husband.' She was seething with anger.

'You're fucked in the head Lizzie - or is it that you're just plain ugly when you're pissed. And let's face it, that's an awful lot of the time these days. What you're doing to yourself is so destructive but it's not just you that is getting dragged down.' Julia pushed herself up from the table and taking her plate moved across to the kitchen to stack dishes in the dishwasher.

'Don't lecture me, Julia. I couldn't give a flying fuck what you think. Your opinion has never mattered to me. You might have men hanging off your every word, but not me. At university, all those guys flocking around you saying, "Pick me, pick me". You loved it and I got so sick of being treated second best.'

Julia turned, all of her grief and pain turning to anger which boiled up inside her.

'Is that why you slept your way through university, Lizzie? Is that why I had to haul you out of a guy's room when it became obvious he'd invited along a few mates to watch and join in the fun? Is that how desperate you were to appear popular? Debasing yourself because you thought you were proving a point by scoring more meaningless sexual encounters than me, Christ, that's sick.'

'I liked sex, what's wrong with that? You have no right to be preaching moral code to me, not when you were sleeping with that Spanish guy. He was all over you. Dance classes, my arse!' She was screaming now, her face distorted with the rage of a drunk. 'That was an excuse, and you fell for it, you're so naïve, just like the way you were over Nick. I warned you about that family. But did you listen to me, no way?'

Julia ignored the reference to her ex-husband, but the anger was turning to ice inside of her.

'Wrong again, Lizzie. Emilio was gay. He was too afraid to come out. He didn't have the hots for me, we were friends and dance partners, that was all.' Julia let the words hang in the space between them.

Julia saw the hesitation in Lizzie and the realisation she'd been wrong about Emilio but unwilling to abandon her rage she pushed her chair back from the table with such force it toppled over, clattering to the tiled floor. She kicked it out of the way and lurched to the fridge to top up her wineglass, pushing past Julia.

The sound of the chair crashing against the tiled floor acted as a trigger for Julia, and she was back all those years ago in her kitchen at the cottage with Nick standing over her, fists clenched. Her stomach churned and for a moment she thought she'd need the bathroom, instead running from the room, away from Lizzie's cruel words. Leaning her head against the bedroom door, she let the tears fall.

A while later, she walked back to the kitchen for her phone and a glass of water to take to bed. Lizzie was standing on the balcony but swung around when she heard Julia and walked back inside.

She sneered. 'Don't run off every time things get difficult Julia, you're such a coward. You've always said you have a thing about people keeping secrets, but it sounds like that's just a load of bullshit. I was your best friend, but you didn't tell me about Emilio did you? You also kept William's sexuality a secret as well and all the time you knew I fancied him. I loved him Julia and you let me go on believing I had a chance, you cruel bitch.' Lizzie was swaying, trying to keep her balance and pour herself wine at the same time. Tears coursed down her cheeks.

'You don't understand how hurt I was that you'd kept that from me. We vowed there'd never be secrets between us. But you've never kept your end of the bargain, never Julia.'

Julia fought to keep control of her voice, to stay with the ice instead of the fire that threatened to flare up again

'That was William's secret, Lizzie, not mine. He was my brother, and he was frightened. I made a promise, and I would not break that for you or anyone else. Anyway, why are you reaching back into the past? What are you trying to achieve, Lizzie? Do you even know?'

'What I know Julia – what I know - I know,' she slurred, 'you're a selfish bitch. Everything is all about you. I've always been the one to pick you up and patch you up. What have you done for me? Standing there with all your judgement. You're not judging that slag of a mother of yours any more though, are you? You've forgiven her sins.'

Julia spoke quietly now, her words precise and considered like a surgeon's scalpel cutting-out something bad.

'Don't talk like that about my mother, Lizzie. I will never forget what my mother did but it's my right to forgive so that I can move on with my life. Maybe you should try it Lizzie, because holding onto the past doesn't look like it's working too well for you.' She sighed heavily before acknowledging Lizzie's statement.

'Yes, you've always been there. And I'm forever grateful for what you did for me. But you're conveniently forgetting how I was there for you when you were out of control at university. You wouldn't have finished your Masters' degree if I hadn't intervened and dragged you away from that rotten group of boozers and drug addicts you'd gotten yourself tangled up with.'

'I was there for you Lizzie when Leighton was running around town shagging anything with a pulse. And despite what you say, I was there for you when Michael died. I was the one accompanying you to that woman's house. I was the one sitting with you for hours as you ranted and raved.'

She saw Lizzie visibly flinch as her words hit a nerve. And watched as the glass Lizzie was holding slid from her hand and smash to the floor, wine splashing across the room. She appeared momentarily distracted by this event, before grabbing Julia's empty wineglass from the kitchen surface and refilling it for herself.

'You don't understand what that was like for me, all that betrayal.'

'I do, Lizzie.' Julia's tone was softer, gentler, recognising Lizzie was in a great deal of pain and, drunk or not, whatever was in her head and coming out of her mouth did not belong to the Lizzie Julia had known and loved since they were young.

'I know all about betrayal Lizzie, but you have to move on, you can't let Michael's secrets keep you in a holding pattern of anger and bitterness. You've got to move on with your life and let this go, and if you can't do it, then go get help. Please, Lizzie.'

Lizzie staggered across to the couch and flopped down like a rag doll, slopping some contents of her wineglass down her front.

'I can't forgive Julia. I can't forgive any of it. You might forgive your mad mother, but I can't forgive mine. She was a weak, pathetic woman who stayed in that shit marriage because she didn't have the balls to leave. She never gave a thought to what it was doing to me, living with a drunk for a father.'

'Your mother did care, she cared very much. She was your shield and took the blows meant for you, that's not the actions of someone who is weak and pathetic,' but Julia could see Lizzie was past talking, her head had tipped forward onto her chest and the glass she was holding was dangerously close to slipping through her fingers yet again.

Julia stepped across and took the glass from her hand and gently laid her down on the couch. Retreating to the bedroom, she brought back a blanket and covered Lizzie's drunken form before returning to the kitchen and sweeping up the shards of broken glass.

In the morning when Julia woke, she lay in bed listening for any sounds from the kitchen, but the penthouse was still and quiet, the only audible sound was that of early morning birds calling out their excitement at the prospect of a new day.

She'd decided before sleep finally overtook her the previous evening, that she didn't have the emotional resilience to shoulder Lizzie's problems as well as her own, so would pack her bag and leave. Now she was awake, she'd phone the airline and change her flight to Dublin, accepting it would be foolish to stay on any longer. Lizzie was out of control and Julia's presence was only making matters worse.

She'd shut out sections of the evening's drunken rage, too afraid to place all the pieces on the table and examine them. The vitriol that had spilled from Lizzie last evening - all that bitterness and resentment of a past that no one could change was not something Julia wished to revisit in any detail. She needed to be in a better emotional place herself before she could deal with Lizzie's problems.

When she had showered and packed and phoned the airline, she walked out to the kitchen intending to make herself a coffee and then phone for a cab. She would sooner arrive at the airport early and wait for her flight, rather than stay in the penthouse with Lizzie a moment longer than she needed to.

As she poured coffee into a cup, she looked up to see Lizzie standing out on the balcony. Lizzie turned and Julia held up her coffee cup. 'Want me to make you one?'

'Thanks. That would be nice,' Lizzie replied, turning back and looking out to sea.

Lizzie joined Julia in the kitchen. 'What shall we do today, anything you feel like in particular?' Lizzie asked, as though the evening before had been nothing more than a disagreement over what channel to watch on the television.

'I'm leaving Lizzie. I don't think it's a good idea for me to be here any longer.'

'What? Why? Can't you handle a little sparring between friends, Julia?' That sarcastic tone was back – it was never far away.

It was no surprise to Julia that Lizzie viewed last night's ugly and destructive argument as sparring – her own mother had been exactly the same.

'Lizzie, can you not see what you're doing, how you're behaving?'

'I could ask you the same questions, Julia. Life isn't all about you and your grief.'

'Shitty behaviour Lizzie; isn't some negative quid pro quo deal. It's not something we trade or build entitlements to. Harming another doesn't heal you but makes the cesspit you're living in even more putrid.'

'Fuck you're uptight, Julia, always have been. Too much to expect you to lighten up a little, I guess.' Lizzie took a sip of her coffee before retreating to the couch and sitting down.

'You've created a swimming pool of crap Lizzie, and you keep inviting me to jump in with you. But I don't wish to swim in the filth of your pool, and nor should you. Pull yourself out and stand on the side – get some help.'

Julia had waited for the explosion, but none had come. Lizzie just looked back at her blankly for a few long seconds, as though trying to process something that didn't make sense, and then resumed cradling her coffee cup.

Julia finished her coffee, put her cup in the dishwasher, collected her packed bag from the bedroom and let herself out of the penthouse, choosing to wait downstairs for the taxi she'd ordered to arrive. As she waited in the sun of a Spanish morning, tears slid down her cheeks as she acknowledged she'd not only lost her husband but also her best friend.

9

———

IRELAND

Flash backs to the moment the two police officers knocked on Julia's door were frequent and painful. Despite the slow pace of life in Baltimore with Rose and Brendan, Julia fell into an ambush of memories. They infiltrated her dreams, leaving her washed out and depressed in the morning.

She could be out walking, and thoughts would drift back to the day Patrick died, and before she knew it, the mugger with his baseball bat would rain down blows on her vulnerable emotions. Was she partly to blame for now being alone?

She hadn't been totally open with Patrick about being unhappy and in return he hadn't been honest about also wanting to move on. Had she told him how she felt, maybe they would have been making plans together instead of him being out late with his lawyer that night so he could surprise her.

She would put her head between her hands and plead for the self-destructive feelings to stop, but the mugger in her head wasn't listening. Had she known somehow what lay ahead that day, would she have behaved differently?

Would she have reassured him of her love and told him that there was no one else in the world with whom she would rather have shared her life? She relived every moment over and over, re-examining every detail of that day as though she were studying a difficult legal case, where if she just concentrated enough on the information before her she'd find the answer.

All these thoughts compounded by remorse and guilt. Remorse because she'd been so angry with him for being late, but late was so much better than never. Guilt, because if she'd been truly *in love* with him, would he have been less reticent about sharing his plans sooner and still be here by her side?

Yes, she loved Patrick deeply but was this her punishment for ultimately marrying a man because he loved her child and that had meant so much more to her than the giddy emotions of being *in love*?

She seldom explored the decision she'd made. Keeping the thought safely tucked away in the back of her mind like a black pearl remaining hidden in an oyster for fear that examining it would reflect the dark truth, to her shame.

WHEN THEY'D TOLD her there had been an accident, that Patrick was dead, Julia could not utter a sound. Frozen. Unable to move. Unable to speak and unable to cry. They'd asked if they could call someone, a relative, a friend perhaps. This question had momentarily shaken her from shock, and she'd asked them to go across the garden to her neighbour, Mrs McAlpine, Nancy. 'Fetch Nancy,' she'd said. 'Go out the lounge doors and across the lawn to the left, there's a gate in the fence which leads to her house,' waving an arm in the general direction.

Julia remembered being huddled in a chair, unable and unwilling to move. Believing if she remained still then this horrible, horrible news, this information which she was sure had to be wrong, would pass on by and all would be well. It wouldn't be real.

It wasn't until Nancy puffed into the lounge; her face red with the shock of finding a policeman at her door and the exertion of rushing to Julia's side and when she'd lifted her bowed head and looked into

Nancy's anguish filled face Julia broke down and cried, although she now remembered it as more of a howling.

Nancy had been remarkable in those first hours which rolled into days when she'd hardly left Julia's side only returning to her own house for a change of clothes and to feed Hagrid who steadfastly refused to eat at Julia's house despite spending most of his time lazing on her terrace. His whiskers twitching and jaw jigging as he uttered pitiful cries to the birds who flew in and out of the garden, the only other moving part was his tail, a quick flick now and then, the effort to stalk and catch a bird far too strenuous a task for Hagrid.

Pushing these memories from her head, Julia reached the top of the hill, panting loudly, her breath creating little smoke rings in the wintry morning air. She decided she would go back to London before Christmas and then arrange a flight back to Melbourne. She couldn't stay in Ireland forever, avoiding the inevitable. Life went on, regardless of her state of mind, and she needed to sort out what she would do about work.

Following the meeting with Patrick's solicitor, she understood there was no need for her to work again. There was enough money. But they still had a mortgage over their house and whilst it wasn't substantial it would need maintaining for the time being until she decided what she would do and where she would live. She couldn't imagine shutting herself away on the mountain and not venturing out to work. She'd worked all her adult life and suddenly to find she no longer had to was both liberating and terrifying in equal measure.

It made her face the reality that she'd made no real friends in the time they'd been in Melbourne other than Nancy. There were no girl-friends she could meet up with for coffee to discuss her options. There was no one she considered close enough to invite back to the house for a wine. Patrick had been her husband, lover and best friend, and she'd foolishly made little if any effort to build meaningful friendships with other women.

She was alone, and it reminded her of the life they'd left behind in London. She'd made more friends in London than Australia. But did she want to move back to London? The week spent in Carrick's apartment with Lizzie had been a wonderful distraction. Catching up with some of their old friends had been both comforting and confronting - all the sadness and reminiscing had left her drained and exhausted. And she couldn't help but notice how much London had changed since they'd left.

She walked along the ridge heading for the boulders on the far side where she liked to sit and enjoy the view. Knowing this was a place Patrick would come to when he was back in Ireland and somehow being up here made her feel closer to him and a sense of peace would blanket her. She let her mind wander as she looked out to Lough Hyne.

Time is a healer everyone kept telling her. Well-meaning fuckwits is what she thought of their platitudes. Time doesn't heal. Time was merely teaching her how to live with the pain. Her wound was still gaping and to heal it she must stop touching it. Stop re-visiting that day - that knock on the door, and then maybe the bat wielding mugger would get out of her head.

She acknowledged she missed the mountain. Missed the wild beauty of the place, but she knew going back would be difficult – a minefield of memories and then what? What would she do with her life in a country she'd never felt connected to? A job she now admitted to herself was stifling her desire to make a difference.

She'd made the move from London to Australia for Patrick's sake. It had been all for him. She harboured no ill-feeling or regret. It was pointless to wonder what if – what if they'd stayed in London? Chances are he would still be alive. But he wasn't and he'd wanted the opportunity in Australia.

It had come as a complete surprise to learn that he'd intended resigning from his post as head of department. That he'd wanted a change. Why hadn't he talked about it with her? He'd kept something as important as a career change from her and now she was here in Ireland, feeling him so near, she questioned how close and in tune they'd really been with each other?

But wasn't she also guilty of not sharing her feelings? She was unhappy at work. Unfulfilled, needing a change and coming to the realisation that she didn't belong nor want to be living in Australia. Had she told him how she felt? No, she hadn't. She'd tucked all those feelings safely away in a private mental box, hoping she would never have to open the lid and spoil Patrick's happiness. But it seemed he hadn't been all that happy either.

It had not been a simple decision to leave England behind and start afresh. There had been many heated discussions well into the night when Patrick first raised with Julia the opportunity to take up tenure in Australia.

'Australia. Christ, that's not exactly next-door Patrick.'

'I know. And I know it's a big change, but I would like you to at least consider it, talk about it with me. That's all I'm asking.'

They had talked and talked and talked some more. So much so, Julia had felt overwhelmed with the enormity of what he was asking of her. England had been her home for many years and the ease of slipping across the water to Ireland and Europe to holiday and to visit Jack had become a part of the natural rhythm of their life.

'I don't have to accept this offer Julia, but I need you to understand that I really want to. This is an amazing opportunity, and it won't come my way again.'

In that moment Julia read in his eyes both fear of a "no" and anticipatory joy that she may just say "yes". She wanted to please him, to give him what he wanted, but she'd done that before in her previous marriage, placated and given in - then punished for her acquiescence.

Julia imagined she could smell the fear on her skin and feel it with every breath she took. The change would be frightening.

She knew and loved the security Patrick shared with her so freely, openly and wisely; enough to make her believe that security now lay inside of her, like thin planks of smooth wood, side by side, a stable resting place that she owned. Now Patrick asked that she discard that security and embrace the challenge of new beginnings.

'It's so far away Patrick. From your parents from Jack and Kat. Have you given thought to how they will feel?'

'Of course I have, but they have their own lives. I've lived away from Ireland for a long time, my parents understand and accept that, always have.'

'What about Jack and Kat then. How do you think they will feel? You and Jack are always on the phone chatting - won't be so easy from Australia Patrick.' Her voice had taken on quite an edge, but at the time she'd been unable to control her anguish.

'Okay, okay. No need to get so aerated.' He'd finished his tea in one rushed gulp, putting his cup down and turning out the light, signalling an end to a conversation they both knew would plunge to lower depths if Patrick kept countering Julia's arguments.

When Julia woke the next morning, reaching out to touch Patrick, her fingers felt the pillow and her hand slipped down to the cold sheet and empty bed. He was already up, so unlike him. Her mind slipped back to the conversation the night before and she knew him well enough to understand if she said no to Australia, he would never speak of it again. He would carry on as he was, teaching, writing, and performing in equal measure.

She also knew she would have to live with the reality that she'd stolen his dream. Hanging on to her fears and letting them dictate their life would prevent Patrick from embracing an opportunity, which, as he'd said, would never come his way again.

She lay in bed a while longer, overwhelmed with the reality of what a new life may bring. Julia loved England, and she had no desire to live anywhere else. They had a life here, a good life. Okay, they didn't have the house and land they both daydreamed about, and England wasn't the same as it had been when she'd first arrived and fallen in love with it. You would have to be blind or rich to not notice the changing social pressures and how much England laboured under the weight of so many people, so many immigrants and too much crime.

They'd lived through the London bombings in 2007, although still tucked safely away in Hambleden it hadn't impacted them in the same way it had Londoners. In 2011 it was the London riots, leaving them shocked and angry that their beautiful city had plunged into such chaos, the summer of disorder and violence. That summer they'd retreated to Ireland to the safety of the family.

Julia wasn't oblivious to the changes, not all for the better, but here was the rub. It was home to her and had been for a long time and she loved it. She was reluctant and a little afraid to say goodbye.

When Julia first arrived in England from New Zealand, she'd been in the Home Counties. Even after she met Patrick, they remained there only moving when Jack left home, and they had the freedom to choose. Not that there had ever been any debate.

Patrick loved London, and it was far more convenient for him to be living in London, closer to the music scene. Petries of Maidenhead, where Julia headed up the Family Law department, also staffed a London office and had done so for the previous two decades, so it had been a seamless move for Julia and the most natural of progressions.

Choosing where to live in London had posed more of a dilemma. Eventually they'd settled on a very modest apartment in Chelsea surrounded by art, culture and music. It suited their needs very well. They could escape to Europe when London's grey days threatened their mostly optimistic mood, and to Ireland in the heat of summer when London crowded with tourists was no place to be. It worked for them - they were happy. Could she give all that up to live in Australia? And could she live so far away from her son?

Julia could hear Patrick's heavy tread on the stairs, relieved he hadn't left the apartment for work without saying goodbye. She heard him curse; and realised he must have spilt whatever he was carrying, tea or coffee?

'Morning. I've made tea although slopped some of yours on the stairs, sorry.'

She pushed herself up grabbing for the extra pillow beside the bed and shoving it behind her back before taking the proffered cup from Patrick.

'Thank you. You're up early?'

'Couldn't sleep.' He did not get back into bed, instead he gazed out the window with his back to her, sipping his coffee; she could smell the strength of it from where she lay. His hair needed cutting, he always wore it collar length, but now it was too long and too straggly. Wisely, Julia decided against voicing her opinion, sensing he was in no mood for her to be critiquing his appearance.

He turned then, catching her staring at him before moving closer to the bed and resting his bottom on the edge of the mattress.

'I'm sorry this business of Australia is causing you so much angst. I hadn't appreciated just how much you love being here - I don't mean London, I mean England. I love Ireland, but I haven't lived there with any permanence in such a long time it doesn't hold me in that same way. You know, hold you - the way a place, a country, can hold you in its embrace, like a lover?'

'Yes, I know, and thank you for being so patient with me.' It surprised her to hear the sadness in his voice, and it made her realise just how much she'd robbed him of the joy of being offered this opportunity. It was selfish of her.

'You're right, I am struggling, but what's more telling is how fearful I feel. I stopped being afraid when you came into my life and I don't want to go back there; it's a dark place for me, uncertainty and insecurity take me back to the darkness of my childhood and my marriage to Nick.'

'I can't change what's happened in the past, I can only promise that I'll keep you safe, loved, adored. That's a promise I can easily keep. You're such a brave woman, Julia, but I have to ask myself - am I demanding too much of you? Am I embracing adventure and an opportunity to do something different because deep down I need to say I've made it? Am I saying to everyone, tenure on the other side of the world, who'd of thought! Am I being selfishly indulgent to want this for myself? If we go, will this impact my parents, Jack and Kat in ways I can't imagine? I don't have the answers.'

'You've earned this, Patrick. You mustn't believe otherwise. I think you should call them tonight, when they are awake over there and tell them yes. "Yes", you would love to accept. We'll work through the decision with Jack and Kat and your parents.'

For a heartbeat Julia had wanted to snatch the words back and scream "No" I can't do it, can't bear to leave here, but she didn't. She let "Yes" sink in and watch the relief flood through Patrick like rushing water released from a dam. She knew he'd been holding onto hope, but probably feeling after last night's heated conversation that hope was not enough. They would go and they would make it work and they would build a new life for themselves.

That decision had set in motion so many changes and so much upheaval. Patrick had phoned Australia that evening, and the procedures were put in place for moving out in three months.

He then phoned Jack and Kat in Geneva and then his parents in Ireland. It thrilled everyone, especially Jack. They were kindred spirits, but Julia couldn't help but wonder if Jack truly felt as excited as he sounded. It had always been so easy to slip across to Geneva to visit or for Jack to drop in to see them when he was over in London for work. That would all change. And she'd never lived far away from him. But as Patrick reminded her, there was always Skype. That idea held little appeal for Julia.

In the weeks preceding their move, Patrick spent hours trawling through real estate websites in Melbourne looking for the perfect plot of land. They had often day-dreamed of buying land and building their own house and it had remained just that, a daydream. A *"One Day"* thought bubble in that giddy space between reality and escapism where you are free to experience your repressed desires without answering to your sensible self.

Driven by a desire to appease Julia, whilst still fulfilling his own fantasy, Patrick emailed several real estate enquiries. Julia was less inclined to rush into committing themselves immediately, content instead to rent for a while until they found their feet. This was the difference between them. Patrick was a restless man with a fearless love for throwing himself at change and challenges.

Julia recounted to Patrick how she'd lived in Melbourne briefly as a young woman. It held bittersweet memories following her escape from home, after a nasty argument with her violent, alcoholic mother only months before she was due to start university.

Gathering a few belongings, her recently gained passport and all her savings from her after-school jobs, she'd booked a flight to Melbourne. Why Melbourne? The airline had a deal on flights, including a week's accommodation. She wasn't the back-packing type, too afraid to sleep in a bunk room with strangers, and this offer was too good to pass up.

A week would give her time to find a job and somewhere to live. Optimistic and horribly naïve, she set off alone, leaving behind Lizzie.

She'd left a note for her brother, William, and her father. Without the ease of mobile phones, email or Skype, they would be unable to contact her and would have to be content to wait until she phoned or wrote. Neither of which she did for several weeks. Her need to find happiness away from her mother allowed little space for concerns about others, and that included William and her father and even Lizzie who, in their airport phone conversation, had alternately said she understood and then pointed out what a shitty selfish thing Julia was doing without even talking it through with Lizzie first.

Her decision had proved to be both challenging and rewarding. She would look back later and know that she'd re-claimed a little of herself. Rising out of the anger and sorrow and self-pity, she'd discovered an inner strength which prior to running off, Julia doubted she possessed.

Melbourne opened her naïve Kiwi eyes to possibilities and opportunities and if William had not come looking for her and persuaded Julia to come back home, back to a university place waiting for her in the faculty of law, she may never have returned.

10

CARRICK

He'd witnessed her pain, her sorrow, and felt powerless. His need to go to her, to comfort, to love and protect was overwhelming, but he'd controlled his emotions. Even on the night she'd been out on the lawn, lying there in the rain.

He'd slowly surfaced from a dreamless sleep to the dulcet tone of Leonard Cohen. Climbing from his bed and moving to the French doors, he'd watched as she turned and swayed as though she were dancing with someone.

He'd heard her crying out Paddy's name and had opened the door ready to go to her, but Jack had come running from the other side of the house and it was he who lay with her, comforting his mother in the way Carrick knew he couldn't do. The memory of that evening still haunted him.

For years he'd been content with his two-bed flat in Chiswick. His bolthole when returning from long-haul flights. The Chiswick apartment block had been his first foray into residential real estate, which had proved lucrative over the years. But more recently, he'd longed for somewhere more luxurious. A place he could call his London home.

He had his house in Lymington, near the shore of the Solent, but that was more of a weekend retreat. He'd kept the Lymington property a secret for years, neither wanting nor needing company when he escaped there, content instead to wander the grounds and listen to nature undisturbed, and if the weather was fine, he'd take his yacht out and sail.

He'd given Paddy and Julia the keys after they married so they could enjoy some time away from the Home Counties and fit in some sailing while they were down there. On two occasions Julia had asked that he come down and join them, but he'd declined her invitations, claiming he had business or prior engagements to attend to. But that had been a lie. The first of many concerning Julia.

Carrick had narrowed his search for a London property to the West End for its proximity to culture, entertainment, and good transport. Patient searching led to finding what he wanted, the end property of a set of Georgian terraces in Bloomsbury. Whilst run down, he could see huge potential if it were sympathetically renovated and he fell in love with it. He knew a good builder familiar with the Georgian era who would deliver what Carrick wanted and at a reasonable price.

When the building work was complete, Carrick hired an interior decorator to make-over the entire space. The result had surpassed even Carrick's dreams. He loved the layout, the décor, the way the rooms caught the sun at different times of the day, the beautifully proportioned rooms with their high ornate ceilings and stunning windows.

A courtyard at the rear of the property was large enough to entertain a few friends, but still keep its intimacy. Overgrown with weeds which hid generations of discarded household paraphernalia, he'd decided he would clean the area up himself. He enjoyed gardening and soon had the Bloomsbury garden space cleared, re-designed and re-planted. Now it was an oasis of peace and calm. With careful planting, he'd created a secluded area to enjoy a wine and a BBQ artfully shutting out the noise and bustle of London.

CARRICK HAD WATCHED Julia's face as he opened the door and welcomed her and Lizzie into his Bloomsbury home.

'Oh, wow Carrick,' Julia had said, 'this is stunning, what a find.' She'd smiled the way he'd seen her do so many times before – before Paddy died, and it relieved him to see that beautiful heart-breaking smile was still there - could still shine regardless of her grief. He wondered if Julia had expected some bachelor pad because the look on her face suggested that what she was seeing was not what she had been expecting.

He explained how he'd found the place and how he'd been so excited at the prospect of restoring it. How he loved that the interior designer he'd used had interpreted his tastes to perfection.

Enthusiastically he'd chattered on, revealing all the details of the restoration, loving Julia's obvious appreciation until noticing Lizzie raise an eyebrow at him as if to say - *'Really Carrick, stop trying to impress her like you're the first boy at school to get a car. She will not fall for that!'*

He'd never quite got the hang of Lizzie. He knew she was Julia's best friend, and they'd been close since their school days back in New Zealand, but on the few occasions he'd been in Lizzie's company he'd found her cool, aloof and sometimes waspish.

She was petite, big brown eyes with long thick lashes in a pixy face. He should have found her looks attractive. Instead, he realised, contained within that petite package were some hard defences and sharp edges, and he sensed that if she were out of her comfort zone, she wouldn't hold back. There was something brittle about her that belied the amiable smile.

He could see Lizzie was loving with both Jack and Julia, but she could be acerbic with comments she made to Carrick and occasionally he'd heard her snap at Paddy.

He'd never raised the subject with his brother. It was none of his business, but he knew his brother well enough to know he would not appreciate her razor tongue.

Carrick had decided, when he'd invited Julia and Lizzie to stay at his home, that he would ensure he was not around to share the time. He had business to attend to in York and he'd catch an early evening flight so he could show them around and then discreetly leave. He knew Lizzie was always watching him around Julia. She was like some over-protective matriarch ensuring her grown-up daughter would remain a virgin.

'I'll show you where everything is and leave you to relax and enjoy being back in London.'

'Where are you off to?' Julia had asked. The image of her standing in his kitchen so clear.

'I'm flying to York tonight. I've got business to attend to up there.' He'd seen her frown and sensed she was disappointed but knew it would be a mistake to stay.

'So, will you be back before we go to Spain?'

'No. Sorry I won't be. I'm up there for a week. But you don't need me here. Enjoy yourselves, rest, relax before you head out to Spain.' He'd turned away, busying himself with making coffee, unable and unwilling to look into those beautiful green eyes without wanting to hold her in his arms and never let her go.

He'd deliberately avoided joining her in Baltimore, recognising the danger. He needed the time apart to force his emotions into order. There was plenty of work in London that needed his attention, and work was always a great distraction.

He'd spoken to his mother, and it was she who had suggested that Julia spend a few days in his apartment before she headed back to Melbourne. He'd agreed this was a good plan, he could hardly have said otherwise, plus he needed Julia to be staying on over Christmas and into the New Year.

Carrick hadn't shared with his parents the New-Year's eve surprise he'd planned. He would wait until he was with them for

Christmas before breaking the news, afraid they may forget themselves in their excitement and let it slip to Julia. He couldn't let that happen. This was to be a complete surprise, and he hoped it would be the start of a more positive year for Julia - for all of them.

11

IRELAND

Julia had enjoyed her walk but was thankful to be back enjoying the warmth of Rose's kitchen. The sun might be brightly shining, but the temperature outside was bone chilling. Warming her hands in front of the Aga, she turned when Rose asked, 'so what are your plans for Christmas, you are welcome to stay here with us, you know that?' The invitation hung in the air between them. Julia was tempted to say yes but knew she had to leave. She needed her own space. Time alone with her thoughts.

Being here for Rose and Brendan had been therapeutic for them - the opportunity to talk endlessly about their son. To reminisce about his childhood, about his success, about everything he achieved and how proud it had made them. But then would come the sadness and pain and the realisation there would be no new stories to tell of the favoured son - only the old to recite, embellish and re-work until all those memories resembled a battered, but much-loved story book whose pages were marked and worn from being turned by loving hands.

Witnessing their sadness and pain only added to her own. She wanted nothing more than to find a peaceful space where she could pull down the blinds, lock the door and turn off her phone.

'I think I ought to think about returning to Melbourne. I love being here, but I have to return sometime. Nancy can't look after Alfie forever, and I need to figure out what I'm going to do about my job.' Her voice trailed off. The thought of dealing with everything that lay back in Melbourne was overwhelming.

'We understand. It's just been so wonderful having you here. You're like a daughter to us Julia, I hope you understand how much you and Jack mean to us?'

Julia clutched at those words. They were words that lifted the blanket and let her crawl right on in, comforted by what she knew was family. She loved Rose and Brendan but recognised she couldn't hide away here in Baltimore indefinitely.

'I love you both very much Rose, but I have such a lot to sort out. So many decisions to make. And yes, I know there is no immediate rush, but I have to make a start.'

'Why don't you go back to London for a few days before you take on that long trip back to Australia? I'm sure Carrick wouldn't mind you staying at his place. He phoned while you were out to see how we were. He's planning to come over for Christmas.' Julia watched as Rose continued to wipe down the kitchen table repeatedly as if she were somehow wiping away the pain with a dishcloth.

'It's the awful hollowness, Julia. The waves of wretchedness that threaten to engulf me – mind and body – it's frightening.' Julia saw the tears slide down Rose's cheeks and wondered if she knew she was crying. Rose seemed to cry a lot without seeming to realise she was doing it, like a scratch she didn't know was bleeding, as if her body excreted grief without her knowledge. She wanted to go to her, to wrap her in an embrace, but she remained standing by the Aga, a spectator to the moment. Her own sorrow was that of a wife. To be a mother grieving for your lost son, must be so much worse.

'It is a beautiful thing to watch a well-loved son grow into a man. You understand that Julia. I see the way you are with Jack.' She lifted her head and smiled at Julia before carrying on her task of wiping the table.

'I watched Patrick grow into a man of integrity, capable of

powerful love. To see him spread his wings, do right by those in his life, and strive to make the world a better place. All those children he taught, especially the disadvantaged ones. He was a blessing to everyone lucky enough to know him.'

Julia wanted to run upstairs to her room. The mixture of love and pain in Rose's words was heartbreaking, and she knew she was right to be leaving.

By the afternoon, Julia had phoned the airline and booked her flight to London. She'd fly out in two days' time. She'd also spoken to Carrick, and he had been more than happy that she come and stay in his apartment. He would meet her flight so she didn't have to worry about a taxi. He'd asked about Rose and Brendan. Julia could tell by his voice that it worried him how they would cope once Julia left.

She'd reassured him they were strong, resolute, and that Carrick returning home for Christmas would be just what they needed.

Rose and Brendan had driven Julia to Dublin airport. The parting had been difficult, and she feared she was being selfish, but she knew in her heart she needed to escape the sadness and sorrow and try to find comfort in the anonymity of London.

12

___

LONDON

Julia sat on the large leather couch in Carrick's lounge. It was a beautiful room and over the past few days she'd wander in curling up on the couch, pulling the throw around herself and read.

Carrick had wall to wall bookcases full of books. An eclectic mix of fiction, biographies and history. She could spend hours reading in this room with its beautiful windows that captured the view across the city, the high ornate ceilings and stunning marble fireplace. She loved everything Carrick had done to this apartment. It was not only beautiful, but it evoked a sense of peaceful serenity every time she walked through the front door.

'Did you collect these books yourself or are they just for show?' She smiled across at Carrick who had poured them both a wine and was standing leaning against the fireplace taking his first sip.

'No. Not for show, thank you very much. I read you know. Always have. But I admit, they are not the result of careful hoarding across decades.'

'I knew it. This collection is quite something.' She grinned, enjoying this light moment of teasing. Over the past few days Julia had unwound and she put it down to this house and the ease of being around Carrick. They'd always shared a special relationship. Comfortable in each other's company. Silences between them had never been awkward. It was as though they could read each other's thoughts without the necessity of incessant talk.

'One of my commercial property tenants in Paddington was retiring. He'd been running this incredible bookshop for decades. He is a lovely man, but old and finding himself alone with just his books for company and with the uptake of Kindle and Kobo, he didn't have the energy nor enthusiasm to compete.'

'How sad. We've lost so many lovely old bookshops. When we lived in London, I would spend entire weekends wandering around bookshops exploring what they had. Buying the odd, rare book.' Julia had a sudden vision of herself finding a battered copy of Pride and Prejudice and bringing it home wrapped in tissue with a wax seal, the trademark of the bookshop.

Patrick was standing in their kitchen making coffee, bemused at her delight. She could still see the look on his face which told her he thought she was bonkers paying a silly price for a battered old book when she could so easily have ordered a beautiful new copy online. He didn't understand her love for old, well-loved and treasured books.

'So, what happened to this old man then?'

'He tried to sell the lease and hoped that someone young would share in his love for books and take the place over. Sadly, that never eventuated, so finally he had to shut the door.'

'And let me guess, all these books,' she waved at the bookcases, 'are the contents or some of the contents?'

'Some of the contents. The rest I sold on his behalf, and I found a new tenant to take over the lease, so he didn't have to pay out the final year. It's a women's boutique clothing shop now. Not the same at all. All shiny. The new tenants spent a fortune kitting it out with modern counters and painting it bright colours. The pitch pine floors are the only reminder of what was before. It appears they are still in fashion.'

Julia thought she detected genuine sadness in Carrick's voice. He loved old buildings, loved the architecture of bygone eras, and whilst he'd renovated this entire apartment, there remained many if not all of the original features. Maybe, she thought, that was why it felt so much like a much-loved home and not a bachelor pad.

'Do you keep in touch with him, the old man I mean?'

'Yes. I do, actually. His name is Edward Schneider.'

'Jewish then?'

'Of Jewish decent. His parents came to England as refugees after the first world war. I visit him when I'm in London. We talk for hours about books, the war, his wife.'

'His wife? I imagined from the way you talked he didn't have a wife or any family.'

'No. He had a wife, but she died about five years ago. It was hard for him after that. They'd worked together in that little book shop for 30-odd years. Side by side every day. No children. They couldn't have children. He also had a brother, but he'd died in the war.'

'God that's awful.' Julia said. Suddenly wishing they could change the subject. This conversation was all too raw.

As though sensing the change in her Carrick looked flustered. 'Sorry. I'm being insensitive. I shouldn't have said that. It only serves to remind you. Forgive me.' He looked across at her curled on the couch and she could see he was visibly upset.

'It's fine. Honestly. You can't wrap me up in cotton wool. Please tell me more about Edward Schneider. How old is he? If he was in the war, he must be elderly?'

'I think about 88 or 89, something like that. He joined up in 1941. He'd been looking after his sick mother and couldn't leave her. When she died, he joined up as soon as they'd laid her to rest. He must have been around 20 years old at that stage.'

'Gosh, I couldn't imagine Jack running off to war at age 20. A blessing the man's mother was dead. At least she didn't have to worry about him being far away in a foreign country fighting a war.'

'Anyway, enough of this maudlin talk. What would you like to eat? I can make a pasta or there's a beef casserole in the freezer that probably needs rescuing. What do you fancy?'

'Actually, the beef casserole sounds wonderful. It's that kind of night, isn't it cold and wet and good old comfort food hits the spot? I can help though. You don't have to run after me.' Julia pulled herself up from the couch and carried her glass through to the kitchen.

They stood side by side preparing potatoes and fresh greens. 'You've hardly mentioned Paddy's name since you arrived. I need to talk about him. I'm sorry if that upsets you, but I really need to talk about him. I need to feel he's still here. I miss him terribly.' Julia glanced across and saw the tears in his eyes.

'It would have been so much easier for mum and dad if it had been me.'

He said the words so matter-of-factly Julia had to think for a moment before responding, concerned she hadn't heard him properly.

'Don't say that, Carrick. Your mum and dad love you to bits. It wouldn't matter which son – it's just difficult for them.'

'I'm not looking for sympathy Julia – I know Paddy has always been the favoured son. It's the way it's always been. I'm not bitter and twisted about it. I disappointed my parents when I chose not to attend university. Even now, they still really don't understand what I do.'

'Rubbish they do, Carrick. They both talked about you a lot when I was there. They're very proud of you and all you have achieved and particularly the philanthropic work you do.' Julia remembered back to a conversation she'd had with Patrick about his parents and their relationship with Carrick.

'Maybe I'm still hanging on to the past then, when they thought I was some kind of shiny real estate agent.'

'Patrick told me once, a long time ago, that he'd spoken to them in depth about what you have achieved. He said it was clear they really did not understand what you did. It had saddened them both that they had so misunderstood you.'

'That's nice to hear. Paddy never mentioned. Anyway, I do what I do, and I will not apologise for the choices I've made and the path I've taken. I love my work.'

'I know you do and so did Patrick. He was very proud of you.' She swiped at a tear that threatened to spoil what had been two days without crying or feeling like the baseball bat mugger wasn't waiting to ambush her again. They carried on preparing the vegetables, dropping the subject.

As they sat at Carrick's dining room table enjoying their supper, Carrick asked about Lizzie.

'What happened in Spain, do you mind me asking?'

'No. I don't mind you asking, although it's difficult to put into words what went wrong. I know I was struggling with grief and probably not the greatest company, but Lizzie seemed filled with antagonism the moment we arrived in Palma, or maybe it started when she was out in Melbourne and progressed when we stayed here that week and became progressively worse when we reached Spain.'

'So, what's her problem then? I sense she doesn't like me much, or at least she doesn't like me being around you?' He stopped eating and took a sip of his wine.

'She's always had this thing that you...' Julia trailed off, unable or unwilling to finish the sentence.

'And what would that be then?' Carrick asked, guessing what was coming next.

'She thinks you are pursuing me while I am vulnerable.' Julia continued to eat her meal, avoiding eye contact.

'She really doesn't like me, does she? I've done nothing which would have made her believe there was some romantic interest between us?'

'I know you haven't. But she's got it into her head and once she seizes on something, she's like a Pitbull with a rabbit. And I think she's put the idea in Jack's head. He's raised it with me.'

'What? When did Jack mention it?' Carrick felt his stomach knot. He loved Jack, thought he was an exceptional young man who'd faced big challenges in his life and risen above them which, to Carrick, showed enormous courage and strength.

'After Patrick died and after Kat returned to Geneva. Lizzie had been out doing supermarket shopping with Jack. She finally had Jack all to herself, she's always been keen to spend time with him on her own. I don't mind. I've never minded. She's his godmother, but it's like something has changed and the relationship has become a competition. I wasn't sure at the time if I imagined it or the vibe I sensed was real.' She hadn't once lifted her eyes from her plate and Carrick was finding the conversation disconcerting, not being able to look into her eyes and read what lay beyond.

'You had just lost your husband, your best friend. Your pain was so obvious, to me. Did Lizzie not see that?'

Finally, Julia lifted her head and glanced at Carrick before taking a sip of her wine. 'Yes, she did, but sometimes I felt something odd pass between her and Jack. Now, saying it aloud, it sounds paranoid, but I know my son. I know him so much better than Lizzie.'

'He's your only child, regardless of how old he is now, he's still your little boy.' She looked straight at him with so much sorrow in her eyes.

'Yes, he is still my little boy, you understand that. Lizzie doesn't. Jack said something to me in the car one day about you, said that Patrick had told him when you were boys in Ireland you had a habit of developing a crush on his girlfriends.'

Carrick ran his fingers through his hair a gesture when agitated or angry. 'I was a right pain. I know that. I was in awe of the female species back then. I was so naïve. I thought girls were amazing, tantalising beautiful creatures, but always unattainable because my big brother had the looks and charisma, and I was kind of shy and awkward.'

Julia laughed, a sound he'd longed to hear. 'It's good to hear you laugh.' He smiled at her and took another sip of his wine, his mind racing with thoughts and questions. Did she know about Katie? Had Paddy told her?

'I feel guilty when I laugh. It feels disrespectful to allow myself this small pleasure. And yet I know it's not what Patrick would ask of me. He would never wish me to be sad and unable to find laughter in small things, but I can't seem to shake these guilty feelings.'

'It will pass. Like everything – it will pass, and other emotions will replace it.'

'I don't know about that. I still feel guilty over Jack. After all these years, I still can't shake that feeling.'

'What, that you should have known, that you should have done more, that you should have protected him? Because you were his mother, you shouldn't have failed him?' He knew when he said the words, they would be painful for Julia to hear, but he believed he understood her well enough that she would know in her heart his words came from a place of love and compassion, not judgement.

'You're the only person who would dare say that to me. And the one person who truly understands.' Tears were coursing down her cheeks. Carrick wanted to push his chair back from the table and go to her. Hold her and let her cry out all that guilt he knew she'd carried around for decades. They'd talked about it before, a long time ago on one of their many walks together in Baltimore when his brother had not wanted to venture out into the cold, content instead to sit by the fire talking with his father. But Carrick knew he couldn't go to her, it would be his undoing.

'It's easy to say, how could I have known. How could I have done anything different? But they're only words, excuses. I know Jack is fine, he has healed. He has a wonderful, loving wife and he's moved on and so have I. But I've never been able to shake off that feeling of guilt and maybe I don't want to. Maybe I want to carry it around with me as a reminder of how fragile life is and how careful we need to be with our children. How important it is as a parent – as a society to keep them safe.'

'Jack is an outstanding young man, Julia. Maybe now is the time to give thanks for the man he's grown into. He's not only a talented musician, but he's kind, caring and from what I've seen a dedicated husband. He'll be a wonderful father when that time comes.'

'But that's not just my influence Carrick, that's the entire family. Patrick, you, your mum and dad, Lizzie, and Michael when he was alive. Everyone played their part - it wasn't just down to me.'

'Yes, that's true, but we were not in his life in those early formative years, you were, that's what you need to acknowledge - your very important role. You have an amazing relationship with him and if

Lizzie believes she has something more special than the mother-son bond you have, she's deluding herself.'

'Back to Lizzie then.' Julia sighed, pushing her plate away from her. 'Shall I clear the dishes and we'll sit in the lounge by the fire?'

'I'll do that. You make yourself comfortable. Would you like herbal tea or something stronger?'

'A tea would be wonderful, anything herbal that you've got, but let me at least stack the dishwasher.' Before he had time to answer, she'd swept up the plates and cutlery and was busy loading them into the dishwasher before washing her hands at the sink. She turned to him, resting her hand on his arm. 'Thank you for this evening, it's been lovely. You are such a wonderful, special friend to me.'

Her hand on his arm felt like an electric shock had passed through him, and he wondered if she noticed the hammering of his heart and could read the guilty thoughts that raced across his mind? She moved away and left him standing in the kitchen, his emotions a mixture of love and fear. He was glad he would leave in another few days for Ireland and Christmas with his parents.

13

——————

LIZZIE

Lizzie had listened to the multiple voice-messages Julia had left, deleting each one after she'd listened. She had no desire to speak with her. Julia had abandoned her once again, running off to Ireland because she couldn't handle some home truths.

She'd phoned Jack the day before and detected a coolness in his tone. Or had she just imagined that? Her Jack, her beautiful godson. She must have caught him at a bad time. That was all it was. She mustn't let her imagination run away with her.

He had been busy since he returned to Geneva after spending a few days here before Julia left and went back to Ireland. It was better Julia departed and had not stayed on for the entire month. Lizzie had been thoughtful, but mistaken, in hindsight, to have invited her out for that long, given her obviously unpredictable state of mind.

Julia had upset Jack with her depressed state, constantly going on about the yachts in the harbour and how Patrick would have loved to have gone out sailing and Patrick would have loved the café they'd been to and the live bands. Patrick this and Patrick that as if Jack wasn't missing him just as much as his mother was, but all Julia could think of was her own loss, not how much Patrick's death was affecting

77

Jack. Lizzie understood. She understood him better than his own mother.

Lizzie had noticed how quiet Kat had been, and she wondered fleetingly if she were pregnant. My god, that would be so exciting. It would be wonderful to be a grandmother to Jack and Kat's child. She knew she wouldn't be an official grandmother; but she'd be a kind of surrogate grandmother –a significant person in the child's life. But she was getting ahead of herself. There was nothing to suggest that Kat was pregnant. Then again, hormones affect you, and Kat had been terse with her, so perhaps she had been a bit hormonal.

The argument after they left had resulted from a build-up of raw emotions. Years of hurt feelings, of jealousies all exposed in an ugly, heated argument. She hadn't meant to unload as much as she had, but once she started Lizzie found she couldn't stem the flow of vitriol. It poured forth like lava – spewing out its ugliness and ravaging a friendship that had lasted decades.

But it was up to Julia to apologise – it was! However harsh Lizzie's words had been that day – well, she'd only spoken the truth after all – so why should she apologise? Julia was the one at fault.

Lizzie had bought Jack and Kat's Christmas present online and couldn't wait to get the call on Christmas day from them to thank her for her thoughtfulness and her generosity. Flights and accommodation to stay at one of the top spa resorts in Paris. It was a crazy amount of money to spend on two young people, but what the hell, she had plenty of money and if she wanted to indulge her godson, then she would.

It was past midday, and Lizzie was already on her second bottle of wine. She'd stop soon and enjoy her siesta. She loved this way of life in Spain. She took a siesta every afternoon, often not waking until early evening, just in time for cocktails at the local bar with her ex-pat friends. She still couldn't decide if they were friends or not. More acquaintances. She didn't really rate any of the women in terms of intellect, but the men were interesting.

Nigel, a retired politician who regaled the group with interesting and sometimes salacious stories of his life in politics. He was fun, although Lizzie sometimes wondered if he suffered from chronic loquaciousness. The man could talk non-stop without appearing to draw breath, such a contrast to his dull bird-like wife who hardly uttered a word and often stared into space, her little feathers all fluffed up, oblivious to the world around her.

Then there was Gerald. Now he was an interesting one, Lizzie thought. A retired university lecturer in English literature. You had to get Gerald alone in a corner to get the best out of him. Lizzie likened Gerald to lifting the lid on a box of exquisite handmade chocolates – each one offering a tantalising delight of velvety chocolate with luscious fillings. He was fascinating to talk to, a real intellectual.

Tammy was just what you'd expect. Cheerfully loud and American, but despite these obvious flaws, Lizzie enjoyed Tammy. She didn't pretend to be anything other than what she was.

As Lizzie drifted off to sleep, she reminded herself she must loan Gerald that biography she'd found tucked away with the books she'd rescued from Michael's apartment in Tarragona. Gerald would enjoy it, she was sure, but she quickly discarded the associated thoughts of Michael which had popped uninvited into her head. There would be no dwelling on Michael – she would not allow him to spoil her siesta.

14

JULIA

Julia had drifted off to sleep but when she woke she realised she needed to get up and find her way into bed. It had been an interesting evening, but she couldn't remember falling asleep and had no recollection of Carrick covering her with a blanket and placing a cushion under her head. The last recollection she had was telling Carrick how she'd run into Sonia when she'd called into the café down the road to pick up a coffee that morning.

As she undressed for bed, she recalled the conversation with Sonia and how she had agreed to go to a yoga class - her old yoga class, the one she'd attended several times a week before they left London. She wasn't all that fussed about Sonia. She was the wife of Geoff, a male nurse at Evelina Children's hospital. Patrick had known Geoff for years and rated him highly, but he had little time for his wife. She was always putting her husband down, appearing to take particular delight doing so in public – watching Geoff blush or turn away to avoid the uncomfortable silence of his friends.

As Julia brushed her teeth, she cursed herself for saying yes, when really, she'd meant no.

'Oh, Julia, you must come to yoga tomorrow. They have a class now at 4:00 p.m. it will be just like old times.' Julia had wondered why Sonia thought it would be like old times. She never went to yoga with Sonia, but Sonia had been part of the larger yoga group who used to all meet up once a month for drinks and a catch-up.

She'd been standing in the queue at the coffee shop waiting, startled by the screeching voice of Sonia. 'Julia. Julia Devlin, is that you?' Why did people say that, she wondered? Is that you? *If you don't know, come over and enquire politely or get new glasses. Just don't shriek embarrassingly across a crowded coffee shop!*

Sonia, a woman who lacked spatial awareness with a terrible habit of getting up close and personal and touching everyone, as though they were her very own adorable litter of puppies that she couldn't resist squeezing and cuddling. She'd looked earnestly into Julia's face, squeezing her arm as she did so.

'It's such a surprise to see you. We were so sorry to hear of poor Patrick's death. Such a waste.' Giving Julia's arm another intense squeeze.

Julia pulled back her pyjama top to see if dear Sonia had left a bruise. She wondered who the "we" was. Sonia and Geoff were no longer an item. Maybe she was referring to the yoga group. Julia had loved her yoga group. She'd made a point of religiously attending her yoga classes twice weekly.

The group, a collection of like-minded lovely women, who had remained friends even after she'd moved out to Australia. Sending emails every few months and threatening to descend on her for a holiday. They never had. It's the thing people say when you leave a place. But as time moved on, the contact became less and less.

Some, she knew, had moved on themselves, across to the west country or up north. One had died from breast cancer, which had made Julia feel sad when she received that email. Maybe one or two from the old group would be there at the 4:00 p.m. class, and that would ease the pressure of Sonia's intensity.

As she climbed into bed, she looked at Patrick's photo on the bedside table. She'd sealed it in bubble wrap before carefully wrapping his jumper around it for extra protection when she'd packed her bags in Melbourne. She'd unwrapped it when she got to Spain, re-wrapped and unwrapped when she arrived in Baltimore and now again at Carrick's.

'Where are you?' She thought. 'I know you came to me that time. I know it was you. It wasn't a dream.' She picked the photo up and placed it against her mouth, gently kissing the face that smiled back at her before returning it to the bedside cabinet and turning out the lamp.

She woke to the sound of cups rattling and sat up as Carrick knocked at her door.

'Come in.' she called. Carrick pushed the door open with his foot and carried in a tray of freshly squeezed orange juice, yoghurt with muesli and a piping hot cup of coffee.

'Here you are.' He waited as she pulled herself up in bed. 'You were spark out last night, it's good to see you relax a little.' He smiled at her. It was Patrick's smile, but not Patrick's eyes. Caught in the memory, she'd wanted to reach her hand up and brush his cheek. She turned away, unable and unwilling to give Carrick eye contact, afraid the moment of tenderness might be misinterpreted.

Being around Carrick had been both soothing and alarming. She struggled with containing the unpredictable ebb and flow of her emotions. The way she'd been in Melbourne. Sudden moments of genuine anger, even rage when she'd wanted to lash out at everything and everyone. But these flashes dissipated in seconds, whereas the feelings of tenderness and intimacy lingered, and she found them disconcerting.

Crying and feeling sad and depressed was one thing, normal in fact when you're grieving, but these feelings were different. They hung around like a bunch of teenagers waiting for some action on a Friday night. She wanted it to stop.

'So, what are you planning to do today, apart from yoga at 4:00 p.m. assuming you are going to go?'

'You remembered then - I wish I hadn't said yes, but maybe it will be good for me. I love yoga. As far as the rest of the day goes, I have no plans. What about you? When are you flying out to Dublin?'

'Day after tomorrow. I want to spend as much time with mum and dad as I can. Christmas will be hard for them, for all of us. But I'm worried about you being here alone.'

'I'll be fine. I need this time Carrick. Time alone to just be. Jack and Kat have a big recording going on. They're intending to work through Christmas, and maybe that's a blessing for Jack, take his mind off things.'

'Have you heard from Lizzie?'

'No. I've tried phoning and left messages, but no response. And maybe that's for the best. I have to get through this first Christmas. He loved Christmas – like a big kid. Even in Australia when it doesn't feel like Christmas at all with the heat and flies and people having BBQ's instead of roast turkey with all the trimmings and hot desserts.' She sighed, remembering.

'It's prawns and salad and steak and whatever else they want to throw on hot charcoal. It's not the same as a northern hemisphere Christmas, but Patrick always made it special.' She could feel the tears well up behind her eyes but refused to let them flow. They could wait for another day, another time.

'Anyway, you never said what you were doing today?'

'I have this special friend.'

'Do you? And just how special is this friend?' Julia could feel a tiny knot of tension in her stomach. When he said friend, she assumed he meant female. She'd not thought Carrick had a current girlfriend.

'Oh, she's extra special, always has been. But she's sad, and I was thinking of a way to cheer her up?'

'Why is she sad?' Julia looked up at him and saw him grinning at her and realised he was referring to her. 'You clown, you had me going there for a minute.'

'I can't remember the last time I had a girlfriend or lady friend.'

'Really. I thought you had a string of females who ran to your side as soon as you crooked your little finger?'

'That's a myth. I've never had a string of females. Anyway, I thought I would take you to one of the last remaining old bookshops in London. It's across town, but we could have lunch on the way back. You up for that? I'll have you home in plenty of time for your yoga class.'

'That sounds like a perfect day. Let me finish my breakfast, which looks delicious, thank you. I'll take a quick shower and be ready to go.'

IT WAS COLD OUTSIDE, but they'd wrapped up warmly and caught the tube across town. The Christmas shoppers were out in force and Carrick didn't think they could get across London, have an exploration in the bookshop, enjoy lunch and be back in time for Julia's yoga class if they drove.

They spent the rest of the morning exploring the beautiful old bookshop. Julia found an original vinyl record of Pink Floyd's second album, *A Saucerful of Secrets*; the first album to feature Dave Gilmour as the guitarist replacing Syd Barrett.

This find would thrill Jack. He loved his vinyl records and over the years had amassed an enviable collection. She knew he didn't have this one. Patrick had made a list of all the vinyl records Jack owned so they could add to his collection without the risk of duplication.

As Julia strolled around the tiny shop, she'd discovered not only book and record treasures, but some lovely pewter pieces, some dating back to the second world war. Kat loved pewter and after a lengthy discussion with Carrick, they agreed on a matching teapot, milk jug and sugar bowl. Julia could imagine them sitting on the tiny shelf in the kitchen of Jack and Kat's apartment. The space would be just big enough to display the set properly.

She'd already warned Jack and Kat they probably wouldn't get anything from her to open on Christmas day. The thought of Christmas shopping had filled Julia with dread. It was something she and Patrick did together every year. It would take them all day, but they loved it and always ended up at the end of their shopping expedition in a bar somewhere discussing their finds.

The thought of him not being by her side to share in this ritual had been overwhelming, and she'd warned everyone they would have to wait until the New Year for any gifts.

Carrick had changed her mind. In bringing her here to this little treasure trove of books and records and other treats, she'd pushed the images of Patrick to the back of her mind and been content to have Carrick by her side to share in the purchasing of special gifts.

After over two hours in the shop, she'd bought everyone something. Even if it were only small, it would be special. At the counter she noticed a case displaying exquisite handmade wrapping paper, so beautiful you could frame it and hang it on a wall. She bought a variety of unique designs with matching ribbon, excited at the prospect of wrapping everything when she got back to the apartment.

Carrying their Christmas gifts in a large carry bag, Carrick steered her out the door and around the corner to a great little pub where they could enjoy a traditional English pub lunch before catching the tube back across town.

As they ate their meal Carrick raised the subject of Lizzie once more.

'Has Lizzie changed since Michael died. I mean, has she grieved properly for her husband?'

'I don't believe so. But then I've been on the other side of the world for most of the time since Michael died. I was here for almost a year after his death and then we moved to Australia. But Lizzie made it clear in one of her drunken rants that she resented me leaving her to deal with her grief. I honestly don't know what I could have done differently.'

'What, she expected you to send Paddy out to Australia on his own and you stay with her for as long as she needed, seriously?'

'That's what she said, not in so many words, but she kept reminding me of how she'd stood by my side when my first marriage fell apart. I'll always be grateful for her love and support during that time and for everything she's done for me, but I could never have let Patrick go out to Australia on his own. He's my husband and needed me by his side.' The memory evoked such emotion, Julia struggled to contain the tears that threatened to trickle down her cheeks.

'The problem is, Lizzie hasn't really got any close friends other than me. But I can't talk. She's been my friend since school and whilst I had good friends when we lived in London, I've made no new friends in Australia. Patrick's my best friend.' She realised she'd again used the present tense and looked across to see Carrick's eyes fill with tears.

She reached across the table and held his hand. 'I miss him so much Carrick and I know you do too.' He smiled back at her, shaking his head like a dog as though he were trying to dislodge the emotion that had suddenly welled up.

'Don't stop, carry on with the story.'

'Well, she's drinking heavily, and that is a surprise and a worry. When Jack and Kat came over to see us in Spain, it was only for a few days. They couldn't spare anymore time, but that decision disappointed Lizzie. She loves them, and she's always had a special relationship with Jack.'

'Maybe it's become too special. She's his godmother, not his mother. I've noticed how effusive she is with Jack, it's, well I don't know - I feel it's over the top.'

Julia wondered if Carrick's and Patrick had discussed it because Patrick had also felt that Lizzie was too possessive where Jack was concerned.

'Was there something funny about Michael's death? I got the impression from Paddy that there was something strange. Or have I got that wrong? Paddy would never discuss other people's private lives – he hated gossip?'

'I know, one of his pet hates.' Julia hesitated, wondering if she should talk about Michael or just leave it, but her need to share as she would have with Patrick was more pressing.

'Michael was in Portugal when he died. He was out there for a golf tournament with his friends and suffered a heart-attack. They'd gone down to the beach for a swim after a game of golf. He'd dived into the surf and didn't surface. It was dreadful for Lizzie getting that call.'

'So why do I think there was something mysterious? Sorry, you don't have to break a confidence if you don't want to. It was rude of me to ask. She's your friend and I can appreciate you may not wish to discuss something so personal.'

'You can stop now.' Julia smiled. 'I don't feel I'm breaking a confidence talking to you. I probably need someone to talk to about it, and I trust you.' She took a sip of her coffee before continuing.

'After Michael died and Lizzie had gone through the ordeal of having his body flown back to England, which was quite a drama - she received a call from his practice nurse asking if she could call by the house with the contents of Michael's office drawers. She'd packed everything up into boxes and wanted to drop it off.' She hesitated for a moment, lost in the memories of the past.

'Joan is a lovely woman, and fond of Michael. She'd been his practice nurse for decades, so his death had been an awful blow to her.'

Julia looked across the table at Carrick and found herself reluctant to reveal what happened next, and Carrick detected her hesitancy immediately. He reached across and put his hand over top of hers.

'You don't have to tell me anymore. There may come a time when you feel ready, but I sense it's not now. Let's finish our coffees. It's been a delightful lunch, but it's time to get back across town so you are not late for your yoga.'

ONCE BACK AT THE APARTMENT, Julia rummaged through her suitcase and found some stretch leggings and a floppy tee shirt. That would have to do for yoga, she thought. She didn't have a yoga mat but assumed they would have spare ones at the centre.

'Bye Carrick, I'm off to Chelsea. Not sure when I'll be back, but don't wait to eat.'

'Okay. Enjoy your time with Sonia.' He was laughing at her as he held open the front door.

'That's not remotely funny. I was foolish to say yes to this. Anyway, it's done now so I better get going or I'll miss the start.'

When Julia arrived at her old yoga studio, it surprised her to note that most of the people standing around chatting and rolling out their mats were fit young women.

There were two yoga instructors at the front of the room with legs folded like origami, eyes staring into space. Julia presumed they were meditating - either that or they were on something and whatever it was she would like some too. They looked serene. She'd never been to a yoga class with two instructors.

This was nothing like her old class, where the instructor had been a woman in her early 60s and no one younger than 45 in the class. She looked about for Sonia, but heard her first, her voice carrying across the room like nails on a blackboard.

'Hi ya Julia,' she screeched rushing into the room, her yoga mat rolled up under one arm and a handbag slung around her chest. Dressed in bright pink leggings and a black glittery top, she reminded Julia of a disco ball.

Finding a spare mat and making herself comfortable, she stretched out and closed her eyes. But Sonia wanted to fill the calm space with idle chatter. Finally, the instructors unwound themselves and looked out to the class. A silence descended on the group and as the instructors began the Ashtanga mantra.

Julia fell into the familiar rhythm as her body relaxed, and the tension loosened. By the time they came back to sitting in the cross-legged position and the last notes of their chant faded away, Julia felt so relaxed and at peace she could hardly believe an entire hour had passed by.

'I thought we might go for a wine, that little place round the corner, you remember the one Julia?'

'Is it still there?' Julia asked as she returned the mat to the instructors and paid the fee for the one-hour session.

'Yes absolutely. You're not going anywhere else, are you? Lovely, let's go then.'

Julia cursed her slow reaction. She'd rather go back to Carrick's and stretch out on his wonderfully comfortable leather couch but had let herself be hustled by Sonia. She bought the first round of wines as Sonia settled herself in a booth.

'So, tell me what brings you here to London Julia, are you thinking of returning?' She leaned across the table as though there were about to be some great unveiling of secrets between the two.

'No, not at all. I've been out in Spain with a friend and then in Ireland with Patrick's parents. I'm having a brief break here before I return to Melbourne.'

'Well, Patrick must have left you comfortable then if you can flit around like a jet-setter.'

The envious remark irritated Julia. She changed the subject away from herself and her perceived jet-setter lifestyle.

'Patrick and I were sorry to hear you and Geoff have parted ways. We were both very fond of Geoff. Is he still living in London?'

'Oh, don't be.' She waved her hand in the air the way one would at an annoying fly. 'It was a relief, frankly. Honestly, Julia I feel like it has lifted a great weight from my shoulders. And no, he's no longer in London, last I heard he was up north somewhere, that's where his family are from.'

'I didn't realise you had been so unhappy.' Sonia's comment surprised Julia as Geoff was a lovely man. Kind, intelligent. Maybe that was the problem. He was a nicer, smarter person than Sonia.

'So, what are you doing job wise? When we left you were in marketing - weren't you with – was it, Vodafone?'

'Yes, that's right. But I left them. I'm working for Sainsbury's now. It's great, I love it. What about you, still in law?'

'Yes, insolvency and liquidation.' She wouldn't add that she hated it and didn't know what she would do when she returned to Melbourne and that since Patrick's death she would no longer have to work ever again if she didn't wish to. She sensed Sonia had a wide green streak of envy that wouldn't allow her to celebrate Julia's good fortune.

Julia watched as Sonia gulped down her wine, pushing back her chair and heading to the bar for a re-fill. 'Same again, Julia?'

'No thanks. I'm fine with this one.' She watched as Sonia sashayed up to the bar, smiling at the barman as she flicked her hair off her shoulder. 'God, she couldn't make it more obvious if she tried,' thought Julia. The poor guy was at least half her age.

'So, you didn't say where you were staying in London? Please don't say you've put yourself up in a posh hotel, Julia?' She laughed, but it sounded so phoney, Julia knew she'd been right not to discuss her finances.

'I'm staying with a friend.' She wouldn't say it was Patrick's brother. A warning light was going off in her head, telling her she needed to be cautious.

'It must be awful for you, suddenly finding yourself alone at your age, it's difficult to find a suitable man, believe me I've been looking.'

She rolled her eyes in that annoying way she had that Julia remembered from the past when they'd all be out for dinner and she'd roll her eyes and sometimes fake yawn at something Geoff was discussing with Patrick. She really was an obnoxious woman. Julia needed to finish her wine and make her excuses to escape.

'I don't want to end up with another male nurse. God Julia, you can't imagine how embarrassed I used to be having to tell people I married a male nurse, so demeaning.'

'Really. What's wrong with being a male nurse? They do a marvellous job - we need more of them.' Sonia looked at Julia as if she'd announced a third world war would be good for everyone.

'I don't expect you to understand. I mean, being married to a musician how could you understand. Especially Patrick.'

She looked across Julia's shoulder as though she were remembering a moment from the past. 'We'd known him for ages before he met you and to be honest Julia, and I know you won't mind my saying this,' she reached out to place a hand on Julia's arm, 'I fancied my chances with him, but then you came along and snatched him up.' Her fingers squeezed Julia's arm as she smiled knowingly.

Julia could feel the little ball of rage growing larger and larger inside of her. She was slightly afraid of these feelings. They came from nowhere and sometimes brought violent fantasies, like right now when she wanted to take Sonia's hand from her arm and break all her fingers one by one. She really didn't want to be with this woman, but the last vestiges of politeness kept her there.

'So, what's happening with your son, wasn't he in Europe somewhere?'

'Yes. Geneva.' Julia sipped her wine quicker in preparation for leaving.

'We couldn't have children. Probably for the best given how our marriage ended and I've no regrets about that. I enjoy being free of the burden of kids.'

'Sounds like you've got the perfect life, Sonia,' Julia said, unable to disguise the derision in her voice. 'Being footloose and fancy-free. Not being tied down with relationships seems to suit you.'

'Do you think so Julia?' Sonia gushed, flicking her hair back from her shoulder like she was auditioning for a hair product advertisement. 'I've always looked after myself, more than I can say for some women. I mean you look good for your age, but I know plenty who don't. Then they wonder why husband's leave them for a better model. Honestly, you can't help some people.'

'My age,' Julia thought, 'that's the second time she's referred to my age. I don't think I need any more of this.'

She looked up to see Sonia waving at someone who had come through the door. She watched the woman wave tentatively back with a stricken look on her face before heading directly to the back of the bar and into the ladies. Probably hoping if she stayed there long enough Sonia would forget about her and the woman could escape. Julia had a sudden image of the stricken faced woman squeezing out through the toilet window and making her escape.

Taking advantage of the distraction, Julia stood quickly. 'I must go, Sonia. I've got things I have to organise tomorrow. Thank you for inviting me to yoga, I really enjoyed the session.' That part was true. She hadn't thought she'd enjoy it, but she did. It was Sonia's company she was finding unbearable.

'Do you really have to run off? I was just going to suggest we grab a bite to eat?' She appeared to not comprehend why Julia would wish to cut short their evening together.

'Sorry. I have a lot to organise and I really must be off. Goodbye Sonia.' And with that Julia grabbed her coat and bag and hurried out the door, rushing along the street to the tube station as though she were being pursued.

Later, as Julia lay stretched out on Carrick's couch cradling a cup of herbal tea, she wondered why Geoff had married Sonia. They were complete opposites. Opposites attract and all that, but their personalities were unsuited. She heard Carrick ending a phone call before coming through to see if she wanted anything.

'I take it Sonia was not a hit then?'

'No. It was awful, awful,' and before she could stop, Julia wept uncontrollably.

'What happened? What did she say to upset you so much?' Carrick was standing in the middle of the room looking bewildered, but with so much tenderness in his eyes, Julia turned away from his gaze. She didn't know why she was crying, maybe just the off-hand way Sonia talked about Patrick.

'Don't take any notice of me, Carrick. I'm just feeling emotional.' She sniffed loudly, before pulling a handkerchief from her sleeve and dabbing at her eyes.

'She had the audacity to tell me how much she'd fancied Patrick and, if I hadn't snapped him up, she would have made a play for him. Who says stuff like that about the husband you've recently lost?'

'It must have been really upsetting. Probably envious of what you and Paddy had.' Carrick closed the gap between them and knelt beside her taking her hand in his.

'My brother loved you, unreservedly. You meant the world to him. He would never have looked at another woman, and especially not someone like this crazy cow.'

Julia laughed. He was right; she was a crazy cow, but her words had hurt in ways Julia didn't really understand. She knew fully that Patrick loved her and would never have so much as glanced at another woman. She'd always felt secure with him in a way she'd never felt with her ex-husband, Nick. It was the casual grubbiness with which Sonia had referred to herself and Patrick that upset her.

'Changing the subject, I've just been on the phone to a courier company that I do business with. I asked a big favour, given it's so close to Christmas, but if you have those presents wrapped and ready to go for the morning, they've assured me the delivery will be in Geneva so Jack and Kat will have something to open on Christmas day.' He remained crouched by her side but had released her hand. She looked at him and was once again reminded of how thoughtful and loving he was. Why had he never married? Any woman would have struck gold with Carrick.

'Well, I better pull myself together and get wrapping,' she said, smiling back at him as he reached out his hand to pull her up from the couch.

They worked in silent companionship as Carrick helped her wrap the Christmas gifts. The presents wrapped and tied with ribbon, Julia sat at the table and wrote the gift cards to go with each. Carrick found a suitable cardboard box to pack Jack and Kat's gifts, and soon everything was complete and ready for the courier in the morning.

'Thank you for making all of this happen. I wouldn't have had the heart to go out searching for gifts if it wasn't for you. The gifts I have in this carrier bag,' she lifted it up from the kitchen chair, 'these are for you to take back to Ireland, so don't forget them or I'll be cross, and you don't want to see me cross.' She laughed as he picked up the bag and called out over his shoulder, 'I'll pack it now just in case. Your being cross is not something I wish to witness.'

As she lay in bed reflecting on the day, she realised she'd allowed Sonia to overshadow what had been a special time with Carrick.

He had known an old original bookshop would be just the place to take her for Christmas gifts, and she'd found everything she wanted for everyone except for Lizzie. She'd talked to Carrick about it and decided she wouldn't buy her anything. Not out of spite, but there seemed no point in trying to find something that would please Lizzie. She felt Lizzie had made it clear by her words and actions, she didn't want or need anything from her.

It had been an awful time and Julia, alone with her own thoughts, was reluctant to revisit it. Eventually, after much tossing and turning, she drifted off to sleep.

15
———

CARRICK

Lost in his thoughts, Carrick almost missed the turnoff to Baltimore. He felt drained of energy and longed for the warmth of his mother's kitchen and the aroma of freshly brewed coffee and sultana cake. She always made one when she knew he was coming.

Thoughts of Julia kept surfacing in his mind. Snatches of conversation, her laughter, her smile. Having her in the apartment for the last few days had been a blissful torture.

So many times, when he'd seen her struggling with her feelings, he'd wanted to reach out and hold her in his arms. Kiss that beautiful mouth, run his fingers through her hair and inhale the smell of her.

He had to learn to control his sea-saw emotions. It was both destructive and exhausting and achieved little. She was his sister-in-law, recently widowed. The last thing Julia needed right now was her love-sick brother-in-law taking advantage of her raw vulnerability.

When he finally pulled up outside his parent's house, he sat in the car for a moment taking in the view and admiring the house. He'd found this property for them after they retired and persuaded them to buy it. It had proved to be the right decision, as he'd known at the time it would be. His mother and father loved the outdoors and having Lough Hyne right on their doorstep had clinched the deal and they'd made such a beautiful home here.

As he climbed out of the car, opening the boot to retrieve his bag, he heard his mother calling to him. 'Hello Carrick. Merry Christmas.' She was standing in the doorway, smiling at him, but he couldn't help but notice how frail she looked and as he got closer, he could see the ravages of grief etched in her features.

Resting his bag on the doorstep, he reached for his mother and pulled her to him in a fierce hug. The tears he'd been holding back for days escaped unheeded, and he did not stop them. This was his mother, he loved her dearly and if he couldn't shed a tear with her then who could he cry with?

'Come on in, it's bone chilling out here.' She turned and taking his hand guided him through to the kitchen where the aromas he'd been longing to smell wafted out from the Aga.

'Would you like a coffee, my boy?' His mother turned to him, seeing her in the brighter light of the kitchen, it shocked him how much she'd aged. This is what grief did to you, Carrick thought. It consumed from the inside out like a fierce fire with flames that licked and burnt until you hardly recognised the face staring back at you from the mirror.

'That would be lovely, thank you. Where's dad?'

'He's taking a nap, been doing that a lot lately. You're looking tired yourself. How's Julia coping? We've been so worried about her.'

'She's okay, I think. There are days when she seems remote, distracted and I can see she's wrestling with her emotions, but other times she's good, more her old self.'

'Jack, the dear boy, has phoned us every week. He's one of a kind, that boy, he really is. He always makes your father laugh and believe me that takes some doing at the moment.' She smiled as she handed Carrick his coffee.

They sat down together at the kitchen table. 'I've made a sultana cake for you. It should be cool enough to cut now. No need to ask if you would like a piece.' She chuckled and ruffled his hair as she stood and walked to the pantry where a large sultana cake was resting.

'This is delicious as ever Mammy, no one makes a sultana cake like you do.'

'Well, better than shop bought.'

'How are you? You and dad?' He finished his coffee and sat looking into his mother's eyes. Eyes so like Paddy's. His brother had inherited his mother's beautiful eyes - Carrick's were different.

He'd often been told as a young boy that he looked remarkably like his mother's much older brother who had died in the war. His mother had carefully preserved old photos of this beloved brother, and in those sepia photographs, Carrick could see the uncanny resemblance.

'We get by Carrick. Just one day at a time. It was easier somehow when Julia was here. I talked her ears off - probably relieved to have escaped when she did.'

'Don't be daft, she loved being here, but she's also got to move on and make plans. She'll be going back to Melbourne after Christmas, well she thinks it's after Christmas, but it will be after the new year is in. I'll tell you about that later, but I am worried how she'll manage out in Melbourne alone.'

'She's a strong woman Carrick, we saw that when she was here. She held herself together much better than we did. I think she's more concerned about how Jack will be. He adored your brother. There will be an enormous gap in his life.'

'I know. It's not a gap anyone else can fill. But Jack's like his mother, he's resilient, adaptable, and he has Kat by his side. She's wonderful. Julia has phoned them most days and I'm sure she'll continue to do that once she's back in Melbourne.'

'Do you think she'll sell up and come back over here, to London I mean?'

'I don't know Mammy. It's too early for her. The changes in London, they shocked her. They've been away long enough to notice. Familiarity with your surroundings often means you don't notice the continuous day by day change to the feel of a thriving city, but she has really noticed and felt the difference this time.'

'In what way?' His mother cut another slice of sultana cake for them both and poured more coffee from the pot.

'I took her shopping for Christmas presents. I thought it would be awful for her trying to manage that this year.'

'You're a thoughtful man, Carrick.' His mother reached across and patted his hand. 'Your father and I are very proud of you and all that you have achieved.' She hesitated for a moment and Carrick was afraid she was going to cry.

'We haven't always understood what you do, I'm ashamed to say, nor did we appreciate how clever you are and how many charitable deeds you have done and continue to do. I want you to know how proud we are of you.' She brushed away a tear before taking a sip of her coffee.

Carrick was speechless, afraid to respond in case he could not control the emotion that had welled up inside, threatening to burst open the flood of tears that seemed to always be so close to the surface since Patrick died. He'd waited a long time to hear these words, and they were a healing balm to him.

'Anyway, you were saying about Julia.'

'Yes, when we were out and about in London, she commented on how frantic everyone was, and I know it's Christmas and people seem to get swept along in a stressful rushing syndrome at this time of year, but she felt it was much more than that, like there was a tension in the air. The winds of change – that's what she said. Like there was something dramatic captured in the wind - that change was coming - and it wouldn't be easy.' He helped himself to another slice of sultan cake before continuing.

'She's sensitive is Julia, and she's always loved London, so it was a surprise to hear her talk about it with such concern and disappointment. It's not the London she remembers.'

'Nothing ever stays the same, Carrick. Change is part of life's rich tapestry. Change can frighten, challenge or excite depending on who you are and how you view life.'

At that moment Carrick's father appeared in the kitchen, rubbing his fists in his eyes, still groggy from sleep. Carrick pulled back his chair and stood to greet his father, surprised at being pulled into a big bear hug.

'God it's good to see you Carrick, it really is. We're so pleased you've come home to us for Christmas.' Carrick could feel the thinness of his father's large frame. He'd always been a tall, well-built solid man, but age and grief had diminished him as it had his mother.

'I think we should break out the Guinness Rosie, enough of coffee and cake, come through to the lounge my son. I lit the fire earlier. It should be lovely and cosy for us to settle down and have a good yarn. I want to hear all about what you have been up to.'

ON CHRISTMAS EVE, Carrick had travelled with his father to find the perfect Christmas tree to bring home to his mother when they would all set about dressing it. It had been a family tradition for as long as he could remember.

They hauled back an enormous tree that would sit grandly in the lounge, and as they mounted it in a bucket of bricks and sand, Rose pulled boxes of Christmas decorations from the under-stairs cupboard. The threesome laughed and joked as they worked together, and it felt wonderful to be sharing a light-hearted moment together without feeling guilty for indulging in a moment of happiness.

With the tree decorated, Carrick went upstairs to his room and brought down the presents which Julia had carefully wrapped. It surprised him to see three parcels. He'd only seen her wrapping two. Placing them under the tree, he couldn't help but notice what appeared to be a bottle, wrapped in colourful Christmas wrapping with a card addressed to Paddy. He smiled. It would be something his parents would do.

When Carrick woke early on Christmas morning, he looked out the window and could see the watery winter sun trying its best to make an appearance. There was no wind, and the lough looked calm and sparkling in the early morning light.

He dressed quickly and quietly let himself out of the house, unwilling to disturb his parents who had stayed up late with him chatting by the fire, reminiscing of Christmas' gone. It had been relaxing and soothing for all of them. Now Carrick wanted to be out on the water. He'd take the kayak and paddle around the lough before breakfast.

The lough lay silver as the early morning light slowly pushed its way through soft clouds. Carrick wore layers of clothing to keep himself warm and pulling himself into the kayak he let it glide across the water, as weightless as the earth in space before he began to paddle. The water always calmed him in a way few other activities did. The only sound he could hear was the soft whispering of the trees and bird song as he made his way around the perimeter of the lough.

His thoughts moved to Julia - she was never far away. He'd received a text message from her late last night asking that he tell family, including Jack, not to call on Christmas day. She was struggling; she said. Struggling with the enormity of what lay ahead when she returned to Melbourne.

'I know you will understand, you are probably the only one who will. I just need to be alone, just for a day, with my own thoughts. Can you do that for me?'

His heart ached for her powerlessness. But he could do this one thing, he would make the call knowing that it would upset Jack and Kat - they may even be angry. But those emotions belonged to them, and Julia needed this time. It seemed little to ask when she'd given so much to everyone else.

He'd watched her in the bookshop in London, her face a picture of delight, and for a moment, he saw reflected in her eyes, the excited little girl she must once have been.

When he returned to London, he would take her to meet Edward Schneider. No, maybe he would invite Edward over to his place, he'd fetch him and bring him back for lunch. Julia was a superb cook and

Carrick was sure she would enjoy preparing a lunch for the three of them and then they could spend the entire afternoon talking books.

He smiled as he paddled around Castle Island, remembering how seriously she'd been wrapping the Christmas presents she'd bought. A small frown creased her brow, and she had a habit of pressing her lips tightly together when she was concentrating as she had been when tying the ribbon, ensuring it was exactly even and sat perfectly in position on the beautifully wrapped gift. This was the perfectionist in her. Patrick used to tease her about it, but he couldn't talk, Carrick thought, he was no different about music.

He questioned what areas of his own personality one could describe as being a perfectionist? Maybe it was contracts. He was a perfectionist with commercial contracts. He read every detail, particularly the small print, his mother's words echoing in his ears all these years later – *the devil is in the detail.*

His attention to detail had often saved him from committing to a deal he would later regret. He knew in business circles they viewed him as hard-nosed, but fair, and admitted that was probably an accurate summation of how he went about his business.

As he paddled back to the house, he wondered if his parents would follow the usual routine on Christmas day of the main meal being eaten in the evening and the day filled with the opening of presents, drinking home-made hot chocolate which his mother had perfected over the years and either being out on the water or taking a walk over the hills. They'd done this for as long as he could remember, and he hoped it would be the same today for he feared there may not be too many Christmas' where his parents would be fit enough and keen enough to be on the lake or on the hills.

Carrick let himself back into the house and quietly made his way upstairs to his bedroom. He made the call to Jack and Kat and as expected Jack expressed concern, then frustration, but it dissipated as fast as it had arrived. He was missing Patrick and his mother, Carrick understood that. They had chatted for a little while, Carrick assuring them he would phone later in the evening so they could speak with Rose and Brendan.

'Julia said you were working through?'

'We are, that's why we couldn't come back to London to spend Christmas with mum. Is she truly okay Carrick - you're not keeping anything from us?'

'No, you have my word. I would never do that Jack, no matter what it was. Your mum has had no time on her own and she's hurting. She needs time to be alone with her thoughts, and sometimes, we need that space even if it is just a day or so, it's part of the process. Changing the subject, did your presents arrive?'

'Yes. Sorry, I should have said. I thought mum mentioned she would send something in the new year?'

Kat's voice came on the line. 'And I said to Jack, that Julia would never leave us with nothing to open on Christmas day. Not that it would have mattered, we are hardly children, but it matters to her, so it was no surprise to me when the courier arrived.' She was laughing, and Carrick was relieved to hear Kat's relaxed tone. It would help soften the day for Jack.

'She didn't think she was up to Christmas shopping. It was such a special event for her and Paddy, something they always did together. I took her to an old bookshop- you know, the type she loves.'

'Oh, she would adore that, Kat said. 'I've known no one to spend so much time in a bookshop as Julia.'

'Anyway, she found something special for everyone, you know how Julia is and I'm glad, as will she be, that they arrived in time for Christmas. I take it you're all set for New Year's Eve?'

'Absolutely. Can't believe they have asked me, it's such an honour. Phil emailed through the details three days ago and he's been on the phone to me. We're planning on flying into Heathrow two days before. I'll text you the hotel details when Phil lets me know.'

'You can stay at my place after though, your mum will want that.'

'That would be great. Have you told Rose and Brendan yet?'

'No. I'm going to tell them today - it will be an extra surprise and hopefully take their mind of Paddy and Julia not being here with us.'

'I better go now, I can hear the rattle of cups. Mammy must be up and making breakfast. I'll phone early evening if that works for you.'

'That would be great Carrick...... and thank you. Thank you for taking good care of mum, we're glad you're there for her.'

'I'm here for all of you. Talk later.'

AFTER BREAKFAST they moved through to the lounge and sat around the tree, Rose handing out the presents.

Julia had bought his mother an early edition of *Wild Flowers of Ireland*. Beautifully illustrated even now after years of handling, the book remained in immaculate condition and the flower colours captured with an artist's brush dipped in water colours had retained their beauty.

Julia had found a book for Brendan depicting some of the earliest photographs and drawings of yacht building. She'd chosen well, Carrick thought, as he observed his parents turning each page with the occasional exclamation. He picked up his own beautifully wrapped present from Julia and read the card.

To Carrick, a wonderful friend, thank you for being there for me. Love Julia xx.

He re-read the card again, his eyes lingering on the two crosses, and wished they were real kisses filled with love and passion. He pushed the thoughts from his mind and opened his gift.

It was an amazing book on Georgian architecture. He didn't have one like it in his collection and he smiled now realising how clever she'd been remembering back to that morning before they left for the bookshop when he found her in the lounge trawling through his bookshelves as though searching for something important.

Now he knew why and he felt overwhelmed with love for her, it was only when he sensed his mother's steady gaze that he looked up.

She was staring at him in that way she had, as she'd done when he and Paddy were young boys and been caught doing something they shouldn't. She could read their expressions so easily, their transparency obvious, and even now he had the same feeling she knew exactly what he'd been thinking. A slow smile lit up her face, and he blushed under her knowing gaze.

. . .

DESPITE THE HOPEFUL start to the day, by early afternoon the weather had turned cold and heavy rain pounded the roof. There would be no sailing and there would be no hiking, still they could enjoy being by the fire and spending time together. Carrick drifted off to sleep. He hadn't realised quite how exhausted he was and was only wakened when he heard his mother preparing the evening meal in the kitchen.

'Your father has taken himself off for another of his naps and I thought I would make a start on our Christmas feast.'

'I'll help Mammy, you don't have to do this by yourself.'

Carrick picked up the potato peeler and began peeling the potatoes harvested months earlier from his parent's expansive vegetable garden. They worked side by side in comfortable silence, each deep in their own thoughts. Carrick remembering back to the time he and Paddy were boys, given a chore to do to help prepare the Christmas meal. Carrick enjoyed cooking, but Paddy had always found it a bore and would slip off as soon as he could to listen to music in his room or play his guitar, leaving his younger brother to finish his chores.

Carrick decided he would break the news to his parents before he phoned Jack and Kat and before they had their meal. They were sitting in the lounge around the fire, his mother satisfied everything was ready and she could safely take a break and enjoy a glass of wine.

'I have something to share with the two of you,' Carrick said, watching as the sets of eyes swivelled around to face him. 'On New Year's Eve in London, there is a musical event being held to raise funds for a variety of charities. One is the charity Paddy set up, "Down But Not Out" and the other is "Evelina London Children's Hospital".'

'That's wonderful news Carrick,' his mother said, her smile beaming back at him and her eyes glistening with tears.

'There's more. As a special tribute to Paddy and his charitable work, they have invited Jack to play drums and saxophone as a guest musician, isn't that the grandest way to end an awful year?'

'That is the best news you could bring us, Carrick,' his father said, his voice shaking with emotion.

'No, the best news is that I intend you both be there, so no protests, you get yourselves to Dublin airport. I've already booked your flights and you'll be met at the airport. I won't be able to get there because I'm going to be busy keeping Julia occupied. She doesn't know, so you can't slip up and say anything when next you speak with her, okay?'

'Absolutely, you can count on us,' his mother said, turning to his father and grabbing his hand. 'Fancy Brendan, going to London for a tribute to our boy and a bonus being able to see Jack play, it doesn't get any grander than that now does it Brendan Devlin?'

They were still chattering with excitement when Carrick phoned Jack and Kat before they sat down to enjoy his mother's Christmas meal. It was a jovial, chatty call, just what they all needed, ending with promises of trips back to Ireland as soon as Jack had finished his latest recording.

Carrick was pleased Jack would make the time to come out to Baltimore. It would mean so much to his parents. They loved Jack as though he were their own grandchild and had always treated him as though he'd been born into their family. Both he and Patrick had disappointed their parents in not producing children. It was too late for that now, but at least they had Jack and now Kat and he assumed, eventually, they would have children and his parents would have grandchildren to watch over as they ran around the garden.

'I'm stuffed, completely and utterly. That was amazing Mammy as usual.' He smiled across the table at his mother, her cheeks flushed from the heat of the Aga.

'You go through to the lounge and I'll tidy up, go on off you go, you too,' he shooed his father away leaving him to the task.

As he stacked the dishwasher he thought back to the earlier conversation with his parents. It had alarmed them when he explained Julia wanted to be alone today. He could see they didn't understand, but he'd talked them through how Julia was struggling and what it would be like for her returning to Melbourne alone with no family to guide her through the maelstrom of emotions, memories, and decisions.

He hoped they understood, but it disappointed them. Having the trump card of the charity event in London had taken the sting out of the disappointment of not speaking with Julia and as he dried the pots and pans and put them away, he could hear their voices from the lounge chattering animatedly about the upcoming trip to London.

16

JULIA

Julia left the apartment to buy a few items from Waitrose. She couldn't bear the thought of cooking something special for Christmas dinner. It seemed pointless, but she still needed to eat so she'd braved the crowds of last-minute Christmas shoppers. She was looking at the window display of an interior design shop when the shop assistant, standing in the doorway, beckoned her inside.

'You look freezing, come in and browse and I'll pour you a glass of mulled wine and you can enjoy a warm fruit mince pie, that's if you would like one, and I hope I'm not being too presumptuous?' she added.

The girl looked about Kat's age, dark hair pulled back from her face held in place with a scarf tied in the fashion's style of the 1950s, in fact as Julia assessed her, she resembled a young woman who had just stepped out of a 1950s fashion magazine. From the hair, to the pretty blouse tucked into tapered trousers and the frighteningly high, thin stiletto heels. She had a pretty face, wearing make-up expertly applied to Julia's keen eye for such detail.

Julia wondered if she owned this shop. It was beautiful, which was the reason she'd lingered at the window. The display was eye catching, and she wished she'd been able to create this look in her own home back in Melbourne. She had never seen furniture or furnishings like this in Australia. That was the difference between the antipodes and Europe – so much more to choose from.

'Presumptuous is fine, it's lovely to be asked.' Julia smiled back at her as she took the proffered mulled wine. 'Thank you, this is delicious,' she said taking a long sip. 'Is it your own recipe?'

'I make it from these,' she held up a sachet. 'I sell them at Christmas time. It's all natural and all you have to do is add the red wine and some oranges.'

'I must buy some of that, it's wonderful. Your shop is amazing, are you the owner?'

'No, wish I was,' she sighed in that exaggerated way of the young and impatient. 'I manage the shop for an interior designer. You may have heard of him, Hugh Rhodes-Brown, he's well known in London?'

'I have, as a matter of fact. He was responsible for the interior design of my brother-in-law's apartment in Bloomsbury.'

'Oh, you don't mean Carrick Devlin's place? Oops sorry, I shouldn't be so indiscrete. Not meant to disclose a client's name.'

Julia laughed, suddenly warmed by this young woman's disarming manner and obvious passion for her job. 'It's fine, no apology needed. You're right, it is Carrick's place. I think it's stunning.'

'Oooh my God, so do I.' her exclamation reminded Julia of some junior accountants she worked with back in Melbourne with their exaggerated Oooh's and Oh My God's.

'Hugh loved that commission. Some of the rooms featured in a design magazine a while ago. We got heaps of work from that. They ran me off my feet in here.'

'You love your job?' Julia asked, taking a bite from the delicious fruit mince pie.

'Absolutely. Hugh is a wonderful boss, and even though I've completed my interior design course, I'm not planning on leaving. To work alongside someone like Hugh is a gift, and he's spent so much time mentoring and encouraging me, I'm very lucky.'

'Well, you're an asset to him and I'm sure he knows that. I'm going to buy some of that mulled wine mix and I love the throw you have on that couch,' Julia pointed, 'the one in the window- I'll take that.'

'Wonderful. You relax, enjoy your wine and I'll wrap these up.'

BY THE TIME Julia had left, she'd had a glass of mulled wine and three fruit mince pies. That would be supper, she thought as she made her way to Waitrose, wishing now that she'd shopped for food much earlier. Waitrose at Christmas Eve was like the Running of the Bulls in Spain. Pushing and shoving with women, because it always seemed to be the women who were the most frantic, thrusting their trolleys at you, skinning your heels without so much as an apology, their strident voices barking orders at husbands who scurried behind gathering armloads of groceries, most of which, Julia wagered, would languish in the fridge over the Christmas holiday.

Still, she needed to get a few things and two of them would now be a bottle of red wine and some oranges. She'd make herself some mulled wine and toast Patrick on Christmas day – it would be just the two of them.

Julia was walking back to Carrick's apartment, her carry bag swinging in her hand and her back-back loaded with food and wine. She turned a corner and there ahead of her was Patrick. She would know that stride anywhere. Her heart raced as her brain tried to process what she was seeing. He had the same collar length hair, the same hair colour. He was wearing jeans and a wool coat, identical to Patrick's with the same stripped scarf Patrick always wore in the winter.

Julia pushed through the pedestrians to catch up, calling Patrick's name, ignoring the stares from Christmas shoppers, oblivious to everything else except keeping Patrick in her sights. She was screaming his name, 'Patrick, it's me. Patrick, turn around.' But he carried on walking as she annoyed more people by pushing past them. She saw him slow for a pedestrian crossing and screamed "Patrick" one more time as she shoved people aside and then tripped and collided with him. He half turned, putting his arm out to catch her as he staggered back.

'Are you alright - are you hurt?' The man asked, and as Julia looked up, she realised he was not Patrick, he was a stranger. It wasn't quite the same coat or scarf. He stared at her, looking bewildered and perhaps she thought, a little apprehensive, as the crowd flowed around them.

'I'm so sorry,' she mumbled, 'I mistook you for someone else. He's dead but when I saw you, I thought you were him, but you're not, are you? He's still dead, isn't he?' Julia stumbled to an awkward silence.

'Please forgive me for startling you.' She could feel her world starting to fragment like the shattered glass in a picture frame. The kind man who she had just frightened the life out of offered to hail a taxi for her. She shook her head.

'There will be none available, it's way too busy. I'm fine, really. A mistake, that was all, I'm only round the corner from here.' She could see from the look on his face he wasn't at all sure she was fine. She stood there dejectedly, crimson with embarrassment, clutching her backpack and the interior design bag, fat tears welling in her eyes.

'If you're sure. Is there someone I can call? You look – distressed.' She could see the concern in his eyes as loneliness and humiliation wrapped themselves around her.

'Honestly, I'm fine. Thank you. Merry Christmas,' she said, with her best attempt at a smile. She walked away, desperate to be gone from the looks and the shaking heads.

Upon reaching Carrick's apartment, she collapsed at the kitchen table and cried. What could she have been thinking? He only vaguely resembled Patrick and, what's more, Patrick had cut his hair when they moved out to Australia and wore it quite short.

What was wrong with her? One mulled wine and she'd accosted a man, who in reality, looked only a little like Patrick, but from years before, not the latest version of Patrick – it had been a London ghost of him.

Resting her head on crossed arms, she half sat, half lay at the table for quite some time until finally, she pulled herself up and unpacked her backpack.

The fun time she'd had with the young girl in the interior design shop had faded, but her humiliation lingered. Her behaviour had been irrational and out of control. For Julia, not having control of her feelings and her actions was terrifying.

She didn't bother to eat, instead retreating to bed where she lay looking at the ceiling, tears streaming down her cheeks soaking her pyjama top. There was no end to her tears she thought, they just kept coming and she let them, there was nothing she could do to stop the torrent of grief.

Thoughts tumbled through the air like space junk keeping her awake when all that she wished was to wipe the day clean as though nothing had ever happened, leaving her with a blank canvas that she could colour in whatever way she pleased.

With a sigh, she turned the lamp on, lifting the framed photo of Patrick from the bedside table. Her fingers traced his face, laughing back at her, so often laughing. She'd photographed him standing on the lawn, glass in hand, toasting the beauty of the mountain. When she'd called his name, he'd turned - her Patrick smiling back at her from behind the wine glass.

'Some days, when I shut out life's noise, when I can no longer hear the London traffic and tooting horns, and people's voices - I close my eyes and talk to this photo of you. It's my favourite and I never tire of looking at it. You know that. You must watch me. I don't know why you don't come - I can't understand. There was that one time, it wasn't just a dream I'm sure of it, but you left me, just faded away as though you'd never been. When I awoke Patrick, I was more distraught than ever. So maybe that's why you don't visit. Is that the reason, Patrick? Are you saving me from myself?' She turned on her back and held the frame out in front of her with both hands.

'There are days Patrick, when my world runs red with blood from the gaping wound that was once my heart. I hear myself whispering my anger to the walls and they answer back with voices of self-recrimination. Those days, of which there are many; leave me feeling burnt and scared with yet another mark of my own wretched aban-donment. But you will know of this, I'm sure.'

Finally, she returned the photo to the table, switched out the light and closed her eyes. Sleep would come, it always did, eventually.

IT WAS Christmas morning and Julia sat in bed with a cup of coffee and a magazine. She didn't have the concentration for a book. Her mind kept slipping back treacherously to the day before and her behaviour, shocked at how completely she had lost control of her rational self in the crowd of Christmas shoppers.

That poor man, he'll probably be sharing his Christmas story over dinner she thought.

'Oh, you'll never guess what happened to me yesterday, walking along minding my own business when I was accosted by some crazy woman. Weird, really. Said she had mistaken me for a dead person. Well dressed, probably not a homeless person, but you never know these days. With drug use so widespread appearances can be so deceptive. Anyway, I offered to help, obviously, but she wished me a merry Christmas and disappeared. I know I'm not high energy, but I've never been likened to a dead person before. I must say though, there was something very genuine about her even if she startled me.'

Julia could imagine him at the head of the table, handing out slices of roast turkey breast, enjoying being the centre of attention. She'd have to disguise herself next time she left the apartment in case anyone recognised her.

Her phone remained turned off - she hadn't changed her mind - she didn't want to hear from anyone. When she'd sent the text to Carrick, it was because of a bad day. All that stuff that Sonia had trotted out about Patrick had left her feeling empty and confused.

She trusted Patrick, always had and, as Carrick said, he would never so much as glance at another woman. It was more the off-hand way Sonia had referred to him like he could be a casual one-night stand instead of her loyal, passionate, kind, and gifted husband.

Not bothering to shower or dress, she wandered through to the lounge and flicked the switch for the gas fire. Not that the apartment was cold, it just felt cosy with the flicker of flames even if they weren't real. She pulled the throw around her and surfed through the channels on the television looking for something, anything that might lift her mood.

She settled for the movie - *My Summer in Provence* and munched her way through a bar of Lindt chocolate with several cups of coffee until she felt like she'd bounce off the walls with caffeine and the movie was only part-way through.

A particular scene where it became clear the wife had once been in love with her husband's brother made her feel sad. She didn't wish to hold that little black pearl in her hand and have its lustre reflect her true feelings- not today. She clicked the remote and retired to bed. She knew if she lay there long enough, sleep would ultimately claim her.

17

———

CARRICK

arrick checked his phone. Ridiculous, she had made it clear her phone would be off, but he couldn't stop worrying about her and had checked for messages every few hours. He was behaving like an abandoned lover. It had to stop - nothing could come of his loving a woman he could never have.

He should know better, he silently scolded himself. The past was a constant reminder of what happens when you love someone you shouldn't. Not that he'd really loved Katie Fitzpatrick, he'd been a sixteen-year-old boy who had mistakenly misread a hormone fuelled crush for something more. Patrick had been in love with Katie, but that had ended in so much heartache.

On Boxing Day, when there was still no message from Julia, he went up to his room and dialled his Bloomsbury landline.

'Hello.' Her voice sounded scratched, jagged.

'Julia, it's me, are you okay?'

'No.' There was silence for a few seconds before he heard the sob. 'Oh, Carrick, I'm so miserable. I can't bear to talk to Jack or Kat when I'm like this, let alone your mum and dad. I don't know what to do.' She cried, and Carrick's heart shattered all over again, the way it had when he'd watched her walk down the aisle to take the hand of his brother.

Carrick had stood alongside Paddy, smiling – a smile he'd maintained throughout the entire weekend of their marriage celebrations. His jaw so tight from the strain of pretence he'd found it ached for days afterward.

He let her cry, and when he could hear her taking a deep breath, he spoke. 'Do you want me to come home? Mum and dad will understand.'

'No. Please don't do that Carrick. Your mum and dad's needs are far greater than mine. I just had an awful night. I've been blocking out a lot of stuff with Lizzie,' she sniffed. 'Maybe it was my way of coping, but it all came out in a dream last night and I feel so despondent this morning.'

'If you're sure. I'm only going to be here for a few more days, but I hate to think of you hurting like this.'

He didn't know what else to say to her, couldn't bear to hear her sounding so broken and wretched. Bloody Lizzie, how could she have dumped all her own unresolved shite on Julia when she'd only just said goodbye to her husband. He had a good mind to phone Lizzie himself and give her a piece of his mind. Almost as soon as he thought this, he knew he wouldn't. It wasn't his fight, and he'd risk making matters worse.

'I'll be fine. I have to be, don't I - can you talk to Jack and Kat for me and your parents?'

'Everyone will understand Julia, don't worry about that, just try to find a place of good memories when you felt at peace with the world. I know that sounds hollow and like some silly platitude, but if you can't let your mind rest, you won't sleep and if you don't sleep, you're going to continue to feel like shite. Sorry, that's all I'm going to say. I'm sounding like some wannabe therapist.'

'No. You're right. I need to relax?'

'I've got a spa bath in my bedroom, use it. It is very soothing. There may even be a bath bomb in the cupboard if you look.'

'A bath bomb? I didn't have you down for a bath bomb kind of guy.' Carrick was relieved to hear a sudden lightness in her tone.

'Thank you. And thank you for phoning. You're my tonic, the best brother-in-law a girl could wish for.'

'Text me later, just so I know you're okay?' He wanted to say so much more, but found words escaped him. If he said what was in his heart, she'd be on the next plane back to Melbourne.

Downstairs he found his mother in the lounge staring out the window to the lough. 'Mammy,' she turned to face him, and he could see she'd been crying. He went to her and pulled her into his arms.

'I'm here Mammy, you're not alone.'

'I know Carrick, but you won't and can't be here forever. Your father and I have to learn to cope, however difficult it is. I'm just so grateful you've arranged for us to make the trip to London. That will be a real balm for your father and I, it surely will.'

'Where is dad, still in bed?'

'No. He's taken himself off for a walk, he wanted some alone time. That's all he seems to do, walk alone and take naps. It's his way, I know that, but some days I just wish he'd sit with me and talk and cry and lance that boil of pain which I know is sitting on his heart.'

'I'm sorry. This must be so difficult for you. What about your friends, are they being supportive?'

'Yes. Yes, they are, but at Christmas they have their own families to think of. In the new year we'll see them again. Do you want a cup of tea?'

'Thank you. That would be lovely. I've just spoken to Julia. She's not in a good place, and can't find the strength to talk to anyone, including Jack and Kat. I said you would understand.' He looked at his mother, raising his eyebrows.

'The poor, poor girl. Of course we understand, she mustn't worry about us. We know she'll phone and have a good old chat when she's ready. I just wish there were more we could do.'

'I feel the same, but she's got to get through this time without worrying about everyone else.'

'She's lucky she has you, Carrick. You will be her tower - she will draw strength from you. You will be the one to help her climb up, out and away from her loss. It's not something Jack can do, he's too close, and it's too much to ask of him right now.'

As always, his mother's words were rich in their wisdom and understanding. He hugged her to him again before turning to take cups from the cupboard. He heard his father stomping his feet on the mat at the back door and pulled out another cup. They could all sit in the kitchen and enjoy a cup of tea together.

He'd have to speak with his father. He wouldn't be happy returning to London knowing his mother was feeling so lonely and abandoned when she needed her husband by her side.

Together they were the pair of mighty oaks planted close enough to reach out and touch, but with enough distance to feel the breeze blow easily between them - ensuring they would always keep their individuality, it's what made them such an amazing couple, but right now his father's touch was out of reach of his mother's grasp.

Later, Carrick phoned Jack. He sounded harassed when he answered. 'Sorry have I caught you at a bad time?'

'No, it's fine. I'm just exasperated with this recording. I can't seem to find my rhythm and every time I think we've found the right tempo for this piece it vanishes, and I'm left with the raw material and I've lost another hour or more. Anyway, I'm sure you didn't phone to hear about my problems. I've been trying to get hold of Mum, but she's still got her phone off.'

'I know. I decided I'd try my landline, and she picked up. She's not great Jack, no point dressing it up. She had a terrible night, something to do with Lizzie.'

'Lizzie, what do you mean?'

'They had a big bust up when Julia was in Spain. I don't know what happened exactly, just that it must have been ugly. Lizzie hasn't spoken to your mum since. It's all a bit shite, really.'

'Jesus! Poor Mum. Why didn't she tell us?'

'I think she's been trying to block it out, it's too much for her to be dealing with right now.'

'Lizzie was a right cow when we were there. Kat thought she was harbouring a grudge, or at least that's how it appeared. But I was pretty pissed-off with her and the way she was treating Mum. It's weird they've been such close friends for decades, but since Michael died, Lizzie has changed. I don't know what's going on with her. She left several messages for us at Christmas but sounded drunk, so I didn't feel like calling her back. I'm glad Mum left when she did.'

'I had the same thought myself. Lizzie's got issues. But whatever is going on, it's not okay to dump it on Julia.'

'Exactly. Lizzie was a bit crazy when she was in Melbourne. I'm ashamed to admit I kind of went along with it for a while. Then I realised she was trying to stir things up between Mum and me. It's not the Lizzie I know from my childhood, she's changed. You haven't invited her to the charity event, have you?'

'No, absolutely not. I want nothing spoiling this for you, for Julia, or my parents.'

'I agree, it's going to be an emotional enough night for all of us. We don't need Lizzie causing problems.'

'I think right now, your mum just needs a little more time to get herself together. She's worried about talking to you and Kat when she's so distressed. I said you would understand and give her the space. She's worried about you.'

'I'm fine, sort of. I have moments when I feel so desperate.' Carrick could hear his voice break and wished he could reach down the phone and hold his nephew, let him cry, the way he himself had cried.

'Sorry, it just catches me, and I can't believe he's gone, that I won't see him again. That he won't phone me to have a chat. He used to do that all the time and I find myself checking my phone for his text messages.'

'I know Jack. I appreciate this must be awful for you and Kat, but there is one thing we must remember – Patrick will forever remain in our hearts. He is in our past through our treasured memories and in our future through the music you create. He will always be close by because we are a family, your family.'

'Thank you. That means a lot to me. When we finish this

recording and get it mastered, which maybe months away if we continue to work at this pace, but that said, once we are free of this, we'd like to come and stay with you in London when you're there. It's going to be such a rush when we come out for the concert, but later, when everything calms down a bit, we'd like to spend some time with you and then go out to Ireland to be with Rose and Brendan.'

'I would love that, and I know mum and dad will. I'll hold you to it.' Carrick said, laughing.

'I'll let you know my schedule once we hit the new year and I can see what's ahead of me travel wise.' They ended the call with Jack promising to let Carrick know when he and Kat arrived in London for the charity event.

18

JULIA

Julia's bedroom and ensuite sat at the opposite end of the house so she'd never ventured up the hallway to Carrick's bedroom. Even when he'd shown herself and Lizzie around the house, he'd never taken them near his bedroom.

Now, towel in hand, she walked up the hallway and opened the door. It was nothing short of sumptuous. Masculine, but not so masculine that you felt you'd entered a *Gentlemen Only* club.

A large spa bath sat to one side of the room above which hung an inset overhang which resembled a hi-tech console with fans, speakers, and lighting. It was a room that subscribed too less is more. Nothing cluttered, Julia hated clutter, and nothing overwhelming. Soft muted tones on the walls and furnishings highlighted the deep rich mahogany coloured timber floor.

A collection of black and white framed photographs adorned one wall. They were all sailing pictures with the people in soft focus giving them an ethereal look. She found herself drawn to each frame, trying to figure out if any of the blurred images were Patrick or Carrick.

She filled the bath and while the water was running, she stood staring at what appeared to be a wall of glass before she realised if she pushed a panel it swung back to reveal an ensuite shower and toilet with a floor to ceiling cupboard.

Opening the cupboard door, Julia found everything neatly lined up, just the way she liked. There was enough toilet paper to supply a small army, soap - both bars and liquid, an array of men's after shave, shaving foam, a collection of serious looking razors, men's hair product and tucked away on a separate shelf were several bath bombs, a jar of Epsom salts and bath foam.

There was something about these brothers. They were both tidy. She had admired this trait in Patrick - his need for order. 'Everything in its place, and a place for everything,' was one of his tenets.

She lay in the bath inhaling the sweet smell of the bath bomb and feeling her body relax, she'd seldom felt like this since that knock on the door.

She looked across the room to Carrick's bed. Simple, nothing ostentatious. Neatly made with the duvet rolled back to reveal fresh white bed linen. One bedside cabinet contained a fancy-looking clock/radio, the other a stack of books.

The view as you sat in the bath was beautiful. She could gaze at the London skyline in total privacy. It was luxurious, and she couldn't help but wonder how many women had sat in this very bath with Carrick and shared his bed.

To distract her wayward thoughts which, she chastised herself, were none of her business, she pressed a button on the bath assuming she would hear the soft rumble of the spa as it pushed bubbles to the surface, but the room filled with music.

She looked up and could see a red light blinking at her from the overhang above. He had surround sound music. Smiling, she lay back down and let her mind absorb the dulcet tones of Melody Gardot, as she sang *Worrisome Heart*. It was an album she had in her own collection.

Julia knew deep inside - when she allowed herself moments of truthful reflection, that Patrick had been her cherished husband, her best friend, her lover, and a wonderful father to her son, but he'd not been her soulmate. The lustre of the black pearl, safely hidden in her deepest self, would reflect the actual truth if exposed to examination.

As Melody Gardot switched from English to French singing the song *Les Etoilesi* – Julia's thoughts were back in France – in Paris remembering the times she'd travelled there with Patrick. She smiled at the treasured memories. Closing her eyes and giving herself up to the music and the water, she drifted half asleep.

Patrick's hand was stroking her lower leg down towards her ankle with a featherlight touch. She looked up into his smiling face across their spa pool. The sun was setting behind him and the air temperature quickly dropping. 'Patrick? I must have nodded off and didn't notice you getting in the spa.' She leaned forward and reached out her hand to cup his face, but his image rippled and vanished before her eyes. She was in Carrick's bathroom lying in rapidly chilling water with sodium streetlights throwing their orange glow through the window. Shivering, she quickly pulled herself up and reached for the towel.

Trembling with the towel wrapped around her, she stood in the bath staring at the water as it swirled its way down the plug hole pulling her peaceful state with it.

The image still clear in her mind, so real she could hear the trees as they whispered their ancient stories and the sound of Patrick's laughter, so elated that they could be enjoying a spa at the end of a sunny Christmas day on their beautiful mountain.

They'd been about to go to bed when Patrick had turned to her excitedly. 'It's Christmas Julia, and we've got a spa pool?'

'Quick, he said, let's skinny dip, it'll be magic so it will Julia, come on, get out of your clothes.' He'd stripped off and ran naked through the house to the spa pool, yanking off the cover and jumping in. Laughing, he called to her to hurry. She'd met no one as spontaneous as Patrick and it had taken her a long time to adjust to someone who could be so intense one minute then in a heartbeat revert to carefree outbursts of boyish exuberance.

Wrapped in a warm oversized dressing gown and wiping the tears from her cheeks she walked through to the lounge and browsed

Carrick's collection of CDs. She was surprised it hadn't all been converted to digital playlists.

At the back of the shelf, she found an unmarked CD case, but when she opened the lid, she saw drawn in marker pen, *Julia's Music*. How peculiar, she thought, why would he have a CD with her name on it? She placed the CD in the Hi-Fi and settled herself on the couch to listen. It was a compilation of the music from the charity event Julia had attended in London at the club Patrick used to play at – the night of Irish music.

That evening had been a turning point for her. It was the first time she'd met Carrick and as she listened it became apparent the CD contained all the songs from that night and also included the performance, several years later when Jack had made his debut on the Saxophone playing with Patrick and his band.

'Why would he have captured all these songs on a CD?' she asked herself. She could ask him next time they spoke, but somehow poking around in his CD collection and finding this, tucked away out of sight, made her feel she'd intruded on something very personal to Carrick. She decided she wouldn't mention it. Instead, when the CD had finished, she carefully returned it to its hiding place, leaving her with a similar guilty feeling as though she had just read someone else's mail.

19

———

CARRICK

Carrick said his goodbyes, watching in the rear-view mirror as his parents continued to wave until he was out of sight, driving slower than normal on the icy road to Dublin. He worried how they'd cope with him gone as he probably wouldn't be able to get back to Baltimore for a few months.

His schedule for the new year was hectic – travel to multiple countries, meetings with commercial developers, decisions about his UK and European property portfolio. And then there was Julia.

She'd sounded so lost and broken on the phone when they'd last spoken and he was anxious to get back to London to see if she was feeling better. He was also acutely aware that he couldn't allow himself to spend too much time in her company. His heart was too vulnerable, foolishly encouraging him to believe there could be something more.

Every time he allowed himself to indulge in wayward thoughts, his conscience would remind him with a guilty jolt, Julia was his brother's wife. The brother he loved so dearly and because of that love and respect for Paddy, Carrick had unselfishly removed himself from the opportunity of getting to know Julia better all those years ago. In his head he was back at the club in London, the night where he'd first met Julia and been captivated by her.

Nothing had changed – he remained captivated. Back then he'd recognised the tell-tale signs that Paddy had feelings for this woman so had chosen to stand aside rather than risk a contest for her affections. He'd removed himself, literally, by pursuing business on the other side of the world. Away from the temptation to pick up the phone to her and feed the spark of attraction he had sensed between them that night. He could not do that to Paddy after the years the brothers had spent dancing around the story of Katie Fitzpatrick. Paddy believing the false rumours that it had involved Carrick. That Carrick had got her pregnant and been responsible for her suicide. Nothing could have been further from the truth. But that knowledge hadn't prevented Carrick carrying for years, the burden of Katie's suicide believing that he should have done more to help her, to stop her taking her father's dinghy out to sea that night and never returning.

As he drove the voice of Maura O'Connell singing *Summerfly* – the words *"who's your partner, who's your darling, who's your baby now"* and the sorrow he'd read in his brother's eyes as he looked out at Carrick from the stage, locking eyes – two brothers who knew the true meaning of this song and the memories it evoked.

A lot of healing had taken place since those dark days and whilst it had taken Paddy quite some time to cease feeling threatened by Carrick and Julia's special connection, eventually the mistrust had evaporated, and they'd regained that special brotherly bond they'd shared as children.

Carrick reached up to brush a tear from his cheek. He missed Paddy terribly, even though they lived on different sides of the world and lived different lives, they connected with each other regularly by phone, or text or Skype calls and he'd stayed in Melbourne with them on multiple occasions when he'd been out in Australia and New Zealand for business. He was already missing the calls - the brotherly banter and knew nothing would ever fill that space again.

Julia was waiting up for him when he arrived back at Bloomsbury.

He'd phoned her from Dublin airport, hoping that she'd turned her phone back on and was ready to connect with the world once more. He learned she'd phoned Jack and Kat, his parents and Nancy, her neighbour back in Melbourne. She'd sounded quiet, distant almost, and he imagined the effort to speak with everyone had taken its toll.

'You look exhausted, long day?'

'Yes. The drive to Dublin airport was slow going, and my flight was delayed, but I'm here now. How are you?'

'I'm okay, actually. I've turned a corner, well at least I think I have.' She bit at her bottom lip in the way she did when she was unsure of something. Carrick knew all her little nuances. He'd been studying that beautiful face for years.

'I've made you some soup. I wasn't sure if they would feed you on the flight or not?' She turned toward the fridge. 'Do you want a beer, wine?'

'A glass of red in front of the fire would be grand Julia. Thank you. You didn't have to worry about food, but I admit, I am famished. Must be all that cold Irish air.' He watched as she moved about the kitchen heating his soup, cutting slices from a crusty loaf of bread and making up a tray. She looked so comfortable in his kitchen, as though she'd always been there.

'How have you been here, did you find everything you needed to make yourself comfortable?'

'Yes. It's been wonderful. I love this place - I really do Carrick. You've achieved something that most of us only dream of. It's so luxurious, what you've done, but you have a gift for the way you've merged original with modern in such a sympathetic way. The whole place has a soothing, homely feeling to it. Not your regular bachelor pad, that's for sure.' She smiled at him and he glimpsed the old Julia.

'And tell me, do you know a lot about bachelor pads then?' He was teasing, keen to keep things light-hearted between them.

'You've got me there. The only bachelor pad I know of was Patrick's apartment in Henley. You must have been there?'

'Yes. I liked it. I thought it was very him. What did you think of it?'

'It was nice. I liked what he'd done. It was simple, and yet still artistic. I can see you share similar tastes in some respects, and yet your home is completely different. Shall I pour you a wine and you carry the tray through to the lounge? Unless you want to sit out here?'

'No, I'd like to be by the fire. So did mum and dad sound okay when you spoke with them?'

'Sad. Missing you as soon as you walked out the door, but I got the impression they were trying hard to move forward. Just a day at a time is what your mum said, and I get that, I really do.'

'This situation has aged them, but only they can work through it. I can't be with them forever and nor can anyone else. Jack and Kat said they would travel out to stay as soon as they've finished this latest assignment. They'll love that, it'll give them a real boost.'

'I spoke with Jack and Kat. They're expecting the project will be finished in another month and then they'll go out to Ireland. Jack said you'd been so thoughtful calling him. He's grateful you're looking out for me.' She looked across to Carrick, her eyes caught in the glow from the lamp. A softer shade of green than the bright sparkling emerald brought out by sunlight. Differently beautiful he thought.

'He's worried about you and he's hurting a great deal. I could hear it in his voice. It's probably fortunate they are so busy with this project that he doesn't have too much time to dwell.'

'He cried on the phone to me. It broke my heart to hear him weep. It took me right back to his childhood and like then, I wanted to take away all that pain. Let it be mine, I can absorb it all - he shouldn't have to feel like this.'

'But he does, Julia. His grief belongs to him. He needs to grieve for Paddy, and you need to let him. Be there for him as a soft-landing place, but let him grieve – he's mourning his dad, because that's what Paddy was to him – a dad.' Carrick could feel his own emotions threatening to spill over and spoil the evening.

He picked up his spoon and sipped his soup. He looked across and saw she was staring into space, no doubt replaying scenes from a past that only she could see. When he finished his meal, he took the tray back to the kitchen, poured himself another wine and one for Julia and returned to the lounge.

'I've given up on reaching Lizzie. I tried and tried, but she didn't pick up or call back, so I'll not waste any more of my time or emotion.' She let the statement hang there and Carrick was unsure what he should say so chose silence. He sensed the dam was about to burst so settled in his chair and waited while she nursed her glass of wine, an emotional tug of war playing across her face.

20

———

JULIA

As the wine and the warmth settled her churning emotions, Julia decided it was time to confide to Carrick what had happened in Spain.

'She was antagonistic from the outset, only I was so caught up in my own feelings, I didn't read the signals. When Jack phoned to say they were delayed, she got really upset. I was disappointed too but when I told her to relax, she bit my head off, angry because I didn't understand how long she'd been waiting for them to visit her and how important every minute with them was to her. It was an over-the-top reaction which left me bemused but now I understand what was behind it.'

Julia took a sip of her wine before carrying on. 'She's envious of me. Envious of everything I have. Everything I represent right back to our days at university. It was such a shock to hear her speak like that. I feel like I've been living in a parallel universe for years – unaware of this other reality around me.'

'You can't hold yourself responsible for Lizzie's unresolved issues, Julia. She's a grownup.'

'I know and I don't. I'm just saddened that it's come to his. All those years of friendship, of loyalty. What did all that mean? She's turned everything we had into a competition of who is the more caring. Who is the more loyal? Staying with Lizzie those weeks was like living inside some bizarre teenage argument – I found it exhausting. And then when she finally exploded, it was so ugly.'

'Friendships are a funny business, and you were more like sisters - well that's what Paddy and I thought.'

'The day before Jack and Kat arrived, I went out for a walk before supper. I asked if she wanted to come, but she'd been in a strange mood all day and didn't want to join me. I walked along the beach and then stopped at a beach bar for a drink and something to eat. I had a lovely time. Alone, without grief for company. They had music on and suddenly I recognised tracks from a Melbourne band that Patrick and I had seen perform. I thought I was going to dissolve into a crying mess at the table, but I didn't - I held it together and ended up staying longer and having a chat with the young barman from Melbourne. I left and walked back feeling upbeat and realised that little bastard with the baseball bat had failed to get me.'

Alarmed, Carrick almost spilt his wine. 'What! A baseball bat - did someone threaten you?'

Julia realised Carrick did not understand what she was talking about. 'No nothing happened to me. Sorry, it's just how I think of it.' She smiled self-consciously at him.

'There are moments when the grief hits me like a physical blow, and I can hardly breathe. It completely overwhelms me, and my emotions run out of control and all the pain and fear makes me want to curl up in a ball on the ground. I picture it like a mugger with a baseball bat has caught me by surprise and assaulted my emotions. Giving it a human form helps me recognise and deal with the triggers for these attacks and defend myself. Saying it aloud makes me sound loopy, but it's my way of taking an active role in healing myself instead of passively waiting for time to fix things for me.' Julia's words tailed off and she looked at Carrick.

'I'm sounding nuts, aren't I?' Her face looked stricken with embarrassment, so he moved from his chair and sat alongside her on the couch, reaching out to take her hand in his.

'No, Julia, you sound like a brave woman who is going to get over this and be stronger than ever, but you don't have to talk about this if you don't want to.'

'But I need to Carrick. That day you phoned, and I was such a mess, I'd had an awful dream – it was ugly and involved Lizzie and Jack so I need to talk it out in the hope that it will cleanse my subconscious such that I don't experience that dream again, ever.'

'I understand.' He gave her hand a squeeze, and Julia glanced at him, but he turned away, his expression unreadable.

'When Jack and Kat arrived, Lizzie was on a real hostess high. She was so hyper I even wondered if she was on something. Anyway, when we sat down for supper that night, she told them I'd been out the night before at a beach bar chatting up the barman who was half my age. She said it in a jesting tone, but there was an edge, and I didn't understand how she knew I'd been at the beach bar.' Julia took a sip from her wine and pulled herself up from the couch, walking to the fire and standing in front of it as though a sudden chill had passed through her.

'She said that she came down to the beach bar, thinking I might have stopped off there, and seen me talking to the barman. 'Your mother looked like she was having a great time, so I left her to enjoy her little flirtation with youth.'

'It was an awful thing to say and untrue, and it made me sound like some old Cougar out on the town for the night. Kat came to my rescue at that point. Jack was too shocked to say anything, but Kat bit back at her and that did not go down well, and everything sort of spiralled downwards from there.'

'I'm surprised Lizzie would be that tactless, especially in front of Jack. She's normally trying hard to impress him with her thoughtfulness, kindness, and wisdom; that's how it comes across to me, but maybe I'm being picky.'

Julia nodded. 'Yes. I know. Patrick used to comment on it, but I guess I'm just used to her fussing over Jack. For a moment I thought nothing of it and then I realised she wasn't just poking fun at me as friends do, she was really putting me down in front of Jack and Kat as though I was an embarrassment to them all.' Julia returned to join him on the couch.

'Do you fancy a tea? I might make myself one, it's a bit of a long story if you're not too tired to listen to more?'

'I'm fine, honestly. A tea would be lovely, thank you.'

Julia returned with tea and a plate of biscuits.

'What are these?' Carrick said, reaching out to take a tiny biscuit from the plate Julia was holding out.

'I made them. They're Amaretti biscuits, a Jamie Oliver recipe, I'm a big fan of Jamie's - a chef groupie you might say, if you were being unkind that is.' She grinned at him. 'They're made with polenta and orange.'

'They're delicious, you can make these anytime.' He smiled at her, taking another biscuit from the plate.

Julia sat down on the couch and continued the story. 'Things settled down for the next day or two but after Jack and Kat left,' she hesitated, suddenly feeling unwilling to unburden herself, but knowing she needed too.

'Lizzie started drinking before lunch and didn't stop till bedtime. I've never seen her drink like that. I'm not a big drinker and she's always drunk more than me, but this was different – like she was on a mission to drown out feelings, thoughts, I don't know. Anyway, that night it all kicked off. It started with her accusing me of upsetting Jack because I was talking about Patrick a lot.' She hesitated, the memory raw and fresh and the familiar lump forming in her throat. She swallowed several times before carrying on with her story.

'Then she got started on how disappointed she'd been when I went out to Australia and didn't stay to help her deal with Michael's death. I told you that part before. It didn't matter that I tried to explain, I didn't have a choice. Her answer to that was *we all have choices Julia, sometimes we just make the wrong ones.* Then it moved on to how much she'd helped me after my separation from Nick. How, if it hadn't been for her, I would have been rotting in the bedroom upstairs with no one to save me.'

Julia moved off the couch again, back to the fire. She was struggling with the telling of this story and the memories it evoked.

She'd been out walking the Baltimore hills with Carrick when they'd all been enjoying a summer holiday with Rose and Brendan. She'd confided in Carrick as they sat on the boulders at the top of the ridge looking out across the lough, how her ex-husband had assaulted her, knocked her unconscious. Lizzie had come out to the house, worried at not having heard from Julia and found her. She could see from the expression on Carrick's face that he was probably remembering back to that same moment when she'd confided.

'I couldn't believe she was saying all this stuff. I thought friends looked out for each other, but apparently her love has conditions. I think that's the part that I find so distressing – all this resentment she must have been hoarding inside herself – percolating away there for years.'

'What's the stuff about Michael's death. I know you alluded to it before, but is there something?'

'Remember, I told you she had all those boxes delivered from Michael's office?'

'Yes, but I could see at the time you weren't ready to talk about it but, at the risk of being nosy, are you going to tell me?'

She hesitated for a moment before carrying on. 'Lizzie found photos of a child, a boy. He was the spitting image of Michael. Long story short, after meeting with Michael's solicitor, Lizzie discovered Michael had a son. He'd had a child with a young woman. Long before he met Lizzie, but he'd never found the courage to divulge his past, and that broke her.'

'Shite. That's a biggie. Was he still seeing this woman after he met Lizzie?'

'Yes - he was, but it appeared there was no ongoing sexual relationship between them. He just went to visit his son, well at least that's how it was presented.'

'How do you know?'

'I don't for certain – and nor does Lizzie. We met her - the mother of the boy, she's German. Michael had bought her a house in London many years before. He wanted to ensure his son was well provided for and Lizzie found all this out from the paperwork and his solicitor. I went up to London with her. She wanted to confront this woman. It was awful.'

'I can only imagine,' said Carrick, reaching out to take another biscuit from the plate.

'She was young – the woman I mean, even then after so many years. It was obvious, she must have been a teenager, maybe even underage, when Michael got her pregnant. I've no idea where he met her and how that came about, only that I assumed Michael must have felt so guilty that he wanted to protect her and his son. And maybe he'd been afraid of Lizzie's reaction - we'll never know.'

'I get that, but why not just come clean to Lizzie at the start, right back when they first met, then there wouldn't be any surprises?'

'I hate secrets with good reason, so I totally get why Lizzie reacted the way she did.' She was looking directly at Carrick and noted his discomfort.

'This was a huge and grubby secret.'

'It kind of explains why Lizzie hasn't been able to deal with Michael's death, all that unfinished business. So many questions and wondering what's real in her marriage.'

'I know. I understand. But it's not this woman's fault and not Michael's son's fault.'

'Where is he, the son, did you meet him?'

'No. He's in Europe somewhere, maybe Germany, his mother wouldn't say. She looked frightened, understandable if you'd seen the way Lizzie was behaving. Anyway, it was soon after that confrontation that Lizzie noticed the house had sold and she'd disappeared. Even Michael's solicitor doesn't know where she is. Just as well really, because I think Lizzie would hound her, she's quite obsessed about this son of Michael's.'

'Like the way she is with Jack?'

'No. It's different, she's kind of haunted by it, but intrigued as well. She wants to know who he is, what sort of man he's grown into. At one stage she hired a private detective at great expense, but that drew a blank. It's like he never existed.'

'What about Michael's Will, does this son stand to inherit?'

'No. Michael had a trust set up for him and he can't make a claim on the estate, so Lizzie is lucky she's in an extremely comfortable position financially, it's just her heart that's damaged. She feels betrayed and I know all about betrayal.' She stopped for a moment and took a sip of her tea.

'Michael should have told her, but I can also appreciate that as every day passed after he met Lizzie the chance to tell her - to explain, slipped away like sand through his fingers. He denied her the opportunity to have children whilst all the time visiting and paying for a son whose identity remained a secret. Lizzie has every right to feel cheated.'

'Yes, I can see that, but it's no excuse to make you her punch bag.'

'I know and she was vicious about all of that, accusing me of patronising her and being smug because I have Jack and she has no children. She seemed to think Jack had phoned her first before me when he met Kat because he felt she was more in tune with him. She was almost foaming at the mouth when I corrected her.' Julia frowned, remembering back to the conversation.

'Jack had sent a text to Patrick and me the day he met Kat. She was working at a bar during her university holidays and Jack had got talking with her. And when she was on her break, she joined him at his table. As soon as he could he was on his phone texting Patrick and I to say he'd met someone special. I think he'd only known her a few hours, but somehow, he just knew. Knew she would be the one. We spoke a few days later, and he mentioned he'd just got off the phone from Lizzie, desperate to share his news. He was so excited - in love I guess.'

She looked away from Carrick, unable to keep eye contact, knowing that she had not felt this way about his brother when they first met. Their relationship had been a slow burn.

'So how do you move forward from this? Assuming you wish to?'

'Yes. I do. I hate there being this destructive antagonism between us, but I will not apologise, nor am I going to keep reaching out. While she's in this dark place, there's little point. I don't have the energy. And yes, I'm sure she'll think that's selfish, but it's five years now since Michael died. She won't get help. Great at telling me when I need counselling but not prepared to take her own advice.'

'Have you talked to Jack about this? He mentioned to me on the phone that Lizzie had been a real cow when they were out in Spain and that she'd left them voice-messages at Christmas, sounding drunk. I got the impression he wants to create some space between himself and Lizzie. Like you, he doesn't need all her baggage.'

'No. We haven't talked about it. I don't want him to worry about what she's said to me. She's his godmother and he shouldn't have to hear about this ugliness.' She sighed, not wishing to dwell on telling Jack.

'You know I never thought I'd hear myself saying my best friend is a drunk, but she is. She was drunk virtually the entire time I was there. You're aware of the story that we both came from homes where alcohol was a problem. I never thought she'd turn to the bottle in search of answers.'

'No one can tell what is going to send someone over the edge. Do you want another tea, I'm going to have one?'

'Yes, please. Thank you, Carrick, - and thank you for listening.'

'I sense there is more. I'll be back in a minute with the tea. Do you want anything else?'

'What you mean is, can I have more of those biscuits please?' She was laughing at him and it pleased him to see her able to enjoy a lighter moment.

'You can read me too well Julia, I'll re-fill the plate. Hope you made plenty?'

'Plenty for a greedy man.'

When Carrick brought the tea back, Julia had once more stretched out on the couch with the throw wrapped around herself. She reached her hand up to take the tea and waved away the offer of a biscuit.

'In the dream I had. Lizzie was sitting amid hundreds of photos scattered all over the floor and then I realised they were of Jack from a baby through until now and she started screaming at me, pointing at the photos saying he was her baby, not mine, her baby. He belonged to her and how dare I steal him.'

'It was so bizarre, but frighteningly real. She looked mad in the dream, her eyes almost black and her face twisted with bitterness and anger.' Julia shuddered at the memory.

'It was clear from the way she spoke, that she thinks I'm the lucky one, have always been the lucky one, able to have men falling at my feet. Great job, plenty of money. She doesn't understand who I am anymore.

When she was out for the funeral, I noticed how she looked around the house, the grounds, everywhere and then when we were having a drink one night, she remarked how she thought I'd fallen on my feet, that if I fell into a pile of pig's shit I'd come up smelling of roses. It was so offensive.'

'Was I still there then when she said that?'

'No. You had gone by then, as had Kat and your parents. It was just Jack, Lizzie, and me. She was going on about the time Jack came with me to New Zealand. Do you remember when I went out to sort my aunt's estate and...' She stopped then, unable to stop the flow of tears.

Carrick put his cup down and knelt down by the couch. He reached for her hand, holding it in his until she regained her composure and continued with the story.

'Apparently she'd seen that as the ultimate snub. That she'd helped me deal with the trauma of learning about my mother and all of that stuff and that she had a right to be accompanying us to New Zealand as though she were the psychologist we needed by our side. She just didn't get it, that it was a time for me, for Jack - it was our journey. Our own private journey and no one, not her nor Patrick, could intrude on that time.'

'Sounds like Lizzie has a lot she needs to deal with, and you are wise to stay away. There is nothing you can do to help her when she's so angry and drinking as she is.'

'I know, but it doesn't sit comfortably with me. I feel like I'm abandoning her in search of my own happiness, but I don't have space for this right now. I've got so much to sort out when I go back to Australia. There is nothing left in the well for her to draw from, and for that I'm sorry.'

She noticed Carrick had continued to hold her hand, and she longed to reach out and let him take her in his arms and comfort her - take away her pain, but she would continue to deny that need - just feeling his hand in hers was enough to calm her, enough of a balm to lighten her sadness.

21

———

NEW YEAR'S EVE

Carrick had occupied himself with organising his schedule for the start of the new year, avoiding spending too much time in the company of Julia. He'd invited Edward Schneider over for lunch days before, and that had proved to be a wonderful distraction. Julia had cooked a delicious lunch and she and Edward had hit it off immediately, as Carrick knew they would.

Now it was New Year's Eve, and Julia didn't know what the night held. She'd gone out shopping intent on making something special before they went out for the evening. He knew she was trying ever so hard to be positive about the beginning of a new year, but he could see the cracks appearing when she thought he wasn't looking.

Carrick would see her swipe a tear from her eyes, before taking a deep breath and carrying on with whatever it was she was doing. Now she was back from Waitrose and unloading food from her backpack.

'So, what are you going to cook?'

'I've probably bought far too much food, but we can always have left-overs. I thought I'd do a Tagine of Venison.'

'What? So, you know a deer stalker now, do you?' He looked at her, his eyebrows raised quizzically.

139

'If you knew London as I do, you would know there is a market that sells wild game. I love venison, so I thought I'd buy some and the rest of the ingredients to make this dish. You'll love it unless you don't like venison?' A look of panic crossed her features as she turned to him.

It would have been so easy to tease her, but the look on her face told him she was genuinely worried she'd made a mistake.

'I love it. Can I help with anything?'

'No. Thanks, you must have heaps of work to do, I'm happy just messing about. What time did you think we will go out?'

'Oh, probably not until around 8:00 p.m. – if we aim for being ready by then. As long as you think you can handle a late night?'

'I've slept better since you returned from Ireland than I have in months. I feel very rested and ready for a night out.' Carrick hoped she could handle the evening's events. It would be emotional for her, but also a time to feel immensely proud.

'Are you expecting a call or something, you keep looking at your phone?' Julia was stirring the pan and the smell of onions and Moroccan spices was tantalising.

'Was I? Few things I'm expecting to fall into place over the next couple of hours.' He walked away into the lounge annoyed with himself that he'd been so obvious, but Julia appeared to be none the wiser. His phone pinged, and he read the message from his parents.

Mammy: Arrived safely, your driver has picked us up. On our way.

Great, Carrick thought, one down. He hoped he would receive another text within the next half hour, otherwise they would be cutting it fine to eat and be ready to leave by 8:00 p.m.

The doorbell rang while Carrick was talking with Julia in the kitchen.

'Are you expecting anyone?' she said, as she lifted the large earthenware casserole dish into the oven.

'Probably just a courier dropping off some papers for me.' He swiftly made his way down the hall and opened the door, putting his finger to his lips to signal no talking. His mother and father grinned back at him like two naughty school children. He quickly grabbed their bags and put them in the hall cupboard before they all walked as silently as they could down the hallway to the kitchen.

Julia turned just as they reached the kitchen door. Her face flushed from the heat of the oven, her apron stained, and a towel draped over her arm.

'Oh, my goodness, what a wonderful surprise,' Julia squealed, rushing to Rose and Brendan and wrapping her arms around them.

'This son of yours is very sneaky,' she said.

'Oh, we wouldn't have missed this for the world Julia,' Rose said, the words tumbling out before she realised. Carrick, standing behind Julia, swiped his finger across his throat to imitate she needed to cut it right now or it would ruin the second surprise.

'Missed what?'

'New-Year's-eve in London.' Rose said recovering herself rather beautifully.

'Come on, you two, I'll show you to your room.' He went back down the hall, collected their bags and opened the door to their bedroom, quickly closing it behind him.

'That was close Mammy,' Carrick whispered. 'I'm expecting a text from Jack any minute. They flew in early yesterday morning and went straight to rehearsals. I was kind of hoping they would be back in time for supper tonight, but it's getting late.'

'So, Julia hasn't guessed?' said Rose, as she unzipped their bags and unpacked.

'No. It will be a very emotional night for all of us, but none more so than for Julia. Jack was lucky his employers were supportive of him coming out for tonight's event, despite the project being behind schedule. Although I think he would have come regardless – he wouldn't wish to miss this opportunity.'

Brendan reached out and drew Carrick into a hug. 'This is the most wonderful gift you could give us, my boy. Your mother and I can't thank you enough for getting us out here at short notice. We felt like school kids doing a bunk, crazy coming from two retired schoolteachers.' He laughed, holding Carrick out from him and looking into his eyes.

'You are right when you say it will be an emotional evening. This is a big night for Julia, we're prepared for that. We'll all be there for her – we're family and she'll need us by her side tonight.'

Carrick brushed a tear from his cheek. 'I imagine we are all going to feel overwhelmed. This is quite something. Anyway, we can't stay in here whispering or she'll know something's up. Come down to the kitchen when you're ready and we'll have a drink.'

When Carrick returned to the kitchen, Julia was busy preparing a couscous salad. She turned to him and grinned. 'You are a devil, Carrick Devlin. Such a surprise to have Rose and Brendan here with us for the new year. They look all fresh faced and excited. Are they coming out with us tonight to this place that you refuse to tell me about?'

Carrick laughed. 'Yes, they'll be coming, probably going to be a late night, but that's what sleeping in is for. Shall I set the table?'

'Yes, please. I'm almost finished with the salad and then I can pour everyone a drink, unless you want to do the honours?'

'You've done all the hard work cooking, I'll pour the drinks, what would you like?'

'I'll have a red thanks. What should I be wearing tonight, is it fancy or casual?'

'I'm not telling you where we're going, so you can stop trying to trick me,' he hesitated, frowning for a moment, 'smart casual, that should be about right.'

'You realise smart casual sounds like where heading to a business conference.' She raised her eyebrows at him.

'You've got that gorgeous wool dress you wore the other day, how about that with boots?'

'Okay, Giorgio Armani', she responded in her best imitation of an Italian accent, sounding more like Danny DeVito. 'That'll be the go.'

Carrick laughed out loud. 'God, you sound so Australian when you say that.'

'That's my best Italian,' she retorted, whacking his arm with the kitchen towel.

'No, I meant, *that will be the go.*' Now Carrick was impersonating an Australian accent, which he thought wasn't half bad.

At that moment Rose and Brendan walked into the kitchen, taking in the scene before them and both grinning widely. 'You two sound like two teenagers,' they laughed. 'It's so good to be here, Julia.' Rose said, lifting her hand up to brush Julia's cheek. 'We missed you after you left.'

Julia took Rose's hand in hers and brought it up to her lips, her skin was soft, but tissue thin, the elastin broken down from years of ultraviolet from an Irish sun a reminder of how much Rose had aged in the past few years. 'It's lovely to have you here to see in the new year together.'

'Right, what do you want to drink?' Carrick asked. 'I'll pour and then we can take them through to the lounge. How long Julia before supper is ready?'

'I would say 40 minutes,' she untied her apron and helped get the glasses out.

'Is that going to give us enough time to eat, change and get out the door, how far away is the venue?'

'You don't stop, do you? Not telling. But that should give us plenty of time as long as you ladies don't dilly dally about with your hair and face and all that stuff.'

'He's become very cheeky, this boy of yours, Rose. You must give him a talking to whilst you're here,' Julia said, laughing as she carried through two glasses of red wine to the lounge.

'Sorry I have to make a call before we have supper. I'll be right back.' He walked swiftly to his office and closed the door. Reading the text that had just come through from Jack.

Jack: Sorry, change of plan, can't make supper. Musicians held up with flights. Will see you at the venue.

Carrick: OK. Mum & Dad are here. See you later. Good luck.

'I'm going to serve supper now Carrick, I'll call you when everything is ready.' Julia left the lounge and returned to the kitchen.

Carrick looked across to his parents, raising an eyebrow, 'haven't given the show away have you?'

'No!' his mother responded indignantly. 'I just got carried away earlier, that's all. I've zipped this,' pinching her fingers together and running them across her lips.

'That was Jack with a text message. He can't make supper, so he'll see us there. He must be so nervous.'

'Supper is ready,' Julia called from the kitchen.

As they all settled themselves at the table, Carrick carried the heavy earthenware casserole to the table and Julia placed a large bowl of couscous salad in easy reach of everyone.

'I hope you both like venison?' She looked at Rose and Brendan expectantly.

'We love it,' they both chorused together. 'Mind you Julia,' Brendan said, 'we haven't had venison for a long while. There used to be a local man who was a deerstalker, but he's long gone and if anyone else is going out hunting, we don't hear about it, let alone see any of the spoils.'

'Well, this will be a delightful treat then.'

22

———

A NIGHT TO REMEMBER

Julia was wearing a plum-coloured merino wool dress that fell just below the knee. A black leather belt loosely fastened at her waist, black leather boots and a plum and black pashmina draped her shoulders.

Carrick whistled at her as she walked towards him down the hall, making her blush. 'You look cool yourself Carrick,' she said, taking in his long legs clad in dark jeans, beautiful teal coloured shirt and dark sports jacket. He was a very handsome man.

It was a surprise for Julia to learn Carrick had a driver. 'I didn't know you had a driver, have you always had one?'

'No. And I seldom use him. I just helped him out by getting him started in a new venture.'

'How do you know him?' They were having this conversation in the hallway while they waited for Rose and Brendan.

Just as Carrick was about to answer, Rose and Brendan stepped out of their room. Rose looked elegant, Julia thought. She was wearing a dove grey maxi dress with beautiful matching accessories. It suited her tall and slim figure and Brendan wearing a wool sports jacket and black trousers, looking equally smart.

'Wow, you two look grand,' Carrick said grinning at his parents, thrilled that they looked so much brighter and happier than when he'd said goodbye to them in Baltimore five days earlier.

'Julia was asking about my driver. Did you recognise him when he picked you up from the airport?'

'No, son, should we have?'

Carrick laughed. 'No, and I told him not to tell you. He's Jacob Nicholson from school, do you remember him?'

'Really! Seriously?' Rose said, looking shocked. 'I would never have recognised him. He was such a skinny waif like boy with hand-me-down clothes always looked half starved. You remember Brendan, the parents were a bit of a lost cause?'

'Yes. I recall. Can't believe he's the same little boy. How did you come across him, Carrick?'

'He was begging outside the tube station and recognised me. He called my name. We got talking. Turned out he was down on his luck, few gambling problems, when I say a few, I mean a lot. Long story short, I persuaded him to go to Gamblers Anonymous, and I found out he loved driving. Selling life insurance had been his previous job until they had made him redundant and - well the rest is history.'

'A driver ah?' Brendan said.

'He loves driving. I set him up with a car, put him in touch with a few of my business associates and now he's got a great little business going. I only use him occasionally, but he wanted to do this job tonight. He should be here in a minute.'

'You and Patrick make your father and I so proud Carrick. Both of you were always looking out for those in need. That was a decent and generous thing to do for Jacob.'

'He did the hard yards Mammy; I just provided the opportunity. It takes real guts to pull yourself up from the dark place he was in. I admire him and he deserves to do well.'

They heard a toot from outdoors and quickly made their way down the steps to the street where Jacob was waiting, holding open both passenger doors.

Julia sat between Rose and Brendan and listened as they chatted animatedly to Jacob, telling him all about their place in Baltimore and if ever he was back in Cork, he was most welcome to visit. It amazed her when she heard the story. Patrick was the same, always ready to help someone in need. It was very humbling to be part of this family.

Julia was startled when they pulled up outside the Royal Albert Hall feeling she was under-dressed for the occasion, whatever the occasion was - she still had no idea what Carrick was taking them to. She noticed Carrick flick Jacob a fifty-pound note and heard him say, 'get yourself a good meal and take a break. I'll text when we're ready to leave.'

As they alighted from the car, Carrick took her arm and together they walked into the main auditorium and took their seats. She glanced across at Rose and Brendan, who appeared to be completely in awe of their surroundings. She leaned across Carrick and asked, 'have you been here before?'

'Yes, we have,' beamed back Rose, 'but not in many, many years, it's grand isn't it? I feel like Lilibet,' she remarked, her eyes sparking with mischief.

'Who is Lilibet?' Julia asked.

'The Queen. Queen Elizabeth. Princess Margaret used to call her Lilibet as a child. I always call her that.' Rose winked and for a flash, it reminded Julia of Patrick. He would wink like that when he was teasing her.

Carrick must have noticed her stiffen and squeezed her hand, and she found herself drawn to his face and his beautiful eyes and the love in that gaze.

'Ladies and gentlemen, for those of you who don't know me, although you must have been living under a rock not to know me.'

Laughter erupted from the audience. 'I'm Dermot O'Leary and I will be your host for this evening's charity event. We have been fortunate enough to secure an amazing line up of musicians and dancers who have given up their New Year's Eve parties to come and join our party.' The audience applauded loudly, whistling out and cheering.

'I won't delay you any further, please welcome to the stage – Adele.'

The audience stood and applauded as Adele made her way to the centre of the stage and the piano intro to Bob Dylan's *Make You Feel My Love* began. Julia loved this song and as the stage was lit by graphic images of children in care, special needs children, homeless and sick children, the words of the song were never more powerful than in that moment.

Sting was the next artist to perform where he sang *Shape of My Heart*. Julia stole a glance at Carrick and saw tears in his eyes and realised, like her, he was thinking of Patrick. They'd both watched Patrick's band play this song.

'Our next performance is by a group of outstanding young dancers who have climbed out of poverty and shaped their own futures, please give it up for *We Ain't Down*.'

The sound of Glenn Miller's *In the Mood* filled the hall and at once a troop of Lindy Hop dancers stepped out on stage. Julia rose to her feet along with most of the audience all swaying in time to the music including Rose and Brendan as people danced in the aisles.

The whole place was buzzing - the audience wild with excitement when all in perfect rhythm and co-ordination the female dancers flipped over the backs of the males; the choreography was extraordinary, and Julia laughed with the sheer exhilaration of the performance, how she loved dance.

'Tonight's charity event is in aid of several organisations who, for a variety of reasons, need additional funding for programmes, medical research and equipment.' Dermot announced.

'One such organisation is Evelina London Children's Hospital. For many years in the week before Christmas, a well-respected and much-loved teacher and musician brought a smile to the faces of the patients at the Evelina Hospital. I'm talking about the late great Paddy Devlin and tonight a special tribute to Paddy's amazing work with not only Evelina, but the charity he set up before he departed our shores for Australia, *Down but not Out*.

Sadly, we lost Paddy earlier this year, but his legacy lives on and tonight ladies and gentlemen, please welcome to the stage as guest musician, Paddy's son, Mr Jack Davis.'

Julia thought she was going to pass out. Her heart was beating so fast, she didn't know whether to sit or remain standing clapping frantically as Jack walked out on stage, his drum-sticks held high, waving to the audience as he settled himself behind the drum kit.

'And now, please give it up for Mr Eric Clapton.'

'Oh my God,' gasped Julia. 'Patrick would be so proud.' She couldn't believe what was happening, her little boy playing with Eric Clapton. She felt Carrick's hand in hers and looked across to find him smiling back at her, looking as emotional as she was.

Julia glanced at Rose and saw she had tears running down her cheeks as Brendan passed her a clean handkerchief from his pocket. She saw them smile at each other, and Brendan take Rose's hand in his.

As the song, *Change the World* ended, the audience stood and applauded. Julia leant across to Carrick, 'is that Phil playing acoustic?'

'Sure is,' he grinned back at her.

'Patrick will be so pissed he's not here tonight - it was his dream to play live with Eric.' It stunned Julia for a moment, Carrick was talking as though Patrick was away for the weekend, as though when he got back Carrick would tease him mercilessly about missing out. It felt strangely comforting that he was still speaking of his brother in the present tense as she found herself so frequently doing, and she loved him for this. She squeezed his hand looking into his eyes as he turned to meet her gaze.

The next song, *I Shot the Sheriff* a more instrumental version than the original and Julia found herself drawn to Jack sitting behind the drum kit and wondered where Kat was, probably back-stage. She'd be loving this, the sound engineer in her would be analysing every nuance of the acoustics.

The song changed to a soft melody with Eric playing a solo riff, making it look so effortless. The big screen captured his face in concentration before switching to Jack and she could finally get a close-up view of her son performing with one of music's all-time greats as Eric turned to Jack for the finale of guitar and drums.

'How awesome was that?' Dermot was yelling out to the audience. 'We'll take a short 15-minute break before the next acts, see you soon.'

Julia looked around and realised the audience included a who's who of musicians old and new that she recognised. This capacity crowd would surely raise an enormous amount for the charities represented tonight -Patrick would be so humbled by this, she thought as they made their way out to the main auditorium.

JULIA AND ROSE were weaving their way between people back to their seats and could see Carrick and Brendan standing waiting for them at the entrance to their row. As she sat down Carrick reached for her hand. 'Jack was amazing, you must be so proud, I know I am.'

She placed her hand on top of his. 'I can't tell you what this means to me, words can't describe, so I won't try.'

'Now ladies, our next performance may get your hearts a fluttering so don't say you haven't been warned, give it up for the sexiest man in town, Mr Bryan Ferry.'

'Oh my God,' Julia exclaimed loud enough for Carrick to turn to her. 'I love him.'

'Please welcome back to the stage as guest saxophonist, Mr Jack Davis.'

'On My God, this is amazing?' Julia squealed watching Jack walk out on stage carrying his saxophone.

Bryan Ferry's distinctively melodic voice launched into *Slave to Love* while the sexy dancers, that epitomised the era of Roxy Music, swayed and gyrated in perfect rhythm. Julia watched in awe as Jack, saxophone slung around his neck, played keyboards before lifting the sax to his lips.

From there they went straight into playing *Don't stop the Dance* and, when Bryan turned to Jack for the solo saxophone piece, it caught Julia in a moment of pure ecstasy. Mesmerised, Julia watched as Bryan, with the familiar flourish of his hand, signalled the end to the song.

Several other acts followed, but they could have included the dancing bear and bearded lady, Julia wouldn't have noticed – still caught her up in the euphoria of seeing Jack play alongside two of music's greats.

'Ladies and gentlemen please welcome back to the stage all the musicians and dancers who not only gave up their new-year's-eve parties to come along here tonight but did so without payment.

A special thanks to guest musician Mr Jack Davis who came all the way from Geneva to be with us tonight and Mr Phil Ulrik, friend and fellow band mate to Paddy Devlin. Phil has been tireless in his efforts to bring all these great artists together this evening as well as playing acoustic guitar with Eric and bass guitar with Bryan. Let's give them all one last round of applause.'

BACK STAGE the party was underway by the time Carrick, Julia, Rose, and Brendan made their way through. Julia spotted Jack with Kat talking to some musicians.

'Hello Mum,' Jack said as he turned and pulled her into his arms. 'You look amazing.'

'Not half as amazing as you, my gorgeous son. You were outstanding Jack. Patrick would be so proud of you and humbled by this event.'

'I know, he'd be stoked.'

Phil interrupted them with arms outstretched, pulling Julia into a big hug. 'My god it's good to see you Julia. I'm so glad you could make it. Carrick said he would do whatever it took to have you here tonight.'

Julia could see he was emotional, and she had a sudden flashback to the funeral and the live streaming of Phil sitting in his studio reading his eulogy to Patrick.

'This is an amazing thing you have done Phil, organising this, it has been an extraordinary night.'

'I didn't do it alone, there were loads of supporters who did all the work, I was just the catalyst. When I heard that Evelina were strug-gling with funding for research, and then I heard about this event being organised for charity, it was good karma and it sort of snow-balled from there.'

'I think what you've done is wonderful. And how good were you on acoustic alongside Eric Clapton and bass for Bryan Ferry - Patrick would be so proud of you.'

'No, he wouldn't. He'd be well pissed, in fact if he could've pushed me off the stage and taken my place, I think he would've done.' Phil lifted his eyes to the ceiling and said 'Sorry, mate, we all miss you. And I know I lost the beat for a moment in the third verse. I was so damn nervous.'

Julia placed her hand on his arm. 'It sounded perfect to me, but it must have been overwhelming to be out there on stage with them.'

'It was.' His face grew solemn and Julia knew that he was about to say more about Patrick when Carrick suddenly appeared by her side as if she'd just conjured him up. He shook Phil's hand, thanking and congratulating him.

'I heard we've reached the $1 million mark already and still climbing. Now I must whisk Julia away. There are people who wish to speak with her. Catch you later, Phil.'

'Thank you for rescuing me. I love Phil, but he was heading into maudlin territory and I need a night off from that.'

'I know. I've been in touch with him a great deal over these last few months and he cries a lot over Paddy, we both do, but not tonight, it wouldn't be what Paddy would want.'

Later, as Julia stood talking with Jack, wondering when she could politely leave, she asked about Jack and Kat's plans. 'Are you coming back to stay at Carrick's tonight?'

'Absolutely, we've got a few days before we head back, so we want to spend that time with you. If this goes on too late, we have a key, so you don't have to wait up.'

'A key. How do you have a key?'

'We use Carrick's place whenever we get back to London, did he not say? He gave us a key after you and Patrick moved out to Australia. Not to his Bloomsbury place, he hadn't found that place then, but to his old flat in Chiswick. Now he has the new apartment we get to stay there. It's awesome, isn't it?'

She didn't appreciate Carrick had been spending that much time with Jack and Kat after she had left for Australia, not that they shouldn't it was more she thought Carrick would have been far too busy flying all over the place.

'Yes, I agree. It's a gorgeous place, he's made a beautiful job of restoring it. I've seen the photos of when he first bought it – you have to admire his vision and dedication to making it what it is today.'

'You look tired Mum do you want to go back? You don't have to stay. And Rose and Brendan look done in,' Jack moved his head to show where Rose and Brendan sat on a couch in the corner looking happy, but exhausted.

'I think I will. I'll find Carrick and let him know - he'll most likely want to stay on and party.'

'Who is going to stay on, and party may I ask?' Carrick appeared at her side.

'You. Jack was just suggesting I go back to your place with Rose and Brendan, do you think you can phone your driver?'

'Sure, but I'm coming too. I'm getting too old for all this late-night partying. Now that we've all sung Auld Lang Syne, I'm happy to retire to my bed.'

'If you're sure then?' Julia asked looking at him trying to read if he was being thoughtful or he was exhausted.

'Absolutely certain, come on let's head out.'

23

JULIA

Rose and Brendan had retired to bed and, whilst Julia felt dog-tired, she was restless and knew sleep wouldn't take her quickly tonight. She lay stretched out in her pyjamas on the couch in Carrick's lounge. Carrick had gone to his room and so, when she suddenly heard a noise close by, she jumped.

'Sorry I didn't mean to startle you. Are you okay?'

'I'm exhausted, but I feel restless. I thought I'd just come and lie here for a little while. It was a lot to process tonight.'

'I can appreciate that. It was amazing to see Jack up there performing, he's an outstanding musician, as Paddy used to remind us all regularly.' He was smiling now, turning towards the fire and stretching his arms out in front of him before turning to face Julia again.

'I was thinking,' Julia said, 'where was Liam Brady tonight? He was so close to you both that I thought he'd be there?'

'He was going to be but, despite the time of year he's been working on an important business deal in the States and the airport got snowed-in. So, he's stuck over there but he gave a very generous donation to Paddy's charity all the same.'

'That was kind of him. He's a lovely man, I just wished he'd been part of tonight's amazing event, shame he had to miss it.'

'He's disappointed too, but it will be available to download so he'll be able to view the entire evening's entertainment at a later date.'

'I also wondered about Lizzie and how she's spent New Year's Eve?'

'Has she got friends out there?'

'Ex-pats mainly, although the way she talked I got the impression, whilst they regularly met up, she wasn't really close friends with any of them.'

'You can't be worrying about Lizzie Julia, she's not your problem.' Julia could sense him not wishing to dwell on Lizzie, but she needed him to understand – to understand why it mattered to her.

'She just wants to be loved, to be noticed, admired. Failing that feared, hated or despised, it's better than walking around unseen. Part of what makes us human is the need to stir up some feeling in others, I think that's what she's doing – consciously or unconsciously. Deep down we all abhor nothingness. I know Lizzie needs professional help, both for her drinking and to deal with the past, and I don't just mean Michael. She needs to come to terms with her childhood.'

'That's deep, but I get what you're saying. My question to you is, does it need to be you taking this on now – now when you have so much to deal with yourself? Time has a way of sifting and sorting, and maybe both of you need time apart to find one another again and regain what you once had. Right now she's just being a real shite friend.'

'I don't intend reaching out if that's what you're getting at and that's not spite speaking, I truly don't believe there is anything I can do. Maybe you're right, it is just about time.'

'I know I'm right. Give yourself permission to let go for a while. I'm going to pour myself a port. Do you want to join me?'

'A port. I haven't had a port in years, but why not, this is not your usual new-year's-eve, well it's new-year's day now, isn't it?' She looked across at him standing by the fire and wondered if he was also giving himself permission to *let go for a while.*

As she sipped her port, which Julia found exceedingly good, the warm dark liquid warming her from the inside out, she wondered how long these festering sores of jealousy and rage had been growing inside of Lizzie?

'You know Carrick, we are all shits at some time in our life. You'd quickly run out of people if you had to disqualify all those who at some point have been shits. I won't give up on her, but I will give it time. Give her time to come to terms with what she's become.'

She looked at him and saw a frown forming. He looked back at her as if he wanted to say something but thought better of it.

'I can't imagine that you have ever been a shit in your life Julia.'

'Oh, but I have Carrick. When I was a teenager and on the rare occasions when my mother was sober, she'd try to reach out to me, try to talk... like mother-daughter stuff. I was a shit.' She raised her eyebrows at him.

'I used to swat her words away regardless of what she said, just because I wanted to punish her - and I probably succeeded. Lizzie said some awful things about my mother and about her own mother.'

'What sort of things?' Carrick moved to sit at the end of the couch.

'She couldn't understand how I'd been able to forgive my mother for all her wrong-doings,' Julia hesitated, unsure whether she wanted to repeat what Lizzie had said.

'She thinks it's a copout, that I'm weak and making excuses for why my mother acted as she did. But I'm not weak, I know that much about myself.'

'I would never describe you as weak, never.' He put his hand out to Julia's foot and rested it there as though he was about to massage away her pain.

'My heart was a frozen block of ice whenever I thought of my mother. When I learned what forgiveness is, there was nothing but water under my ice, everything was crystal clear and forgiveness brought with it the liberty to love again, to heal. It was imperative I forgave. I finally understood she didn't hate me for me, she hated what I represented. She hated what had happened to her and the powerlessness that came with it.'

Her mind drifted back to that time, the day she'd received the letter from Grace and how she'd completely fallen apart.

'I was a rotten seed planted in her womb from an act of violence, a violation. She must have felt so broken inside to know there was nothing she could do about it. My father refused to let her have an abortion, and he raised me as his own. I understood what love was, just not a mother's love.'

Since she and Jack had travelled out to New Zealand all those years ago and she'd been able to say goodbye to her mother and be at peace with their relationship, she'd seldom re-visited that time. It felt liberating to talk about the past in this way without tears or recriminations, and that's what Lizzie failed to grasp.

'I know you said she'd been awful, but I hadn't imagined quite how awful.'

'It was dreadful and the next morning at breakfast when I announced I would leave, that I'd phoned the airline and changed my flights she was astonished, bewildered even, before lambasting me for overreacting.' She released a long sigh, 'we should go to bed, well at least I should. What time is it?'

Carrick looked at his watch. 'It's just after 2:30 a.m. and you're right, I need some sleep. Kat and Jack are obviously still having a great time. It will be good for them, it's been an intense time working on this project, I think Jack is regretting taking it on.'

'I know. He sounded so tired when I spoke with him over the phone recently, it was a relief to see him so upbeat after the show. I hope they can relax for a couple of days before they fly back.'

'Me too. Anyway, night Julia. I'll see you in a few more hours.' He smiled wearily, reaching out his hand to pull her up off the couch. He kissed the top of her head, before turning and heading down the hall to his bedroom.

The song is ended. But the melody lingers on

Irving Berlin

PART II

24

—————

MELBOURNE

The farewells at Heathrow Airport had been painful. Jack and Kat were heading back to Geneva, and Rose and Brendan were intending to stay for another few days before they too would leave and fly back to Ireland.

Jack had held onto his mother for the longest time, and she wondered how many months would pass before she would see them both again.

Rose and Brendan had been more upbeat, and she wondered if they'd been putting on a brave act just for her, but it was Carrick's face that she kept seeing every time she closed her eyes and tried to sleep on the long-haul flight.

He had drawn the curtains, pulled the blinds downs, closed the shutters, whichever analogy she chose, the conclusion was the same, he'd withdrawn from her.

He once said on one of their many walks that he believed he hid his emotions from the world because of his business, because it demanded that he project an air of complete confidence and control when he was dealing with lawyers, bankers, and architects, so this had become the norm for him in his everyday life.

Julia had been surprised to hear this perception of himself.

Maybe in business he could conceal his emotions and wear the correct persona for a successful businessman, but to his family, to those that knew and loved him, he could never conceal his emotions.

One could see it in his eyes, his movements, how he ran his fingers through his hair in moments of anguish or anger. How his shoulders would slump when he was told of something sad, or violent, or unfair. The vibes of inward weeping were so obvious that Julia felt you could take a tissue and mop them up.

Until the goodbye at the airport, she'd always believed she could read him like a book. That was one of the many things she loved about him, his openness, and his ability to both show and share emotion. Now she doubted herself. Perhaps there was a deeply hidden side to Carrick, one she'd never glimpsed.

WHEN SHE LANDED at Tullamarine airport in Melbourne, she saw Nancy waiting for her in the arrivals lounge.

'You look worn out Julia, come on let's get you home. I didn't bring Alfie with me, it's just too hot today for him to be in the car even with the air con.'

'It's so lovely of you to come and meet me, Nancy. I know you don't enjoy driving across town, so I am ever so grateful.' She leaned across and patted Nancy's knee before fastening her safety belt.

'I wouldn't have let you catch the bus into town and then, what, a train out to Belgrave? No, that would never do.' She glanced across at Julia and smiled.

'So, Sarah and Jason have left the house then, I know they mentioned in an email to me where they've bought, but I can't remember?'

'They bought an end Terrace in Middle Park. They showed me the brochures, said it reminded them of England. It seemed a lot of money for so little. Still, they want to be in the city and city prices are extortionate.'

'The emails I received showed they enjoyed staying on the mountain, I thought they may have bought locally,' Julia said, surprised when she'd learnt they'd purchased in the city's heart.

'Oh, they liked it well enough and enjoyed keeping the garden under control, but I think they like to go out a lot to restaurants and bars, and you really can't do that easily on the mountain, well not like in the city where so much entertainment is just a short walk or tram ride away.'

'They would have been used to the local pub scene in the UK, it's not always easy to adjust. Anyway, enough of Sarah and Jason, how are you doing Nancy, have you been okay?'

'I have days Julia probably like you do where I can't believe a car crash has taken Patrick from us. I keep imagining I'm hearing him calling out to let me know he's going to cut my grass. I even went outside one day. I was so certain he was there. I felt ancient and foolish.'

'You needn't. I chased a man down the street in London, calling out to him, convinced it was Patrick. I must have frightened the life out of him. I can laugh about it now, but at the time it was humiliating and frightening.'

It was Nancy's turn to lean across and pat Julia's knee. 'You poor dear, it's the shock - it affects you in so many ways that sometimes you don't even know what is real and what isn't.'

Nancy took a different route home. Relieved, Julia released a sigh. She did not wish to drive along that stretch of road. She'd still not made herself get behind the wheel of a car which was ridiculous really, it wasn't her that had crashed.

There would come a time when she had to get over this irrational fear and she would have to drive that route so she could confront and banish the ghosts but today was not that day

'Now do you wish to come to my place for a cup of tea or should I take you straight home, make you a cup of tea and then leave you to settle back in?'

'It would be nice to just be in my own home Nancy. I have to get used to being there, so may as well be sooner rather than later.'

'I left Alfie in the laundry room, it's lovely and cool in there and he seemed pleased to be back in his own home again. I let him walk through the entire house this morning so he could get re-acquainted with everything.'

'I can't thank you enough for looking after him for all this time. He's a lucky boy to have had you.'

'I'm the lucky one. I'd have been lonely if I'd been at home knowing you weren't right next door. Hagrid is a lovely cat, but he really has little to contribute in the way of conversation.' Julia burst out laughing, glancing at Nancy and seeing her serious expression made her laugh even harder.

'How is that cat of yours? Did, he mind having Alfie staying and making himself comfortable in Hagrid's territory?'

'They got along well, considering how much of a bully Hagrid can be. Alfie was awfully quiet for the first week after you left. He kept going to the gate in the fence and just sitting there waiting. After a while I think he realised no one was going to come and let him through into his own property, so he settled and perked up. But he's missed you.'

'I've missed you both,' Julia said. They turned into the drive and Nancy clicked the remote to the automatic gates. She watched as they slowly swung back and she could see the avenue of trees standing to attention as they drove up the long drive to where the house sat on the rise of the hill, her heart thumping – overwhelmed with so many memories, Julia quickly brushed a tear from her cheek.

She looked at the car's temperature gauge, it was 18 degrees Celsius inside the car but 38 degrees outside. Opening the car door was like stepping inside a full-size pre-heated oven. With a fine sheen of sweat forming on her skin she ferried her luggage from the car to the terrace reflecting that the cold of London wasn't so bad after all.

Alfie, as Nancy had predicted, was ecstatic to see her, running around in circles, fetching his favourite toys to present to her before rushing outdoors to tear around the lawn before collapsing in a heap enjoying the coolness of the kitchen floor tiles.

'Everything looks spotless, I hope you didn't have to clean after Sarah and Jason left Nancy?' Julia looked across at her neighbour as she filled the kettle and stood thinking which cupboard the cups were in. She'd gotten so used to Carrick's kitchen it took her a minute to re-acquaint herself with her own.

'No. They left everything immaculate, just how you like it. I didn't do a thing, other than make sure you had some basics to get you started. I'll be going to the shops tomorrow, so maybe we could go together if you feel up to it and need to get in groceries?'

Julia knew instantly Nancy had remembered her phobia about driving, and gratefully accepted the offer. She'd need to spend some time going through the pantry and freezer to see what was there and what needed throwing out.

WHEN NANCY LEFT and Julia was finally on her own with just Alfie for company, she wandered through the house. Every room looked the same. She couldn't think why it wouldn't, but somehow because her life had changed, she thought the house would also feel different, look different.

She walked to the far wing where Patrick's music room was. She'd locked it before she left, not wishing anyone to intrude on what had once been Patrick's special place of creativity and relaxation.

Julia had not been in this room since he died. She turned the key in the lock and the door swung open.

Through the windows of her mind, she could see Patrick sitting at his desk or standing with headphones on, listening to music or strumming his guitar.

But he wasn't there, even though the room still held a faint scent of him, and Julia noticed one of his jumpers remained draped across the back of his chair. She picked it up, holding it to her nose and smelling. He was there in those fibres and the tears which she'd held back made their way in a steady stream down her cheeks, unrestricted.

Later, after she'd unpacked, taken a shower and was lying awake in their bed, she picked up the framed photograph of Patrick which she'd carried everywhere with her and spoke to him.

'So, I'm back alone without you and it feels so wrong.' She pulled herself further up in bed and placed the pillow that should have cradled Patrick's head behind her back.

'I'll not hear your footsteps in the hallway, as you turn out the lights and come to bed. I won't feel you reach out to run a finger down my cheek and across my lips, the way you did every night for as long as we've been together, before you whispered - "good night, my beautiful darling".

I won't lay my head on your chest and feel the peaceful rhythm of your heart beating. I won't turn in the night and know that you're there. And when I wake from a bad dream, I won't be able to reach out and feel your comforting presence. The shape of your back as you sleep curled up on your side, the way you fold one leg around mine with your arms around my breasts, drawing me in toward you, keeping me close and safe.'

She kept staring at the photograph and wondering where he was, what he was doing. Was the other side nicer, calmer than the earth plane?

'I've accepted, finally, after a few false starts, that you have gone. You will never come home to me and I must move forward without you. You dismantled the protective walls I'd so carefully erected around myself, one brick at a time, until you revealed the Julia of old. The Julia who loved life and laughed so freely.

You discovered that sense of humour lost to me; now found. And you handed me the most precious gift of all - security in your love without conditions or expectations,' her hands were shaking, holding the photograph in front of her.

'How am I to hold on to those gifts you gave me? When you placed them in my fragile heart, it was your strength beside me that ensured it would be a safe stronghold for gifts so precious. I don't know if alone I can keep those gifts you gave me safe. I can't promise you I won't lose them again, the way I did in the past, but I have to try, if not for me then for you. The legacy you left I must try to preserve.'

25

JULIA

Julia had not intended going back to work, but after returning from London and spending time at home, she'd longed to be away from the house and the memories. Patrick was staring out at her from every space, every nook and cranny, even out walking with Alfie in the bush, she felt his presence or a sudden flash-back to a time, a moment and conversation. Returning to her job in the city appeared a better option, at least for the time being.

They'd been kind, her colleagues, thoughtful, and she found the routine of working through legal proceedings with insolvency cases was better than drifting around at home wondering how long it would be until she could retire to bed with a book and could safely loose herself in someone else's story – someone else's life – so much better than dwelling on her own.

She'd tried to get behind the wheel of her car, sitting in the garage for an eternity, unable to even turn the key in the ignition. It was ridiculous; she kept reminding herself, but nothing changed until Nancy took charge.

'Come on now, I'm right here beside you, turn the key, and drive down your driveway and then back again. Just small steps – that way you'll build your confidence up and in no time at all you'll be back to normal.'

Simple though it was as a plan, it worked, and soon Julia found herself driving again. She hadn't been in the car with Patrick; she wasn't there to witness what happened, so why had she behaved so irrationally? Nancy had suggested she attend some grief counselling sessions, but Julia was unsure if she was ready for that.

She'd sought refuge on the couch of a wonderful psychotherapist in England following the revelations about her mother. Joanna had been special, and Julia feared she wouldn't find someone as skilled as Joanna had been, so she parked grief counselling to one side. Maybe she'd phone Joanna in the UK and see if she could have some on-line therapy. She didn't even know if this were possible, but she could ask – she'd do that soon.

Soon never came and as the months marched on, Julia became more and more withdrawn. She performed her duties at work competently but unenthusiastically, having little interaction with her colleagues, but one evening in mid-July as she neared Southern Cross station, she could hear Latin American music. The distinctive drumming and repetitive bass lines were unmistakable. As she entered the station, she saw an area cordoned off where a small band, singer and dancers were performing.

Glancing at her watch Julia realised if she stopped to listen, she'd miss her train, but she found herself drawn into the crowd already gathered to watch the performance. A young and beautiful dark-haired woman was handing out pamphlets, thrusting one at Julia with a big smile.

'Here you are Señora, come join our dance classes.' She glided off before Julia had time to hand the brochure back. As the performance ended, Julia took the escalator to the concourse to wait for her train.

Once seated, she looked at the pamphlet she was still holding and read. A woman boarding the train at the next stop jostled her way past other passengers and sank her enormous frame unceremoniously into the seat beside Julia. She was carrying a bulky faux leather bag which was half open revealing papers and a laptop. The woman moved her bag, hitting Julia's leg. She didn't apologise, instead pulling out her mobile phone she began a loud and argumentative conversation with some equally loud person on the other end of the call.

Passengers glanced at the woman, but she was oblivious to the annoyed stares and sighs until an older woman who was standing holding onto the support rail called out.

'Hey, keep it down. Your life interests no one. Have some thought for your fellow passengers.'

Smiles were exchanged, delighted someone had the courage to call out the loudmouth but all the older woman received for her courage was a hard stare as the woman continued with her conversation.

Fortunately, as the train pulled into the next stop, the loudmouth heaved herself up, still talking on her mobile, and shoved and pushed her way down the carriage to the door.

'Would you like a seat?' Julia asked, smiling up at the woman who had dared to call out a fellow passenger for poor behaviour.

'Thank you, it will be a relief to sit.' Julia moved across to give the woman room so she could place her bag at her feet.

'I'm so over people like her, the one that was sitting here. They never think of other people, just about themselves.' She had a soft Canadian accent, well at least Julia was as sure as she could be it was Canadian.

'You were brave to call her out, not that it made any difference, but I'm glad you did.' Julia usually avoided conversation with fellow passengers. If asked, she would say she hated anyone talking to her on a train, a bus or especially a plane.

She had zero interest in hearing about some stranger's children, their grandchildren, the aunt's cousin's haemorrhoid problem, the death of their dog last summer – she wanted to be alone with her own thoughts and not bother herself with the cumbersome ritual of polite meaningless conversation. To find herself engaged in conversation with this woman felt unfamiliar to her.

'Did you see them performing at the station?' The woman asked, nodding her head at the pamphlet Julia still held in her hand.

'Yes, they were wonderful, did you see them?'

'Absolutely, I missed two trains to watch them, I'll be home late, but it was worth it. Gave me a real buzz. Are you thinking of joining the dance classes?'

'Me? No. They just thrust the pamphlet at me.'

'Don't you like dancing?'

'I love it. But I've had little practice in, probably decades. I used to belong to the dance club at university. It was fun.' Why was she telling this woman her life story? She was behaving like one of the boring people she was normally so quick to criticise. These confused thoughts were swimming around in her head when she realised the woman was asking her another question.

'Was that in the UK? I detect an English accent?'

'I'm a Kiwi actually but lived in the UK for a long time. I went to university in New Zealand.'

Whilst uncomfortable at talking about herself to a stranger Julia was inexplicably drawn to this woman. She was older than Julia but didn't disguise her age as many women did.

Her hair was silver grey, short and stylishly cut. Her faced lined, but with wisdom and experience more than the ravages of age and she wore bright colours, not garish as though she were trying to hold onto a bohemian youth, but lively – perhaps a reflection of her personality.

It wouldn't be until late in the evening when Julia was lying awake in bed re-hashing the conversation in her mind that she realised the woman had been non-threatening because she exuded a sense of freedom – as though she didn't give a damn what anyone else thought, life was for the taking.

Julia realised she hadn't felt like that in a long time, and it wasn't just since Patrick died. She'd been feeling used up and spent before that. Little or no job satisfaction and the realisation that she would never fit in nor feel she belonged in Australia.

She'd asked the woman if she was from Canada? The woman flashed a smile at her.

'I sure am, Quebec. I'm out here on secondment. Most Australian's think I'm an American, and we sure don't like that. Probably, I'm guessing, like you Kiwi's - you don't like being mistaken for an Aussie, am I right?'

'You're right. We don't.' Julia laughed. It was strange to laugh out loud in public, an unfamiliar sensation and yet it had brought a little thrill of optimism.

'I'm getting off in a moment.' Julia looked up at the sign and saw the next stop was Surrey Hills. 'My name's Gloria,' she twisted in her seat to shake Julia's hand.

'I'm Julia, perhaps I'll see you again sometime, have a lovely evening.'

'I intend too. You know,' she said gathering her bag and preparing to stand as the train pulled into Surrey Hills station, 'you ought to go see what the dance lessons are like, you never know, you may just remember all those dance moves from university.'

She laughed and gave Julia a brief wave as she moved down the carriage and out the door. Julia watched from the window as Gloria made her way along the platform and out of sight through the exit.

That night Julia dreamed she was back at university dancing with Emilio Perez a student on a scholarship from Spain and the man Lizzie had so crudely referred to in one of her drunken rants.

In her dream they danced the Tango and Salsa before the music changed and Emilio swung her around to the Lindy Hop. In the dream she was laughing as he pushed her through the moves that were much more familiar to him than they had ever been to her.

She woke, the dream still so real in her mind that she believed she could hear the thrum of the music. She hadn't thought of Emilio in a long time, well not until Lizzie had mentioned him.

When they met at university, he was studying to become a linguist, hoping to work for the diplomatic service. He had the look of a young Fernando Rey, with bold features and dark brooding eyes.

Female students did their best to seduce him, but Julia knew, from the moment he first danced with her, he was gay.

They became good friends and dance partners, neither mentioning his sexuality. It remained an undisclosed secret between them. Julia never minded that Emilio didn't confide. She understood how hard it was to come out. It had taken real courage by her brother William before he confessed he was gay.

As she pulled herself up in bed, debating whether she should get up and make herself a cup of herbal tea, she recalled the conversation with William from all those years ago as though it happened only recently.

'Julia, I'm going to tell you something that you need to keep a secret, you mustn't tell anyone, not even Lizzie. Can I trust you to do that?'

Julia lay stretched out on her bed reading a book and wondering how long they would have the house to themselves before their mother came stumbling in from wherever she'd been. She turned on her side to face her big brother and saw immediately something was worrying him. She was 14 years old.

'Have you heard the term *gay* before, like... someone is gay?'

'I have. I am 14, you know, I'm not a child anymore.' She turned back over and continued to read.

'Julia, can you look at me please, I'm trying to tell you something important.'

She sighed and this time, swinging her long legs off the bed, she sat up straight and looked at him. 'What's wrong, you look terrified?'

'I'm gay, Julia. I wanted you to hear it from me in case – well, in case someone at school says something.'

'I know you're gay. I've known for ages silly, what's the big deal. Does Mum know, is that why you're frightened?'

'I'm not frightened, I'm nervous. I'm nervous saying it out loud.' He sat down beside her and hung his head, and Julia noticed his entire body was shaking. Her big brother, the person who tried to protect her, now needed her protection, her love and support.

'Your secret is safe with me, I won't tell anyone, not even Lizzie. It changes nothing, you know - I mean between us. You're still my big brother and I love you - always,' she'd reached out and draped her arm around his shoulder. 'Do you have a boyfriend?'

'No, I don't. But one day I will, and that might be difficult for you when that time comes.'

'Why? I only want you to be happy, the way you want me to be happy, which probably won't happen until I can leave this place and go to university.'

'I promise I won't leave you here alone, even when I go to university. I'll stay living at home until you're ready to leave.'

'Do you mean that? Would you stay, even when you start university? I thought you wanted to go to Australia to study?'

'I thought about it, but I can start my degree at Lincoln and then transfer to the veterinary school in Australia later on if I wish to. That's the plan, anyway.'

'You'll make a great vet, you really will.' She reached across and took William's hand in hers. 'You're the best brother ever and I'm so proud of you.' She'd lifted his hand to her lips and kissed it, realising that this decision to share his secret was huge and she could appreciate why he'd looked so frightened.

'Does Mum suspect something?'

'No. She'd never handle it, and I don't think Dad would either.' It was then they heard their mother arrive home, and the conversation broke off.

Over the years Julia wondered if her father knew and if he did, he neither condoned nor condemned. Fortunately, her mother died without the knowledge her treasured son was a gay man. If life had taken a different course, Julia was sure her mother would have been supportive of William, but that was something she could only surmise.

As it was, her mother was such an angry alcoholic Julia wasn't at all sure how she would have coped knowing William was gay. She looked at life through a bitter alcohol-distorted lens – it wasn't surprising, therefore, that William never wished his mother to know.

Their mother had reached the end of her life as a gin soaked, urine-stained, hollowed-out wreck of a person. It was cruel to think of her in such terms, but it was the reality of how her mother had allowed a rapist to trap her in his power leaving her a victim – her only solace - the bottom of a bottle.

Julia tried unsuccessfully to go back to sleep, but sleep was elusive – so many memories. She remembered Lizzie had been jealous of her relationship with Emilio. Looking back, the signs had been there, as long ago as their university days when Lizzie's jealousy would raise its ugly head.

Lizzie had been convinced Julia was sleeping with Emilio and had confronted Julia in the cafeteria where they'd been having lunch together between lectures.

When Julia vehemently denied it, Lizzie had made a throwaway remark challenging the validity of their long-standing friendship and stormed off. It was ridiculous and Julia had thought no more of it. She would not betray Emilio, not even too Lizzie. Similarly, she never disclosed William's secret to Lizzie - that only came to light when William found the courage to come out, which he did by bringing his partner to a party.

Julia had kept in touch with Emilio for many years after they graduated from university. He had forged a successful career in the diplomatic service in the UK until his death. His life cut short by a brain aneurysm.

As she made herself a cup of herbal tea, she thought back to those days of dance and how much she'd enjoyed it. When the tedium of legal torts became overwhelming, the university dance club had been a beacon of light which helped her relax and she'd tackle her studies the next day with renewed vigour.

The pamphlet lay on the kitchen counter where she'd left it, and as she sipped her tea; she opened it up and read about the dates and times for the classes.

By the time she woke the next morning, she'd decided she'd go. Why not? She could go to one class and if she hated it or felt out of place amongst a room full of young, fit, beautiful dancers, then she didn't have to return.

26

CARRICK

arrick had been busy since Jack and Kat had visited London. He'd spent a lot of time in Europe and now back in London he was looking at his itinerary for Australasia.

He phoned Julia regularly to check-in, ensuring she was managing and not drowning in a sea of memories, but he missed her a great deal. His London apartment seemed devoid of colour without her presence.

From conversations they'd had, he'd learned she really didn't enjoy living in Australia, and he wondered if she'd return to London. It seemed unlikely, but one could always live in hope. In a recent conversation Julia mentioned the bewilderment she felt over Lizzie.

'I couldn't stand the silence any longer and phoned her landline. She answered and told me to fuck off, before slamming the phone down. I feel the longer this impasse continues, the harder it's going to be to rekindle the friendship that we had. I've been thinking back to years ago when we were at university together and how jealous she could become over silly things, usually men who she perceived showed an interest.'

'Well, I imagine you were an exceedingly popular student,'

Carrick had laughed, trying to bring a lighter tone to the conversation. He could hear Julia becoming more and more agitated.

'I guess, what I'm trying to say Carrick, is that perhaps I haven't been a good friend all these years. I've been blind to situations which vexed Lizzie, and maybe she had a right to expect more from me.'

'Why do you always work a situation around to a place where you blame yourself?'

'Do I? I don't think I do that. I'm just trying to work through events in the past where perhaps I could have been more thoughtful.'

'Julia, Lizzie is very envious of you, for whatever reason. Maybe you have to accept there doesn't have to be a valid reason – that the problem lies with her. Maybe it's her job to make herself better - to take that negative energy she's poured in your direction and turn it into something positive for herself. You've told me she had a difficult child-hood, not unlike your own, so perhaps that's at the heart of her issues and Michael's death was the touch-paper – once lite, difficult to extinguish.'

'Jack said something similar to me last time we spoke. He's worried about me, but he also intimated he's worried about Lizzie's state of mind.

Apparently, she's been sending text messages, leaving voice messages trying to contact him on Facebook Messenger all the time wanting him to call and chat. She's obviously very lonely, but Jack sees her need to contact him is more about competition. Like she's trying to compete with me for his affections. He's finding that difficult.'

'I'm inclined to agree with Jack. I've always thought she doted on him in a way that was, well, if I'm being frank, unhealthy.'

'I don't see that, so maybe I really have a blinkered view. I have involved her in Jack's life ever since we left New Zealand and moved to the UK. She helped me a lot in those early months with caring for Jack when I had to be at work. She looked after us when my marriage broke up. She's always been there for me and Jack, so I find it difficult to believe that her actions had an ulterior motive.'

'Do you think you owe her?'

'Yes. Loyalty is a rare commodity these days – I've always been loyal, and even convinced myself that we never had secrets, but that's not true and I've had to ask myself recently how many secrets have I kept from her over the years? And has that been a contributing factor as she sits there in her penthouse brooding over the past?

I've got a hang-up about secrets since Nick. Prior to that I wouldn't have placed so much emphasis on needing to know everything. I'm such a hypocrite. I've kept things from her I shouldn't have.'

'Like you said to me when you were out here, we all have our secrets.'

Carrick had a sudden flash-back – sitting opposite Julia at his kitchen table and hearing her say those very words, and wondered what specific secret she'd been referring to.

'What do you think I should do Carrick, try calling her again, email, send a text message, what?'

'It's not for me to advise you about your friendship with Lizzie, Julia. From what I've heard from you and Jack, Lizzie is in a dark place, angry and bitter –she's capable of starting a fight in an empty room, so consumed is she by her emotions and unresolved issues.'

'I'm probably guilty of that. Some days my anger has no beginning and no end, and my thoughts are a raging torrent as though if the opportunity presented itself - I could walk down the street sweep the white cane out from under a blind person and punch a dwarf - crazy stuff like that fills my head.'

Carrick couldn't hold back his laughter. 'You're right, it sounds a little crazy Julia either that or you have re-kindled your delightful satire humour. Grief has many disguises.'

'I don't know Carrick. I detest feeling like this, it's so random, and it really feels mad. I just loath this out of control feeling. Sometimes I'm travelling to work on the train and I see couples holding hands. I want to scream at them - *don't get too cosy you two, don't delude yourself that there's a happily ever after.* I despise their affection, their love, their touching, their kiss goodbye when they part ways. Sometimes I have to turn away because I'm so afraid I'll speak my thoughts out loud.'

'Have you thought any further about seeing someone, some counselling...' His words trailed off, afraid of her reaction.

'I have thought about it, but I keep saying *soon* but soon never comes. I'm afraid a counsellor, therapist, whatever you wish to call him or her, will pick away at the loose thread of my emotions and I'll completely unravel.'

'What about the person you saw over here, is it worth contacting her by phone?'

'Joanna. Yes, I have thought about that, but she fits into the *soon* category and another week, another month drifts by and I remain the woman standing in the lake, slowly sinking.'

27

JULIA

Julia sat at Nancy's scrubbed pine kitchen table. It reminded her of the pitch pine table that took pride of place in Patrick's kitchen in his Henley apartment.

Alfie lay his head across her lap. Instinctively, she reached down to stroke him. He was such a different dog to Patrick's Finn – the beautiful Irish terrier who had died before they moved out to Australia.

Patrick had been inconsolable for months and it was not until they bought Alfie as a puppy from a Sydney breeder that she felt Patrick had finally given himself permission to cease the mourning of his adored companion and concentrate on training and raising a new puppy.

Julia had wanted to get a cat when they moved into their house, but Patrick had admitted that whilst he liked Chino, the Burmese Julia had inherited in England and who had died not long after they moved from the Home Counties to London, cats were not his favourite. He was a dog man.

This revelation stunned Julia. She'd been angry with him for allowing her to believe he liked cats. His argument back- he'd never said he liked cats, and he'd also never said he wished to own one. At the time she'd let the matter drop, but it had remained a thorn in the side of their otherwise peaceful relationship. Every now and again she could feel the piercing barbs of that thorn, especially when she received an email from an animal shelter with pictures of abandoned kittens desperate for new homes.

As she observed Nancy removing a hot tray of biscuits from the oven, she realised now she was on her own she could have an entire house full of rescue kittens if she wanted. She could foster, adopt, do whatever she liked. She was free to make her own choices, one of which was that she no longer wished to remain in Australia and with that acknowledgement came the realisation she could not submit a kitten to so much uncertainty – it would be hard enough for Alfie.

Her internal battle with trying to fit in, with trying to belong, with trying to suppress all her genuine feelings had recently ended in a truce of sorts. She'd kept her thoughts secret from Patrick, as he had also done with her. She'd feared that if she were open and honest, it may have robbed him of his passion for being here in Australia.

How could she have known that his passion had been subsiding of its own accord. Instead of being relieved that he'd been ready to end his Aussie love affair, she felt resentment gnawing away at her fragile emotions making her question just how honest their relation-ship had been? Great that he'd been ready to finally leave but where was the sharing, and why was it all on his terms?

These treacherous thoughts were the edge of a slippery slope toward recrimination from which no good would come so, as she sat waiting for Nancy to pour the tea, she breathed deeply and willed herself to let go of the wish to punish Patrick for leaving her like this.

'Penny for them?' Nancy remarked, holding out a plate of warm biscuits.

'I love these Scroggin biscuits you make. I can never get mine to taste exactly like yours, are you sure you didn't leave out an essential ingredient Nancy when you gave me your recipe?' Julia managed a laugh as she bit into the biscuit, avoiding answering Nancy's question, although she knew Nancy wouldn't let it slide.

'You seemed deep in thought Julia, anything you wish to share? And no, I didn't leave out any ingredients.'

Julia sipped her tea and took another bite from her biscuit. The fusion of melted chocolate, rolled oats, sultanas and sunflower seeds was a delicious treat Julia loved.

'I was thinking about my future – more to the point, whether I wish to stay in Australia.'

'And have you come to any conclusions?' Nancy asked.

'I think I have and that means I need to decide where I want to live. Is it back in the UK or somewhere else?'

'Well, I have some news of my own which I wanted to share with you this morning, that's why I asked you over.' Julia looked up from her tea and noticed Nancy appeared uncomfortable as though she were about to disclose something personal.

'Oh, what news is that then?' Julia tried to sound upbeat but couldn't help but think the news had something to do with Nancy's health, she hoped her dear friend wasn't ill.

'My sister has been nagging me for ages to move closer. We're both getting older, and I guess she's feeling desperately lonely after Tom passed away last year. It's made her realise how vulnerable we are, widowed and alone in different countries. She has a big house, and her suggestion is that I move in with her.' Nancy hesitated, taking a sip from her cup of tea and crunching on another biscuit, letting crumbs fall to the floor where Alfie quickly hoovered them up.

'She asked me a while ago – around the time Patrick died actually, but I didn't want to mention it then. It was too distressing learning about Patrick - but while you've been away, I've given it a great deal of thought.'

'Goodness, okay. How would you feel about that, I mean living with your sister in the same house, are you close?' Julia asked. She herself could never imagine living with, say Lizzie, who would be the closest thing to a sister that Julia had, not that that was saying much anymore.

'We are close, always have been close even as wee bairns back in Aberdeen before our parents moved out to Australia. There is only a two-year age gap between us. It made it easier that our husbands were good friends, always helps, don't you think?'

'Yes, it's tricky if you have a sibling or friend who doesn't get on with your partner or their partner doesn't like yours. Lizzie was like that with my ex-husband Nick, she couldn't' stand him, mind you, she was right.' Julia raised an eyebrow at Nancy.

'Ainsley and I have a lot in common and sharing a house would save on costs and mean we would both have more funds to see us into our old age. You never know when you need an operation and if you can go private, it helps. I don't have private health insurance. I haven't been able to afford it.'

'Patrick had a policy subsidised through his work, otherwise we wouldn't have any either. I need to leave these biscuits alone, or you'll have none left,' Julia said, reaching out to help herself to another one. 'Your sister lives in New Zealand, doesn't she, is it Auckland?'

'North of Auckland, at Red Beach. It's a beautiful spot. Roy and I used to visit every few years, but I've only been back out twice since Roy died. Now that Tom has gone, I guess Ainsley feels lost in that big house all alone. I think it could work, what do you think?'

'I'm flummoxed, Nancy. You've caught me by surprise. I mean I knew your sister was in New Zealand, but I'd never thought of you leaving the mountain – well leaving Australia. I guess I always believed you were really settled here?'

'I have been as much as you can be when you're a foreigner.'

'You're not a foreigner, surely, you've been here since you were, what 15, 18-years-old?'

'I was 16 and Ainsley was 14 when we came out. It was a big adventure back then, but I'm probably like you Julia, I've never really felt like I have my roots in the soil, if you know what I mean. It's a funny thing to say after all these years, and I have travelled during that time. Ainsley and I went back to the UK when we were, let me see now, must have been about 22 or 24. We went back home to Aberdeen and then travelled around the UK, that's where I met Roy.'

'I thought you met Roy in Scotland?'

'No. He's from Edinburgh, but we met in London at a dance hall.

Ainsley and I loved to dance in those days, and we used to take ourselves off to dance halls any opportunity we got. That's where I met my Roy. Poor lad, he couldn't dance to save himself, but he had a beautiful smile, and that was enough for me.'

Julia imagined a young Nancy swept off her feet by a smiling Roy. 'How did you know he was the one just like that?'

'You just do, Julia. There's something that clicks, and suddenly, you're swept away by a feeling of contentment, of everything being just right. Well, at least that's how it felt for me and Roy,' a wistful tone creeping into her voice.

'You must have felt that when you met Patrick? You two were so close, such a loving couple.'

Julia busied herself, pouring them both another cup of tea, aware that she hadn't felt like that about Patrick. She wouldn't share with Nancy that she hadn't liked Patrick at all when they first met, in fact she'd been really bitchy toward him.

Over time, that had changed when she saw the impact he had on Jack and how much Jack admired, adored, and loved him. It was only then that she gave herself permission to allow deeper feelings to occupy the space in her heart.

'I guess it's different for everyone. I had been on my own for five years by the time I met Patrick and I wasn't looking for a relationship. I had Jack to think of and he was all that mattered to me.' She was about to add that having a child changed the dynamics. Julia would never have introduced a man into her life without first considering Jack, but if she said this, it would only emphasise to Nancy that she and Roy had not been able to have children.

'So where did Ainsley meet Tom?' Julia was eager to steer the conversation away from her love-life.

'She met Tom here, he was travelling around Australia at the time having what the young ones now days call a gap year before he went to University. They courted long-distance for a while, and then Tom was here in Melbourne at the veterinary school. He became a vet, had a practice in Auckland on the North Shore for years before retiring to Red Beach.'

'My brother was training to be a vet, but he died before he qualified, such a waste.' Julia could feel her emotions rushing to the surface, remembering back to William, and visiting the hospice before he passed.

'I'm so sorry, Julia. You've mentioned William a lot over the years. He must have been a special brother to you?'

'He was - is. He's always in my thoughts.' Julia reached across the table and took Nancy's hand in hers.

'You've been an amazing friend and neighbour to us, and I think this is a lovely idea, take Ainsley up on her offer. No one should be alone as they get older. Life designs few of us to live alone. You've done really well coping since Roy passed over, even though I know you miss him still, but maybe it's time for a change, time to move on to the next chapter?'

'Thank you. That means a lot to hear you say that. I've not spoken with any of my friends, I'm not sure they'd understand. The girls at bridge club only ever seem to complain about husbands, children, grandchildren and siblings. I sometimes wonder how they would feel if they suddenly found themselves all alone. Who would they moan about then?'

'People like that always find something to complain about. But you're not like that, Nancy, you're a step above. Would you sell your house, or rent it out?'

'Oh, I think I'd sell, in fact I was going to seek your advice about that. Things like real estate agents and dressing your house for sale if that's what you call it these days. I'm naïve about all of this. I was hoping, if you didn't mind, that I could ask for your help. I know you have a lot on your plate, but your opinion is the one I would value more than anyone else.'

'That's sweet of you and I will help in whatever way I can. You never know we may both be selling at the same time.' Julia laughed, wondering if she really meant what she'd just said. Could she bear to part with their beautiful home, the culmination of so much love and hard work from both her and Patrick?

28

CARRICK

Following his conversation with Julia, Carrick had decided he would travel first to Australia and then onto New Zealand. There would be no time to get back to the UK in between. He'd stay out there until Christmas, when Jack and Kat would join him, and then return to London with them in the new year.

He was travelling so didn't pick up Julia's message until he was back home in Bloomsbury. He listened to the voice-message and whilst she said little; he sensed something was wrong. He felt exhausted and longed for a cold beer and was tempted by the thought of a curry takeaway. There was nothing in the fridge anyway, so he phoned for a delivery.

After a quick shower and change of clothes, he heard the doorbell, and was already salivating at the thought of a creamy, spicy curry. He'd eat, then phone Julia.

Mopping up the last of the delicious sauce with his Naan bread, he wondered whether he would disclose to Julia he was coming out to Australia soon. He wouldn't spoil the surprise that Jack, Kat and himself would all be spending Christmas with her and was ready to evade any questions she might ask around his Christmas plans. He pressed Julia's number at the top of his phone's favourites list.

'Hi Carrick, are you back in Bloomsbury?'

'Yes, arrived home today, how are you? You sounded sad on the voice message you left, what's up?'

'Sorry, I didn't mean to be dreary, but it's difficult to hide sometimes. Our lovely neighbour Nancy is planning to sell up and head to New Zealand.'

'Oh, is that sudden or has she been planning for a while?'

'Apparently she's been contemplating the move since around the time Patrick died, but didn't wish to burden me with her thoughts and emotions around making such a big decision.'

'Has she put her property on the market yet?'

'No. She wants my advice about real estate agents and what you have to do to sell. She's not got any experience and it will be good for me to help her for a change. Nancy's always been there for us, and it will take my mind off myself. Frankly, I'm tired of being in this state – this holding pattern, or at least that's what it feels like.'

'You're good at presenting a house for sale, I saw what you did with your place in Chelsea. I have to pay people a lot of money to do that for me, so Nancy will be grateful for your input. What else has been happening, how is work?'

'Hideous. I don't know why I keep going in day after day. It's a routine I guess, I've needed a routine since I came home. I can't bear being in the house all day long on my own. There are too many memories.'

'I understand. That must be hard, but maybe you have to think about finding another interest, a hobby, and let go of that job. Sometimes you need to let go of the lifebelt to discover you can swim. Good heavens! Listen to me now, I'm sounding like Dr Phil.'

Julia laughed. 'I have found something actually, I'm going to start dance classes next week, I love dance, so I thought I'd give it a go.'

'Wow, dance, I never knew you liked dance – I mean, Paddy's got two left feet so I just assumed you can't have been interested either.'

'Your right. Patrick has so much musical talent, but it didn't transfer to his feet. We sway danced. If there is such a thing – that translates to not moving your feet or learning steps.'

Carrick had a sudden image of that night when he'd heard Leonard Cohen singing and saw Julia swaying around on the lawn before Jack raced out to rescue his mother. He could imagine his brother swaying along to music in this way.

'As for dance,' Julia continued, 'I went to dance classes at university, but I've hardly danced since. When I was a young girl, I used to dance around the kitchen with my brother William. He was a talented dancer, not sure where he learnt all his moves, but he had them. Anyway, I may not enjoy it the same as I once did, but only one way to find out and that's by going to a class.'

'I think that's grand Julia, I truly do. Dance can be a therapy just like music can be. You'll be able to tell me all about it soon. I'm flying out to Australia and then going on to New Zealand, not sure of the dates yet, but I'll let you know.'

'Wonderful,' she shrieked down the phone at him, so loud he had to hold his mobile out from his ear, but it made him laugh to hear her enthusiastic reaction.

'Sorry, that was loud. It will be wonderful to see you. It's been hard since I came back. Anyway, I'll not keep you, let me know your dates and I expect you to come and stay here.' He heard an intake of breath before she added, 'unless you need to be in the city's heart for work, if you feel it's easier for you?' Carrick interrupted before she talked herself out of having him to stay.

'I would be delighted to stay with you. It will be lovely to be up on the mountain, an enjoyable break from the city. I'll send you a copy of my itinerary as soon as I've completed it. Take care and enjoy the dance class.'

'Wow,' he thought, grabbing another beer from the fridge and walking through to the lounge. 'Dance classes, who would have thought,' he said aloud. Carrick struggled to recall a time when he'd seen Julia dancing, mind you, the opportunity had probably never arisen in the past.

They wouldn't have been dancing at Baltimore with his parents and any gigs they went to were to watch Paddy perform or to see some band he was interested in and they were big venues or small intimate clubs. Regardless, he was pleased she was getting out and doing something different to lift her spirits.

'I should have told her I love to dance, why didn't I?' he asked himself, but no answer was forthcoming.

He sat down on the couch and opened the post that had piled up in his absence. Opening a large envelope, he flicked through a glossy property brochure. He felt unsettled with the property market, both in the UK and in Europe. This Brexit business was completely out of hand, Carrick thought, and likely to have an impact on his portfolio.

He would make time to talk with his solicitor and accountant this week and think seriously about divesting his investments in Europe and possibly even the UK. With Theresa May gone and Boris Johnson in charge, who knew what Britain would look when the dust settled, and Carrick didn't like carrying too much risk. Julia had been right to comment on the changes. What had she called it? - *the winds of change*. Maybe her instinct that something far reaching was about to happen should be listened too.

29

JULIA

Julia stepped out of her car and walked the few steps to the entrance of the dance studio. Pushing open the door and taking the stairs with more determination than she felt, she made her way to the first floor.

A young woman sat at the reception desk. Looking up, she beamed and welcomed Julia. Registering her name, contact details and paying the fee, she looked about her.

It was not a huge dance space, but that made it all the more intimate and less intimidating. The wall immediately in front of her was a floor to ceiling mirror. Large windows allowed light to penetrate the space giving it an open airy feeling. Two comfortable couches tucked away in the corner near reception and a water cooler sat perched on a work bench alongside pamphlets, a large first aid kit and dance pumps for $45.00.

The walls around reception were adorned with framed photographs of Latin American Dancers in various stages of performance. She was early, but that didn't matter, she told herself; she was happy to be the first one here; she hated being late as she settled herself down on the couch and prepared to wait for the next arrivals.

She wondered if the woman on reception was the instructor? She looked familiar and Julia realised she was the woman handing out the pamphlets at Southern Cross station.

By 7.30.p.m. all twenty pupils had arrived, completed forms and paid their fees. Suddenly a burst of loud Latin music filled the small dance studio and a door to the side of reception opened and in walked a handsome male. He spoke briefly with the receptionist and then looked out at the class.

Dressed in jeans and a T-shirt, black dance shoes on his feet and the unmistakable stance of a dancer, he made his way to the centre of the room, signalling for the group to follow. Tall, dark and handsome, he announced in a heavy Russian accent, 'welcome everybody to Latino Dance Studio. This is the first step towards your.... I guess an unfamiliar experience, maybe... just something that you would like to do, or something you think you would like to do.'

He smiled reassuringly at the group, and Julia could already see several young women flicking their hair back across their shoulders and thrusting their hips out.

'First, my name is Serghei and I guess I'll find your names later on and I'll remember them too.' He said with a laugh and an impish grin.

'I would also like to introduce Carolina who you met on reception. Carolina is also a qualified and highly successful dancer. She will work with the men in the class, as I will work with the ladies.'

As Julia glanced across to the two young hair flickers, she saw their faces light up with obvious glee. The poor guy would have his work cut out with them, Julia thought.

'So, we are going to start with our warm-up routine. Can you all take a partner; and we will rotate around the room, changing partners as we go. Just the basic steps to begin with and then we build ourselves up.' Julia looked around and found herself face to face with a tall, string bean man who looked as uncomfortable as she felt.

'Would you mind if I danced with you?' He looked so terrified Julia didn't hesitate in agreeing to partner with him.

'Now Salsa has eight beats, right?' Serghei was saying. 'But we are going to use one, two, three, we're going to hold on four and then we are going to go five, six, seven and hold on eight. Has anybody done Salsa before?'

One or two hands went up, including Julia's, and she heard a sharp intake of breath from the string bean beside her. She didn't know whether this signalled reassurance or the knowledge that Julia had danced before made him want to run out the door and down the stairs to the safety of his car.

'Ok, so what do you think is the most important part of Salsa?'

'Grinding ya hips,' shouted out one of the hair flickers.

Serghei smiled whilst avoiding looking at the hair flicker. Wise, Julia thought, she'll be trouble.

'I'll tell you quickly. First, it's the connection between two people, the trust they have for their dance partner, then allowing yourself to relax and feel the rhythm. We're going to start with the first little step and I just want you to get comfortable with that and then we'll add to it. I will show to begin.'

Taking a stance in the centre of the room, a microphone strapped to his head, he talked and moved his way through the basic steps.

'Step forward on your left foot, weight back on your right and together. We pause and then we step back on the right, rock our weight back onto the left, and then back together. One, two, three hold on four, then five, six, seven and hold eight. Now your turn. Try it, and one, two, three and five, six, seven, again one, two, three, and five, six, seven then from there we are going to try the Cucaracha step. Funny name, yes? But basically, it's a side-step. Let me show you.'

Everyone stopped to watch, a great relief for Julia as the string bean at her side had two left feet and zero sense of rhythm.

'Start on the left foot, replace the right, bring together. Then we're going to start on the right, replace the left, bring together. Now we try with partners, and ladies remember you will start with stepping back on your right while the man steps forward on his left.'

As he moved through the basic steps Julia could see the group were in awe of Serghei's smooth fluid movements and the rhythmic sway of his slim hips made the dance look easy and sensuous. They would soon learn it was far from easy.

In the beginning the tension in the room was tangible, but as the time ticked by, the dancers gradually unwound and forgot their inhibitions as they struggled to master the basic steps and rhythm required to become a good Salsa dancer.

Apart from Serghei's professionalism and obvious skill as a dancer, a genuine warmth radiated from him. A tenderness mixed with an unmistakable Russian passion which quickly put his pupils at ease.

He worked his way around the room, dancing with each woman as Carolina danced with each man.

The pupils moved around the room, changing partners every two minutes, and Julia caught several glimpses of the two hair flickers vying for Serghei's attention and smiled to herself. They didn't stand a chance. Julia had guessed Carolina and Serghei were an item. When they'd danced together to show to the class the importance of being at one with your partner, she could feel the passion that moved like an electric current between them.

After thirty minutes there was a short five-minute break to get water and use the bathroom if anyone needed. Filling a plastic cup from the water reservoir, Julia flopped down on the couch, surprised at how physical the past thirty minutes had been.

The music started up signalling the break was over. Julia loved the sound of the sultry music as it pulsed and beat out its message, calling the dancers to their partners, their hips moving in sensuous time to the music and now as they returned to the floor, she danced with Serghei.

'You are good. I'm sorry, what is your name?'

'Julia. It's been many years since I danced. Is this class only Salsa?' she asked as she concentrated on moving in time to the music.

'I take private classes where I teach most genres. We just had a lot of interest for the Salsa. You have excellent rhythm, Julia.' The way he pronounced Julia sounded like Youlia, which made her smile. He moved off to dance with another female and Julia found herself commandeered by an older man who had no difficulty placing his hand on her butt instead of her back. She moved slightly and could feel his hand firmly re-establish its grip on her butt.

'Your hand should be on my back, not my butt.' She glared at him, but a reptilian smile creased his face, so Julia walked to the back of the studio and sat down. As the dancers moved to new partners, Julia watched Carolina step in to dance with the reptile. She moved in close to him and said something in his ear, before taking his hand and placing it in the correct position on her back. She looked formidable, and Julia thought he would be foolish to not heed the warning.

When the class finished, Julia picked her bag up and walked downstairs. Unlocking her car, she knew that, whilst tonight had been a fun distraction, it wasn't for her. For a start, most of the others were young, apart from the reptile and string bean there was no one else around her age and although she enjoyed Salsa, she wanted a more varied dance class. Maybe she'd do a Google search when she got home and see if there were classes that offered more of a dance mix but not just lessons for ball-room dancing.

The next morning, sitting at her desk poring over a report from their forensic accountant, her phoned rang registering a number she didn't recognise.

'Hello Julia, this is Carolina from Latino Dance Studio, do you have a minute to speak?'

'I'm at work, but I can talk.'

'Thank you. I was calling to see how you felt about the Salsa class last evening. We like to phone pupils at the start of a new term to see how they feel and if they wish to continue?'

'I enjoyed it, but I don't wish to learn only Salsa. I'm more interested in a dance class which offers multiple genres. I hope you don't mind me being so direct.'

'That's perfectly fine. We appreciate honesty. How would you feel about private classes? Serghei runs private sessions which can be a mix of different dance styles or just one style if a pupil wants to master one, in particular.'

'He mentioned that to me last night, but it was only a fleeting conversation. I think I would really enjoy that. I don't have time to discuss this further, I've got a report to get out, but if you email me all the details I'll come back to you?'

'Not a problem. I'll get something out today.'

When Julia checked her personal email later in the day, she found an email as promised from Carolina setting out dates, times, costs and a list of the dance genres Serghei taught. For the first time since Patrick died, she felt a flutter of excitement – to try out some formal dance lessons felt like the beginning of a healing process which she'd so desperately been seeking.

She replied to Carolina's email, her fingers fuelled with a mixture of adrenaline and fear moving swiftly across her keyboard. If she didn't reply instantly, right this minute, then she may lose her courage. Too afraid to leave her job. Too afraid to take on anything new. Too afraid to make life-changing decisions.

She wasn't that woman. She'd never been that woman, so who was this imposter that inhabited her body? This charlatan who walked around inside of her all day every day robbing her of the courage to confront life's opportunities. It was time she took control again.

Later that evening when she had completed the report which she'd been working on all day, and emailed it out, her mind returned to the Googling expedition she'd undertaken, searching out information on Serghei Lebedev. From what she'd read, he was an outstanding dancer and teacher. She smiled as she shut her laptop and was about to pour herself a wine when her landline rang.

Hardly anyone ever called her landline, apart from Nancy, so she was surprised to hear Jack and Kat's unmistakable voices singing down the line to her - *I just called to say I love you*. She waited until they ended their rendition of one of Julia's favourite Stevie Wonder songs before applauding.

'Just thought we'd spread the love Mum, how are you?'

'I'm better, thank you.' Her face crinkling into a smile and her voice sounding, even to her own ears, more like her old self.

'Wow, that's wonderful to hear. Anything in particular that's making you feel great?'

'I've enrolled for private dance lessons.' The statement burst out of her before she had time to consider what she was saying. There was no changing her mind now.

'Dancing, that's fab, Kat will probably want to get on the next plane and join you. She loves dancing, don't you?'

'I love it,' Kat exclaimed loudly. 'I'm so pleased, Julia. It will be a therapy I'm sure of that. I did not know you loved the dance.'

'Well, not something I've done much of in decades, but I thought why not, it will help get my fitness back?'

'It will thrill Carrick,' Jack said laughingly.

'Carrick, what's Carrick got to do with it?'

'He's a fab dancer, didn't you know? I forgot to mention we went to Paris for a long weekend and used that spa voucher Lizzie gave us for Christmas. Carrick was already out in France on business, so he joined us on the Saturday night. Kat had found a fab little bar with a dance floor. Well, the rest is history really. They stole the show.'

'Who stole the show?'

'Kat and Carrick. The DJ played some disco music and did Carrick have all the moves down, even the arm roll thing John Travolta did back in the day.'

'Gosh. I didn't appreciate he was a dancer.' This news was such a surprise, but Julia quickly changed the subject.

'How was Paris then, did you enjoy the spa place?' Julia felt her world had tilted slightly. She couldn't grasp Carrick and Kat dancing the disco, it seemed incongruous. She'd seen Kat dancing around their apartment in Geneva, while Jack cooked supper, she'd laughed at the time loving Kat's enthusiasm and the fact she didn't seem to mind that whilst Jack wasn't a dancer, it didn't stop her enjoying a boogie.

When Kat said goodbye and left Julia with Jack on the phone, she said to him, 'you know Jack you ought to learn to dance especially as Kat loves it. Trust me, a woman who loves to dance needs a husband who enjoys it.' Her voice had taken on a more reflective tone. She'd never considered it important where her own relationships were concerned, she'd accepted that neither Nick nor Patrick were dancers and so she became a non-dancer.

'Really, dancing? I enjoy watching, but I always feel like such a Muppet on the dance floor. I'm like Patrick, he couldn't dance, he was a swayer.' Julia burst out laughing, amazed at how wonderful it felt to enjoy a spontaneous burst of laughter.

'That's so true, but you need not be. I'm serious Jack, have some lessons, I'll pay.'

'You mean this, don't you? It's that important?'

'Yes, I think it is. It's something you and Kat can share apart from work.'

'I hadn't thought of it like that, but maybe it's a good point. Anyway, I'm glad you're doing something for yourself and you sound so much better, Mum.'

'I feel better, although the sad news is Nancy is planning to sell up and move to New Zealand, so that was a bit of a shock, but I'm pleased for her she's going to live with her sister. It's hard as you get older and have no one.'

'Gosh, that's a big move for her, but like you say, maybe a better solution for the future. Have you heard from Lizzie?'

'Not since she slammed the phone down on me. I haven't tried again. Has she been in touch with you?'

'I sent a text message to thank her for the spa weekend, but she didn't reply. She'd left several very drunken messages on my mobile over that Christmas period and countless messages on Facebook Messenger which I ignored, partly because I was so pissed with her over how she's treated you and her behaviour made me feel uncomfortable, but also because we were so busy with work. I didn't have the head space to deal with Lizzie, which probably sounds heartless. I phoned about a month ago. She seemed okay then, but on that occasion, she wasn't drunk, but it's odd she hasn't sent a text back or tried to phone me.'

'She's on Facebook. I'm not or I'd check myself, but maybe you could look and see if she has posted anything recently. I would hate to think she was unwell, or something had happened – that would be awful.'

'I should have thought of that, I'll check her Facebook page. Anyway, I better go now Mum, glad you're okay, speak soon. Love you.'

After the call, Julia poured herself a wine and sat down in the lounge, enjoying the view out across the lawn to the bush. As she gazed it seemed everything about the star-lit sky was a beautiful, beguiling mystery, a backdrop to the glow of the moon, that mother of the night sky watching over every beating heart, steady and true. Julia found herself immersed in a state of tranquility, as though she was standing beneath a warm pool of light and transparency where her life lay before her – full of hope and possibilities.

~

Dance is the hidden language of the soul

Martha Graham

PART III

30

DANCE

Julia had been attending weekly dance classes with Serghei for several months and recalled her tentative start convinced that muscle memory was a fallacy and that, when faced with dancing the Tango, Swing, modern or any of the other dance steps she'd mastered at university, she'd fail spectacularly.

Muscle memory was a real thing – she rediscovered that the brain-to-muscle connection speeds up the more you practise, like your internet browsing history and loading up a page, or at least that was how she thought of it, not that she didn't make mistakes and spend hours practicing at home to salvage her pride.

Serghei was an amazing teacher, patient, kind but a hard taskmaster pushing her when she really didn't believe there was any more to give. But his approach worked, and because of his desire for perfection, Julia had overcome both the physical and psychological hurdles needed if she were to become more than just competent.

The perfectionist in her strove for every step, every movement to be as seamless as she could manage. Being okay, average, adequate would never do.

Every now and again Julia sat at her desk in the evening and wrote a letter to Patrick. Nancy had suggested that she try writing as a therapy. She herself had written to Roy during the last months of his life when she was nursing him at home. It was her way; she said, of saying goodbye whilst he was still physically with her.

Julia took her advice and had been writing occasional letters to Patrick. Tonight, she had something important to share with him.

Hello, it's me again. I haven't written in a while mainly because I was filling my letters with so much grief and sorrow that I believed they were not helpful to you or me. Getting through the first anniversary of your departure was a struggle. People were thoughtful, no more so than your mum and dad and Carrick, but for me and for Jack it was an awful time. I've relived that day so many times in my head – it's pointless, I know, but until recently I've not stopped myself.

I'm better today, much better. Do I miss you any less... no. The house is sad, empty, and soulless without you and you remain a constant in my thoughts.

I'm contemplating selling our home... you will probably think me impulsive, and way too emotional to be making such a big decision. You could be right, but I've reached an impasse and need to take the risk. It won't be immediate, maybe early next year.

I hate the thought of strangers tramping through our home, looking at our treasures, commenting on our tastes. I wish they could buy it from a picture or stand at the front door and take a quick peek down the hallway without invading our space – just enough to satisfy their curiosity so they'd sign the contract there and then for fear of missing out. You can probably tell I have unrealistic expectations!!

My need to move-on is great Patrick. This home, our home, is cloaked in memories, beautiful memories, which are now sources of great pain. They seek me out at every opportunity and leave me wounded and bleeding with their glimpses of a beautiful future together had you not left me, and I recognise I will not heal if I keep touching the wound. You will come to understand my decision in time – at least I hope you will.

My other news is of a more personal nature – I've taken up private dance lessons. And no, I haven't mentioned it before, because I wasn't at all sure how I would feel stepping onto a dance floor again.

I used to dance at university. I'm sure I told you that once, ages ago now. Anyway, I stopped when Nick and I got together; he wasn't a dancer and he would never have permitted me to attend dance lessons for fear that I'd meet someone else or fall in love with the dance instructor – his capacity for jealousy appeared endless.

Jack mentioned this evening when he phoned, that you are more of a swayer than a dancer... sorry, it's a comment meant in the spirit of good humour, not a criticism, but he is right, it wasn't your thing, and I know you would never have prevented me from taking up lessons – I can't say why I didn't – it never seemed important, there were too many other matters vying for my attention.

I find dance helps banish my sadness – it enables me to find myself and lose myself at the same time. When I dance, I turn into a better version of me – and I've learned to accept that I have no power over the choice of music that life plays for me, but I get to choose how I dance to it.

My dance teacher, a Russian called Serghei, has helped me find the song in my heart, the beat in my feet and helped me regain a passion for life. That passion had left me a long time ago, long before you went. It was all to do with work and living here, not this beautiful home we built, but here – in Australia. I want to leave this place – I need to find somewhere else – somewhere I can start afresh, that doesn't mean I leave you behind, lost in the unpredictability of this country – you will always be a part of me – how can you not?

Before I go to bed, there is more news I need to share. Nancy is selling up – leaving Australia. And no, that didn't influence my decision... well, maybe a little. She's moving out to live with her sister in New Zealand. I will miss her enormously, another void I will have to fill, but I'm happy for her. She is here all alone without family and it makes sense to join her sister and find comfort and friendship – growing old together, supporting each other rather than both living alone in separate countries.

I'll write again soon. I love you. J XX.

IT FELT LIBERATING to be writing to Patrick with her news, some may think she was crazy writing to a dead husband, but he was still very much alive in her heart and her thoughts, but now her actions had to be her own. She had to decide and make choices for herself without the need to consider a partner. She was still no nearer deciding on where she wanted to live. Being back in London had been a source of happiness and sorrow so entwined, she'd found it difficult to unravel those emotions and examine them clearly.

Time is what she needed, even though she hated that expression, particularly when it referred to grief, so she knew she mustn't be tempted to rush life changing decisions. She hadn't even told Jack and Kat about selling, but Patrick needed to be the first to know, it was right to share her news with him, even though she'd intimated to Nancy previously that she would move on, she'd not elaborated with any detail since their discussion that morning when Nancy had told her of her decision to sell up and move.

Since then, Nancy had been spending her time de-cluttering, sorting, selling, and taking carloads of goods to charity shops scattered around Melbourne. Julia had helped dress the house ready for sale and sat with Nancy as they heard the sales pitches from three separate real estate agents before finally selecting one. The photographer would come next week to take pictures, and then Nancy's house would be officially on the market.

The entire process had been a roller-coaster of emotions for Nancy. Like Julia, her home held so many wonderful memories and leaving it behind had somehow felt like a betrayal of her love for Roy. They'd talked all this through over coffee, tea, wine, and food. Julia found having Nancy share her emotions had been cathartic. Even if the circumstances were different, the baseline was still the same.

They'd both lost husbands, and both loved their homes – letting go and moving on would be difficult.

Nancy had decided regardless of whether her house sold before or after Christmas, she wouldn't travel out to New Zealand until January. It was easier; she kept reassuring Julia for the shipping companies if she were to go in late January. They'd have time to clear the Christmas backlog of containers belonging to families desperate to move during the school holidays.

'What happens if your buyer wishes to take possession earlier, like prior to Christmas?' Julia asked Nancy.

'I realise that could be a possibility, but I am hoping I can spend one last Christmas here. There is no rush for me to be in New Zealand so if that were to be the case, could Hagrid and I stay with you?'

'You don't have to ask. You can stay as long as you need. I thought you would spend Christmas with your sister, but I'd much rather you spent it with me.' Julia said, putting an arm around Nancy and giving her a hug.

'Well, that's settled then. Sale or no sale, I'll be here for Christmas.' Nancy announced, waving over her shoulder as she walked back across the lawn and through the gate to her property.

31

CARRICK

Carrick was putting the last touches to his itinerary before emailing it to his accountant, his solicitor and Julia. He'd arrived back from Ireland the evening before, having visited his parents before he departed for Australia. He'd asked if they would join him for Christmas with Julia.

'That sounds wonderful Carrick,' his mother had said, 'but Elizabeth and Martin, you remember they taught the junior school when you were a boy?'

Carrick had a vague memory of them and had heard his parents talk of their friendship over the years but had not set eyes on them since his school days. He'd been sitting in his mother's kitchen watching as she kneaded soda bread.

'Well, they are coming to stay with their son and his two children. Sad, the son's wife left him two years ago, but he's maintained a great relationship with his children, anyway it's his turn to have them for Christmas so they are coming over to us from Dublin. You know we would love to be with you all for Christmas, but I can't disappoint them and to be honest Carrick, your father and I are not so good on the long-haul flights anymore.'

'But I would pay and have you travel in business class.'

'Yes, I know you would dear, but we've planned, and you know what your father is like at Christmas, his preference is always to be in his own home. Why do you think you all came out here every Christmas you could manage when Paddy was still with us? It was your father, not wanting to budge from the hearth of his own home.' She'd smiled at Carrick, giving the dough one last punch before covering it with a clean tea towel and leaving it to rise.

'He's always been the same Carrick, so let's leave things as they are – and before you say it, no I won't give the surprise away when next I'm talking to Julia and nor will your father.'

Carrick was checking his emails when a new message appeared in his Inbox. It was the contract for his Lymington property. A real estate agent had contacted him several weeks ago asking if he wanted to sell. He'd thought about it a great deal and decided it was time to let go of that property. It had served its time as an escape pad – a place to unwind, to walk in the countryside and to sail, leaving all his worries and concerns behind on the waves.

Life was different now. Since buying the Bloomsbury apartment and the renovations that followed, he seldom visited Lymington, and the need to use it as a bolt hole had diminished with the passing of time.

He opened the attachment and printed off the contract. The price was ridiculously good, not that he would tell the agent or the buyer that. It was way above the average price for the area, the land, and house. According to the agent, the buyers were an American couple who'd been living in England for some time but never found a property they both liked and agreed they could call home.

He was pleased for them and that their happiness had resulted in this quick profitable sale. 'It's grand when everyone gets what they want', he thought.

Carrick signed and dated the contract, initialling the pages as instructed before scanning and returning it to his solicitor and the agent. There was no chain of buyers to hold anything up, just one cash buyer. It couldn't have been easier and a feeling of release, a letting go of the past washed over him.

This was the beginning, well not quite the beginning. He'd already started the process for the sale of multiple properties he owned in Europe. He'd walked away from the investment in Geneva, something inside of him saying no, it wasn't the right time to invest in a resort redevelopment in Andermatt. He would learn months later that his decision had been a wise one.

In the morning he would meet with his accountant to go over his financial position now that much of his property portfolio in the UK and Europe was sold or under contract.

Over lunch the next day, his accountant raised retirement. 'You should give this some thought Carrick, I know you don't wish to sit idly on a beach somewhere in the world, although why on earth not, I do not know.' He raised his wineglass at Carrick and smiled.

'I would be happy to find myself in your position. There's not a hint of retirement in site for me, not because I don't wish to – I still have those expensive daughters at university. I'm thinking they'll be lifelong students at this rate. Each time I say to myself, finally they'll graduate this year and I'll be free of the burden, they insist on doing another Masters' degree, or obscure but essential study project that never seems to translate into an offer of paid work. I envy you.'

'I'm lucky, I know. I've got choices, maybe sometimes too many.' Carrick took a sip of his wine.

'Luck has nothing to do with it Carrick, you've worked bloody hard to get where you are. Remember, I've been a passenger on this journey with you, right from the start. I remember when you could barely afford to pay your own rent after you purchased your first property. You deserve this, you really do. Also, too many property developers are greedy and fly too close to the wind with the deals they're doing. You have never cut corners. You've never chased every pound, always content to manage risk and above all you're honest.'

He'd never heard Douglas talk like this before and tucked the compliment safely away where he could bring it out later and examine it - a reminder of where he'd been and how far he'd come. He knew there were plenty of property developers far richer than he'd ever be, but how well did they sleep at night?

He'd invested in a trading and analysis course with the LSBF, after his business turned its first profit - the most study he'd undertaken since leaving school. He'd enjoyed the challenge, and the skills he'd gained helped him to read the trends in global markets. As a result, he would sell out his investments in any country where he believed there was likely to be a financial downturn.

As a result of his dedication to detail and his interest in world economies, he'd made substantial profits selling out a property portfolio ahead of a real estate collapse. He made a rule to spread his portfolio between commercial and residential and to date that had proved to be a winning formula.

Reviewing the figures in Douglas' office before they retired to lunch had been a surprise. Whilst Carrick tried to keep abreast of his actual wealth as opposed to paper wealth. The startling figure at the bottom of the page made him realise he could comfortably retire now, years ahead of when he'd planned. What did the future hold for him? Or what did he want from his future - now that he had choices?

'What does Bill say about your divesting in Europe and here in Britain?'

'He's a solicitor, Douglas. Bill is more interested in ensuring no deal I sign up to is going to come back and bite me on the arse. He's a brilliant lawyer, loves all the detail, well we both do if I'm honest. I've been lucky to have both you and Bill on my side. We make a great team and it's not over yet. I'm going out to Australia and then on to New Zealand next week. I'm particularly interested in bees, Douglas.'

'Bees, you mean the buzzing kind?'

'Yes, the buzzing, honey making kind. There's a little company with great ideas, but weak on capital to get their venture off the ground – I'm going to look at their operation and see whether I can help. The returns won't be great, not initially anyway, but I would look at the long term. I'm not interested in the short term.'

'Interesting. I'll look forward to hearing more about that once you've looked. Anything else grabbing your attention out there?'

'Maybe farmland. Buying up some land where there's been overstocking, poor farming practices and little if any ongoing investment or care of the land itself. Properties where the land is no longer fit for grazing. I'm thinking of buying these properties, if I can, and planting them out in trees, or sustainable crops like quinoa. It would mean hiring a manager and probably investing in some heavy-duty expensive equipment, but I'm giving it some real thought. Nothing definite yet.'

Douglas laughed. 'That's quite an undertaking for a man who can afford to retire and sit on a yacht in the Greek Islands?'

'I can't be idle Douglas, you know that's not me, but I also don't have to be travelling all over the globe either. To be honest, I'm tired of the travel. It's fine when you're a young man starting out and hungry for your first deal – I'm neither these days, but I'll still want to be doing something and the more time I spend in New Zealand the more I love the country, the people. It's a different way of life. Kinder, gentler somehow. I think that's what I'm looking for and probably what I need after all these years of living in the fast lane.'

Douglas nearly choked on his food, recovering himself, patting down his mouth with the serviette. 'What - are you contemplating moving out there permanently?'

'No. Just that I may spend more time out on that side of the world than here. I'll hang on to Bloomsbury, I love it and can't imagine selling it. It's more that I need time away from here, from Europe.'

Douglas grinned at Carrick. 'Okay, pleased to hear we won't be losing you to the colonies, just yet anyway.'

They said their goodbyes at the restaurant door, Carrick promising to keep Douglas in the loop once he was out in New Zealand.

32

JULIA

Carrick had arrived in Australia and was spending the first few days in Sydney checking on his property investments before travelling down to Melbourne. He'd be spending the day in the city before coming out to the mountain, he'd said in his email.

Julia had let him know she'd be in the city herself that evening at her dance class, and perhaps they could meet up after and he could drive back to the mountain with her.

'Serghei, I have my brother-in-law in town tonight, I've asked him to meet me here at the studio. I'd like to ask a favour of you?'

'Okay, what is this favour?'

'I understand, although I've never witnessed it, but Carrick, that's my brother-in-law, is an exceptionally good dancer, in particular disco dancing.'

'The disco.' He raised an eyebrow at her. 'What red-blooded male doesn't think he is good at the disco.' He was shaking his head and grinning at her.

'No, really Serghei. Apparently, he has all the moves. I have it on good authority. So, I was wondering if when he arrives, you could put some disco music on, and we could see if he really is as good as I've been told.'

'What time is he coming?'

'I said I'd meet him here after my class finished at 5:30 p.m., but you and I both know I don't finish until 6:30 p.m. So, will you do this for me, please?' She put her hands together in the sign of the prayer.

Serghei laughed at her antics. 'You are a very sneaky fox Julia - you make us Russians look like pussycats in comparison. But regardless of your sly ideas, we were going to be working on some modern this evening anyway, so let's do this. It will be fun.'

As it transpired, Carrick played Julia at her own game and arrived before 5:30 p.m.

Julia was in the middle of a dance perfecting the routine Serghei had taught her to Donna Summer's *Last Dance*. She'd worked doubly hard over the past weeks improving the arm moves and the head roll.

'Loosen those shoulders, Julia,' Serghei shouted from his position on the opposite side of the room to where Carrick stood.

'Watch the foot work, come on Julia, you can do this, hold the rhythm.'

She knew exactly where she'd missed the beat, distracted by Carrick's sudden appearance. It was one thing running her hands over her body as she sashayed up the dance floor followed by sexy head and shoulder rolls in front of her dance tutor, but quite another when her brother-in-law was present.

When the song finished, Carrick slowly clapped. 'Amazing, how didn't I know you were this good.' He was grinning at her.

Julia walked across, flushed from the exercise and embarrassed by Carrick's presence.

'It's so good to see you, I didn't expect you until later. And how didn't I know, Carrick Devlin, that you were a dancer?' Carrick pulled her into a gentle hug, kissing her on both cheeks.

'Because I'm a private man, that's why.'

They made introductions before Serghei winked at Julia and clicked the remote in his hand. At once the sound of the Bee Gees *You should be Dancing* echoed around the room.

Serghei took his place in the centre, beckoning Carrick with his finger to join him. With his microphone strapped to his head, he called. 'I hear you are a disco king Carrick, come join me and show us what you have.' He was laughing, his face a picture of mischief.

Julia was astonished to see Carrick slip off his jacket. She'd half expected him to decline gracefully. Instead, here he was joining Serghei. She perched herself on a stool and watched in awe as the two men competed to the audience of one. Jack had been right - he had all the arm rolls down, the strutting up the dance floor such a distinctive element of John Travolta's performance decades earlier.

What she was witnessing was a different Carrick – a foreign Carrick. A Carrick who had shed his businessman persona and morphed into this sexy dancer. Dance transformed him the way, she knew performing did for Patrick, who was a different man on stage. Now it appeared his brother also had a talent for performing. The only part he omitted from his routine was the sliding splits, which Serghei managed with ease. Being a professional dancer helped, Julia thought.

At the conclusion, she saw Serghei say something to Carrick, but was too far away to hear, and then the room filled with the saxophone of Kenny G playing *Girl from Ipanema*.

'I want to see the two of you dance the Rumba, off you go.'

Julia slid off her stool and joined Carrick on the dance floor. She knew Latin dance well, thanks to Emilio's expert guidance all those years ago.

Carrick took her in his arms and as they stepped together, her movements flowed with dazzling grace as she felt herself become one with the music and unleashed her emotions into the dance. She'd discovered she needed dance as badly as she needed to breathe. They moved with perfect timing to the slow-speed Rumba beat. The music reminding Julia of Jack when he'd first learned to play this piece on the saxophone.

When Julia turned her body in one sensuous move so her back was leaning against Carrick's chest, he moved against her his hips gyrating slowly and she felt that strange little flutter she'd tried so hard to suppress, before Serghei's voice instructing her to keep her head in position brought her back from that split second of an emotion she didn't care to name.

'That was excellent,' Serghei called out.

'Now Julia, we need to go back to your lesson. Take your position.' The sound of David Bowie's *Let's Dance* reverberated around the studio and Julia moved through the steps to the contemporary piece Serghei had been teaching her.

She glanced across at Carrick as he made his way to reception and sat on a stool to watch. She tried to focus her attention on the routine and shut out all other thoughts, concentrating only on the dance steps. When she finished, she heard Carrick clap and looked up to see him smiling back at her, a look in his eyes she didn't recognise.

'How long are you staying, Carrick?' Serghei asked. 'You could join Julia in her class, she's just increased the number of dance classes to three times per week so plenty of days to choose from.' He was grinning at both of them, waiting for a response.

'I must see if I can fit dance around my schedule,' Carrick said. 'I've got business to sort in New Zealand so I may be back and forth a little.' Laughing, his eyes twinkling with naughtiness.

'I'm sure Carrick has way too much work to do Serghei to be taking time out for dance classes.' She wasn't sure what answer she wanted to hear as tonight's performance had shaken her emotions in ways she didn't understand - or at least that's what she told herself. Exploring her emotions was risky territory.

'Julia is every dance tutor's dream student,' Julia heard Serghei saying to Carrick.

'She works hard and concentrates, it would be good if you found some time to join us while you're in Melbourne.' Serghei said, patting Carrick affectionately on the back as though they'd known each other for decades.

'Have you learned the dance in – where – London?' Serghei asked of Carrick.

'Yes. I started lessons when I was 20 and I've kept up regular private lessons ever since.' He looked down at his feet like a schoolboy admitting to an embarrassing secret.

'Well, it shows. You have great rhythm and grace on the dance floor. Ah, here is moya lyubov,' Serghei announced as Carolina arrived with food and coffee for Serghei. As she rested the meal on the reception counter Serghei went to her sweeping her up in his arms and kissing her tenderly.

Julia looked away, straight into the eyes of Carrick before she blushed and turned to pick her bag up from the chair. She made the introductions to Carolina before saying goodbye and heading down the stairs.

THEY WERE DRIVING BACK to the mountain, the earlier emotions Julia felt now strictly tucked away in her private mental box – safely out of harm's way.

'It's great to see you're driving again Julia. Have you regained all your confidence?'

'Mostly, I think. I still haven't driven on the side of the mountain where Patrick died, but that will come in time and if not – does it really matter?'

'You don't have to visit there, unless you think it will help you heal – it's your decision.' She could feel his eyes on her as she took the exit onto Ferntree Gully road and wondered if this had been such a good idea inviting Carrick back to the mountain. It would bring back a lot of memories for him, and she knew he missed his brother a great deal.

'What are your plans for Christmas, or don't you know yet?'

'I'm probably going to be out in Ireland.' Julia flicked her eyes across to look at Carrick, but he'd turned his head and seemed to be intent on looking at something out the window.

'Jack and Kat said they have to work through again this Christmas. It seems crazy that they've found themselves back in the same position as last year, working these long hours. Still, they're young and have the energy.'

'Their skills are in great demand, so I guess they're thinking they need to make the most of the opportunities. Jack has made a proper name for himself in Europe, especially with his musical scores. He just gets better and better. I think he's reached the stage now in his career where he could work anywhere in the world – all this new technology has provided more flexibility.'

'Really? I hadn't realised that. I just assumed he would always base himself in Europe somewhere, or maybe the States. He's extraordinarily talented and with Kat's sound engineering skills, she's such a perfectionist, they make a great team.'

'Absolutely.'

'How is business back in Europe? I hear you were out in Paris with them recently?'

'Yeah. The timing couldn't have been better. I was completing the sale of two properties outside of Paris. It was wonderful to see them both. They looked great. Rested, especially after the spa treat. Have you heard from Lizzie?'

'No. Not a thing, nor has Jack. We were speaking about it the other night. I've asked him to check her Facebook page – just in case something has happened.'

'Like what? An accident or something?'

'Oh, I don't know – anything, really. I would hate to think she was ill or in need of something or someone and we didn't know.'

'You dance extremely well, Julia.' The sudden change of subject away from Lizzie caught her by surprise and she could feel his eyes on her as she drove, but dare not look at him, afraid of what she may read.

'I'm loving it.' She responded. 'Why have you never told me you loved to dance?'

'I guess I never figured it would be important. I'm not used to sharing stuff about myself. Too many years as a single man.'

'What made you take up dancing in the first place?'

'It was Liam. He talked me into going along to a dance class in London – he said it was a great way to meet girls.' Julia glanced across at him and could see the embarrassment contained in his smile.

'I discovered later that Liam had never been to a dance class in his life, but he recognised the importance that I overcome my shyness around women and thought it was worth a shot. I recall him saying *–Carrick, dance is a certainty for pulling the girls. They love a man who can dance, so they do.* I was terribly naïve. But Liam was right, despite my nerves, I fell in love with dance. It transports me to a different place - if that makes sense?'

'Yes, it makes perfect sense. You were right to say dance is a therapy – the way music can be. I feel more like my old self. It's a strange transition – strange in a good way, like an exotic snake looking dull and scuffed then starting to shed its old skin to reveal bright, fresh new colours underneath – does that sound weird?'

Carrick laughed, reaching his hand out to rest on her arm. 'Not at all. It's a grand description actually – just don't celebrate your rebirth by flicking your tongue out and eating rodents.'

'Oh, I'll try my hardest not to give in to those urges.' She smiled at him, his hand pausing on her arm before slipping back to rest in his lap, leaving her skin feeling scorched from the heat of his touch.

33

———

CARRICK

Carrick felt guilty for the lie he'd told Julia about his Christmas plans. But it was a necessary lie if he wished to surprise her with the arrangements already in train.

As he complimented her on her dancing, he watched her face in profile, seeing that beautiful smile that had first captured his heart. He rested his hand on her arm as she spoke - the warmth of her skin beneath his touch electrifying. Reluctantly he pulled back and let his hand rest in his lap, aware touching her was an indulgence he shouldn't allow himself.

As they chatted on the journey up the mountain, Carrick decided he would cook supper. Julia probably had not enjoyed the indulgence of being looked after since she returned to Australia.

'What's in the fridge at home?'

'Plenty of everything – why?' Julia glanced at him before returning her eyes to the twisting curves of the road.

'I'm going to cook supper, that's why, just checking we didn't need to stop off anywhere.'

'Well, I won't turn down a wonderful offer. Thank you, that would be lovely, and I'm sure you'll find everything you need to make something.'

Carrick would tell her this evening of his plans to invest in New Zealand and the sale of most of his properties in the UK and Europe. It would be a surprise to her. He'd surprised himself at the time as he'd had reservations, but as the months had dragged on with no real clarity around Brexit, he was relieved he'd made the decision.

With perfect timing of the remote gate opener, Julia swung off the road and onto her tree-lined driveway.

'Wow, these trees have grown, they look amazing. How are you managing with the lawns and gardens or do you have someone in?'

'I've hired a local guy who comes regularly. That might sound lazy but I'm not sure the ride-on mower is safe under my guidance, and as for the Strimmer - in my hands it could be described as a lethal weapon.'

Carrick laughed. 'I'm sure you're not that bad.'

'Oh, but I am Carrick. Patrick encouraged me to try the ride-on and I nearly gave him a heart attack. I took off too quickly, veered off across the lawn, mowed the edge of a flower bed and only just stopped with the front pushing into the hedge separating our garden from Nancy's vegetable patch!'

'Okay, best you have someone in then,' Carrick laughed as he lifted his bag from the backseat of the car and followed Julia indoors.

Showered and changed Carrick was in the kitchen preparing supper. He'd found steak and salad in the fridge and new potatoes in the pantry, apparently fresh from Nancy's garden.

He looked up as Julia walked into the kitchen fresh from a shower and changed from her dance clothes into a dress. She looked radiant and Carrick struggled to take his eyes off her.

'Can I get the chef a drink? I'm making myself a fizzy water and lime juice.'

'I'd love a beer, thank you.' She poured him a beer before retreating to the terrace. From the kitchen window, as he washed salad leaves, he could see her gazing at the sunset, Alfie lying beside her - it was a blissful scene, and he was so glad to be here on the mountain by her side.

Dance had changed her in ways he wouldn't have expected, and yet he should – didn't it have the same effect upon him? But it was more than dance, he thought. It was as though she'd reached a place of peace where she could stretch out and accept the future was going to be different – not always easy, but perhaps she'd glimpsed an image of the future without Paddy that wasn't dominated by a sense of loss.

34

___

JULIA

Julia sat out on the terrace. The mountain air cooler and fresher, a relief from the earlier heat. As she watched the sun fall behind the horizon, painting the sky shades of red and pink, Alfie lay at her feet content to enjoy the coolness of the evening, punctuated by the occasional growl as he reacted to a Wallaby crashing and thumping its way through the bush at the edge of the property. The loud distinctive call of the laughing Kookaburra echoed around the valley - it too rejoicing in the beauty of the evening.

Carrick had insisted on making supper for them. She'd happily let him get on with it. There were plenty of choices. She'd stocked up the pantry and the fridge in readiness for his arrival and was enjoying him fussing over her.

As they ate their meal Carrick announced he'd divested virtually all his investment properties both in the UK and Europe. Julia rested her cutlery on her plate, shocked at this revelation.

'Why, what's brought on this big change?' She took a sip from her glass of water, waiting for him to respond.

'I'm worried about the economic uncertainty over there.' He hesitated, his head down.

'There's Brexit and the EU drama and a general sense of restlessness everywhere. Remember, you said when you were there – that you felt there was something coming – winds of change you said.'

'Yes. I do recall, but that's probably as much about my state of mind as it is about the state of the world. I wouldn't be putting too much weight on it.' Julia pushed a new potato around her plate, trying to figure where Carrick was going with this conversation.

'I met with my accountant and it seems I'm in a very stable position to retire if I wish to, even if I invest heavily in New Zealand, which is my intention. I have enough passive income to live comfortably without the need to be jet-setting around the globe actively growing and managing my business.'

'That's wonderful, but I thought you enjoyed the cut and thrust of all that,' Julia queried.

'I do – or rather I did. But I'm tired, Julia. For a while now I've been feeling like little more than a grain of sand being blown around the world – it's a lonely life.' Julia looked across the table at him, but his face remained impassive, offering no further insight.

'It's time for me to look at other sources of income and I'm keen to see what New Zealand has on offer. Remember, I told you months ago I was looking at that bee company, the small start-up.'

'The people who needed more capital to build their production and distribution for the domestic and overseas market?' Carrick looked up at her in slight surprise. 'Just showing I pay attention to what you say, so put that astonished look away before I start to feel patronised.' She smiled at him to show him she was only teasing.

'Yes, that one. Plus, there are other ideas I've got which I won't bore you with now, but once I've been out there and taken another hard look, then I'll decide.'

'You never bore me, I'm genuinely interested. My life, dancing apart, is rather dull, and now that I've resigned from my pointless job, I need to find something fulfilling – something meaningful. I've loved helping Nancy these past weeks, it's been a welcome distraction and has made it easier for her. Lovely to give back when she's been so generous to us.'

'How's the sale coming along? Any interest?'

'Yes, plenty of interest, but it's an auction so we have to wait. Unless she receives an acceptable offer beforehand and then she can cancel the auction. She really doesn't like the Open Homes, the sense of intrusion as strangers examine the fruits of your life and put a price on your love and hard work.' She hesitated for a moment, unsure whether she should keep this news to herself for the time being – but why? What was the point, she'd decided?

'I've got some news and now you are here, I can tell you face-to-face.'

'What's that then?' Carrick asked.

'I'm going to sell this property, not immediately, but early next year or maybe later next year. I haven't decided, but I know I need to move on from here, from this house and from Australia.'

'Wow. So, you really are moving on with your life in every sense? Any thoughts on where you want to be?'

'None. Stupid, isn't it? I shouldn't even be considering selling until I know where I want to settle, but just being able to say I'm going to sell makes me confident I am in control of being free again. Not free of memories of Patrick, I don't mean that - like I'm leaving everything that reminds me of him. It's more that it wasn't my choice to come to Australia'

'Why did you then – for Paddy?'

'Yes, and I would do the same again in those circumstances. She added hastily, afraid she may sound critical of Patrick.

'It's just now I can decide for me without the need to consider anyone else. It was Patrick's dream to take up this offer at the university. I understood that, and couldn't steal it from him, but as we now know, his excitement and sense of achievement faded with the passage of time.

You were with me at his solicitor's that day. It came as an enormous shock to hear that he was prepared to leave. Did he ever mention anything to you about resigning from his position and leaving Australia?'

'No. Like I said at the time, I didn't know. My brother was a private man. He often kept things to himself until he was ready to share.'

Julia pushed her plate away, unable to finish the last of her salad. Carrick's news was a lot to process. A song came on her playlist as they sat talking. The first few bars made her reach for the remote to turn the volume up.

'I love this song, haven't heard it in ages. I only just changed the play list this week. I try to rotate so I don't end up listening to the same old tunes day in, day out.'

Carrick stood up from the table and coming around to her chair, he reached his hand out to take hers.

They danced on the terrace as the moon rose high in the night sky and stars winked their approval. Julia followed Carrick's lead, matching his steps avoiding looking into his eyes, but conscious of the words to Lauren Wood's Fallen – ...*And you should know that you are life in my vein...*

Carrick's timing and natural rhythm were a perfect match to Julia's, and for a moment she was back dancing with William remembering the joy dancing with her big brother had given her, the violence and unhappiness of her home life banished as they whirled and twirled their way around the kitchen, dodging the kitchen chairs as they went.

'I couldn't resist that – hope you didn't mind me taking advantage of the song. It's one I like.' Carrick was sitting back at the table, flushed in the face but smiling at Julia in that way he had which made her feel glad to be alive.

'I haven't mentioned to Jack and Kat yet about selling, so please say nothing if you happen to be speaking with them?'

'My lips are sealed,' he said, smiling at her.

35

CARRICK

As he undressed Carrick glanced across at a grouping of framed photographs on the wall. Unbuttoning his shirt, he walked across the room to look at them. He'd slept in this room when he was last here and knew the photographs were a recent addition.

Up close he could see they were photographs of sailing. A young Paddy standing on the deck using the winch, his legs spread wide apart, his body arched as he looked directly ahead – his hair caught in a wind-generated quiff. The other photograph showing their boat anchored and Carrick caught in mid-air as he leapt into the water.

He studied the two photographs, searching his memory for who was likely to have captured these moments. A vague recollection of being out on the water – the three of them. Paddy, Carrick, and Katie Fitzpatrick – but there was no hint of Katie's presence. It had to have been that time – he'd embarrassed himself that day trying to impress Katie with his acrobatic dive. Arms outstretched as he leapt overboard laughing, hoping she would notice him and be impressed by his juvenile act of bravado.

The next photograph sitting below the two above was one he remembered well - sailing in Ireland one summer when they'd all been out for a holiday with his parents. Julia caught in a moment of joy as she aided Paddy in trimming the mainsail. Carrick had taken that photograph, intent on capturing that look on her face. He'd done well, he silently congratulated himself.

He stood staring at all three photographs, remembering back to the days of his youth with Paddy, how close they'd been and then how far they'd drifted apart.

As tears ran down his cheeks, Carrick's overwhelming sadness at the years they'd lost overcame him– that wasted time the brothers had spent estranged from each other, all because of a misunderstanding. He wondered if Julia knew about Katie. She'd mentioned nothing, but he felt certain his brother would have shared that time in his life with the woman he loved. He'd been a young man, his first love and his heart broken. It had become a huge barrier in his life and Carrick believed his brother would have shared that experience with Julia – they talked about everything, that's what Julia had told him once.

It had surprised him to learn she was still planning to sell the house and leave Australia. He'd thought that, once she'd worked through her grief, she'd stay out of loyalty to Paddy and because she could afford to without needing to ever work again. It made him realise just how much she'd sacrificed moving from England.

She'd said as much when they'd been back in Ireland, but he'd not thought her feelings would extend to selling the house.

As he lay in bed thinking of Paddy, his heart ached with the loss of his much-loved brother and the guilt he felt that his every waking moment was filled with thoughts of Julia, of wanting her to be his woman. He agonised between knowing he could not have her but feeling unable to let go, to leave well enough alone. He tried to imagine the unimaginable, of walking away. He'd walked away from Julia once before, and that's exactly what he should do now.

It was the song that did it, he could admit that now in the darkness of his room where there was no one to witness his guilt. He could have ignored the song and continued chatting, oblivious to the words, to the feelings overtaking him once more. When he stood from the table and reached his hand out to her, the longing for the closeness that dance could legitimately provide him was overwhelming.

As he held her in his arms their feet moving in perfect rhythm to the beat of the music, he could smell her perfume and feel the heat from her skin as her bare arms touched his and he longed for the song to be on a continuous loop allowing him to hold her in his arms for eternity.

Waking early and feeling wretched after a restless night, Carrick resolved to complete his business dealings in Melbourne and get on the first available flight to New Zealand to distance himself, as he had in the past, from Julia. It was the only way he could control his feelings. Being in proximity to her brought irresistible desires.

He ached in ways he never knew were possible. His heart accelerating every time he looked at her. And as for dancing – well, he'd be giving that a miss. He'd been foolish to have invited her to dance with him last night – the feelings it aroused in him were all-consuming. He resigned himself to getting the hell out of Melbourne and staying away. Coming back for Christmas would be fine – he wouldn't be alone with Julia and Jack and Kat's presence would change the chemistry.

He showered and dressed, walking barefoot through to the kitchen where he found Julia making a smoothie. She turned, smiling at him, holding up a glass of what resembled green gunk.

'Good morning. Thought I'd make you one of my special smoothies for breakfast.'

'What is that exactly, something healthy no doubt?'

'It's swamp juice – avocado, spinach, mint and water – try it. It's delicious.'

He reached for the glass and took a tentative sip. She was right; it was delicious, aware she was watching him - waiting for a response.

'See wasn't that bad was it?'

'No. You were right. It's rather nice, even if it looks gross. Thank you. I'm going to head off early into the city, I've got some meetings today about those apartments in Docklands. Would you mind dropping me to the station?'

'Why don't you take my car. I'm not going anywhere today. No dance class, and I thought I'd help Nancy with sorting some more of her stuff to take to charity before the next Open Home.'

'Okay if you're sure. I'll drive back up tonight, but I'll be leaving for New Zealand tomorrow.' He looked away, unwilling to let her see the pain behind his eyes.

'That soon. I thought you'd be here for longer.' She sounded disappointed, but he averted his gaze from hers.

'I can take you to the airport tomorrow. Do you want a coffee before you head off?' She'd turned back to the sink, rinsing the glasses before stacking them in the dishwasher.

'Thanks. That would be lovely, I'll just go finish getting ready.' He hurried back to his room, feeling wretched that his performance was all a big act. He'd been friendly, but aloof, putting back in place the familiar walls he'd erected to protect himself and which had served him well for so many years.

36

JULIA

Julia looked across the counter-top at Carrick. Something was wrong. His mood was different. She thought the previous evening had been special, but this morning it was as though Carrick had erected a barrier between them. Maybe that wasn't a bad thing, she thought, looking into her coffee cup – he'd exposed feelings that she'd been suppressing since London.

Last night, the food, the dancing, the moonlight, it had the hall-marks of romance attached to it and in the morning light this felt so wrong. Wrong to be giving what they shared last night a name. She loved Patrick. Thought of him every day, missed him every day. What happened last evening had been a mirage, a second of madness where two people who loved the same person had found themselves caught in a tender moment, that's all it was. She'd been telling herself that since she climbed beneath the sheets last night. She poured herself another coffee, offering Carrick a top-up.

'I'm not looking forward to the serious conversation I'm going to be having today with the builders of the apartment block in Dock-lands, it's going to be pretty heated I imagine.' He looked across the counter at her.

'Why, what's happened with that development to have you stressed about it?'

'The cladding. The plans specified how it had to meet all building regulations, particularly in relation to fire. I've had a builder friend of mine from the UK, who's living out here now, to check on it. He thinks it's some cheap shite from China. One way to keep costs down, but not what I'd specified and not what they guaranteed when they tendered. So, someone is going to be in for an enormous shock today.'

'You're scary when you're angry,' Julia said, pursing her lips, trying not to smile.

'I've already spoken to my solicitor back in London and he in turn has instructed a firm out here to handle any disagreement if the construction company plays hard-ball.'

'If it's in the contract and you've stated the product, then they don't have a leg to stand on. Unless you're saying that there is no clear evidence the product is defective?'

'Oh, there's evidence alright, but like a lot of construction companies, they'll threaten a big delay to the build and hope I'll back down to keep things on track. That's not going to happen because it will be my future tenants who occupy that building who would be the ones in danger. If a fire broke out, it would burn ferociously and fast and the aftermath would be a finger-pointing battle in court between the construction company, the suppliers, the manufactures, the building inspectors, and myself that would do nothing to repair the broken lives. The time to fix it is now,' said Carrick whilst thumping the bench-top with his fist to emphasise the point.

'Good for you! Let me know if I can look over any contractual matters if it will help. Sometimes a set of fresh eyes – who is the Melbourne solicitor?'

'Duncan, James and Lovington. They're specialists in this area. I met with the senior partner when I flew in from Sydney and he's instructed their Melbourne office to assist. Hopefully, it won't become litigious, but they're on standby just in case.'

'I've heard of them, but don't know anyone there. Fingers crossed it doesn't get nasty. What time do you think you'll be back tonight – I'll cook?'

'Probably by six or thereabouts, but I'll text you and you don't have to cook. Take a night off, why don't I pick up a takeaway?'

'Because Carrick Devlin, I've got a lot of food in and if you are taking off to New Zealand tomorrow, I'll have a fridge full of food which I'll struggle to get through by myself – so I'll cook.' She pushed her car keys across the counter to him before collecting their coffee cups and placing them in the dishwasher.

'I'm going to shower, so I'll see you later tonight, hope today works out better than you expect.' She reached up to peek him on the cheek before heading down to her bedroom.

37

CARRICK

Carrick drove into the city thinking through the day ahead. This was a set-back, but he would not let it rest until he had a guarantee they'd replace the cladding with the specified safe product on his development.

The kiss on the cheek this morning, however innocent, had stirred his emotions yet again. He was furious with himself for his lack of control. He'd spent years compartmentalising his relationship with Julia and now that safety net had developed great, gaping holes with no quick and easy way of mending it.

His focus moved to his flight to New Zealand. He'd fly into Auckland first and drive down to Wellington. He'd taken this option before, loved the scenery plus it would allow him to check out the bee farm and surrounding area.

He wondered, as he manoeuvred his way into the Collins Street car park, if he should tell Julia about the apartment in Wellington? He shouldn't have kept this from her and Paddy, but at the time it seemed the right thing to do and he believed there was no pressing need for her to know. It had been a hard time for her and no telling how his brother would have reacted. Would the jealousy of old raise its ugly head again? That had been his logic back then, but now there was no reason at all not to tell her. He'd do it tonight when he got back to the mountain.

He arrived early at the construction company's head office in Docklands so made himself comfortable in their reception area and reviewed his notes on the contract. He knew it by heart but the perfectionist in him meant he would recheck every clause to ensure there were no loopholes.

Checking his emails, he saw one from Duncan, James and Lovington – Thomas Keneally, his name at the bottom of the email, the solicitor assigned. They had emailed the construction company early this morning

He smiled as he read the contents. Pleased that despite him saying to the senior partner days before that he wanted them on standby if things turned sour, they had taken it upon themselves to intervene sooner rather than later and reviewed the contract themselves and highlighted to the construction company the contract specifications, financial liability for failure to comply, and the futility of taking the case to court with the certainty of incurring legal costs on top of the remedial work on site. Carrick smiled to himself, thinking the construction company would be foolish indeed to make a fight of it.

They weren't foolish so, by the conclusion of Carrick's meeting, he'd achieved what he wanted. Works would start on replacing the defective cladding within a month. Now he would head up to the offices of Duncan, James and Lovington to complete the details.

Thomas Keneally was younger than Carrick had expected, but he was sharp and engaging. They'd gone out to lunch in a fancy restaurant after an exchange of emails between themselves and the construction company's solicitors. Everything agreed and confirmed, Carrick could leave Australia knowing matters were in hand.

'Future tenants ought to be grateful that as a landlord you are ensuring their safety. I can tell you now, there are a number, quite a large number in fact, of apartment blocks such as yours, where the cladding is inadequate, and no one is addressing the elephant in the room – that is the Council whose building inspectors signed off on works which did not comply with current building guidelines. It's shameful.'

'Corrupt is more accurate a word, I would have thought,' Carrick said, shaking his head in disapproval. 'It goes on everywhere, doesn't matter which country. So many players in the market, so many opportunities to cut corners. It's not my style and never has been.'

'Are you planning on staying in Melbourne long Carrick?'

'No. I'm heading off to New Zealand tomorrow. Looking at investment opportunities out there.'

'Whereabouts – North or South Island?'

'At the moment, I have properties in the North Island and that's where I'll be concentrating my efforts, but the South Island, I'm sure, holds possibilities.'

'I was born in Auckland. Came out to Australia about ten years ago now.'

'So how do you find living and working in Melbourne?'

'It's different – really different actually and I miss New Zealand, but I enjoy working here. Interesting clients and no two days the same. So, for the time being, I'll remain. Who does your legal work for you in New Zealand?'

'I use Parker O'Connell. They're connected with my solicitor in London, so it's been easy getting things done and ensures my London solicitor is across my Australasia portfolio.'

'I understand you have a large portfolio in the UK and Europe, how are you finding business - I mean with Brexit and all that fiasco?'

'Well, I've divested virtually all my investments in the UK and Europe. I'm not happy with the way matters are being handled over Brexit. The whole situation has been a disaster from the beginning. We got into this situation on a wave of emotion, without appearing to have done any serious business modelling on what Britain would look like if we left the EU.' He took a sip of water before carrying on.

'Anyway, let's not get into the swamp of politics, I'm glad I divested – it was the right time.'

'You may well be correct. I've friends in the UK who are looking at how they could immigrate to Canada or Australasia, but you know what they say about the grass looking greener?'

'You're right, who knows what will happen, but I'm looking forward to seeing what New Zealand offers.'

'What about Australia, no further interest here?'

'I'm comfortable with the investments I have in Sydney and Melbourne – I'm not a big player, Thomas. I'm small fry compared to my peers, but what I do, I like to believe I do well and with care and consideration. It's not all about the bottom line for me, never has been.' Carrick signalled the waiter to bring the bill.

'Anyway, I'm sure I've taken up enough of your time today. Thank you for the work you've done and for heading off at the pass, what could have been a turbulent meeting this morning. Perhaps we'll catch up next time I'm back in Melbourne?'

'I'd like that. You could join me and my wife for dinner, maybe. Let me know when you're back?'

They shook hands before Carrick waved goodbye and headed back to Collins street to retrieve Julia's car. It was only 3:30 p.m. and he'd told Julia he wouldn't be back until around 6:00 p.m. He sent her a text message to say he was on his way early, but did she need him to pick anything up?

He heard nothing from her and as he drove through Burnley tunnel to the freeway; he wanted nothing more than to relax with a beer on the mountain. The city was hot and sticky – Melbourne was becoming more humid like Sydney, he thought as he turned up the air conditioning – the mountain, with its clean air would be a welcome reprieve.

He pushed the button for the car stereo and the unmistakeable husky voice of sound of Chris Isaak filled the car singing *Wicked Game* and Carrick couldn't help thinking how apt this song was as his thoughts lingered on his feelings for Julia.

38

JULIA

Julia didn't see Carrick's text until much later. Realising he would almost be home there was no point in responding. She'd been busy helping Nancy sort through the last of her treasures. Items that deserved a new home. Julia had driven Nancy's car down to Belgrave to drop them off at the Op Shop, leaving Nancy to tidy and clean up.

It had been a day of mixed emotions as they worked side by side sorting into two piles, one for the Op shop and one for recycling. Nancy holding-up an item that had belonged to Roy, calling out to Julia, 'Look at this, it must be thirty years old or more,' before placing it in the pile for the Op shop.

'They are not sentimental things, and it seems silly to hold on to them, where they will languish in a cardboard box, never opened.' Nancy repeated this many times to Julia – if she said it enough times, Julia thought, she could convince herself the box ought to be irretrievably handed to the Op Shop.

Julia imagined she was going to be experiencing something not too dissimilar in the months ahead when it came time to sell her home. She wasn't a hoarder, but there would still be a lot of items she would probably wish to sell or give away, and what would she do with all of Patrick's musical equipment and instruments? She made a mental note to speak with Jack about that. And where would she go?

On nights when sleep eluded her like an indefinable shadow - she agonised over how she had mentally and emotionally committed to selling her home when she still didn't know where she really wanted to be, hoping that instinct or fate would guide her unerringly in the right direction when the time came.

In daylight hours, she'd chastise herself for depending on such whimsical concepts to decide her future. What was she thinking selling her home before she knew where she wanted to live - ridiculous?

When Julia opened the gate from Nancy's property to her own, she heard a vehicle and realised Carrick must have returned. She checked her watch; it was almost 5:00 p.m. thankful that she'd thought to prepare supper before going to Nancy's.

The day had slipped by in a blur of boxes, cobwebs and reminiscing, but she was glad she'd been able to help Nancy so all that remained was to wait for the auction day, unless she was lucky enough to receive an offer beforehand.

'Hello. You're earlier than I expected. Sorry I didn't see your text until it was too late. But I didn't need anything extra.' Carrick was standing in the kitchen looking hot and tired as she came near. He reached out a hand and plucked something from her hair.

'A cobweb. Is this the new look now Julia?' He laughed, but Julia could see closeup he looked tired and she hoped this morning's meeting had not been too fraught.

'You look exhausted. Why don't you change, and I'll pour you a beer, sound like a plan?'

'That would be marvellous, thank you. I might jump in the shower if that's okay?'

'You don't have to ask silly?' She smiled at him, picking up her car keys from the counter-top and hanging them on the hook in the pantry cupboard.

'I've organised supper, so we can sit outside and enjoy a drink before we eat.'

'Sounds grand to me. I'll be back shortly.' He picked up his jacket and laptop bag and headed down to his room.

Julia was intrigued to know how he'd got on this morning. She'd been thinking about his meeting off and on all day and wished she'd had the chance to look over the contract herself – but he'd not taken her up on her offer of help last evening and she did not want to push it.

Julia went to shower and change. She felt dusty and sweaty from hours of rummaging through Nancy's garage. She slipped into some loose-fitting linen trousers and a sleeveless silk shirt, pulling a brush through her hair and spraying Yves Saint Laurent's *Libre* liberally across her chest and behind her neck.

Barefoot she returned to the kitchen, opening the fridge she lifted out a bottle of Guinness, took a tall beer glass from the cupboard and began pouring. She looked up as Carrick joined her at the counter.

'I assumed, rightly or wrongly, that you might like a Guinness?' she asked, not lifting her eyes from pouring.

'You assumed correctly. That's exactly what I feel like. Thank you. What can I pour for you, Red or White?'

'I'll have a Pinot Gris – there should be one on the fridge door.'

Seated outside enjoying the warmth of a beautiful mountain evening, Carrick talked to her about his day. Julia listened. 'I'm glad things worked out between you and the construction company, that must be a tremendous relief?'

'It is. I hadn't realised until it was over, just how stressed and tense I'd been feeling. But it's in hand now, and I can leave tomorrow without the worry of litigation. What have you been doing today?'

'Helping Nancy sort and tidy the last of her possessions, which she's decided she needs to hand over to the Op shop or recycling. It was quite a job and emotional for her.'

'How will you handle that side of things when your time comes to sell?'

'I was thinking about it today, actually. I need to speak to Jack about Patrick's music equipment and his instruments – but to be honest, I'd rather not dwell on that tonight. Tell me about your New Zealand trip – are you flying into Auckland?'

'Yes, I've got two meetings lined up, then I'm going to drive down to Wellington. I want to visit the apiary on the way down. It's outside of Whanganui. I'll be in touch with the owners once I get to Auckland and set up a time.'

'You're keen on this bee business, aren't you?'

'It's intriguing – and for me it's not just about a profitable invest-ment. If I get involved, I'll not be thinking of making a quick profit. Managing the environment is important and the need to keep our bees safe. Anyway, I won't bore you with bee stories.' He took a sip of his beer and Julia noticed once more how tired he looked.

'You mentioned about buying up some farmland – are you still looking at that?'

'Yes. I have my eye on something in Wairarapa, which reminds me, I must email that contact before I go to bed tonight.'

'It'll be a busy trip then?'

'Yes. I'll have plenty to do when I get out there, but I'm looking forward to it.'

'And then are you flying back to Ireland or stopping off in London?'

Carrick looked up, startled by her question. 'I haven't thought that far ahead, but you're right to remind me. I must book flights once I see how things fall into place.'

'Do you want another?' Julia stood, not waiting for his reply, walking back inside and taking another bottle of Guinness from the fridge, handing it to him to re-fill his glass before he could protest.

'I want to ask you something that has been bugging me for a while?'

'Okay, fire away,' Carrick said, concentrating on a perfect pour to create a creamy head to the top of his glass.

'Who's Katie?' Julia was watching him intently and noticed when he rushed the last of the pour, causing the head to overflow the glass.

'She's a girl we knew back in Ireland when we were young.'

'Was she Patrick's girlfriend?'

'Yes. His first love. I thought he would have told you?'

'No. He never mentioned her, not once, why would that be Carrick? Why would he not tell me about his first love? I told him about every fumble and sexual experience I've ever had. I never wanted secrets between us... not that sort of secret.' Julia, arms crossed fixed him with a steady gaze.

'How did you know about Katie?'

'I was sorting through a box of his old photos. I found some, the ones I've had blown up and framed which are hanging in your room. The inscription on the back of one - *Patrick & Carrick – may summer never end*. Not in Patrick's writing nor yours. So, I assumed it was the person taking the photographs. Then I found a photograph of her, she's beautiful. On the back she'd written *For Paddy, my only love, Katie.*'

'I'm sorry Paddy never told you about Katie. It was a long time ago and maybe in my brother's defence, he never felt it was important enough to share.' Carrick ran his fingers through his hair and immediately Julia knew mentioning Katie was a source of anxiety for him. She figured there was much he wasn't saying, but she wanted to know. Patrick may be dead, but it didn't stop her wanting to understand what went on in his past and why he'd kept it a secret from her.

Patrick's first love was music, she'd always known this from the very beginning, they'd even talked about it before they moved in together. He'd never denied that whoever was in his life had to understand music came first. It didn't mean he didn't love her passionately, but music would always dictate how much time he could dedicate to loving her.

He'd talked to her about other women he'd spent time with over the years, including his bandmate Phil's sister Erika. Julia had met Erika at a gig one evening and clocked the coolness with which Erica addressed her. She'd known immediately that Erika had most likely been an old flame. She was in a stable relationship with a financial advisor at the time, so Julia was at a loss to understand Erika's hostility.

She'd quizzed Patrick later that evening when they'd driven back out to Hambleden, and he'd been open and honest about his relationship with Erika. So, finding these photos of Katie with their personal inscriptions was both intriguing and disappointing that Patrick had never shared this with her.

She'd sensed something, looking at the beautiful young face sunlit in the photograph, standing facing the camera onboard the yacht the boys had sailed when they were young.

'The photo, Carrick, the one of Katie taken on the yacht you and Patrick used to sail as boys. I've seen pictures of it enough times to recognise it immediately. Why all the secrecy?'

Carrick settled himself into his chair, gazing out across the lawns to the bush beyond the look on his face told Julia he was revisiting another place, another time.

'Katie Fitzpatrick was a Catholic girl from a poor family. Back then, in those days, Catholics didn't mix with Protestants, but Katie did. She was our secret friend.'

'A secret friend, what do you mean?' It confused Julia, annoyed with the obvious hesitation in Carrick. And what was so special that they had kept this girl a secret?

'They fell in love – Paddy and Katie. They kept it a secret, except I guessed something was going on between them and so I provided a cover - I used to go out sailing with them. Everyone thought it was just me and Paddy, but Katie was often with us.'

'Is she one girl you had a crush on? And is that why Patrick was so touchy about the relationship you and I shared?'

'Yes. I had a monumental crush on her. I was 16, immature and easily influenced. Later Katie became a friend.'

'So why didn't Patrick ever tell me this, it seems so silly really. Your first love, always the one you find hardest to forget – sometimes you don't wish to forget - holding onto that time of innocence – that time before you have to grow up and life becomes complicated.'

'Paddy was in love with Katie, but his first love was always music and he was going away to university in Edinburgh to study. They'd made plans once he finished university, he would return to Baltimore and they would go off to London together and start a life where no one knew them. Where there was no space for religious or social judgement.'

Julia could feel her stomach somersault at the words *Paddy loved Katie deeply*. How could he not have shared with her how important this time had been in his young life? He'd talked endlessly about university and his first band, Platonic. He'd regaled her with stories of their success, life on the road touring, he'd left nothing out, even the bits she'd have preferred not to hear. Why would he not tell her about this?

'They argued the night before he left for university. She'd begged him not to go, to change universities and attend Dublin or London. It shocked and angered Paddy. He'd made it clear from the outset that he would go to Edinburgh.'

'So why did she wait until he was about to leave? Why not tell him earlier, when maybe he could have changed his mind about universities?'

'Katie didn't think like that – she wasn't very sophisticated. The world we'd grown up in was so different to hers – like night and day, in fact. Her home life was grim. She saw Paddy as a way out – a chance to escape. They never saw each other again after that night.'

'Really, why? Didn't Patrick come home in his breaks?'

'No. Not that first year. He was working in a bar to help pay his fees, and life at university was so different for him. You know how he was about music, his passion, his dedication. That dedication wasn't something that grew as he matured - it was always there, right from the beginning.'

'That must have been hurtful to Katie – you were all so young. It would be difficult to understand or accept?'

'I guess so. But you're right, we were young.' Carrick stopped talking and took a sip of his Guinness.

These revelations had definitely taken a turn Julia had not expected, but there was more to this and she'd keep probing Carrick until she knew everything – there would be no more secrets.

'So what happened to Katie, where is she now?' She watched Carrick's face change. A flash of pain – a memory from the past.

'Katie died. She committed suicide.'

'Oh!' It shocked Julia to hear these words - it wasn't what she expected. 'Why? What happened to her?' She had a horrible feeling Carrick was going to tell her Katie had been pregnant with Patrick's child, or something equally shameful as it would have been back then.

'After Paddy left, Katie and I became friends. I'd realised by then that my all-consuming schoolboy crush was just that – it could never be anything more, but I did want to be her friend, her link back to Paddy and I wanted to help her.'

'What do you mean help her?'

She watched Carrick trace his finger around and around his glass before he looked up at her, and she sensed the hesitancy and braced herself for the worst.

'She had a drunk for a father, violent to both her mother and to Katie. That's why she wanted to escape to London.'

Julia could feel all the old emotions of fear and anguish weaving a tight knot around her. She knew first-hand what it was like to be on the receiving end of the vicious hand of a drunk. 'Was she pregnant?' There, she'd said it and she knew this was something Carrick would not lie to her about.

'No. She wasn't pregnant. She felt rejected by Paddy and couldn't understand why he'd left, or more to the point, didn't wish to under-stand. She kept telling me he'd used her. Made promises he'd never intended keeping just to get sex.'

'Patrick would never behave like that. He'd treat no woman so callously.' She hissed the words across the table at Carrick.

'I know, my brother's a good man, she was wrong, and I realised that even if Paddy had returned to Katie, it would never have worked. She was just too different, too damaged, and she'd never have coped with Paddy putting music ahead of everything else, including her. I gave her money, all that I had saved so she could escape Baltimore and go some-place else. Somewhere she'd be safe from her father.'

'Where did she go?'

'She didn't. Her father found the money and thought she'd been on the game, so he beat her up. She felt wronged and powerless, and despondent that she would never escape her life, both of poverty and as a victim of men. It was the last straw - so she took her father's dinghy out to the open sea and drowned herself. I should have realised how fragile she was and helped her through the blackest days, but I didn't, and then it was too late.'

'Oh Carrick. I'm so sorry. That must have been awful for you and Patrick. Were you parents aware - didn't they guess something was amiss?'

'No. They never suspected. We were all incredibly careful. I suspect Mammy thinks something might have been going on, although she'd direct that accusation at me, not Paddy.'

'Why you? Did people just gossip because you were her friend?'

'There were other boys from Baltimore who were at Edinburgh university with Paddy. They spread rumours that I'd got Katie pregnant, that we were an item. It got back to Paddy.'

'Did he believe them? Please say he didn't?' Carrick looked across at her and Julia could read the pain in his face, the hurt that his big brother had believed malicious rumours. It was hard for Julia to imagine Patrick being so taken in and judgmental of his own brother.

'He did. I tried to explain, but he wouldn't listen.'

'Why wouldn't he listen Carrick, it seems so unlike Patrick?

'He felt guilty Julia. I think part of him wanted to believe I had caused Katie's suicide rather than face up to how the self-centredness of his departure and failure to return during holidays had contributed to her state of mind. Who knows? I'm just glad that we finally had that long overdue conversation and were able to find each other again. We were so close as boys it still saddens me deeply to think of all those lost years as we grew into men.'

His voice broke and Julia watched as he bent forward, dropping his head, the hand holding his glass shaking. She'd never witnessed him weep like this before. It was painful to watch, but she stayed sitting and didn't rise to go to him, to offer comfort. He needed to cry, to express his grief – his loss. She knew all about that.

The conversation with Carrick had disturbed her a great deal.

Reconciling the Patrick she knew and loved with this other Patrick – the one who had not only kept something from her -an important part of his prior life – but his inability to reconcile with Carrick. All those years. What a waste she thought – but it was Carrick's face, the hurt he couldn't disguise, that confirmed this was how it had played out.

Carrick must have spent years trying to escape the memories, the rumours. It explained why he'd spent so much of his time flying around the world. Yes, work was a factor, but so many trips away, had they all been necessary? Or had he too, like Patrick, been escaping into his work? Is that what he meant when he'd referred to himself as a grain of sand being blown around the world – was this his admittance that beneath the surface, lay a lonely man.

How stupid of Patrick to have kept this from her. He'd been so open about everything else. It was one of his many attributes she'd loved and respected. Her previous husband couldn't lie straight in bed – he was incapable of being honest, even with himself. But Patrick wasn't Nick. She'd always thought him to be a straightforward, honest man not someone who would unfairly bear a grudge for years, and not someone who would keep this core part of himself from her.

As she lay in bed, her arms behind her head unable to sleep, her mind racing with thoughts, she sensed a movement, and watched as her half-shut bedroom slowly opened, and Alfie appeared at her side. Since Patrick's death he'd taken up residence at her bedside and she'd allowed him - loving the feeling that he was close by protecting her.

She rested her hand on his head, his wet muzzle pushing into her open palm before he moved across to his large dog cushion, turning several times before releasing a long sigh and settling down for the night.

Knowing sleep would evade her, she rose and sat down at her writing desk. This letter couldn't wait until morning.

I learnt a lot about your past tonight, Patrick. It shocked me, shocked me in a way I didn't expect. I found the photos. I wasn't snooping, merely tidying up and sorting. I framed several photographs of you and Carrick when you were boys and I've hung them in the spare room. I go in and inspect them every so often. I touch your face, your hair, caught in the wind. I trace my fingers across your mouth. You were both so young, so vibrant - so alive with so much to look forward to, so many possibilities.

Why didn't you tell me about Katie? This must have hurt you a great deal and yet you never thought to share it with me when I've always been so open and honest with you – even the awful bits embarrassing for me to reveal. But in you I trusted – always I trusted.

To estrange yourself from Carrick for so long, the brother I know you love passionately and who you are so proud of. What a waste, Patrick. I'm so angry with you – it feels like a betrayal of your family – of me. I've had enough betrayals to last me a lifetime.

I don't understand why you would keep this from me. It was a major event for all three of you. And yet you bury it away in a box of old photographs, which had you not died, I probably would never have found and therefore never have known. Unless you planned on waiting until we were so old, I wouldn't have the strength to be angry with you.

I'll get over it, the anger I mean, but you've disappointed me, and it's made worse because you are not here to defend yourself or explain. Maybe you never felt the need to share. It was a long time ago, long before me, and therefore none of my business. Perhaps you're right, but your hurt and pain is my concern, will always be my concern.

It's hard for me to understand how you could have carried this around with you for all those years without feeling the need to unburden yourself. Did you think I would judge you?

I understand – have always understood that music was your first love. Everything and everyone else took a back seat behind music. Did I resent that? Sometimes. Sometimes when you were out late at night and I was home alone - those feelings were fleeting – they came and went like the rush of an ocean tide and I could never say I didn't know what I was in for.

The honesty you shared when we got together still astounds me. It was a risk - you must have known that. You must have wondered would I say *no thanks*, I'd rather stay on my own with Jack. That we settle for friends with benefits - no attachment. You knew me better than I knew myself. For I didn't hesitate to agree to our relationship moving forward.

I will confess to you now, because I think I should – I love you, will always love you, but your love and commitment to Jack was the defining moment in our relationship – I've said it now, so I can't take it back.

It doesn't diminish the love I have for you and that you have for me, even death can't rob us of that, but in the spirit of being open and honest, the love and bond which grew so strongly between yourself and Jack meant more to me than the love of a man and a woman ever could. Did you know that anyway? Probably, you were always so astute.

I'll write again when I've had time to process everything.

39

CARRICK

'There's something I want to talk to you about this morning before I leave. Something I should have told you a long time ago and before you ask, it's got nothing to do with Katie.'

They were standing in the kitchen together, Julia pouring cereal into two bowls and chopping a mixture of fresh fruit which she sprinkled on the top before adding oat milk.

He sat ramrod straight on his bar stool clearing his throat waiting on her to pass the bowl across as she sat down opposite him.

'So, what is it you should have told me Carrick?' He could see from the tightness of her jaw she was nervous.

He placed a spoonful of cereal and fruit into his mouth and began eating, stalling for time, realising Julia was looking at him expectantly. He needed to tell her what he'd done all those years ago and hope that she wasn't angry or disappointed with him, that he'd never mentioned it.

'You're making me nervous, Carrick. What is it you need to tell me?' He looked up from his cereal bowl, noticing how her face registered a mixture of intrigue and fear.

'It's about your aunt's apartment in Wellington – the one she left you in her Will.'

'I remember Carrick. She's the only aunt I have or had; I should say. What about the apartment?' He could see from the set of her jaw and the flash of anger that she blinked away before fixing Carrick with her steady gaze. She would not take this well.

'I should have told you back then – but I didn't. I thought you were dealing with such a lot and your relationship with Paddy had only just begun.' He hesitated, watching as her mouth hardened and her eyes took on that steely look he'd witnessed in the past.

'I bought the apartment Julia. I'm the owner. A managing agent has been acting on my behalf, organising corporate leases. I bought it because I sensed it had meant something to you – a link to your family in some small way... was I wrong to have assumed that?'

'Why the secret? Why didn't you tell me? I don't accept it was because I had too much on my plate. Knowing you were the owner wouldn't have added to my burden. I hate secrets Carrick, you know that.' She almost spat the last words at him before rising from her stool, leaving her untouched cereal behind.

'I know. I'm sorry, I truly am. My withholding what I'd done I appreciate was stupid, thoughtless.' He looked across at her. She hadn't sat down again and was standing staring at him with undisguised anger and disappointment.

'Do you know how many times in the intervening years I wondered if I'd done the right thing selling the apartment? That maybe I should have held onto it. At the time I needed the money, but later, when Patrick and I were together, I really regretted selling it. You of all people should know how much I detest secrets. What was wrong with just telling me then? Was Patrick's reaction what you feared?'

'For a long time, Patrick felt threatened by our relationship, you know that. I didn't want to cause problems between the two of you. I didn't want him thinking I'd bought the apartment to...' he trailed off, unable to finish his sentence.

'Thinking what Carrick, that you had feelings for me, that I would suddenly stop loving Patrick and run off with you because you'd bought my aunt's apartment?'

'I'm sorry, Julia. I truly am. My intentions were honourable.' He gulped down the last of his cereal and looked across at her, wishing she would come back to the counter and sit down.

'Why now? Why tell me now?'

'Because it's been bothering me for ages and when you said you were intending to sell this place, I figured that you may need a safe landing place until you decided where you wanted to live.'

He could see his last words resonated at some level with her, but she was far from happy with him and now all he wanted to do was pack his bags and get on a flight to New Zealand. Time and distance would help heal her disappointment, or at least he hoped it would.

Carrick slunk away liked a whipped dog into his room to finish packing. He'd hurt and disappointed the one person in his life who meant more to him than anyone else. But maybe that was a good thing. Maybe, as long as Julia could get past him keeping a secret from her, then their friendship would remain intact and he could let go of the stronger emotions of love and wanting her to be so much more than a friend.

No good could come of their union. How many times do I need reminding? He asked himself. It wouldn't be right to lie beside his brother's wife. And everyone else in the family would agree with him. Now all he had to concentrate on was winning back her friendship and respect, and the best way he could do that was being absent from her.

Seeing her every day was too difficult, painfully exquisite, but ultimately reckless. He'd stayed awake for hours the night before, restless and unable to sleep, unable to stop his mind reliving every word of their conversation about Katie. And now he'd added to her burden.

Buying the apartment had been the right thing to do, of that he was certain, but keeping it from her had been a huge mistake. She was right to think it was because of Paddy. He would have been furious that Carrick had taken control and purchased a property, knowing it would have a sentimental impact on Julia.

Back then, Paddy would have perceived Carrick's actions as an inappropriate display of his greater wealth. It had taken a long time before his brother had accepted Julia and Carrick shared a special bond together. One that was not a threat to him – Julia loved him and would never betray their love.

Carrick had seen a slight lessening of the anger in her eyes when he'd mentioned that the apartment could be a temporary soft-landing place. If she sold and still had nowhere to go, then there were far worse places to live than central Wellington.

He hoped, given enough time, the calm, rational Julia would understand his motives. The last thing he wanted was to leave Melbourne with tension and hostility raging between them.

Now he had doubts about surprising her at Christmas. Maybe she wouldn't even want him here?

He'd phone Jack when he got to New Zealand and discuss it with him. Maybe he would appreciate the thought behind the action less emotionally than his mother.

40

___

JULIA

Julia cleared away the breakfast dishes before going through to her ensuite to shower. Carrick's news had not only been a shock, it angered her that he'd never thought throughout all these years to share this information.

What a stupid, stupid secret to have held onto – and for what? As she showered, she thought of her ex-husband Nick – he'd been the master of secrets and in the unravelling of all his secrets, part of Julia had also unravelled, and she'd never quite been able to wind back and control her emotions when it came to secrets.

Then there was Lizzie and all her long-held jealousies and perceived slights – such a tangle of emotional mayhem and she couldn't deal with any of it – she was sick and tired of dramas – especially other peoples.

Everyone has secrets, small or large, silly or outrageous, necessary or evil. She told herself as she let the water cascade down her body.

Hadn't she kept secrets from Patrick as he had from her? Her job for one. She'd not been happy in her job for a long time, yet had she confided in Patrick? No, she hadn't. Had she confided her feelings about Australia, that she didn't belong, felt no connection? No, she'd shared none of these feelings with the one person she should have.

And then there was her own special secret which seldom saw the light of day. She didn't wish to remove that black pearl from its hiding place and see reflected, the biggest secret she'd kept from everyone.

There was a lot to process and right now she didn't have the mental space to deal with any of it.

41

CARRICK

arrick glanced at Julia. They were sitting at traffic lights on the way to the airport. He wouldn't see her again until Christmas, only she was oblivious to this, believing he would be flying from New Zealand to Dublin to spend Christmas with his parents.

She'd been unusually quiet since they left the house. Perhaps, like him, she was all talked out. This morning had been exhausting, but at least now she knew. The last secret, well almost, he'd never share with her how much he loved her, longed for her. It would be the greatest betrayal of his brother and so once more he would surrender his chance to be with the only woman he'd ever fallen in love with – it was for the best – for everyone.

'Keep up your dance, won't you? You're a natural and it's a wonderful therapy.' He watched as she glanced across at him before returning her eyes to the road and accelerating as the lights turned green.

'I have no intention of giving it up.' Her tone was flat, and Carrick realised she was not ready to forgive him.

'I should have told you about the apartment, Julia. I understand I've disappointed you and for that I'm sorry.' He could see from the set of her mouth there was nothing more he could say to ease the situation between them.

When they entered the airport, Julia took the lane for drop-off. It was now abundantly clear there would be no lingering goodbyes. He felt wretched, furious with himself that he'd never thought to tell her about the apartment a long time ago. He'd been reckless, holding back something as important as this, but there was little he could do about it now.

As he collected his bag from the boot of Julia's car, she got out of the driver's seat, leaning her arms on the roof of the car, she had sunglasses on so he couldn't read any messages from her eyes as she called across to him.

'Safe journey Carrick. I hope you find some great investment opportunities in New Zealand.' He thought she was going to say something more. Instead, she climbed back behind the wheel and drove away.

Carrick settled himself into his business class seat. It wasn't a long flight, but he still felt like sleeping. The way things had ended with Julia had left him emotionally drained.

He wondered how she would process all the information they'd talked about. It may not be easy for her to understand everything that happened with Katie. If she hadn't discovered the photographs it was unlikely, he would ever have told her. To do so would have felt like a betrayal both to Katie and to his brother, and the matter of her aunt's apartment had been the nail in the coffin.

He didn't regret telling her; she had a right to know, and he fervently hoped, given time, she would accept his reasons for not divulging that he'd been the buyer.

42

JULIA

As Julia drove away from the airport tears streamed down her cheeks. It was silly. Stupid, stupid tears, unnecessary tears, but whilst she inwardly chastised herself the tears continued to flow.

She kept telling herself it was the anger, the feelings of betrayal by Patrick and now Carrick. How could both brothers keep such big secrets from her? Unnecessary secrets, but secrets all the same, and that's what she couldn't accept.

By the time she drove through the gates to her home she'd composed herself, taking in the view of house nestling itself into the landscape, still marvelling at how beautiful it was. Some lucky family would walk in her garden and sit on her terrace admiring her view.

She opened the garage door with the remote, parking the car and sitting there for a moment as a feeling of loneliness wrapped her in its chill embrace. Christmas was not far away, and what would she be doing? Christmas with Nancy here at the house, no Jack and Kat and no Carrick. There were worse things. "Really?" she said aloud, her voice breaking the car's silence. She stifled a sob. What could be worse than no family at Christmas?

The following morning, as Julia sat in Nancy's kitchen with a cup of tea, Nancy received a phone call from the real estate agent. She came back into the kitchen, flustered and out of breath.

'What's up?' Julia asked, taking a sip of her tea and a nibble from the freshly baked shortbread that Nancy had piled on a plate.

'That was the agent. Oh, Julia, what should I be doing, they've received an offer prior to auction, he's coming round at lunchtime to present it. Would you be kind enough to be here with me?'

'Did he say if it was an excellent offer?' She knew the agent wouldn't reveal the price.

'No. He just said it was an offer he needed to present and that I ought to consider it.'

'That's agent "speak" - meaning "an excellent offer". Do you want to go to auction?'

'Not particularly. A friend of mine auctioned her house a few months back, and she found the auction night so stressful, she almost withdrew her property before it went under the hammer. It has influenced the way I feel about the whole auction business. Perhaps I should have gone with a fixed price, if that's what they call it?'

'I'm assuming the agent talked you into an auction. They make a lot of money from the process, but you also have the opportunity of having several interested buyers in the room at one time. If a bidding war starts, then chances are you will achieve a much higher price, but that's not always the case. Anyway, let's not panic. We'll wait until he comes by at lunch time. Call me and I'll come straight over.'

'Haven't you got a dance lesson today, I thought you said you had?'

'I do, but not until 3:00 p.m. so plenty of time. I love this shortbread as you well know - that whole plate will disappear if you don't take it away.' She smiled at Nancy, but Nancy was a million miles away, Julia assumed, thinking of all the possibilities.

The reality of selling was an emotional roller coaster, but Julia offered support as much as she could. It was scary at Nancy's age, not just the sale of her home, but moving to another country. There was so much to organise and change, even if it excited you - the journey to new beginnings was not always smooth sailing.

THE PRE-AUCTION OFFER was exceptionally good, but Julia urged Nancy to consider sleeping on it before responding to the agent.

Later in the afternoon when Julia walked into the dance studio, both Carolina and Serghei were there to greet her.

'Carolina is going to instruct today, Julia. I want to work with you on Swing and the Quick-Step. It will be easier if Carolina can watch and instruct. You okay with that?'

'Sure.' She dropped her bag in the corner and changed shoes. 'What music have you chosen?'

'Two fresh pieces. *In the Mood* and *Bright side of the Road*. This session will exhaust you.' He looked across at Julia and laughed.

'Well, I'm game, let's do it,' sounding more confident than she felt inside.

By the end of the first set of Swing moves, Julia was panting. She went to the water cooler, gulping down one cup before pouring herself another. She thought with all the dance lessons she'd been having she would have not tired so easily. Now she had the Quick-Step to tackle which was much faster.

'We'll take it slowly, just listen to the music and allow your body to relax into the rhythm.'

By the time she climbed into her car to go home, her calf muscles were screaming and a soak in the spa was all she could think of as she drove back to the mountain. Despite her aching body, she'd enjoyed the challenge. This was something Serghei loved to do with her. He made her work hard and each session she not only became more skilled; she relaxed more, letting go of her worries one step at a time.

She found the process so empowering. She would miss Serghei when she left, but that wouldn't be for some time, so she pushed that thought from her mind as she drove through the gates to her home.

Julia had just enough time for a soak in the spa before Nancy arrived to talk through her options. As she soaked, her muscles finally releasing the tension they'd been holding onto for several hours, she acknowledged how lonely she was without Carrick, regretting they'd parted on such tense terms. It had only been days, but it felt more like weeks, the house feeling empty without him. When Nancy moved away it would be even worse so Julia hoped matters wouldn't progress too quickly.

She'd never been lonely after her marriage broke up. Even with no romantic interests and Jack at boarding school during the week, her job had been busy and pressured, but one she loved and never once had she felt lonely.

She'd known what being alone was like and the feelings that went with that emotion, but it wasn't the same as being lonely and in need of company. But perhaps her loneliness now was due to the absence of one person and one person only. She shut the thought down as fast as it had materialised.

Glancing at her watch, she pulled herself out of the spa and rinsed quickly under the out-door shower before drying herself down and heading inside to change.

Sale and Purchase Agreements were not Julia's area of legal expertise, but she would look over the offer carefully. She wished Carrick were here. His knowledge was so much greater. By the time she'd read every line and explained the process to Nancy, they needed a drink.

'Would you like a wine Nancy, before we phone the agent?'

'Absolutely, thought you'd never ask. This is both exciting and stressful. Do you still believe I'm doing the right thing?'

'You mean moving to New Zealand or accepting this offer?'

'Both.' Nancy took the glass of wine from Julia and sat back in her chair, releasing a heavy sigh, stretching her legs out in front of her and kicking off her shoes in one movement.

'Absolutely I do. This is an amazing offer and I think moving out to share a home with your sister is going to be marvellous for the two of you, I really do Nancy.'

'I think I will wait until morning before responding, Julia. I have 48 hours, don't I to respond?'

'Yes. You do. I think that's sensible. If it will help, phone your sister before it gets too late in New Zealand and talk it through with her?'

'No need for that. Ainsley's a darling but she's always been a bit of a flibbertigibbety sort of girl with no head for numbers, she'll only confuse matters.'

Nancy's pronouncement was so matter-of-fact Julia couldn't help but laugh. 'Are you going to be the sensible one then?'

'Yes, that will be my job. I don't mind. I'm used to it with Ainsley. She's got a heart of gold, would do anything for anyone, but not so good with making big decisions. We make a great team when we combine our strengths.' She swirled the wine around inside her glass before looking across at Julia.

'When you sell Julia, will it be by auction or fixed price, have you thought about that yet?'

'No. I haven't, but I guess I should start thinking about a sales strategy. I just want to get through Christmas. I'm glad I'll have you here with me.' She raised her wineglass to Nancy in salute.

'Changing the subject completely. When I got back from dance today, a courier had left something at the door. It was an extra-large Christmas card – from Lizzie.'

'Oh, your friend who has been so difficult?'

'That's the one.'

'Julia, when I met Lizzie, you know when she was out for the funeral – well I couldn't put the two of you together as friends. You're not alike. I hope I don't sound harsh or offend you, but she seemed to me to be a spiky little woman.'

'Well, she never used to be, but sadly that's what she's become. It's a relief to know she's okay - sort of. I won't bore you with the details, but I'm pleased she's made contact.'

'That's good then. In this life, a good friend is not a majestic mountain peak or the fireworks on Guy Faulks night. They're not a fine wine or an aged cheese. A friend is fresh air and clean water. A friend is all the things we don't realise we need or love until they're gone.'

'That's very profound, Nancy. I like that.' Her sage words helped Julia understand and accept the place where Lizzie had landed and where she needed to stay until she'd healed.

43

CARRICK

Carrick had been busy checking his properties in Auckland before driving down to Wellington, stopping en route to view the apiary. He'd not had time to dwell on the situation with Julia, steadfastly refusing to let it distract him from his work.

Later that evening, sitting out on the balcony of the apartment, the apartment that had caused so much upset, he thought about phoning Jack and Kat in Geneva, checking his watch to ensure it wasn't too early for them. He dialled the number.

'Hey Carrick, how is my favourite uncle?' Kat sounded happy to hear from him.

'Tired, but I'm fine Kat. How are you?'

'Like you, exhausted. Anyway, what's happening? And where are you? Australia or New Zealand?'

'I'm in New Zealand, Wellington actually. I was hoping to have a chat with yourself and Jack about Christmas, is Jack around?'

'Sure, I'll put the phone on speaker.' Carrick could hear her calling out to Jack to come into the kitchen.

'I'm here Carrick, everything still good for Christmas? Mum hasn't guessed, has she?'

'No, nothing like that,' he hesitated, unsure how to proceed. 'It's just something happened when I was with her in Melbourne and I'm not at all sure I should join you for Christmas. I'm not Julia's favourite person right now.' He laughed self-consciously, knowing full well it would upset them hearing his words.

'Why, what's happened, is Mum alright?'

'Yes, she's fine. She's much better than when you last saw her. Going to dance classes has been an amazing therapy. But I must confess I'm the one that's caused the problem, and I may as well tell you both before she does.' He took a deep breath and ploughed on.

'So,' Kat said, have I got this straightened in my Swedish head. You bought Julia's aunt's apartment so it could stay in the family, but you didn't tell her.'

'Yes, that's the sum of it Kat. Julia feels I've betrayed her - kept a secret that should never have been kept, and she's right. I should have told her a long time ago.'

'In Sweden we have a saying - *Kommer tid, kommer råd* which translated, goes something like this - comes time, comes counsel. For some problems, if there is no good solution at the moment, then given enough time, probably there will somehow be solutions coming up.'

Before Carrick responded, Jack interrupted, 'Carrick, can I ask something? Did you keep this from Mum because of Patrick?'

Jack was so perceptive and there was no hiding the truth because that was the reason he'd kept it to himself.

'Yes. I didn't think Paddy would have handled my purchasing the apartment very well back then. But it doesn't excuse me not telling Julia in the intervening years. It was stupid of me and now I've hurt her a great deal. You know how she is about secrets.' He let this statement sit between them, unsure of how Jack would react.

'I do. But Mum needs to get over this, she can't keep letting the past influence the now and you absolutely must spend Christmas with us - I insist. Kat and I will sort this out.'

'God! Don't go saying that you've spoken with me Jack, she'll feel even more betrayed, she's very raw right now. I'm not sure I should tell you this, but it might help you understand why it may seem like she's overreacting.'

Carrick told Kat and Jack briefly the story of Katie. Somehow telling it for a second time so soon after the revelation to Julia felt much easier, and he hoped Jack wouldn't judge Patrick harshly as he thought Julia would be doing.

'Wow. That must have come as an enormous shock to her Carrick. She didn't believe there were any secrets between herself and Patrick. I can imagine she's feeling pretty hurt right now. Even though it was a long time ago, it's not something you should keep a secret.'

'I know, but Paddy must have had his reasons. It was difficult for him. I know he felt very guilty about Katie's suicide. We both did. Enough said. Look, I'll leave it with the two of you to guide me as to Christmas. I won't come if it's going to be awkward. I care too much for Julia to make her feel uncomfortable.'

'She'll be fine. Leave it with us. We want you there, so you're coming,' Jack laughed.

They said their goodbyes, leaving Carrick less worried than he had been when he'd left Melbourne.

44

JULIA

Even the mountain wasn't cool this evening as Julia tossed and turned, unable to get comfortable. She rose and took a cold shower before returning to bed still damp, lying on the sheet with the cover thrown back seeking relief from the sticky, unpleasant closeness of the night.

As she lay, her mind drifting – first, Nancy's accepting of the offer and finding she needed to be out the week before Christmas, which was only a fortnight away, and thoughts of Carrick.

She'd not heard from him since he left Melbourne. Carrick had bought the apartment believing it was what she would want, only he'd just not bothered to tell her. And then there was the story of Katie and how that made her feel. Patrick had kept something from her that had affected his and Carrick's lives. Once more she was back in the past, the victim of secrets and betrayal.

She naively believed the therapy she'd undergone years prior meant she could let go of the past, but she found herself back there again revisiting that rather old and worn chestnut.

She hated these feelings - they were irrational and often unpredictable taking her on a journey back to a time and place she'd tried so hard to forget.

269

The sound of her mobile ringing startled her. Sitting up in bed, she reached across and grabbed the phone from her bedside cabinet. It was Jack, unusual for him to phone so late she thought.

'Hi Mum, sorry it's probably late for you, but we thought we would call when Kat and I are both able to chat. How are you?'

'I'm okay. How are you two doing, how's work and your project?'

'Work is work, busy trying to meet unrealistic deadlines, but that's the nature of the beast.' Julia thought Jack sounded jaded but didn't think he would appreciate her saying so.

'Julia how is your dance coming along. I'm interested to hear how you are doing with the dance?' Kat asked.

'I love it, Kat. I really do, it's the one bright light in my life - keeps me sane. I told you Nancy is leaving, didn't I? Well, she's accepted an offer on her place and needs to be out the week before Christmas.'

'Wow, that was quick,' Jack responded. 'Is she going to stay with you over Christmas?'

'Yes. Which will be lovely for me, but I shall really miss her when she's gone. Which leads me to something I should have mentioned to you weeks ago – if I'm honest, I've been avoiding telling you because I feared you would think I'm being selfish. But I've given this a great deal of thought and - well, I'm going to sell up. I don't want to be here alone. The place is too big for me and everywhere I turn I see Patrick and that anchors me to what I've lost instead of being able to move forward.' She trailed off, unsure how Jack and Kat would react.

'That's a big decision Mum. Have you talked about it with Carrick?'

'Yes, he knows. He understands. Although he's probably wondering why he should even care. We had words before he left for New Zealand. It's been a difficult time.'

'Words about what?' Kat asked

'You remember when my aunt Grace died, she left me her apartment in Wellington, which I'd wanted to hold on to, but couldn't afford to. The person who bought it was Carrick. He said nothing at the time because he believed Patrick would have reacted badly, and I accept that is probably true, but he never told me in the intervening years that he owned it. He fessed up before he left for New Zealand.'

'Why would he buy the apartment Julia, do you think?' Kat asked.

'To keep it in the family and it was, is, a lovely gesture so I ought to be grateful instead I feel angry that he never told me.'

'I know you have a thing about secrets, but Carrick isn't your past. You can't keep revisiting what went before.'

Julia, startled by Jack's response, thought he would be more in tune with how she felt.

'There was other stuff which I won't bother you with, but I feel that both brothers have kept things from me,' she said defensively. 'Stuff that should have been out in the open.'

'Is it important stuff? Really, in the big scheme of things?'

'It is to me Jack,' she sighed, realising she was sounding like a petulant child.

'I haven't handled this very well, have I? Don't answer. I can't keep blaming everything on grief, it's just me, my hang-ups.' She wanted them to know she wasn't blind to her own weaknesses.

'Julia - Carrick adores you, he wouldn't willingly do anything to hurt or upset you. He's the kindest person I know, well apart from my husband. We have a saying in Sweden – the longest journey is the journey inward. Maybe you need to take a rest from the journey and accept the present moment is significant, not as the bridge between past and future, but because the contents of the moment can fill that void – that place of emptiness.'

'Gosh, that's very profound Kat,' Julia could hear the tremble in her voice, afraid she would break-down and cry.

'Let it go Mum. Let it all go. Kat's right, give yourself permission to live. Patrick's sudden death shouldn't be in vain. We all have to learn to live in the now, we can never know what's around the corner. Don't deny yourself happiness all because you're holding onto crap from the past.'

'When did you become so grown-up Jack, and you too Kat? What you've said makes sense, I need to let go. I have to let go or I'll drown in memories which are not the sort I wish to hold to my heart and cherish.'

'Call Carrick Mum, he's been there for you, don't push him away. He's grieving too, remember – we all are.'

'Okay my wise children. I will call him. I will put it right between us.' She hesitated a moment before asking, 'neither of you have said what you think about me selling?'

'If it's what you want, Julia, I think you should. I know you don't enjoy living in Australia, I've always known that, even though you have never said those words to me, I've known. Now it's time for you to make your own way, your own decisions, isn't that right, Jack?'

Laughing, he said, 'I've learned never to disagree with my wife. You need to do what's best for you, for your future. If staying in the house and living in Australia is not what you want, then do something about it, we'll support whatever decision you make.'

'Thank you. You don't understand what a relief it is to hear you say those words. And whilst we are on the subject, would you like all of Patrick's music gear and instruments?'

'Absolutely. I was going to ask you ages ago about that. But thought it might be too soon for you to make a decision. But we'd love all of it, wouldn't we, Kat?'

'Yes, like the apartment, it can stay in the family.'

'Great, that's good to hear. I better let you go. It's late now and I need to get some sleep, but thanks for the call and the words of wisdom. I love you both.'

'Mum, just before you go, there is something we were keeping as a surprise, but we've talked about it and think you should know. We are coming out for Christmas and Carrick is also coming.'

'Oh, my God,' she squealed, 'that is the best news ever, but I thought Carrick was going back to Baltimore?'

'That was a little white lie we've been keeping from you. Forgive us, but it was to be a big surprise – but Kat thought maybe you would like to know ahead of time so you can plan and also appreciate you won't be alone this year.'

'You are right Kat, now I know I can enjoy the build-up and excitement and plan the food, presents – oooh this is going to be a great Christmas.'

45

CARRICK

Carrick had heard nothing further from Jack and Kat since his call to them and no phone calls or emails from Julia, but he decided he wouldn't chase her nor would he make any plans for Christmas that involved flying back to Ireland to be with his parents. They weren't expecting him, so it was easier to stay where he was and if that meant a lonely Christmas in the apartment then so be it.

He was standing on the balcony enjoying his first coffee of the day, his gaze roaming over Lambton Harbour and Oriental Bay.

Despite how Julia felt, he had no regrets about buying this apartment. It had proved over the years to be a very lucrative investment and he was lucky that he'd been able to secure two weeks for his own personal use.

A truck rumbled by on the street below, and the noise of it almost drowned out the ringing of his phone. He only just answered before it rang off.

'Carrick it's me. How are you?'

The sound of her voice sent his fragile heart into over-drive, and he grinned from ear to ear. Even if she hadn't forgiven him, she was phoning, and that was a start.

'I'm fine, Julia. It's so lovely to hear from you, how are you? I've just realised, it's barely dawn in Melbourne, there's nothing wrong is there?' Suddenly wondering if she was phoning with bad news.

'I'm foolish, is how I am Carrick. I'm foolish to have pushed you away and overacted. I'm sorry.'

'No need to apologise, but I'm so glad you've called. I really am.' He glimpsed himself in the ornate French mirror that hung on the lounge wall and realised he was still grinning like some silly schoolboy.

'I wondered how busy you were?'

'What like now you mean?'

'No, over the next few days, I was thinking of making a lightening trip out, just three or four days. I can't spare anymore time because Nancy has sold her place, and she must be out the week before Christmas, but I could spare a few days. I thought it would be nice to see Grace's apartment, but only if it won't interfere with your work?'

'Even if it did, which it doesn't, I hasten to add, that would be wonderful. I'll book you a flight, how soon can you leave?'

'Today, later today or is that too impulsive and a little crazy, since I know you are coming back for Christmas. I'm afraid Kat and Jack spilled the beans.' She was laughing, and he had a sudden image of her standing in the kitchen leaning on the counter, her face breaking into that beautiful smile she had and her emerald eyes sparkling with mischief.

'It's perfect. I'll hang up and book flights, expect the eTickets to come through shortly. I'll see you soon, Julia, bye for now.' He didn't know whether to laugh with excitement or cry with relief. The impasse was over, she'd forgiven him, all would be well.

IT WAS early evening as he stood in the arrivals lounge at Wellington airport, hardly able to contain his boyish excitement that any minute now she'd walk through the doors - head held high, scanning the crowd - elegant and beautiful as always and as he was thinking these thoughts, there she was standing in front of him, her smile so warm and beautiful the whole airport lounge would sparkle with her radiance.

He hugged her to him and could smell her perfume and feel the heat of her body through the linen dress she was wearing. He carried her bag to the car, and they drove back into town to the apartment.

46

NEW ZEALAND

Julia had seldom been this impulsive in her life, smiling as she packed her bag, maybe Patrick's impulsiveness was rubbing off on her. It would only be three days, but it would be an exciting three days.

As her flight touched down in Wellington and she made her way through to arrivals, she saw Carrick standing waiting for her. He wasn't looking her way, and she studied him before he spotted her.

He looked tanned and rested, dressed in jeans and a short-sleeved shirt, then turning towards her as though he sensed someone watching him. His faced creased into a beautiful smile and her treacherous heart skipped a beat in a way it had no right to do.

He took her bag, but not before he'd hugged her close to him and kissed the top of her head before he abruptly pulled away, leading her outside to the short-stay parking area.

The drive to the apartment took just twenty minutes and when she stepped inside and gazed about, everything appeared as it had in her mind's eye all those years prior except for the furniture.

She'd shipped all the big, beautiful pieces that Grace had left her to London, and they now occupied pride of place in her Melbourne home. The apartment was furnished in keeping for a corporate lease, sophisticated, but not ostentatious.

'It looks amazing Carrick, it's in such incredible condition. You must have re-painted...' she trailed off, distracted by the view, unable to stop herself walking out onto the balcony drawn by the sight of the water.

Carrick joined her, and she turned to him, putting her hand on his arm, feeling the warmth of his bare skin against her palm. He looked into her eyes, his smile radiant, his eyes sparkling with joy.

'It's beautiful isn't it, this view? It's what I loved about the place and knew it was the right thing to do to buy it. Even if you never wanted to come back. This is a million-dollar view and if I'd been buying something similar in London – well, we both know I wouldn't have been able to afford it.'

'So, it's been a great investment property for you then?' She said teasingly.

'Absolutely, but that's not the only reason, in fact it was never the first consideration. It was always about you. About protecting something which I believed may be precious to you. If not immediately then – later when you'd had time to come to terms with everything.'

'What you did Carrick was so caring and, like I said on the phone, I was very foolish in the way I reacted.'

'And like I said, no need to apologise. Do you feel like food? I have some anti-pasta in the fridge - or I can order in if you want something more substantial?'

'No, anti-pasta would be perfect. I'll unpack first though and then maybe a drink?' She walked through to the spare bedroom where a king-size bed occupied the space. It was masculine but tasteful, with a leather headboard. The bed linen was high quality, in fact everything about the apartment was high quality and she realised looking around that Carrick must have spent quite a lot of money ensuring the interior was in immaculate condition.

Although it was summer Julia knew Wellington could be cold and very windy, so she was delighted her first night back was warm and still.

She joined Carrick on the balcony as he opened a bottle of champagne, lifting his glass to her in a toast. 'May this lightening trip back to your native country be everything you wish it to be.' He grinned at her as they clinked glasses.

'How about you enjoy the view and put your feet up and I'll bring out the anti-pasta, I think it's warm enough to eat on the balcony.'

She'd missed him fussing over her and settled herself at the table, eyes roving over the houses climbing the hillsides around the harbour, their lights twinkling upon the water.

Later, as they sat in the lounge, the night air too chilly to remain on the balcony, Carrick asked what Julia wished to do the following day.

'Christmas shopping. I confess I've done nothing. And now I know who is coming for Christmas, I need to get my skates on.'

'Need help? I'm free, happy to carry your bags.'

'Absolutely, I'd love you to help me. How about I take you somewhere nice for breakfast and we make an early start?'

'Sounds like a plan. I had wondered, if you're not too tired tomorrow after shopping, would you like to go dancing? There's a club in town that runs regular dance nights. It's open tomorrow night. We could have supper here and then head out, only if you feel up to it?'

'Fab. I'd love that.' She smiled at him. 'I might head off to bed now. I'm suddenly feeling worn out. Thanks for a lovely evening Carrick, see you in the morning.'

She hadn't realised how exhausted she felt. Undressing and sliding beneath the sheets, she could no longer keep her eyes open, sleep quickly overtaking her.

47

EVENING BEGINS

When they arrived back at the apartment, it was early afternoon and Julia kicked off her shoes and flopped down on the couch.

'I'm all shopped out, but I'm so glad we did that. I don't have to think about it when I get back. Thanks for being my shopping assistant today. You have great taste. I wouldn't have thought of half the things you did.'

'Nonsense, you're excellent at buying the right gift, I just offered alternatives.'

'Regardless, I'm grateful. What time do we need to be out tonight? I might have a little Nanna nap so I can be ready to boogie tonight.'

'I don't think it opens until 8:30 p.m. or something like that, so we don't have to rush. You go off and have a rest and I'll check my emails.'

Later, Julia busied herself making a light supper of grilled salmon and a fresh salad. It was another beautiful evening, warm enough to dine on the balcony. Carrick had disappeared out somewhere while she was still sleeping, so she showered before he returned.

When Carrick arrived back hot and sweating, Julia realised he'd been for a run, she poured him a beer and waited until he'd had a shower before grilling the salmon.

'I've already showered, but haven't changed yet, I'm not going out in my trainers.' She laughed as he joined her in the kitchen. 'Thought I'd wait until we'd eaten in case I spill something over myself.'

'This looks delicious,' Carrick remarked as she carried their plates outside to the balcony. 'I'll fetch the salad. May I pour you a wine?'

'Yes please. Half a glass will do, thanks Carrick.'

They settled down to their meal, eating in silence as they enjoyed the food, each caught up in their own private thoughts.

When Julia forked the last of her salmon into her mouth, she reached for her glass and took a sip of wine and glanced across at Carrick. 'Tell me about the bee business, did you get to see the apiary and talk to the owners?'

'Yes, I spent a night there. I'm going to invest. It's an exciting opportunity and so different for me. It won't happen for a while yet - they have to provide a full business plan to my accountant, and we'll take it from there.'

'That's great. I'm glad it's worked out. Anything else you've been looking at, I thought you were checking out some farm-land?'

'Yes. I've done that. Putting it on hold for the time being. Something else has caught my eye. It's something I'm just mulling over.' He avoided Julia's gaze, instead swirling the last of his beer in the glass before drinking it down in one gulp.

'What are you mulling over?'

'I'm thinking of buying a property in Russell as a residence, so I can spend more time out here, a lot more time.'

'Oh. What, you'd no longer be in London?'

'I'd have two properties. My Bloomsbury apartment and something out here, if not this one, then another. I sold my Lymington property before I left, I think I mentioned that to you before?'

'Yes you did, but I didn't understand you were thinking of buying something more permanent out here.' Julia took another sip of her wine, intrigued by Carrick's decision.

'Being in New Zealand again, it's kind of consolidated my thoughts. I love it here. The gentler pace of life, the people. It's a kinder space to work and live. I love London, but I don't wish to spend twelve months of the year there.'

'I think that's a great idea. You can divide your time between both countries and as you said you can retire now at an unseemly young age I might add, and you don't have to be on the move all the time.'

'That's the plan, I'll have to see how it pans out.'

'Goodness look at the time.' Julia announced. 'I better change.'

48
———

DANCING

Julia slipped into the dress she'd bought whilst out shopping with Lizzie in London. Lizzie had spotted the dress in the shop window and insisted Julia try it on. Thinking of Lizzie now saddened her mood. It still felt like she was grieving for two people she loved letting her thoughts drift back to the letter Lizzie had written tucked inside the very large and glamorous Christmas card.

Dear Julia

I bought the biggest card I could find. It doesn't make up for what has happened between us, but I wanted the size to reflect how much you mean to me – how much our friendship means.

I have behaved disgracefully. I ask for your forgiveness and your patience. I have booked myself into a clinic – probably could buy a small island for the fees they're charging, but I don't care. I need specialist treatment. I've been denying this for so long. I convinced myself I didn't need help of any kind. That others caused my problems and my unhappiness. I know better now.

I won't explain how I got to this point – that can wait for another time. I merely wanted you to know, I'm getting the help I need and I'm asking that you don't contact me. My therapist's advice is that I opt out for a while until I'm in a better, happier place emotionally and free of my demons... if one can ever be free of one's demons, but I must try.

Please understand I never intended to hurt you or anyone else, but I know I have and for that I am deeply sorry.

I'll be back in touch when the time is right. In the meantime, have a wonderful Christmas Julia and know that I love you.

Lizzie XX

SHE LOOKED at the dress hanging on the back of the bedroom door. That day they'd been out in London, ostensibly to pick up a few things from Waitrose, but en route Lizzie had darted down a side street to a tiny boutique tucked in between two large shop fronts.

'Oh, look at that dress, it's divine. You should try it on Julia, it would suit you.'

Julia had turned away, disinterested in trying on anything. *What would be the point, where would I ever be going now to warrant spending money on a beautiful dress?* But Lizzie had nagged and pestered until Julia relented. Lizzie had been right to nag.

The dress did suit her. It was stunning - a dusky pink embroidered Bardot A-Line mid-length dress that sat slightly off her shoulders and emphasised her height and slimness.

'See I knew it would suit you, it needs someone tall to pull it off, it's perfect, buy it.' Julia could hear Lizzie's voice as though she were standing in the room looking at Julia's reflection in the full-length mirror. She swiped at a lone tear, aware that she'd been holding back so much emotion, thoughts of their ugly argument in Spain still so clear and raw and now the letter. Lizzie had been at her best that day – a day when she wasn't pre-occupied with imagined slights and petty jealousies.

Reaching her arms behind her head, Julia fastened the necklace

Patrick had given her on the occasion of their first wedding anniversary. A single diamond in an exquisite setting and matching diamond stud earrings.

Pushing her feet into heels, she wondered how she'd last the night wearing them. It wasn't as though they were six-inch stilettos, but she'd not worn heels since she resigned from her job.

If you didn't think you could manage Julia, why did you pack the shoes and why pack the dress if you hadn't intended going out somewhere special so you could wear it. She was inwardly chastising herself and cursing as she tried to fasten the tiny pearl button that sat above the zipper, she'd have to get Carrick to do it.

'You look lovely, beautiful dress.' Carrick was standing in the lounge as she walked out of the bedroom, Julia felt herself blush under his penetrating gaze.

'Would you mind securing the button at the top of the zipper, I can't manage it?' She turned her back to him and immediately felt the warmth of his hands against her bare neck, making her skin tingle.

'All done, you won't come adrift.'

'Thank you,' she turned back to face him, but he'd turned away and walked to the balcony door, pulling it to and locking it.

'If you're ready I'll order an Uber, it's a bit too far to walk?' He turned back to face her, pulling his phone from his jacket pocket.

'Yes, I'm ready, thanks for cleaning up. I'm looking forward to his club. Do you know what sort of dance music they play?'

'Uber will be here in three minutes, just enough time to get downstairs. And no, I'm not sure what they play. Their website showed a mix of jazz, modern, Latin American.'

'Sounds great, let's go then.'

Carrick held the door open for her and soon they were in the Uber, ready for a night out.

'What will you have to drink Julia?' Carrick was at the bar about to order, but Julia was still gazing around. The club was full of people, surprising she thought for a weeknight, it was obviously a popular place.

'I'll have fizzy water to start, thanks Carrick. Should I grab us a table while you get the drinks?'

'Good idea.'

Julia found a table in the corner slightly separated from others, but with an excellent view of the dance floor.

'Here you go, one fizzy water for the beautiful lady,' Carrick smiled as he handed her the drink and sat down with his own beer. 'It's groovy this place, isn't it? I was worried it might be seedy, but it's not at all, much more sophisticated than I imagined. You can never tell from the websites. They often take very moody, sexy photos which can be misleading.'

'It's great, I'm surprised how many people are here for a week-night.' Julia responded, taking a sip of her fizzy water.

'I think they only do the dance stuff on certain nights, it's not every night, hence the crowd I guess.' As they sat people watching, the music started up and immediately couples walked to the dance floor in readiness.

Carrick and Julia looked on as couples moved around the dance floor in time to the Latin American music. Some were professional while others were those who just loved to dance, and steps or timing didn't matter. When the music changed to a Marvin Gaye number *What's Going On*. Carrick stood reaching his hand out inviting Julia to dance.

'How's your waltz? Been practicing lately?' He grinned at her, taking her hand in his. As they moved gracefully around the floor other dancers moved aside and some abandoned the dance floor alto-gether and returned to their tables.

'You're good, excellent in fact.' Carrick beamed. Julia could see from the bright sparkle in his eyes he was in his element dancing. She'd seen the same look when he'd danced at Serghei's studio.

The Marvin Gaye song ended, followed by a quick-step tempo to Van Morrison's *Bright Side of the Road*. She knew this, having only practised it with Serghei weeks before and to this very song.

It wasn't until they were part way through their routine that Julia noticed the floor had emptied and couples sat watching as the two danced in perfect rhythm to a fast quick-step, Julia matching Carrick's perfect timing. She felt exhilarated – immersed in the music, the way she knew both Patrick and Jack immersed themselves as musicians, only she found that special place with dance.

As the song finished the small crowd clapped and cheered. Julia blushed, but Carrick seemed to be oblivious to the crowd - to the clapping, he was looking at Julia his eyes dancing and sparkling with mischief as the music switched to Latin once more.

Couples joined them on the floor for the Argentine Tango and as the slow seductive rhythm produced some outstanding dancing from younger couples, Julia whispered in Carrick's ear.

'Don't expect me to lift my leg too high, I'm way past risking that.'

He whispered back, 'Don't ask me to do the Travolta splits and you've got a deal,' pulling her closer to him as her body moved against his in time to the music. When the song ended couples returned to their tables and Julia and Carrick went up to the bar to order more drinks, before returning to their table.

'You dance so well, Julia. Wherever you end up living, please don't give up your journey with dance.'

'Like I've said before, I have no intention of doing so,' taking a sip of her fizzy water. 'I can't believe I've let dance slip out of my life for so many years, but now it's back, I won't be letting it go.'

As the evening was drawing to a close, a dance troupe took the floor and performed an outstanding dance routine to Donna Summer's song *On the Radio*. Carrick and Julia stood to applaud. 'They're professional,' Julia commented, looking across at Carrick.

'I would say so. The lead male moves beautifully.' Carrick took Julia's hand as he steered them through the milling crowd, pausing briefly at a table by the front door to pick up a card.

'What was that you took?' Julia asked as they emerged into the cool night air.

'The business card for that dance troupe. I'm interested to know who they are. I've sent a text for an Uber, so shouldn't be long. Are you cold?'

'Just a little, but I'll be fine.' Before Julia had time to protest further, Carrick had taken off his jacket and draped it around her shoulders.

When they arrived back at the apartment, Carrick excused himself to use the bathroom and Julia walked immediately to the couch, kicking her shoes off as she went. Her feet were aching and as she sat rubbing her soles her gaze drifted out across the city, the cloudless sky offering an unfettered view of the star-dusted heavens.

Julia was still lost in her own thoughts when Carrick walked back into the kitchen. 'I'm going to take a shower and go to bed Julia, see you in the morning.' He did not join her on the couch and chat about their evening - he'd shut down again, the way she'd witnessed him do before.

49

———

CARRICK

Carrick undressed quickly and stepped into the shower. He felt hot and uncomfortable and needed the coolness of water to wash away not only the stickiness of the night, but the emotions that had boiled up inside of him.

Stretched out in bed unable to sleep, he relived every moment of the night from when she'd stepped out of the bedroom in that stunning dress. He'd been unable to keep his eyes off her and fastening the top button had almost been his undoing.

The touch of her bare skin beneath his hands, the exposure of her upper back revealing smooth, olive skin without blemish and all he'd wanted to do was to bend and kiss her neck, her back and so much more.

Remembering the feel of her, the smell of her perfume, the way she'd moved in tightly against his body when they danced the Argentine Tango – so seductive.

Alone in bed, he admitted to himself, having her here in the apartment with him in such close proximity was nothing less than sweet agony. He'd never realised until now, not even when they were alone together in London, that Julia completed him as a man.

Business deals and travelling all over the world had been a necessary focus – he needed to prove he could be successful as a property developer, not only to himself, but to his parents. But a desperate need to shut down his desire for a woman he could never have had also driven him.

Was it possible that after all these years of suppressed feelings he would find the courage to explore the possibility that Julia could be in his life as more than his friend, his sister-in-law? Or was he holding out for a love that could never reach fruition? The guilt, the betrayal, because he felt sure that's how Julia would view his love, and how others would feel vindicated in sharing their opinions, and judgements about such a union.

Restless and unable to sleep, Carrick rose and quietly crept out to the kitchen where he poured himself a scotch.

50

JULIA

Julia sat looking out across the balcony to the night sky reflecting on the past 14 months since Patrick's death. So much had happened in the intervening period and she could tell herself it was the friendship, the connection to Patrick, to Rose and Brendan and yes, that was part of it, but she knew there was another part, a more important part – a longing she'd been denying for so many years it felt reckless to be examining it sitting in Carrick's apartment while he lay in his bed only metres away.

The dancing had been amazing. He was an excellent dance partner and until she'd started lessons with Serghei, she'd denied herself, not only the opportunity of dancing, but even thinking about it. She'd shut out the memories of dancing at university and how much joy she'd gained from those weekly classes – why? Why had she let Nick dominate her in such a way? And why, once she'd married Patrick, did she not take it up again?

Jack had been her sole focus and, apart from work, he was all that mattered to her until Patrick came into their lives and then she'd taken a back-seat to her son's and her husband's relationship and passion for music. Music had become the focus in their household.

The only focus. She'd never resented it – accepted from the beginning that music would always be Patrick's first love

This is crazy, all these feelings, all this longing. Do nothing you'll regret. Her words swirled around inside of her head as she lay back and tried to relax and free her mind of rogue thoughts. She drifted off to sleep, and it was the sound of liquid pouring into a glass that startled her awake.

Carrick was standing in the kitchen. From her position on the couch, she could see it was a scotch he'd poured himself. His chest was bare, but she could see he was wearing baggy pyjama bottoms.

A sudden image of sailing and swimming in Baltimore flashed before her eyes and she was back there that very first summer when she'd struggled to stop her eyes darting intermittently to look at Carrick, topless and tanned his shoulder muscles rippling in the sunlight as he loosened the ropes to the mainsail. Patrick had been at the other end of the boat out of sight and she remembered how wicked she'd felt gazing at his younger brother with interest.

'Sorry did I disturb you? I thought you'd gone to bed.'

'I meant to - must have dozed off, but I ought to take a shower and get some sleep.'

She moved from her position on the couch and joined him in the kitchen. Later she would recall it was the way he was looking at her, his beautiful chocolate eyes smouldering with unrequited longing, and that should have been the warning. It was the warning, but she was tired of obeying her head and for once had let her heart be the decision maker.

'Can you undo the pearl button on my dress?' She turned her back to him and waited. She felt his fingers unfasten the button and then the zip being pulled down to expose her back. She let the dress fall and silently stepped away, leaving it crumpled on the floor like a deflated meringue.

Once he kisses my neck, my resistance will crumble - just a few delicate touches of his warm lips and my hands will do his bidding. Now there is only one desire, one wish, and I know it's just a matter of time before it

happens. Lover come close. Run your hands up my bare arms. Let your lips cover my skin with kisses.

His breath was warm against her skin as the kisses started at the nape of her neck and moved down her back one vertebra at a time.

He rested his hands on her shoulders and turned her around to face him. Reaching out his hand and touching her cheek before letting it drift down to her throat, her chest, where palm outstretched, he rested it on her heart, before gently pulling her in close, tilting her chin up so he could look into her eyes before he bent to kiss her lips.

She opened her mouth and let his tongue explore. A soft moan escaped from somewhere deep inside of him.

Her hands caressed his back before straying to his firm buttocks. She felt him unclasp her bra and let her arms fall to her sides - where her bra joined the abandoned dress.

He dipped his head and kissed her breasts. She could feel his tongue tracing the outline of her areola and his lips pull her nipple inside his mouth. She let go and gave into the desire, the longing.

51

THE MORNING AFTER

When Julia awoke, she was alone in her own bed, looking across to the clock on the bedside table which told her it was past 9:00 a.m. She couldn't believe she'd slept so late.

She lay back, her thoughts a jumble of fragments from the previous evening. A wave of guilt trapped in her heart making her struggle for breath, she pulled herself up in bed catching site of her reflection in the bedroom's full-length mirror.

She got out of bed and examined her face close- up in the mirror, looking for the tell-tale signs of a cheat, an adulteress. But the face staring back at her was her own, her eyes did not reflect guilt, instead they appeared greener than usual, sparkling almost. How traitorous, she thought.

Pulling on her dressing gown, she padded through to the kitchen and filled the kettle. While she stood in a trance waiting for the water to boil, she wondered where Carrick was. There was no sound from his room. It would be easier if she didn't have to face him.

She'd have to leave and catch the first available flight back to Melbourne, but she remembered she was to meet Malcolm Braithwaite, her late aunt' solicitor, for lunch, they'd kept in touch after her aunt's affairs settled and over the years had become close friends. She could still meet him and then catch an early evening flight if she could get a seat.

It was another beautiful day, so she opened the sliding doors to the balcony. The city was alive with cars and the sound of voices carried up to the apartment as people made their way along the parade to work oblivious to what had happened last night in this apartment.

What had she done? Well, she knew what she'd done, asking Carrick to undo her dress.

It had been her fault. They'd not had sex, he'd pulled apart from her in the kitchen, running his fingers through his hair. The anguish of their intimate moment obvious in his face, gazing at her through guilty eyes. What would he think of her now? She'd been the initiator.

She flicked through the contacts on her phone and pressed Malcolm's number. They agreed to meet for lunch at 12:30 p.m. She finished her tea and opened up her laptop.

Quickly she logged in to the airline website and changed her flight to one leaving early evening. Then she showered, changed into a navy linen dress, and packed her bag. She'd catch an Uber from the restaurant to the airport and that way she'd avoid having to come back here.

She looked about the apartment, saddened that she'd sullied what had been a special time. Hesitating at the dining table, wondering if she should sit down and write a note to Carrick, but afraid he would return from wherever he was, she let that thought slip and let herself out of the apartment, catching the lift downstairs to wait for her Uber.

Upon arrival, she took the lift to Malcolm's floor and waited in reception. Minutes later Malcolm came bustling out, arms outstretched and a beaming smile.

'Julia. Oh, I can't tell you how good it is to see you. You look glorious as usual.'

Julia realised the last time she saw Malcolm was at Patrick's funeral when she'd been so distraught, she'd hardly been able to string two words together. Now, caught in the moment of joy that radiated from Malcolm, she laughed at his boyish enthusiasm.

'Your eyesight is failing you Malcolm, but it's so wonderful to see you too.' They hugged before Malcolm took Julia's hand and led her to the lifts.

'I've booked a table. Hope you've allowed plenty of time? We've got so much to catch up on.'

'I'm catching a flight back to Melbourne early evening, so I've got a few hours.'

Seated at their table in a very high-end restaurant, Malcolm shook out his table napkin, waiting until the waiter had poured their wine and moved away before he spoke.

'Now, let me see, bet you're staying at Grace's apartment? I shouldn't refer to it as Grace's any longer; old habits.'

'I am. But how did you know that?'

'Well, when you gave me instructions to sell, the market was flat, and the place sat empty for ages. Then out of nowhere I received an offer from an interested party, all very mysterious, but turned out to be legitimate. So, as you know, we sold the apartment but, given I'm such a very inquisitive chap, I couldn't help but do a bit of digging.'

Taking a sip from his wine, he looked across the table, waiting for a response.

'And you would have found that it was my brother-in-law that bought the apartment.'

'I didn't understand his need to keep it all so hush-hush, but I was not of a mind to question. I assumed he had his reasons. Anyway, I eventually got to meet your handsome brother-in-law.' He grinned and winked at Julia, enjoying the telling of this story.

'Oh, I didn't realise you two had met, how did that come about? I know you're dying to tell me Malcolm.' Julia responded, raising her eyebrows at him.

'Well, I know all the repairs and maintenance crew who handle that building and I heard that some upgrades were being done. So, I was in the area one day and thought I'd check in.'

'In the area, my arse - you were snooping.' Julia laughed, taking a sip of her wine as the waiter arrived at their table to take orders.

'Yes. You're right, I just couldn't help myself. Long story short, I met Carrick, and we discussed at length the upgrades he was planning, including the décor. He's got a brilliant eye I'll say that for him. He invited me back to look once they finished it and I thought he'd done a beautiful job, don't you agree?'

'I do. And yes, he has an expert eye. The apartment is beautiful. I only learnt recently that he was the buyer. He never told me. I won't bore you with the reasons, but it was a beautiful gesture on his part and I'm really thrilled he's preserved the last bit of family connection for me.'

Julia was aware of Malcolm watching her intently. It was making her feel uncomfortable. Finally, he spoke.

'It would have thrilled Grace to know you're staying there. Is Carrick with you?'

Julia could feel herself blush - she took a sip of her wine before answering. 'Yes, he's been out here for a while sorting out some investments. But like I said, I'm going back to Melbourne later today, I just wanted to slip over and see what the apartment was like after all these years.'

Their food had arrived and whilst Julia felt hungry having skipped breakfast, she pushed the food around her plate for several minutes before taking a forkful of the grilled chicken.

'I wanted to ask how you're doing? It's been over a year now. I've often wondered if you would stay in Australia because of the memories or whether you would sell because of the memories. How do you feel about those options?'

He really was very astute, Julia thought, despite his exaggerated gay affectations, which could easily mislead someone who didn't know Malcolm, to believe he was shallow.

'It's no longer about options, it's definite, Malcolm. I can't stay there. Well, more to the point, I don't want to stay there. So many memories and I've never felt like I belonged in Australia. Going back to London really confirmed that for me.'

'So, are you thinking of returning to London?' Julia noted the star-tled tone in his voice.

'No. That's in the past, a beautiful time in my life. Well, not all of it was beautiful, but you know what I mean. I am shocked at how much London has changed. I felt like I'd returned to London to take up with an old lover, only to find they'd moved on and what we once shared was no longer relevant or meaningful. It's silly really, but it was painful for me.'

'It's not silly. You were there a long time, and you met Patrick there. I wish I'd met him. How do you get on with Carrick, are the two brothers alike?'

It was ridiculous, Julia inwardly scolded herself, why was she feeling so embarrassed every time Malcolm mentioned Carrick. She was behaving like a silly schoolgirl but avoided eye contact when she answered.

'Carrick's a lovely man, they're both lovely men, but, in some ways, completely different from one another.' She quickly brought the conversation back to Patrick.

'When we moved to Australia his job occupied his every waking moment and come holiday time it was always Baltimore for his parents or Geneva to see Jack and Kat. He never appeared interested in visiting New Zealand.'

'I've never shared this with you before but years, well many years ago now, I was in a relationship with a musician. I naively thought it was the real thing.' He took another sip of wine before continuing, whilst signalling the waiter for another.

'There is a part of growing up that is joyous, and a part that subjects us to the greatest pain we can ever know.' He speared a prawn popping it into his mouth and Julia sensed talking about a past love was still difficult for him.

'I'm sorry. What happened?'

'Music was his first love - his only love, and I was secondary. I believe he loved me, but he would never have put me first, never. Back then I wanted to be the sole focus of someone's love, not in the back seat noticed only when they glanced in the rear-vision mirror. I was naïve. I also learned to understand and accept that love is like the burlesque fan dance – you are teased by the knowledge that for everything that is revealed, there is that which is mysteriously hidden.'

Julia felt the food she'd just swallowed catch in her throat. This was not a conversation she'd been expecting, but it resonated on so many levels - she couldn't pretend otherwise.

'Can I ask how you managed with Patrick? He was an extraordinary musician, and he must have been away a lot?'

He didn't need to say anymore, Julia knew exactly what he was getting at. Being in the company of Malcolm reminded her so much of the times she'd spent with her brother William, so it felt natural to open-up and share her feelings with someone she trusted.

'I won't deny sometimes I resented the time Patrick spent at rehearsals - at gigs, often coming home in the early hours of the morning. I was also aware he'd been a single man for a long time. He'd successfully avoided commitment and long- term relationships until I came along.' Julia pushed her plate away from her, having eaten little.

'Do you want dessert, cheeseboard, coffee? Sorry to interrupt, but I may as well grab the waiter's attention while I can.'

'Actually, a cheeseboard with coffee would be perfect, thank you Malcolm.'

'Right, where were we? I kind of figured it wouldn't have all been plain sailing.'

'No marriage is plain sailing. It's always about compromise, and there is usually one partner that finds they have to compromise more than the other. Patrick loved me passionately. He was loyal, but his greatest attribute was his dedication and love for Jack. They shared the most amazing relationship. It's been difficult for Jack dealing with his death.'

'I can only imagine, but he has a wife for support and that's worth so much. Who is there for you?'

'Jack, Kat, Carrick, Patrick's mum and dad and you. Once I would have said my best friend Lizzie, but we had a huge bust up. It's going to take time for the wounds to heal for both of us.'

'When did this happen -when you were in London?'

'Oh, I suspect it had been brewing for ages, only I was unaware. She was stirring the emotional pot when she came out for Patrick's funeral and then I stayed with her in Spain for a few weeks and, I don't know Malcolm,' Julia sighed, 'being in each other's company every day was enough for the cauldron of bitterness and resentment to boil over, who knows. It was ugly and painful.'

'My darling Julia, you deserve so much more than that. If Grace were still with us, she'd have given this Lizzie a piece of her mind.' He glanced away, but not before Julia saw the tears in his eyes and it reminded her once more of how much he'd loved her aunt. It was far more than a solicitor client relationship.

'You know your beautiful aunt treated me like a son. She was more of a mother to me than my own. There isn't a day goes by when I don't think of her and even now – occasionally I reach for the phone to dial her number before I remember.'

'I wish I'd got to know her, but in some-way I feel I know some-thing of the woman she was, especially after reading those diaries. The place I scattered her ashes, Chedworth, it's a beautiful spot. I feel she'd have approved of my choice.'

'Did Patrick go with you, to scatter her ashes I mean?'

'No, he couldn't spare the time. But Jack came with me. It was a special weekend that we spent in the Cotswolds.'

'She would be thrilled to know you visited the village that meant so much to her. I'm grateful that you made that happen Julia.'

'Tell me, are going to sell up, and if so, where are you planning to live?' He cut himself a slice of soft brie and picked a grape from the board. Placing the grape precariously on the slice of brie before sliding it into his mouth.

'I'm giving serious thought to coming home. Home to New Zealand. I never thought I'd hear myself say that, but time is a healer and, even though this time I've only been here five minutes, I feel comfortable. It's like slipping your feet into a comfy pair of old slippers. But I can't go getting ahead of myself. I have to sell my place and pack and all that horrible stuff that goes with a move.'

'I can take some leave and fly across to help you. You only have to ask Julia. I'm here for you.' He reached across the table and took her hand in his. 'Having you back here would make my life complete again. No pressure.'

He grinned, helping himself to more cheese. 'Are you planning on getting back into law out here?'

'No. That part of my life has ceased to be. And, at the risk of sounding vulgar, Patrick has left me very well off, which means I don't have to work again if I don't wish to.'

'Well, well, well, footloose and fancy free the lady is. I'm delighted to hear that. It gives you time to decide not only where you want to live, but what you want your life to look like there's a lot to consider and no need to rush, well, apart from selling up and getting out here quick smart.'

Julia laughed. 'You're not at all subtle Malcolm, but it's great to know I can come back, and you'll be here.'

'Absolutely, I'm not going anywhere. I just had a thought Julia, one of my more brilliant ones I might add. Do you want more coffee?'

'No, thank you. What's the brilliant idea.' It frequently threw Julia off centre the way Malcolm steered conversation switching from one subject to another in a millisecond.

'Oh, sorry, easily distracted me. Once you have moved out. Note I'm using the word "once" not "if", then you could stay at my holiday home for a while until you feel grounded. You know, take a brief rest and put your feet up, good idea - don't you think?'

'It's a great idea. I can't stay at Grace's apartment because Carrick will need to be letting it out.'

'I'm sure he would leave it vacant for you if you needed it. But being in the Bay of Islands would be more relaxing and peaceful. That's what you need. It's a lot to be coping with on your own, selling up, moving to a different country - you'll need some headspace and you loved it last time you were there with Jack. Regardless, the offer is there.'

'Thank you. That's very generous. I'll keep you posted with everything once I'm back in Melbourne.'

Julia drained the last of her coffee, checking her watch it was past 2:30 p.m. She kissed Malcolm goodbye, promising to keep him updated with her plans, before climbing into the Uber and heading to the airport.

It had been lovely spending time with him, but there were moments she'd felt overwhelmed by the flood of memories. Admitting that being married to a musician had not been all wine and roses was not what she'd expected herself to reveal and it had left her feeling uncomfortable that she'd been disloyal to Patrick.

It had been Malcolm's revelation about his past love and the pain which it still caused that had forced her to admit to something she'd barely acknowledged to herself. She now had to come to terms with Patrick's flaws. It wasn't as though she didn't know he had flaws it was more that she'd ignored them, choosing to focus on all Patrick's wonderful attributes.

She'd been denying for years the aspects of their marriage that were not perfect, making excuses for how she felt – tired, work stress, missing London, many creative justifications in defence of what had been an issue for her and one which she'd chosen to ignore. Now there was no need to ignore it. Now was the time to be honest with herself and those around her.

ONCE JULIA HAD CHECKED in and made her way through security, she pulled out her phone and called Carrick. He answered on the first ring, his voice sad and broken. Her heart ached for him and with the ache came the guilt of what she'd done and how much pain she'd caused him. She hesitated before she spoke.

'I'm at the airport Carrick. I thought... after last night... I thought it best to leave. I'm sorry, please forgive me for letting things get out of hand.'

She couldn't finish the sentence - tears were coursing down her cheeks as she dug in her bag for a tissue to dab at her face, afraid people sitting opposite her would notice her distressed state.

'I need to say this Julia just this once. I love you. I've always loved you since the first time I met you. But this can't happen between us, it's not right. I can't betray my brother. I just can't. I shouldn't have allowed myself to get carried away.'

She didn't know how to reply, what to say. Words failed her. Finally, after a lengthy pause, she said, 'I'm so sorry. I'll phone you when I get back.' She ended the call, shaking and desperately trying to contain her emotions, she tucked her phone into her bag and made her way to the departure lounge.

The seat belt sign was off, drinks were being offered and passengers were deciding which movies they were going to watch. Julia was numb with grief for Carrick with no way of reaching out to comfort him.

Her thoughts drifted back to lunch with Malcolm and whilst it had surprised her to hear he knew Carrick she'd not felt angry that he'd not told her. She acknowledged this was not a secret, not something Carrick had deliberately kept from her, choosing instead to believe he wasn't used to sharing information the way most couples do. She was pleased that they knew each other, it somehow drew her little circle of family and friends closer together.

It was obvious, talking to him, that Malcolm missed her aunt. Reading Grace's diaries had been an enlightening time for both Julia and Malcolm.

They'd learnt so much about Grace's past. The time she'd spent travelling between London and Chedworth, a little village in the heart of the Cotswolds. From the entries in her diaries there appeared to have been a love interest in Chedworth, someone she kept travelling up from London to visit.

Before Grace took up her position at the Te Papa Museum in New Zealand, she travelled back to England. After that entry which described her journey, there was nothing further to read and nothing more to learn about that time.

It was intriguing, leaving Julia and Malcolm to create their own fantasies about the enigmatic Grace. Finally, Julia drifted off to sleep, only waking when the pilot announced their decent into Melbourne.

52

JACK

~

When I saw her dance – no inhibitions, the control that had always ruled her life now given over to the control of the position of her feet, the movement of her arms and hands – I didn't recognise this woman, my mother. The woman who sacrificed so much for me has finally set herself free, and I couldn't be happier for her.

When Patrick came into my life, he forever changed how I viewed myself. Damaged and afflicted by the emotions of anger and fear that had once dominated my young life, I was healing; I knew that, but I was struggling with my identity. Did my abuse define me, would it always be there, a darkness that shadowed my every step as I struggled with life? A constant reminder of a time when robbed of my innocence, I was a victim, and that state of mind defined me.

My mother did everything possible to help me heal. She was there, loving and absorbing my hurt every step of the way. But she couldn't give me the gift that Patrick so readily and easily shared. He became my therapist, the person who could reach inside of me and pull out my absolute best even when I was doubting my own abilities – Patrick never once doubted me.

I love Patrick way beyond normal father and son, beyond friends. Our love for each other extends outside all of this. It blossomed and thrived in a place of mutual trust. A place where I gave myself to music and Patrick grasped hold of my talent and expanded it into something so much bigger than the trauma I'd experienced as a child and the doubts I'd lived with growing up.

He took my fears, my anger, my anxiety, and he shaped all those emotions into musical scores, quavers, beats, rhythms, and words.

When he phoned me in Geneva to tell me he was taking up tenure in Australia, I could only pretend to be happy for him. I feigned delight that they had offered him the opportunity. Kat understood, she knew how much I relied on him being close, on my mother being close.

The man who had become my father figure was asking so much of my mother. I knew better than anyone the sacrifice by mother made in giving up her life in London and starting a new life in a country I knew she'd never desired to live in. But my mother's loyalty to a husband she'd grown to love because of me, would dictate her decision, she would make this sacrifice.

Kat was my tower, the person I grieved with, the person who understood my loss. Patrick phoned, he found ways of keeping in touch all the time, but it was never quite the same as knowing they were there in London and I could reach out and feel my mother's strength, the power of her love, her wise words.

Kat knew. Call it a woman's intuition. She loved both brothers, but it was always Carrick she gravitated toward. He reminded her of the father she'd lost as a young woman. They talked to each other regularly over the phone. Carrick would visit when he was travelling in Europe and then when Patrick and my mother moved to Australia, it was Carrick who was there for both of us. Visiting when he could, letting us use his apartment when we were in London.

He was the constant in our lives. But it was Kat who guessed his secret. She didn't even share her thoughts with me until recently.

Now we are in Australia for Christmas and my mother is radiant, she's beyond excited at our news – becoming a grandmother has lifted her spirits to another level, only it's not just that - she's happy and appears finally free of the demons of the past.

But it's the dance, that's when I see it, when I know - when Kat turns to me and smiles her beautiful encompassing smile, and we silently acknowledge and can't help but be pleased. How could we not?

Carrick loves my mother. He's loved her for the longest time, and now they can put aside feelings of betrayal and guilt and let the past stay where it belongs – in the past. Finally, their love can grow and blossom.

THE END

~

ACKNOWLEDGEMENTS

The greater the love, the greater the grief.

This third and final book in the *Julia Series* is a love story. But grieving is often the process through which we can let go of one love in order to find another. How we deal with grief is complex, and wide ranging.

Dance as a therapy is thankfully becoming more widely acknowledged. Understanding movement reflects a person's pattern of thinking and feeling and dance and movement facilitate emotional, mental, spiritual and social growth. So those moments when you want to boogie around the kitchen, don't hold back!!

There's a famous quote by Friedrich Nietzsche, the German philosopher – *"And those who were seen dancing were thought to be insane by those who could not hear the music"*.

Listen to the music inside of you and dance your heart out.

My grateful thanks to the only person I would trust with a first draft – my husband, my amazing editor, best friend, and soul mate. Thank you for your humour, wisdom, and love.

Thank you to Cheryl, Jane, and Andy for taking the time to read my completed manuscript. Your feedback, inspirational words, and belief in me is treasured. The phone calls, emails and words of encouragement have kept me going when those moments of self-doubt rise-up to choke my words.

A special thanks to Serghei Bolgarschii, professional dancer, tutor, and competitor in the television series *Dancing with the Stars*.

Many years ago, Serghei you gave unselfishly of your time and knowledge as we sat in the New Orleans Café, Crows Nest, Sydney, Australia drinking copious coffees while I recorded our interview on my Dictaphone - the recording of which helped create the dance scenes in this novel together with a big pinch of imagination and I apologise in advance if I've misinterpreted the Salsa steps!! Thank you Serghei – a true professional.

And finally, I want to thank you my readers, you have purchased a copy of this book - I am eternally grateful for your continuing support. I have enjoyed writing the story of Julia's journey across the three books, but now it's time to say goodbye to Julia and Jack and I look forward to introducing you to my new characters in 2021.

MUSIC REFERENCES

Music referenced and which influenced the writing of this novel

Leonard Cohen - *Dance Me to the End of Love*
    Flyying Colours – *Goodtimes*
    Flyying Colours – *Long Holiday*
    Flyying Colours – *Mellow*
    Melody Gardot – *Worrisome Heart*
    Melody Gardot – *Les Etoiles*
    Adele – *Make You Feel My Love*
    Sting – *Shape Of My Heart*
    Glenn Miller – *In The Mood*
    Eric Clapton – *Change the World*
    Eric Clapton – *I Shot the Sherriff*
    Bryan Ferry – *Slave to Love*
    Bryan Ferry – *Don't Stop The Dance*
    Donna Summer – *Last Dance*
    Bee Gees – *You Should be Dancing*
    Kenny G – *The Girl from Ipanema*
    Chris Isaak- *Wicked Game*
    Lauren Wood – *Fallen*

Marvin Gaye – *What's Going On*
Van Morrison – *Bright Side of the Road*
Donna Summer – *On The Radio*
Gloria Gaynor – Never Can Say Goodbye
Bee Gees – *How Deep Is Your Love*
Bee Gees – *Stayin' Alive*
Bee Gees – *More Than A Woman*
Bryan Ferry – *Johnny & Mary*
Iyeoka – *Simply Falling*
Womack & Womack – *Teardrops*
Billy Ocean – *Caribbean Queen*
Roxy Music – *Avalon*
Sting – *A Thousand Years*
Chris Isaak – *Only the Lonely*

ALSO BY ADRIANA GUYTON

Consequences

Can we ever really escape our past?

New Zealand expat, Julia Davis, arrives in England hoping for a new beginning. It's a chance for her son Jack to heal, and for Julia to finally rid herself of the guilt that torments her daily thoughts.

The arrival of her husband Nick should complete Julia's family. But as Jack runs into trouble at school and Julia and Nick's frayed relationship begins to unravel, secrets are exposed with devastating consequences.

Can Julia cling on to her fragile happiness – and all she holds dear?

Consequences is a novel about the ties of motherhood and marriage, about confronting the past and finding the courage to face the future.

Reviews:

Consequences is phenomenal, so eloquent and powerful. **Dr Lucinda Molan (Australia)**

Not just a story for women, men need to read this too -What a lovely story that lifts you, bangs you down hard, and picks you up again - I was completely immersed in it! Not only will this particularly touch the emotions of anyone who has witnessed violence or abuse, but it shines a light as to how we have choices and responsibilities whatever the path we take. Enjoyment apart, I learned things from this story that as a husband and father I ought to have known, but didn't, so this is a book that deserves a place on many couple's reading list.

Al Richard (Australia)

Consequences gripped me from the first page. A lovely story and a powerful message.

Karen Copper (UK)

An easy, organic and relatable read. Adriana's writing made it easy to form vivid pictures of the characters & their surroundings. I'm not much of a reader yet I looked forward to returning to this story each evening. I look forward to more material from Adriana Guyton. **Stella (USA)**

From the prologue to the last page I loved every word of it. Along with the characters, I felt I was "living" in the book. **Amazon Customer (USA)**

I really enjoyed reading this book. I didn't know what to expect and was pleasantly surprised. I'd highly recommend it.

Capstar68 (USA)

The Music Teacher

Julia is getting her life back together after the tumultuous events following her move from New Zealand to England. Focussed on her job at a thriving legal firm and fiercely protective of her son Jack, life has become calm and measured just the way Julia likes – no more secrets or surprises, everything under control and predictable. The last thing she needs or wants is a man complicating their lives again.

Jack is a teenager who dreams of becoming an awesome musician. Music is his safe place when he needs to escape dark memories - it lifts his self-belief and makes him feel worthwhile in other people's eyes, not just his mother's. He has the passion and talent but needs the right teacher to nurture his potential.

Patrick Devlin left his native Ireland to pursue his passion for music and now runs a prestigious teaching academy. He's known love and heartbreak and has found that life is simpler when you follow your passions but, where women are concerned, commitment is to be avoided.

When Julia grudgingly allows Jack to be accepted as a student of Patrick's academy, the journey of self-discovery for three damaged people begins. Sibling rivalry, a tragedy from the past, and the healing power of music will change their lives forever.

Adriana Guyton's second novel explores the ties of brotherhood, a mother's sacrifice and a young boy's search for contentment where music becomes the healer and the teacher the cycle breaker. The Music Teacher is the second novel in the "Julia Series"

Reviews:

A very well written novel portraying the total devotion and love of a mother and son. I enjoyed the Irish connection integrating the relationship between the two brothers and the music theme throughout the book. I thoroughly recommend it and look forward to Adriana's next novel.

Jane O'Reilly

From the first chapter I was immediately engaged and taken by this novel, could not put it down. A wonderful story bound together by strong characters both young and mature, filled with inspiration, hope, heartbreak and romance. Having not read the first book of the "Julia Series" did not seem to matter, however I'm now compelled to go back and read

"Consequences". A beautiful novel written by a writer who clearly knows how to construct a good, compelling story.

Andy – Good Reads

WHERE TO GET HELP

If you find yourself in need of support, please contact one or more of the organisations listed below:

- **Grief Counselling**
- **Grief UK**
- https://www.griefuk.org/
- **Grief Anonymous - USA**
- https://www.griefanonymous.com/
- **Australian Centre for Grief and Bereavement**
- https://www.grief.org.au/
- **Grief Centre NZ**
- http://www.griefcentre.org.nz/
- **Alcohol Support Services**
- **Drinkaware UK**
- https://www.drinkaware.co.uk/advice/support-services/alcohol-support-services
- **National Institute on Alcohol Abuse and Alcoholism (NIAAA)**
- https://www.nih.gov/about-nih/what-we-do/nih-almanac/national-institute-alcohol-abuse-alcoholism-niaaa

- **DrinkWise – Australia**
- https://drinkwise.org.au/drinking-and-you/support-services/#
- **Alcohol Drug Help NZ**
- https://alcoholdrughelp.org.nz/